Spiriting a child away from the Tithing Festival
wasn't going to be easy.

The census takers made sure that all children who had turned eight years old attended, so I'd need to find a way to strike his name from the list. But I'd dealt with census takers before, and Imperial soldiers, and even the Emperor's constructs.

I smoothed the front of the uniform jacket and went to the door. I should have drawn aside the curtains, or cracked the door to look beforehand. But the quake had unsettled my nerves, and I was close to finding the boat that had taken Emahla. I was close to an answer. So instead, I stepped back into the narrow street, the sunlight hot on my face, wide-eyed and unsteady as a newborn lamb.

And found myself in the midst of a phalanx of Imperial soldiers.

Praise for
THE BONE SHARD DAUGHTER

"[A] richly told, emotional, action-laced debut. . . . Readers will finish this eager for the follow-up."

—Library Journal (starred review)

"*The Bone Shard Daughter* . . . deserves as much attention as it can get."

—Locus

"Stewart's debut is sharp and compelling. It will hook readers in and make them fiercely anticipate the rest of the series."

—Booklist

"[An] action-packed, must-read epic fantasy. . . . One of the best debut fantasy novels of the year." *—BuzzFeed News*

"Andrea Stewart's *The Bone Shard Daughter* is not just an amazing start to a new trilogy. It's likely the best fantasy novel you'll read this year." *—Culturess*

"Original and intricately written." *—Ms.*

"*The Bone Shard Daughter* is one of the best fantasy novels I've read in a long time. With stunningly intricate worldbuilding that leaps off the page and characters who are so vibrant that you wish they were real, it grabs you by the heart and the throat from the first pages and doesn't let go until long after it's over. This book is truly special."

—Sarah J. Maas, *New York Times* bestselling author

"Epic fantasy at its most human and heartfelt, concerned with the real lives caught in the gears of empire and rebellion. Inventive, adventurous, and wonderfully written."

—Alix E. Harrow, author of
The Ten Thousand Doors of January

"Stewart gives us eerie, grungy bone magic that permeates through every layer of a fascinating and dangerous world. Strange monsters—some friendly, most not—unsettling rituals, and a cast of wonderful characters trying to fix a world on the brink of shattering, *The Bone Shard Daughter* is utterly absorbing. I adored it."

—Emily A. Duncan, *New York Times*
bestselling author of *Wicked Saints*

"There's a bold, ambitious imagination at work here—and this is a world you'll want to linger in."

—M. R. Carey, author of *The Girl With All the Gifts*

"A triumph of fantasy and science fiction populated with memorable characters and bone-chilling secrets that keep you turning the pages."

—K. S. Villoso, author of *The Wolf of Oren-Yaro*

"*The Bone Shard Daughter* begins with a spark of intrigue that ignites into a thrilling adventure you cannot miss—with a unique (and painful!) magic system to boot."

—Hafsah Faizal, *New York Times*
bestselling author of *We Hunt the Flame*

"A grand, ingenious, and sweeping tale of power, magic, and heart, *The Bone Shard Daughter* is groundbreaking epic fantasy for a new age." —Tasha Suri, author of *Empire of Sand*

"Stewart etches this story into your heart, filling it with everything I love about fantasy: a well-realized world, dark magic that challenges your presumptions, and deep questions about identity. Highly recommended."

—Marshall Ryan Maresca,
author of the Maradaine Saga

THE BONE SHARD DAUGHTER

Book One of The Drowning Empire

ANDREA STEWART

orbitbooks.net

Copyright © 2020 by Andrea Stewart
Excerpt from *The Bone Shard Emperor* copyright © 2021 by Andrea Stewart
Excerpt from *The Mask of Mirrors* copyright © 2021 by Bryn Neuenschwander and Alyc Helms

Cover design by Lauren Panepinto
Cover art by Sasha Vinogradova
Cover copyright © 2020 by Hachette Book Group, Inc.
Map by Charis Loke
Author photograph by Lei Gong

Orbit
Hachette Book Group
1290 Avenue of the Americas
New York, NY 10104
orbitbooks.net

First U.S. Paperback Edition: March 2021
Originally published in hardcover and ebook in Great Britain and in the U.S. by Orbit in September 2020

Orbit is an imprint of Hachette Book Group.
The Orbit name and logo are trademarks of Little, Brown Book Group Limited.

The publisher is not responsible for websites (or their content) that are not owned by the publisher.

The Hachette Speakers Bureau provides a wide range of authors for speaking events. To find out more, go to www.hachettespeakersbureau.com or call (866) 376-6591.

Library of Congress Control Number: 2020933516

ISBNs: 978-0-316-54143-5 (paperback), 978-0-316-54144-2 (ebook)

Printed in the United States of America

CW

7 9 10 8 6

For my sister, Kristen, who has read nearly everything I've ever written. I owe you.

1

Lin

Imperial Island

Father told me I'm broken.

He didn't speak this disappointment when I answered his question. But he said it with narrowed eyes, the way he sucked on his already hollow cheeks, the way the left side of his lips twitched a little bit down, the movement almost hidden by his beard.

He taught me how to read a person's thoughts on their face. And he knew that I knew how to read these signs. So between us, it was as though he had spoken out loud.

The question: "Who was your closest childhood friend?"

My answer: "I don't know."

I could run as quickly as the sparrow flies, I was as skilled with an abacus as the Empire's best accountants, and I could name all the known islands in the time it took for tea to finish steeping. But I could not remember my past before the sickness. Sometimes I thought I never would – that the girl from before was lost to me.

Father's chair creaked as he shifted, and he let out a long breath. In his fingers he held a brass key, which he tapped on the table's surface. "How can I trust you with my secrets? How can I trust you as my heir if you do not know who you are?"

I knew who I was. I was Lin. I was the Emperor's daughter. I shouted the words in my head, but I didn't say them. Unlike my father, I kept my face neutral, my thoughts hidden. Sometimes he liked it when I stood up for myself, but this was not one of those times. It never was, when it came to my past.

I did my best not to stare at the key.

"Ask me another question," I said. The wind lashed at the shutters, bringing with it the salt-seaweed smell of the ocean. The breeze licked at my neck, and I suppressed a shiver. I kept his gaze, hoping he saw the steel in my soul and not the fear. I could taste the scent of rebellion on the winds as clearly as I could the fish fermentation vats. It was that obvious, that thick. I could set things right, if only I had the means. If only he'd let me prove it.

Tap.

"Very well," Father said. The teak pillars behind him framed his withered countenance, making him look more like a foreboding portrait than a man. "You're afraid of sea serpents. Why?"

"I was bit by one when I was a child," I said.

He studied my face. I held my breath. I stopped holding my breath. I twined my fingers together and then forced them to relax. If I were a mountain, he would be following the taproots of cloud junipers, chipping away the stone, searching for the white, chalky core.

And finding it.

"Don't lie to me, girl," he snarled. "Don't make guesses. You may be my flesh and blood, but I can name my foster son to the crown. It doesn't have to be you."

I wished I did remember. Was there a time when this man stroked my hair and kissed my forehead? Had he loved me before I'd forgotten, when I'd been whole and unbroken? I wished there was someone I could ask. Or at least, someone who could give me answers. "Forgive me." I bowed my head. My black hair formed a curtain over my eyes, and I stole a glance at the key.

Most of the doors in the palace were locked. He hobbled from room to room, using his bone shard magic to create miracles. A magic I needed if I was to rule. I'd earned six keys. My father's foster, Bayan, had seven. Sometimes it felt as if my entire life was a test.

"Fine," Father said. He eased back into his chair. "You may go."

I rose to leave, but hesitated. "When will you teach me your bone shard magic?" I didn't wait for his response. "You say you can name Bayan as your heir, but you haven't. I am still your heir, and I need to know how to control the constructs. I'm twenty-three, and you—" I stopped, because I didn't know how old he was. There were liver spots on the backs of his hands, and his hair was steely gray. I didn't know how much longer he would live. All I could imagine was a future where he died and left me with no knowledge. No way to protect the Empire from the Alanga. No memories of a father who cared.

He coughed, muffling the sound with his sleeve. His gaze flicked to the key, and his voice went soft. "When you are a whole person," he said.

I didn't understand him. But I recognized the vulnerability. "Please," I said, "what if I am never a whole person?"

He looked at me, and the sadness in his gaze scraped at my heart like teeth. I had five years of memories; before that was a fog. I'd lost something precious; if only I knew what it was. "Father, I—"

A knock sounded at the door, and he was cold as stone once more.

Bayan slipped inside without waiting for a response, and I wanted to curse him. He hunched his shoulders as he walked, his footfalls silent. If he were anyone else, I'd think his step hesitant. But Bayan had the look of a cat about him — deliberate, predatory. He wore a leather apron over his tunic, and blood stained his hands.

"I've completed the modification," Bayan said. "You asked me to see you right away when I'd finished."

A construct hobbled behind him, tiny hooves clicking against the floor. It looked like a deer, except for the fangs protruding from its mouth and the curling monkey's tail. Two small wings sprouted from its shoulders, blood staining the fur around them.

Father turned in his chair and placed a hand on the creature's back. It looked up at him with wide, wet eyes. "Sloppy," he said. "How many shards did you use to embed the follow command?"

"Two," Bayan said. "One to get the construct to follow me, and another to get it to stop."

"It should be one," Father said. "It goes where you do unless you tell it not to. The language is in the first book I gave you." He seized one of the wings and pulled it. When he let it go, it settled slowly back at the construct's side. "Your construction, however, is excellent."

Bayan's eyes slid to the side, and I held his gaze. Neither of us looked away. Always a competition. Bayan's irises were blacker even than mine, and when his lip curled, it only accentuated the full curve of his mouth. I supposed he was prettier than I would ever be, but I was convinced I was smarter, and that's what really mattered. Bayan never cared to hide his feelings. He carried his contempt for me like a child's favorite seashell.

"Try again with a new construct," Father said, and Bayan broke his gaze from mine. Ah, I'd won this small contest.

Father reached his fingers into the beast. I held my breath. I'd only seen him do this twice. Twice I could remember, at least. The creature only blinked placidly as Father's hand disappeared to the wrist. And then he pulled away and the construct froze, still as a statue. In his hand were two small shards of bone.

No blood stained his fingers. He dropped the bones into Bayan's hand. "Now go. Both of you."

I was quicker to the door than Bayan, who I suspected was hoping for more than just harsh words. But I was used to harsh words, and I'd things to do. I slipped out the door and held it for Bayan to pass so he needn't bloody the door with his hands. Father prized cleanliness.

Bayan glared at me as he passed, the breeze in his wake smelling of copper and incense. Bayan was just the son of a small isle's governor, lucky enough to have caught Father's eye and to be taken in as a foster. He'd brought the sickness with him, some exotic disease Imperial didn't know. I was told I got sick with it soon after he arrived, and recovered a little while after Bayan did. But he hadn't lost as much of his memory as I had, and he'd gotten some of it back.

As soon as he disappeared around the corner, I whirled and ran for the end of the hallway. The shutters threatened to blow against the walls when I unlatched them. The tile roofs looked like the slopes of mountains. I stepped outside and shut the window.

The world opened up before me. From atop the roof, I could see the city and the harbor. I could even see the boats in the ocean fishing for squid, their lanterns shining in the distance like earthbound stars. The wind tugged at my tunic, finding its way beneath the cloth, biting at my skin.

I had to be quick. By now, the construct servant would have removed the body of the deer. I half-ran, half-skidded down the slope of the roof toward the side of the palace where my father's bedroom was. He never brought his chain of keys into the questioning room. He didn't bring his construct guards with him. I'd read the small signs on his face. He might bark at me and scold me, but when we were alone – he feared me.

The tiles clicked below my feet. On the ramparts of the palace walls, shadows lurked – more constructs. Their instructions were simple. Watch for intruders. Sound an alarm. None of them paid me any mind, no matter that I wasn't where I was supposed to be. I wasn't an intruder.

The Construct of Bureaucracy would now be handing over the reports. I'd watched him sorting them earlier in the day, hairy lips fumbling over his teeth as he read them silently. There would be quite a lot. Shipments delayed due to skirmishes, the Ioph Carn stealing and smuggling witstone, citizens shirking their duty to the Empire.

I swung onto my father's balcony. The door to his room was cracked open. The room was usually empty, but this time it was not. A growl emanated from within. I froze. A black nose nudged into the space between door and wall, widening the gap. Yellow eyes peered at me and tufted ears flicked back. Claws scraped against wood as the creature strode toward me. Bing Tai, one of my father's oldest constructs. Gray speckled his jowls, but he had all his teeth. Each incisor was as long as my thumb.

His lip curled, the hackles on his back standing on end. He was a creature of nightmares, an amalgamation of large predators, with black, shaggy fur that faded into the darkness. He took another step closer.

Maybe it wasn't Bayan that was stupid; maybe I was the stupid one. Maybe this was how Father would find me after his tea – torn to bloody pieces on his balcony. It was too far to the ground, and I was too short to reach the roof gutters. The only way out from these rooms was into the hallway. "Bing Tai," I said, and my voice was steadier than I felt. "It is me, Lin."

I could almost feel my father's two commands battling in the construct's head. One: protect my rooms. Two: protect my family. Which command was stronger? I'd bet on the second one, but now I wasn't so sure.

I held my ground and tried not to let my fear show. I shoved my hand toward Bing Tai's nose. He could see me, he could hear me, perhaps he needed to smell me.

He *could* choose to taste me, though I did my best not to think about that.

His wet, cold nose touched my fingers, a growl still deep in his throat. I was not Bayan, who wrestled with the constructs like they were his brothers. I could not forget what they were. My throat constricted until I could barely breathe, my chest tight and painful.

And then Bing Tai settled on his haunches, his ears pricking, his lips covering his teeth. "Good Bing Tai," I said. My voice trembled. I had to hurry.

Grief lay heavy in the room, thick as the dust on what used to be my mother's wardrobe. Her jewelry on the dresser lay untouched; her slippers still awaited her next to the bed. What bothered me more than the questions my father asked me, than not knowing if he loved and cared for me as a child, was not remembering my mother.

I'd heard the remaining servants whispering. He burned all her portraits on the day she died. He forbade mention of her name. He put all her handmaidens to the sword. He guarded the memories of her jealously, as if he was the only one allowed to have them.

Focus.

I didn't know where he kept the copies he distributed to Bayan and me. He always pulled these from his sash pocket, and I didn't dare try to filch them from there. But the original chain of keys lay on the bed. So many doors. So many keys. I didn't know which was which, so I selected one at random – a golden key with a jade piece in the bow – and pocketed it.

I escaped into the hallway and wedged a thin piece of wood between door and frame so the door didn't latch. Now the tea would be steeping. Father would be reading through the reports, asking questions. I hoped they would keep him occupied.

My feet scuffed against the floorboards as I ran. The grand hallways of the palace were empty, lamplight glinting off the red-painted beams above. In the entryway, teak pillars rose from floor to ceiling, framing the faded mural on the second-floor wall. I took the steps down to the palace doors two at a time. Each step felt like a miniature betrayal.

I could have waited, one part of my mind told me. I could have been obedient; I could have done my best to answer my father's questions, to heal my memories. But the other part of my mind was cold and sharp. It cut through the guilt to find a hard truth. I could never be what he wanted if I did not take what I wanted. I hadn't been able to remember, no matter how hard I'd tried. He'd not left me with any other choice than to show him I was worthy in a different way.

I slipped through the palace doors and into the silent yard. The front gates were closed, but I was small and strong, and if Father wouldn't teach me his magic, well, there were other things I'd taught myself in the times he was locked in a secret room with Bayan. Like climbing.

The walls were clean but in disrepair. The plaster had broken away in places, leaving the stone beneath exposed. It was easy enough to climb. The monkey-shaped construct atop the wall just glanced at me before turning its limpid gaze back to the city. A thrill rushed through me when I touched down on the other side. I'd been into the city on foot before – *I must have* – but for me, it was like the first time. The streets stank of fish and hot oil, and the remnants of dinners cooked and eaten. The stones beneath my slippers were dark and slippery with washwater. Pots clanged and a breeze carried the sound of lilting, subdued voices. The first two storefronts I saw were closed, wooden shutters locked shut.

Too late? I'd seen the blacksmith's storefront from the palace walls, and this was what first gave me the idea. I held my breath as I dashed down a narrow alley.

He was there. He was pulling the door closed, a pack slung over one shoulder.

"Wait," I said. "Please, just one more order."

"We're closed," he huffed out. "Come back tomorrow."

I stifled the desperation clawing up my throat. "I'll pay you twice your regular price if you can start it tonight. Just one key copy."

He looked at me then, and his gaze trailed over my embroidered silk tunic. His lips pressed together. He was thinking about lying about how much he charged. But then he just sighed. "Two silver. One is my regular price." He was a good man, fair.

Relief flooded me as I dug the coins from my sash pocket and pressed them into his calloused palm. "Here. I need it quickly."

Wrong thing to say. Annoyance flashed across his face. But he still opened the door again and let me into his shop. The man was built like an iron – broad and squat. His shoulders seemed to take up half the space. Metal tools hung from the walls and ceiling. He picked up his tinderbox and re-lit the lamps. And then he turned back to face me. "It won't be ready until tomorrow morning at the earliest."

"But do you need to keep the key?"

He shook his head. "I can make a mold of it tonight. The key will be ready tomorrow."

I wished there weren't so many chances to turn back, so many chances for my courage to falter. I forced myself to drop my father's key into the blacksmith's hand. The man took it and turned, fishing a block of clay from a stone trough. He pressed the key into it. And then he froze, his breath stopping in his throat.

I moved for the key before I could think. I saw what he did as soon as I took one step closer. At the base of the bow, just before the stem, was the tiny figure of a phoenix embossed into the metal.

When the blacksmith looked at me, his face was as round and pale as the moon. "Who are you? What are you doing with one of the Emperor's keys?"

I should have grabbed the key and run. I was swifter than he was. I could snatch it away and be gone before he took his next breath. All he'd have left was a story – one that no one would believe.

But if I did, I wouldn't have my key copy. I wouldn't have any more answers. I'd be stuck where I was at the start of the day, my memory a haze, the answers I gave Father always inadequate. Always just out of reach. Always broken. And this man – he was a good man. Father taught me the kind of thing to say to good men.

I chose my words carefully. "Do you have any children?"

A measure of color came back into his face. "Two." He answered. His brows knit together as he wondered if he should have responded.

"I am Lin," I said, laying myself bare. "I am the Emperor's heir. He hasn't been the same since my mother's death. He isolates himself, he keeps few servants, he does not meet with the island governors. Rebellion is brewing. Already the Shardless Few have taken Khalute. They'll seek to expand their hold. And there are the Alanga. Some may not believe they're coming back, but my family has kept them from returning.

"Do you want soldiers marching in the streets? Do you want war on your doorstep?" I touched his shoulder gently, and he did not flinch. "On your children's doorstep?"

He reached reflexively behind his right ear for the scar each citizen had. The place where a shard of bone was removed and taken for the Emperor's vault.

"Is my shard powering a construct?" he asked.

"I don't know," I said. I don't know, I don't know – there was so *little* that I did know. "But if I get into my father's vault, I will look for yours and I will bring it back to you. I can't promise you anything. I wish I could. But I will try."

He licked his lips. "My children?"

"I can see what I can do." It was all I could say. No one was exempt from the islands' Tithing Festivals.

Sweat shone on his forehead. "I'll do it."

Father would be setting the reports aside now. He would take up his cup of tea and sip from it, looking out the window at the lights of the city below. Sweat prickled between my shoulder-blades. I needed to get the key back before he discovered me.

I watched through a haze as the blacksmith finished making the mold. When he handed the key back, I turned to run.

"Lin," he said.

I stopped.

"My name is Numeen. The year of my ritual was 1508. We need an Emperor who cares about us."

What could I say to that? So I just ran. Out the door, down the alleyway, back to climbing the wall. Now Father would be finishing up his tea, his fingers wrapped around the still-warm cup. A stone came loose beneath my fingertips. I let it fall to the ground. The *crack* made me cringe.

He'd be putting his cup down, he'd be looking at the city. How long did he look at the city? The climb down was faster than the climb up. I couldn't smell the city anymore. All I could smell was my own breath. The walls of the outer buildings passed in a blur as I ran to the palace – the servants' quarters, the Hall of Everlasting Peace, the Hall of Earthly Wisdom, the wall surrounding the palace garden. Everything was cold and dark, empty.

I took the servants' entrance into the palace, bounding up the stairs two at a time. The narrow passageway opened into the main hallway. The main hallway wrapped around the palace's second floor, and my father's bedroom was nearly on the other side from the servants' entrance. I wished my legs were longer. I wished my mind were stronger.

Floorboards squeaked beneath my feet as I ran, the noise making me wince. At last, I made it back and slipped into my father's room. Bing Tai lay on the rug at the foot of the bed, stretched out like an old cat. I had to reach over him to get to the chain of keys. He smelled musty, like a mix between a bear construct and a closet full of moth-ridden clothes.

It took three tries for me to hook the key back onto the chain. My fingers felt like eels – flailing and slippery.

I knelt to retrieve the door wedge on my way out, my breath ragged in my throat. The brightness of the light in the hallway made me blink. I'd have to find my way into the city tomorrow to retrieve the new key. But it was done, the wedge for the door safely in my sash pocket. I let out the breath I hadn't known I'd been holding.

"Lin."

Bayan. My limbs felt made of stone. What had he seen? I turned to face him – his brow was furrowed, his hands clasped behind his back. I willed my heart to calm, my face to blankness.

"What are you doing outside the Emperor's room?"

2

Jovis

Deerhead Island

I hoped this was one of my smaller mistakes. I tugged at the hem of the jacket. The sleeves were too short, the waist too roomy, the shoulders just a bit too broad. I sniffed the collar. The musky, star anise perfume went straight up my nose, making me cough. "If you're trying to attract a partner with that, best try a little less," I said. It was a good piece of advice, but the soldier at my feet didn't respond.

Is it still talking to oneself if the other person is unconscious?

Well, the uniform fit enough, and "enough" is what I could hope for most days. I had two full, standard boxes of witstone on my boat. Enough to pay my debts, enough to eat well for three months, enough to get my boat from one end of the Phoenix Empire to the other. But "enough" would never get me what I truly needed. I'd heard a rumor at the docks, a whisper of a disappearance similar to my Emahla's, and I'd be cursing myself the rest of my life if I didn't suss out the origins.

I slipped from the alleyway, resisting the urge to tug at

the jacket hem one more time. Nodded to another soldier when I passed her in the street. Let out my breath when she nodded back and turned away. I'd not checked the yearly Tithing Festival schedule before stopping. And because luck rarely worked out in my favor, this meant, of course, the Festival was here.

Deerhead Island was swarming with the Emperor's soldiers. And here I was – a trader without an Imperial contract, who'd had more than one run-in with the Empire's soldiers. I held the edge of my sleeve in my fingers as I navigated the streets. I'd gotten the rabbit tattoo when I'd passed the navigational exams. It was less pride and more practicality. How else would they identify my swollen and bloated body if I washed ashore? But now, as a smuggler, the tattoo was a liability. That and my face. They'd gotten the jawline wrong on the posters, the eyes were too close together and I'd cut my curling hair short since then, but aye, it was a likeness. I'd been paying gutter orphans to take them down, but then five days later I'd see some damned construct putting another one back up.

It was a shame that Imperial uniforms didn't come with hats.

I should have taken my witstone and fled, but Emahla was a string in my heart that fate couldn't seem to stop tugging. So I set my feet one in front of the other and did my best to appear as bland and blank as possible. The man at the docks had said the disappearance was recent, so the trail was still fresh. I didn't have much time. The soldier hadn't seen me before I'd clobbered him, but he'd patched a section of the left elbow and he'd recognize his uniform.

The street narrowed ahead, sunlight filtering down through gaps between the buildings and laundry hung to dry. Someone inside called out, "Don't keep me waiting! How long does it take to put on a pair of shoes?" I wasn't far from the ocean, so the air still smelled like seaweed, mingled with cooking meat and hot oil. They'd be preparing their children for the Festival, and preparing the Festival meal for when their children returned. Good food couldn't heal wounds of body and soul, but it could soothe them. My mother had prepared a feast for my trepanning day. Roasted duck with crisped skin, grilled vegetables, fragrant and spiced rice, fish with the sauce still bubbling. I'd had to dry my tears before eating it.

But that was a time long past for me – the scar behind my right ear long since healed. I ducked beneath a shirt hung too low and still damp, and found the drinking hall the man at the docks had described.

The door creaked as I opened it, scraping a well-worn path along the wooden floorboards. This early in the morning, it should have been empty. Instead, Imperial guards lurked in dusty corners, dried fish hanging from the ceiling. I made my way to the back, my shoulder against the wall, my wrist hidden by my thigh, my head down. If I'd been a better planner, I'd have wrapped the tattoo. Ah well. My face was the bigger problem, and I couldn't wrap that.

A woman stood behind the counter, her broad back to me, hair tied up in a handkerchief with a few loose strands stuck to her neck. She hunched over a wooden cutting board, her fingers nimbly pleating dumplings.

"Auntie," I said to her, deferential.

She didn't turn around. "Don't call me that," she said. "I'm not old enough to be anyone's auntie except to children." She wiped her floured hands on her apron, sighed. "What can I get for you?"

"I wanted to talk," I said.

She turned around then and gave my uniform a long look. I don't think she even glanced at my face. "I sent my nephew along to the square already. The census takers would have marked him by now. Is that what you're here for?"

"You're Danila, right? I have questions about your foster daughter," I said.

Her face closed up. "I've reported everything I know."

I knew the reception she'd received upon her report, because Emahla's parents had gotten the same – the shrugged shoulders, the annoyed expressions. Young women ran away sometimes, didn't they? And besides, what did they expect the Emperor to do about it?

"Just leave me in peace," she said before turning back to her dumplings.

That soldier in the alleyway might be waking up right now with a splitting headache and a good many questions on his lips. But – Emahla. Her name chased itself around my head, spurring me to action. I slid around the end of the counter and joined Danila at the cutting board.

Without waiting for any sort of approval, I picked up the wrappings and the filling and began to pleat. After a startled moment, she began again. Behind us, two soldiers bet on their game of cards.

"You're good," she begrudged me. "Very neat, very quick."

"My mother. She was – *is* – a cook." I shook my head with a rueful smile. It had been so long since I'd been home. Another life, almost. "Makes the best dumplings in all the isles. I ran about a lot, sailing and studying for the navigational exams, but I always liked to help her. Even after I passed."

"If you passed the navigational exams, why are you a soldier?"

I weighed my options. I was a good liar – the best. It was the only reason I still had a head on my shoulders. But this woman reminded me of my mother, gruff but kindhearted, and I had a missing wife to find. "I'm not." I slid my sleeve up enough to show the rabbit tattoo.

Danila looked at the tattoo, and then at my face. Her eyes narrowed, then widened. "Jovis," she said in a whisper. "You're that smuggler."

"I'd prefer 'most successful smuggler in the last one hundred years', but I'll settle for 'that smuggler'."

She snorted. "Depends on how you define success. Your mother wouldn't think so, I'd guess."

"You're probably right," I said lightly. It would deeply pain her to know how far I'd fallen. Danila relaxed, her shoulder now touching mine, her expression softer. She wouldn't give me away. Just wasn't the sort. "I need to ask about your foster daughter. How she disappeared."

"There isn't much to tell," she said. "She was here one day and then gone the next, nineteen silver coins left on her bedspread – as though a silver phoenix was all a year of her life was worth. It was two days ago. I keep thinking she'll walk back in the door."

She wouldn't. I knew, because I'd thought the same for a year. I could still see the nineteen silver coins scattered across Emahla's bed. Could still feel my heart pounding, my stomach twisting – caught in that moment of both knowing she was gone and not being able to believe it.

"Soshi was a bright young woman," Danila said, a quaver in her voice. She struck the tears from her eyes before they could reach her cheeks. "Her mother died in a mining accident and she didn't know her father. I never married, never had any children of my own. I took her in. I needed someone to help."

"Was . . . ?" The word thudded from my mouth; I couldn't form the question.

Danila picked up another wrap and studied my face. "I may

not be old enough to be your auntie, but to me you are still a boy. If the Empire had anything to do with her disappearance, she's already dead."

I have never been in love. We never met as children, we never became friends. I never took the chance, never kissed her. I never came back from Imperial Island. I told myself the lie, over and over. Even so, my mind layered on top her teasing smile, how she rolled her eyes when I made up a particularly silly story, the way she leaned her head onto my shoulder and sighed after a long day. But I needed to believe the lie. Because every time I thought about living the rest of my life without her, panic fluttered up my chest and wrapped itself around my throat. I swallowed. "Did you look for her? Did you find any trace?"

"Of course I looked," she said. "I asked around. One of the fishermen said they saw a boat leave early that morning. Not from the docks but from a nearby cove. It was small, dark and had blue sails. It went east. That's all I know."

It was the boat I'd seen the morning Emahla had disappeared, rounding the edge of the island, the mist so thick I wasn't sure I'd seen it at all. In seven years, this was the best lead I had. If I was quick, I might be able to catch it.

One of the soldiers in the hall laughed, another groaned and cards hit the table. Chairs scraped against the floor as they rose. "It was a good game." A beam of sunlight warmed the back of my neck as they opened the door. "Hey you. You coming with us? The captain will bite your head off if you're late."

No one answered, and I remembered the soldier's jacket I wore. He was talking to me.

Danila seized my wrist. The one with the tattoo. Both her voice and her grip were intractable as tree roots. "I've done you a favor, Jovis. Now I need a favor of you."

Oh no. "Favors? We didn't speak of favors."

She talked over me, and I heard footsteps approaching from behind. "I have a nephew. He lives on a small isle just east of here. If I have it right, you'll be headed in that direction anyways. Take him before the ritual. Get him back to his parents. He's their only child."

"I'm not one of the Shardless Few. I don't smuggle children," I hissed. "It's not ethical. Or profitable." I tried her grip and found her strength greater than mine.

"Do it."

By the sound of the footsteps behind me, there was only one soldier. I could handle him. I could lie my way out of this. But after all these years, I still remembered the trickle of blood from my scalp, running down my neck. The cold touch of the chisel against my skin. The wound felt like fire. The Emperor says that the Tithing Festival is a small price to pay for the safety of us all. It didn't feel like so small a price when it was your head bowed and your knees digging into the ground.

I am hardened to the suffering of others. Another lie I told myself because I couldn't save everyone; I hadn't been able to even save my own brother. If I thought too much on all the suffering, all the people I couldn't help, I felt like I was drowning in the Endless Sea itself. I couldn't carry that weight.

Mostly this worked. But not today. Today I thought of my mother, her hands on each side of my face: "But what is the *truth*, Jovis?"

The truth was that someone had saved me. Sometimes one is enough. "I'll take him," I said.

I was a fool.

Danila let go of my wrist. "He owes me for a mug of wine. He'll be along shortly," she told the soldier.

The man's footsteps retreated.

"My nephew's name is Alon," Danila told me. "He's dressed

in a red shirt with white flowers embroidered on the hem. His mother is a cobbler on Phalar. She's the only one on the isle."

I brushed the flour from my hands. "Red shirt. Flowers. Cobbler. Got it."

"You should hurry."

I'd have snapped at her if her grief wasn't so obvious. She'd lost a daughter. I'd lost a wife. I could be kind. "If I find out what happened to your foster daughter, I'll figure out a way to let you know."

She wiped at her eyes again, nodded and turned back to pleating dumplings with the ferocity of a warrior on a battlefield. It seemed the lie she told herself was that these dumplings were the most important thing in the world right now.

I turned to go and the earth moved beneath me. Mugs rattled in their cupboards, Danila's rolling pin fell to the floor, and the dried fish swayed on their strings. I put my hands out, unsure of where to steady them. Everything moved. And then, just as quickly, it settled.

"Just a quake," Danila said, though I knew already. She said it more to soothe herself than me. "Some people think it's the witstone mine causing them – it runs deep. It's nothing to worry about. They've been going on for the past few months."

A lie she tells herself? Quakes happened sometimes, but it had been a long time since I'd felt one. I took an experimental step and found the ground steady. "I should go. May the winds be favorable."

"And the skies clear," she responded.

Spiriting a child away from the Tithing Festival wasn't going to be easy. The census takers made sure that all children who had turned eight years old attended, so I'd need to find a way to strike his name from the list. But I'd dealt with census takers before, and Imperial soldiers, and even the Emperor's constructs.

I smoothed the front of the uniform jacket and went to the door. I should have drawn aside the curtains, or cracked the door to look beforehand. But the quake had unsettled my nerves, and I was close to finding the boat that had taken Emahla. I was close to an answer. So instead, I stepped back into the narrow street, the sunlight hot on my face, wide-eyed and unsteady as a newborn lamb.

And found myself in the midst of a phalanx of Imperial soldiers.

3

Jovis

Deerhead Island

I f only the street were busy, or loud, or anything but quiet and still. Ten uniformed men and women turned their attention to me. Sweat prickled in the small of my back.

"Soldier," one of them said. The pins at her collar marked her as a captain. "You're not one of mine. Who is your captain?"

Lies were well enough when you had substance to back them with. "Sir, I was with the first company to disembark."

She peered at my face, frowning, offering me nothing.

"Lindara's?" another soldier in the phalanx asked.

"Yes," I said in a tone that implied this was obvious, and the soldier foolish for verifying.

But the way the captain examined my features had me wanting to sink my chin into the collar of the uniform. Still studying me, she said, "You should be with your captain. This isn't a pleasure outing."

"I understand. It won't happen again."

"Did you happen to see another soldier around? Short, stocky, big nose and stinks of star anise."

I'd seen him, though we'd not become acquainted. His uniform and I had become intimately acquainted, however. I hoped fervently that the smell of fish and seaweed covered the scent lingering on my jacket. "No, I'm afraid not, sorry. And you're right, I should be with my captain." I turned to go.

A hand landed on my shoulder. "I didn't dismiss you," the captain said.

Oh, I would have made a terrible soldier. "Sir?" I pivoted back and did my best to wear "deferential" better than I wore this jacket.

Her fingers tightened around my shoulder and she squinted at my face. "I've seen you before."

"Probably digging latrine ditches. Lindara doesn't like me much." The other soldiers cracked grins, but the captain was uncrackable. I ran through all the tried and true tricks in my mind. Flirting with her would probably get my head chopped off. Self-deprecation didn't throw her off. Flattery maybe?

"No," she said. "There's something about your face."

Damn the Empire and their pettiness over a small bit of stolen witstone. Damn their power over both men and magic. But most of all, damn their stupid posters. "My face?" I said, to buy some time. "Well, it's—"

The ground beneath me shook again, and this time it shook harder. Everyone eyed the buildings above, hands out in vain attempts to stave off falling walls with fingers. A tile fell from the roof behind me, shattering on the stones by my feet. The shaking stopped.

"That's another one," one of the soldiers said. "Two in one day." He sounded anxious. Truth be told, I didn't like it much either. Sometimes there were small aftershocks, but this one had been stronger than the first.

The captain turned her attention back to me. Her eyes narrowed.

I cleared my throat and straightened my shoulders. "Should we be at the square, captain? It's nearly time for the Festival."

I'd finally hit the right note – respect and discipline. The captain's hand dropped from my shoulder. "We'll have to find our comrade later. We've a duty to fulfill." She strode up the street, beckoning for the others to follow.

I saw a couple of hands reach behind right ears to touch their trepanning scars. I wondered if they remembered that day as crisply as I did. I fell into step behind them – I had business at the Tithing Festival too after all. I might be a liar, but I kept my word. Always kept my word. So I put my legs into it and climbed the hill with the rest of them. The stones beneath my feet shifted as I trod upon them, loosened by the quake. The street opened up at the top of the hill, joining with two others.

The man in front of me turned around to check the view when we reached the top. His face paled, his eyes widening. "Captain!"

I whirled, wondering what it was he saw.

The narrow street wended behind us, buildings looming over it, pressed together like teeth. Dust glittered in the air, but this wasn't what had captured the soldier's attention. Down by the ocean, something had changed. The outline of the harbor had widened. The docks lay at strange angles to one another. There were dark shapes near the shore, jutting from the water.

The tops of bushes. The harbor had sunk.

The captain regarded this revelation with a grim set to her mouth. "We go to the square," she said. "We tell the other two phalanxes. Keep calm, keep order. I don't know what this means, but we stick together."

It was a testament to her leadership that the soldiers fell into step behind her.

I eyed the docks behind us. Promises were well and good, but I'd also promised Emahla I'd find her – and I couldn't very well do that if I were dead. I thought of Danila folding dumplings for her nephew's Festival feast. After mine, my normally reticent mother had held me close, kissed the top of my sweaty hair. "I wish I could have protected you," she'd said. She hadn't known then that I'd been spared. I'd barely known it myself. The square wasn't too far now, and I was a quick runner.

So despite my dread, I followed the soldiers. The air had gone still; no voices, no birds calling, only our footsteps scraping against stone. After another turn and a climb, the stillness gave way to murmuring. Ahead, the street widened into the city square.

Deerhead Island wasn't the largest of the known islands, but it was one of the wealthiest. I'd heard natives brag about their spicy fish soup, their vast markets, and had even heard one claim that Deerhead floated higher in the water than other islands. Their witstone mine produced a good deal of the Empire's supply, and the square was yet another reflection of this wealth. The stones beneath our feet became smooth, laid in patterns. A raised pond adorned the center of the square, bridges leading to a gazebo in the middle. The vine-like carvings on the gazebo marked it as one of the few Alanga-era structures still standing in one piece. It would have been a place I'd liked to have visited with Emahla. She would have given me a sly, sidelong look: "So why did the Alanga build that?" And I would have launched into a story about how this graceful building was merely one of their outhouses. She would have laughed and added in her own details. "Of course. Who doesn't dream of relieving themselves in a gazebo?"

But she wasn't actually here.

I stopped at the mouth of the street, waiting until the soldiers in front of me had made their way to the other end of the square. Dozens of children stood there, hemmed in by Imperial soldiers.

Like sheep being led to a slaughter. Some were calm but most looked nervous, and several of them openly wept. They'd have been dosed up with opium to make them docile and to dull the pain. I strode closer and searched their ranks. Red shirt, flowers on the hem. Too many children in red.

It shouldn't have been me doing this. It should have been one of the Shardless Few, with their romantic ideals about freedom and an Empire ruled by the people. I wasn't an idealist. Couldn't afford to be.

The earth moved. Dust shook loose from the tiled roofs and I struggled to keep my feet underneath me. Panic jolted to the tips of my fingers. An aftershock, fine, yes. Three quakes in one day, and the sinking of the harbor – this wasn't anywhere close to normal. At the other end of the square, the soldiers crouched around their charges, hands going to weapons as though that might help. The census taker presiding over the Festival hunched over his book. The children watched the buildings shake with wide eyes.

I steadied myself at the edge of the fountain, counting. One, two, three, four . . .

At five, my throat tightened. At ten, I knew this shaking might not stop. Something terrible was happening. I could feel it to the very marrow of my bones. As soon as I felt it, I could walk again. If the world was ending, then just waiting around for it to end would help no one, least of all myself.

A boy in the group of children seemed to sense the same thing I did. He rose from his crouch and ran. One of the Imperial soldiers caught him by the shirt.

Red shirt, flowers at the hem. Alon, Danila's nephew. Short for eight years old, with a mop of black hair that threatened to overwhelm him.

Duty held the soldiers together like a piece of fishing string. A hard push and they'd snap. I ran toward them, stumbling as the ground shifted. "The island is sinking! I've seen this happen before," I lied. I didn't have to try at all to sound panicked. "Get to the ships, get out of here before it takes us all with it!" I couldn't be sure if I was exaggerating or not, but I wasn't about to stick around to find out.

The soldiers stared at me for a moment, stricken, the buildings behind them rumbling.

"You!" the captain called to me. "Get back in line."

With a sound like thunder, a building on the opposite side of the square collapsed. With that, the string tying the soldiers together snapped. They ran. Children and soldiers buffeted me, threatening to knock me to the ground. I reached through the crowd and seized Alon's arm. So small I could fit my entire hand around it. "Your Auntie Danila sent me," I told him, shouting to be heard above the rumbling earth. I'm not sure if he heard me, but he didn't try to slip from my grasp. That was something. "We need to run. Can you do that?"

This time, he nodded at me.

I caught a glimpse of the faces of the other children – panicked but still placid, their steps unsteady. Their parents, their aunts and uncles would come. *A lie, a lie* – my mother's voice. I shook it off. I couldn't help them all. "Deep breaths," I said, and then ran, still holding on to Alon's arm. The boy might have been short, but he could keep a decent pace. We dashed around the pond and back toward the docks.

My heartbeat pounded in my ears. The narrow street now felt like a chasm, one into which we were falling without hope of escape. Another building to our left teetered, beams breaking. The soldiers behind us screamed as I yanked Alon forward, just out of the way of the collapsing facade. Dust swept across the paving stones, climbing into my nose. I tried not to think of the soldiers now buried in the rubble, the people that might have been inside. I had to focus on keeping us alive. Alon began to cry, a high-pitched keening sound. "I want my mother!" he sobbed, pulling at my grip.

Oh, child. I did too. She'd sat through hurricane winds, ignoring the rattling shutters and the wailing wind as if they were merely overwrought children. I promised myself – I would find a way to visit home again if I lived through this. "Listen," I shouted, "you need to run. If you don't, you'll never see her again." The words shut him up more cleanly than a slap. There wasn't time to regret them. I wasn't big or strong enough to carry him.

I thought I recognized the doorway to the drinking hall, but Danila would have to make her own way out. The ground jolted, throwing me into the wall of a building, my shoulder catching the brunt of it. I pulled on Alon's arm to keep him upright. The air was hazy; it made my eyes water. But between the gaps in the buildings I could see blue ocean and blue skies. We skidded down the uneven stones. A falling tile hit Alon on the shoulder and he reached for the wound. I pulled him along before he could touch it, merciless.

And then the air cleared and we were at the docks, a cloud billowing behind us as though we'd brought this destruction with us. Despite the shaking and the destruction, people hadn't yet filled the harbor. They hesitated on the edge of that precipice: is it bad enough? Will I feel foolish when this is all done? What of the belongings I've left behind?

Fear nipped at my heels, and I knew by now to pay heed to my fear. The thought of remaining on this island filled me with a dread I couldn't name. Maybe this would all stop, the island having sunk only a few measures. But maybe it wouldn't, and it was the second maybe that roared in my mind.

A few people tried to get into the Imperial boats – searching for protection – but were warned off by the soldiers. Others made for their fishing boats. A hulking construct with the face of a long-beaked bird did its best to stop each of them. "Please declare your goods before leaving," it croaked out. "The shipping and sale of unauthorized goods may result in fines and imprisonment. Sir, I need to perform a randomized search of your cargo hold." Bureaucrat constructs were my least favorite. I waited until it was occupied with someone else. "Alon," I said to the boy, "that's my boat out there, at the end of the dock." Wood creaked and groaned behind us; stones ground against one another. "The dock is unmoored. We need to swim. I'm going to let go of your wrist now, but you'll need to follow me. Kick off your shoes if they weigh you down."

I didn't wait to see if he nodded; I ran for the water while the construct's back was turned. It couldn't do much without Imperial soldiers backing it up, but this wasn't the time I wanted to be attracting undue attention. The ocean's surface jittered with the shaking earth, obscuring my reflection. I saw, with a shock, that the backs of my hands were gray with dust and dotted with blood. No time to check for injuries. I plunged into the water. Here, in the harbor and at the end of the dry season, it was as warm as the surrounding air. I took my own advice, kicking off my shoes as soon as the water came to my chest.

Anchors still weighed the docks to the ocean floor, so they'd only shifted instead of completely floating free. Each stroke felt surreal, brought me back to swimming in the ocean as a child, even as the island behind me fell to pieces. I seized the edge of the dock and climbed up, splinters digging beneath my fingernails.

Alon was only a short distance behind me. Good boy – he'd kicked off his shoes. I bent to help him onto the dock. My boat was moored at the other end, swaying gently in the water. It was a small thing – big enough for some decent cargo and for weeks at sea, but smaller was quicker. Smaller meant less witstone used when I had the use of it at all. This far from the dust and falling buildings, my mind cleared. "There's my boat," I told the boy, and this time I didn't have to shout. "We're going to your parents."

He followed me like a little lost lamb.

As soon as I was aboard, years of training took over. Checking the lines, undoing the docking line, hoisting the sail. The cacophony from the island faded to a dim sound in the back of my mind. My father had started teaching me to sail as soon as I could walk. Here, on the boat, my feet were steadier beneath me than on the quaking island.

Alon found a seat at the bow, and he sat there, mute and shivering.

A *crack* filled the air, loud as thunder. I looked back and swallowed. The island *was* sinking, the harbor now nearly fully submerged, the buildings at the edge creeping into the water. This wasn't going to be enough. I had to do something, get away faster.

The witstone. I scrabbled at the cargo hatch, and then at the loose boards below. The boxes of witstone lay beneath. Anyone who knew my boat could see it was sitting lower in the water than it normally did, but there were few who knew my boat the way I did. I grabbed a handful of the white, chalky stuff, pushed myself up and dumped it into the brazier.

I could have been gone, long gone if I'd not stopped for the boy. If I'd not stopped to ask after the boat that had taken my Emahla. But ifs couldn't save me now. I fumbled with the flint and then struck it against the side of the brazier. Sparks showered onto the witstone; it caught fire as easily as if it had been chaff.

White smoke surged forcefully from the brazier, bringing with it a gust of wind that caught the sail and filled it. My ship lurched forward toward the harbor opening – which was now twice as wide as it had been when I'd arrived. Sweat traced tracks down the side of my face. The sun had risen higher in the sky and the heat of it licked at the back of my neck. It didn't seem fitting that the world should end on a cloudless day.

I blew on the flaming witstone and adjusted the mainsail. We weren't the only ones speeding out of the harbor, but we were among the first. On the ocean, my heartbeat calmed, though my fingers still trembled. I caught a look at Alon, still sitting and shivering at the bow, arms wrapped around himself. The swim hadn't washed all the dust from his face. His eyes widened as he stared at the island behind us. I risked a glance back.

The scale of destruction stole the breath from my lips. Half the buildings in the city had collapsed – nothing more than rubble. A gray plume of dust and smoke rose into the air, obscuring the trees. Flocks of birds had risen from the trees, dark specks among the plume.

"Auntie Danila . . ." Alon said.

Sometimes one was enough. One *had* to be enough. I swallowed. "She might have made it out, lad – don't despair yet." Around us in the water, I saw other shapes moving away from the island – goats, deer, cats, dogs, even rabbits and mice – all swimming, all abandoning the island. The deep stirred, the scales of some giant creature breaking the water briefly before it dove back down. I caught glimpses of fins and bright spots of luminescence. Even the beasts that lived on the underside of the floating island were leaving. Dread burrowed at the base of my neck, prickling down my spine.

The island trembled more violently, sending more of the city tumbling to the ground. The ground began to sink in earnest, as lazily as a person slipping into a bath. My mind calculated out the problem before my heart could believe it. If the island sank completely, the water would rush to fill the space left behind, creating a whirlpool.

If we did not get far enough away, we'd be pulled in. "By all the Alanga," I murmured. We were moving quickly, but not quick enough. We'd barely cleared the harbor. I threw more witstone onto the fire, wiping the chalky dust off on the jacket. My little boat jumped in the water, but then slowed once more. I could see the eddies and currents, moving other boats about without regard for the wind. Someone on one of the boats screamed.

The witstone. I had to dump it. It was slowing us down.

Even with death staring me in the face, my mind scrambled for other options. I clamped down. No. I wouldn't be like those people still at the docks, still hoping the quake would end, that they'd be able to return to their homes. They were still there if they weren't drowned already.

"Alon, give me a hand with this, would you?"

The boy unfroze when I gestured to the hatch door. People always responded better in a crisis when given something to do. He held the door up as I dug for the boxes and heaved them onto the deck. A wealth of witstone, illicitly acquired, but mine. Enough to pay my debt to the Ioph Carn.

I reserved a handful for the brazier and then tossed the boxes overboard, one after another, before I could change my mind.

Enough – now not enough. Island sinking or no, the Ioph Carn would find me and demand their payment. But for now I was alive, my boat skimming across the water, my heartbeat quick and strong.

Alon crept back to the bow of the ship like a wounded animal. I'd pushed him hard, but I hadn't wanted to leave him behind.

He curled in on himself and began to keen. The opium was likely wearing off right about now too.

"Your auntie might still have gotten out," I said. I knew it wouldn't help as soon as I said it. He was eight; he wasn't stupid. Although he lived on a smaller island, he probably came to visit his auntie often; he probably knew this place like a second home. And it was gone, dissolving into the ocean, Danila with it too.

He glanced at me, red-faced, from beneath his elbow. "They're gone," he wept. "The people are dead, the island is dead, the animals –" He lifted his head to look at the animals swimming alongside our boat. "They're going to die too."

The island behind us shook once more, and that last rumble broke down the walls I'd built around my horror. What had caused this? In all the old stories – even the ones of the Alanga – there was no mention of islands sinking. Quaking, yes, but not this. Not an entire island destroying itself, taking everything with it. I did my best to bolster my feelings. It wouldn't help me or the boy if I fell apart, no matter how badly I wanted to.

I leaned over the side of the ship and saw a brown kitten, struggling in the waves. It had nowhere to go, but still it swam on. It scrabbled at the side of my boat, hoping for some purchase. I knew the feeling. Its brown eyes met mine, and I could feel its desperation.

On an impulse, I took my net, reached over and scooped the creature from the sea. It didn't move when I deposited it on deck; it crouched, bedraggled and shivering. "Look here," I said to Alon. "This one won't die if you can take care of it. Open up that bench over there. There's some blankets on the left side and some dried fish buried beneath them. See if you can get this fellow cleaned up and eating."

Alon wiped his tears on the back of his sleeve and crept from the bow to the kitten. He cupped the little creature in his arms, and though he still sniffled, he stopped keening.

One more life saved. It was a pittance, unutterably small against the scale of the lives lost. But it was there. And one life certainly made a difference to the one living it.

4

Lin

Imperial Island

I stared at Bayan, my throat tight, feeling my expression shift to shock and surprise. He'd scrubbed his hands and had removed the apron, all traces of blood washed away. I seized control of myself, wiping my expression clean, making sure that was all Bayan saw. He opened his mouth to ask me again what I was doing outside my father's room. I spoke over him, my mind running just one step ahead of my mouth.

"I was trying to get in, of course," I said lightly. I reached out and rattled the doorknob.

Bing Tai growled, the sound echoing up and down the empty hall.

We both jumped back. I caught Bayan's eye. For a moment we just regarded one another. His black eyes were wide, his lips parted, hands outstretched to ward off an attack. I wasn't sure if he laughed first or if it was me, but for a brief moment our gazes locked and then we both laughed. The door was locked and we were safe. Relief and an odd, forbidden giddiness swept through me. I'd never shared a laugh with Bayan before. I'd laughed at him and him at me, but that was the nature of rivalry. He had seven keys and I had six, and though I was the natural-born heir and Bayan an outsider, he had his eye on the crown. We couldn't be friends when we both yearned for the same thing.

As if he'd remembered that at the same time I did, his face sobered.

"And besides," I said, "what are *you* doing outside my father's room? I've more reason to be here than you."

"Is that so?" Bayan's hand went to the keys around his neck. "I'm the one with more access to the palace than you. I was on my way to the library – the secret one."

"The secret library," I said flatly. "It's not a secret if you've told me about it."

He put a finger to his chin. He had to know the gesture only emphasized his firm jawline. "What should I call it then? The magic library? The construct library? The library forbidden to Lin because she just can't remember?"

My insides boiled like a pot ready to accept a feast of crabs. I breathed out the heat of it and kept my face cool. "If you're seeking a name that descriptive, might I suggest the library primarily utilized by the pompous boy of no station?"

Bayan clucked his tongue. "The Emperor's daughter should have better manners. I am his foster-son – that's no small station. He wanted me to look up the correct command for my deer construct, and I finished my nightly meditations so I'm off to do some research."

He said it nonchalantly, and it fed my envy. What I would give to find myself in that library, to run my hands over the books, to smell their pages. To learn everything they had to offer. It was my birthright, not his. "You think so highly of yourself.

Knowledge can only be wielded by those who dive into its depths and know the shape of it. Reading—"

"—without true understanding is only wading in the shallows without a care for the monsters that lurk beneath," Bayan finished. "I'm familiar with *Ningsu's Proverbs*."

I hated him; I hated my inability to remember; I hated locks and the keys I needed to open them. What would be worse? My father casting me out and elevating Bayan in my place, or elevating Bayan and leaving me here in the palace to serve him?

Bayan might not have been any good at reading expressions, but he softened regardless. "You spend a lot of time skulking around the palace and playing around with the constructs."

"I'm not playing," I said, though I sounded petulant even to my own ears. "I'm studying them."

"Whatever it is you're doing –" He lifted his hands, palms to me. "I've seen you doing it. The Emperor has seen it. I've recovered many of my memories, and it wasn't by speaking to constructs. I meditated and spent some time on my own. Perhaps if you did the same – if you went to the courtyard or the pond or even just sat in your room and meditated on yourself as you are – you might get your memories back."

"So simple?" I couldn't put the bite into it I wanted to. I studied Bayan's expression – his steady gaze, his thick black brows raised, entreating, his full lips closed but not pressed together – and I realized he did not hate me. He should have hated me. When I had more keys in my possession, after I'd stolen more of them, I'd set up an easy way to frame him, just in case Father caught me. I didn't have much choice. Bayan wouldn't be a good Emperor. He was too much like my father, too concerned with secret places and experimental magics.

The Constructs of Bureaucracy, Trade, War and Spies were higher-level constructs that helped Father rule, but it seemed more and more that he hid behind their base competence while he worked on his own mysterious projects.

"Perhaps I will try that," I said, and Bayan actually smiled at me. I frowned, waiting for the trick, the insult.

"Bayan. Lin." Father's voice echoed down the corridor. He coughed into his sleeve but kept limping toward us.

A flush worked its way up my chest, making the air around my neck feel like a furnace. I was an idiot. I'd stood here, trading barbs with Bayan while my father had been finishing his nightly routine. I should have been long gone instead of letting Bayan waylay me. Had he done it on purpose?

But he looked as surprised as I did.

Father's phoenix-headed cane rapped against the floor as he approached; his slippered feet were silent. One of my earliest memories once I'd awoken from my sickness was seeing my father's foot, bloodied and bandaged, and asking him what had happened. "An accident," he'd said gruffly. He'd said it in a way that brooked no more questions.

Father stopped in front of us. "What are you doing outside my room?"

The piece of wood I'd used to hold the door open lay heavy in my pocket. The tips of my ears burned. Be like ice, I willed them. Like the ice at the tops of the tallest mountains. I avoided his gaze and waited for Bayan to answer first. My father would see it on my face if I looked him in the eye. He would study my face and know exactly what I'd done.

Bayan said nothing, and the silence stretched – too long.

"Bayan said he'd show me the secret library." It was the only thing I could think to say.

Both Bayan and my father took in a breath at the same time, both ready to speak.

A soft tapping came from the window at the end of the hall and we all looked to the source of the sound. A hand appeared on the windowsill, and then two, and then four. Ilith, the Construct of Spies crept through the window, one leg at a time.

I wasn't sure on which of the floating islands Father had found the abomination that made up the bulk of the Construct of Spies. But I knew I never wanted to visit. The construct looked like nothing so much as a giant spider, dark brown and glistening, as tall as my chest when it stood to attention. Human hands were attached to the end of each of its spindly legs, and an old woman's face adorned the abdomen. I wanted to look away from the creature but always, inevitably, found my gaze tracking its every movement even as my spine prickled. There was a strange beauty in its grotesqueness. "Your eminence," the Construct of Spies said. Its voice was hazy, as though spoken through layers of cobwebs. It held a folded missive in one of its front arms. "I've received word from our fastest Imperial ships. There has been a disaster."

My father's attention slipped from me and Bayan. He leaned on his cane and took the proffered parchment. "A disaster? Have the Shardless Few rebels attacked another island? A mine collapse?"

"No, my master," the Construct of Spies rasped. "It is Deerhead Island. It has sunk into the sea."

5

Phalue

Nephilanu Island

Ranami had more than made a difference in Phalue's life – she'd changed it irrevocably, much as Phalue didn't want to admit it sometimes. Times like now, when she just couldn't concentrate because of her.

Sweat stuck Phalue's hair to the back of her neck. The sword in her hand dipped, but she adjusted her grip and gritted her teeth. She'd dive into the Endless Sea before she'd lose a match to Tythus. They were of similar ages, heights and weights – her skill should win out, though. True, she was distracted. As if to prove that point, Tythus darted in, nearly scoring a hit on her pouldron. She batted the attack away just in time.

"Ah, Phalue," Tythus said, grinning with this near-victory, "you're not yourself today. A lover's quarrel perhaps?"

Phalue grimaced. It was an old joke between them. A few years ago, she'd often come to their sparring sessions moody and out of sorts. And he had gently chided her for courting, as he liked to say, "half the island". He hadn't been far off, if she were being honest with herself. She'd been an incorrigible flirt, taking up with women both highborn and low. But then she'd met Ranami, and the hot-cold passion had cooled to something more comfortable, more livable.

Lately, though, yes – they'd fought.

Tythus broke through her guard and struck her on the leg. She jumped back, too late, and hissed in pain. That would leave a bruise. She tore off her helmet and sucked in the air. It was still moist with rain from earlier in the morning, making her feel a little like she was drowning on dry land. Perhaps she wasn't ready to dive into the Endless Sea just yet.

Tythus' expression sobered, and he lowered his sword. "Really? Something is bothering you. Don't tell me you've broken things off with Ranami. She's the best thing that's happened to you."

Phalue hobbled across the stones of the courtyard, walking off the pain. "No, we're still together. I just . . . don't understand women sometimes."

He crowed with laughter. "Oh, that's richer than my auntie's seafood stew."

She scowled. "I don't understand *other* women." Or perhaps it was just Ranami she didn't understand. Ranami reminded Phalue of a spotted dove – all soft and brown, quiet and elegant, with round black eyes that evoked gentleness. But there was a thing of sharp edges beneath the feathers, and sometimes Phalue could feel herself brushing up against it if she dug too deep. She walked past the fountain at the corner of the palace courtyard, glancing at it. It was one of the old remnants of the palace, one of the parts built by the Alanga. They'd taken their last stand against the Emperor's ancestors here on Nephilanu. Her father's palace was one of the few buildings that had remained mostly intact.

She nodded at the fountain. "Did it open its eyes again?"

Tythus shifted uncomfortably. "No. They were open for five days, but haven't been open since. Gives me the shivers, honestly."

A figure stood in the fountain, a bowl in her hands from which the water flowed. The palace had been in an uproar when the statue's eyes had opened a few months ago, sightless. Her father had been about to order it destroyed when the eyes had closed again. Nothing had happened. No trumpets, no rumblings, no sudden appearance of people who had old magics. There were whispers in the streets that this meant the Alanga would return and take back rule of the islands, and that it would happen first at Nephilanu. But even frightening stories lost their bite sun-bright day after sun-bright day. "If they did come back, they'd go to Imperial first," Phalue said.

Tythus frowned. "It's bad luck to speak of the Alanga coming back."

"Don't tell me you're that superstitious."

He only pressed his lips together.

Phalue shook out the leg and sighed, her mind turning back as it always did to Ranami. "I asked her to marry me. Ranami," she said. She wasn't sure why she was confessing this to Tythus, except that he had always listened when she'd had a problem.

He sheathed his sword. "Well, I certainly didn't think you meant the fountain. And?" He read her face. "Ah. She didn't accept."

Phalue brushed sweat and hair from her forehead. "I've asked before. It's not the first time. But she keeps telling me she doesn't want to be a governor's wife. What am I supposed to do with that? Abdicate? I'm not fond of my father's policies either, but if she were my wife and I inherited, she could help me shape them."

Tythus only shrugged. He was one of the palace guards; he

wasn't going to speak ill of her father, no matter how freely she might.

"She hates that he ships all the caro nuts away to Imperial. She hates the way the farmers are treated. She thinks it's not fair. Then what is she doing with me? I'm the governor's heir. If she's truly not interested in improving her station, shouldn't she be courting someone whose station doesn't repel her? Am I a joke to her? A passing fancy? I took her to the docks where we first met, had set floating lanterns in the water, and she wanted to talk about my father's taxes! I should have known she would say no." Phalue was pacing the length of the courtyard. She stopped, took a few deep breaths.

"Phalue," Tythus said. "I've been married for five years now, and I've two children. I'm no governor's child. I'm no governor. Beyond that and most importantly, I am not Ranami. You should probably ask her."

"I don't know how to talk to her," Phalue said, and hated the edge of a whine in her voice. She'd tried to explain to Ranami that her father was urging her to marry, that she would give Ranami free rein to change things once she was installed as governor, that they'd been together for long enough. She'd even once thrown a fit and had walked away, resolving to leave her and court someone else. But she could no sooner leave Ranami than the world could leave the sun. So she'd crawled back into orbit, begging forgiveness – which Ranami had granted with a lingering hug and a kiss to the cheek. No one could ever claim she was not magnanimous.

"Perhaps," Tythus said, his head tilted and thick eyebrows raised, "you could try listening?"

"You think I don't listen," Phalue said flatly.

Tythus lifted his hands in a half-shrug. "Listening is an art. It's not so much sometimes in letting the other person speak as in asking them the right questions."

"What are the right questions?"

"I'm just your sparring partner," he said lightly. "Remember?"

A door on the second floor opened briefly to the balcony, spilling the sounds of music and murmuring voices into the courtyard. Phalue eyed the palace with distaste. "Still going, is it?"

"Your father likes his parties." Again, his voice was perfectly neutral. "He might enjoy it if you stopped in."

Stopped in? It would be like a crow trying to roost among songbirds. Phalue's mother and father had dissolved their marriage when she'd been young, and though her mother had sent her to live at the palace, she never felt like she quite fit in. Her excesses were not drinking and dancing. She shook her head. "Tythus, I would no sooner stop in than you would. You know that."

He put a weighty hand on her shoulder. "Talk to Ranami if you want to know her thoughts. I'm no soothsayer. You're prying at a rock and hoping to find a nut inside."

Phalue sheathed her sword and then redid the tie in her hair. "We haven't spoken since last night. I left angry."

"Was she angry?"

Phalue slammed a hand against one of the teak pillars. "No. Just . . . sad. And that just makes me angrier sometimes."

"Well, you'll have to talk to her sooner or later," Tythus said. "Or just never talk to her again."

"You're only two years my senior," Phalue said, rolling her eyes at him. "I'm not a child."

"Then go," Tythus said, waving a gloved hand. "Go be an adult. Go make adult words and sort out your differences. I'd very much like to end on the high note of winning."

"Unfairly," she said, a finger raised. And then she shook her head. "We'll finish this tomorrow morning."

"Fair enough."

She didn't bother to change out of her armor; she preferred it to street clothes or – heaven forbid – to the embroidered silken tunics her father was always trying to get her to wear. And Ranami liked her in armor. She'd confessed to Phalue after one breathless night that Phalue seemed the most comfortable in it, her truest self. And Phalue loved that.

Her heart skipped at the memory, before sinking as she remembered their fight. Always, always at the end of these fights, Ranami would say that Phalue just didn't understand, and Phalue would say, "Well, then make me understand!" and then Ranami would look at her as though she'd asked a dog to sail a boat. It was like they stood on two different islands when they argued, and neither of them could find a way across.

The forest outside the palace walls was damp and green, just at the beginning of the wet season. The tree branches Phalue brushed out of the way were wet, the street still slick. In the distance an iyop bird repeatedly sang *iyop-wheeeee* – one last desperate attempt to attract a mate before the heat of the dry season faded and raising young became difficult.

The palace stood at the top of a hill, insulated from the city below. Phalue's knees jolted as she strode the winding switchbacks, trying to keep her footing. Despite the unrest among the farmers, and despite the unpopularity of her father, the people of Nephilanu Island seemed to like her. They liked her discipline, her lowborn mother, the fact that she often walked down to the city to visit her. Her visits, accompanied by a retinue of guards, had been the inspiration for Phalue to learn how to fight. If she could fight, she'd argued with her father, then surely she could visit her mother on her own.

When she'd beaten two of his best men in a brawl, he'd relented. At first, she'd walked down to the city just to visit her mother. Then it had been to see the markets. And then she'd caught the eye of a visiting governor and had fallen in love for the first time. She'd been a late bloomer at nineteen, but she'd more than made up for lost time.

Halfway down, she had to walk into the mud at the side of the road to let a cart pass. It creaked beneath its burden, the oxen at its front straining to pull the load. More supplies for the palace. She wondered sometimes what it had looked like when the Alanga had built it. After all the renovations her family had made to it, it probably resembled the original as much as a lapdog resembled a wolf. The caro nut farms had made her father rich, and he'd ordered the construction of a new hall just outside the palace walls – one he was convinced the Emperor himself would some day visit.

Phalue scanned the city as she waited for the cart to pass, trying to pick out Ranami's home among the sloping, tiled roofs pressed too close together. What would she say to her? "Sorry" was the most obvious opener, but oftentimes seemed inadequate. "I understand" would be what she'd most want to hear probably, but it wouldn't be true. "I love you"? So true that it swelled her chest every time she looked at her.

On the odd morning, she missed her days of philandering. A new woman every few weeks, a new passionate tryst. But the day she'd met Ranami at the docks had knocked the wind from her. If Phalue took a long view of things, Ranami didn't seem overly special. She'd been crouched at the edge of the dock, long lashes shadowing her face, slender fingers pulling a crab trap up from the depths. Who fell in love with the way someone drew up a crab trap?

Phalue had noted Ranami's beauty first, and then her gracefulness, and then the way her lips parted a little as she concentrated, her brows forming the smallest of lines at her forehead.

Her approach had . . . left much to be desired. She'd offered to buy a crab, and they clearly weren't for sale, and Ranami had frowned, confused, and had said they were for her personal use. Ranami knew who she was, and what use would the governor's daughter have for a random crab from the docks? And then she'd guessed Phalue's intentions soon enough, and had turned her down.

"I'm not interested in being toyed with."

"Is it that you're not interested in women?"

Ranami had given her a long look, like she couldn't believe what she was hearing. "It's not that you're a woman. It's you." Not the most auspicious of beginnings. She'd left Ranami alone, as she'd asked, but her words had given Phalue cause to reflect. She had broken things off with her latest paramour, and endured three full months of celibacy. Had she been so reckless with others' feelings? And then, to her surprise, Ranami had sought her out at the palace. "Perhaps I'm making a fool of myself," she'd said, eyes downcast, demure, "but if you've still some interest . . ." She'd handed her a basket with a crab inside.

Phalue tapped her fingers against her scabbard, Ranami's words echoing in her head. It's you. Was it something about her again this time? She tried to shake off the uneasy feeling that it was. It lay slick over her heart like oil over water. If it was, she'd make Ranami say the words, make her break it off – because Phalue just couldn't.

She picked her way through the narrow streets near the dock, the gutters clean from the rain but still smelling faintly of fish. A few gutter orphans caught sight of her and followed her down the street. "Please, Sai. Please." She reached into her purse and tossed them some coins. Her father gave her an allowance every tenday, and what else was she to spend it on? She always made a point of helping the orphans or the shard-sick when she strolled into the city.

Ranami lived in a small one-room apartment above a merchant who sold steamed buns. She smelled it before she saw it – fish sauce and scallions, and the sweet scent of steamed bread. The merchant lifted a hand when he saw her, and she gave him a quick nod before turning into the alleyway where the stairs were, feeling a little foolish as she dodged dripping remnants from the rooftops. If her father had his way, she would be dressed in silks and sent to other islands to treat with them. She'd have learned diplomacy rather than battle. As her father's only child, she was an asset, and he often moaned that she was going to waste. But he never seemed to gather the willpower to set against hers.

Phalue laid a hand against the stair railing and froze. Something was wrong. She should have sensed it before, but she'd been too caught up in daydreams. There was no sound coming from the upstairs apartment. And the door, which should have been closed, lay slightly ajar. She put a hand on her sword. "Ranami?" she called.

No answer.

"Uncle," Phalue called out to the bun merchant, "have you seen Ranami this morning?"

"I've not seen her at all today, Sai," he called back.

She would have gone to set her traps by now, and she always liked to buy two buns from the merchant before she set out. Phalue's heartbeat quickened, her lips numbing. Keeping her hand on her sword, she barged up the rest of the stairs and into Ranami's apartment.

Part of her had expected to find Ranami here, startled, wondering what Phalue was doing. The curtains were drawn; the room dark. She drew her sword, but as her eyes adjusted, she could see – there was no one here.

Ranami's normally pristine home had been turned upside down. The linens were stripped from the sleeping cushions, belongings pulled from cupboards, chairs overturned. The books on philosophy and ethics Ranami had practically begged her to read lay scattered across the floor. Phalue's head pounded. She shouldn't have been so stubborn. She should have come back sooner to apologize, should have never left Ranami's side. Who would want to ransack Ranami's home? She made only a modest living as a bookseller. And where was Ranami?

Phalue sheathed her sword and picked up a dress strewn across the floor. It was the one Ranami had been wearing the day they'd met – the golden cloth bright as turmeric, setting off her dark skin and darker hair.

"Ranami?" she called again, and she could hear the desperation in her own voice. This couldn't be real. She felt like she'd stepped through into a mirror world, and if she just tried hard enough, she could step back through to her own. She squeezed her eyes shut and opened them again. The same dark room greeted her. But this time, she saw the piece of parchment on the table.

She marched over, the floorboards creaking beneath her boots, and snatched it up. She had to pull a curtain aside to have enough light to read by.

If you want to see Ranami again, come to the Alanga ruins at the road leading from the city.

6

Sand

Maila Isle, at the edge of the Empire

The bark of the mango tree was rough beneath Sand's fingers as she climbed. She'd harvested nearly a full bag, but she needed just two more mangoes to bring back to the village. So she climbed. Higher and higher, her breath ragged in her throat, her arms and legs aching. She never returned without a full bag. None of them did. If you did not return with a full bag, you did not return at all. She'd seen one of them before – Waves was his name – sweeping his net in the water for fish, over and over until the tide rose and he fell from his perch into the sea. He was gone. Dashed upon the reefs surrounding Maila. It happened sometimes. Someday, it would likely happen to her. The thought gave her no feeling at all; her heart was as gray and cold as a foggy morning.

But today she saw the blush of two mangoes among the branches above, peeking from beneath the leaves like shy cour-tesans. Sand searched for footholds and tested them, making sure she wouldn't slip. The branch bent a little beneath her weight as she pushed herself further up, but it held. The first mango was above and behind her a little. She had to twist and reach out for it with her smaller hand, the one missing two fingers. Her fingers brushed the smooth outside of the fruit; she walked her fingertips across its surface, trying to pull it closer. Her other arm strained, her palm growing sweaty.

The others had likely all returned from their daily tasks. She stopped to breathe and scanned the rest of the tree for easier targets. None. She was Sand and she always returned with a full bag. So she tightened her grip on the branch and reached again for the mango. This time, she got a grip around the bottom, and she pulled, trying to break it free. The mango slipped from her grasp and she slipped into a memory.

It wasn't the mango she was touching. It was a curtain of rough linen. She drew it back – and her hand had all her fingers. A sliver of sunlight fell across her face, warming her cheek. When she blinked past the golden hue of the rising sun, she could see the green-tiled rooftops of a palace, shrouded in mist, the jagged mountains beyond cradling the buildings as though offering up a precious jewel. A rush of feelings swirled in her breast. Awe, anxiety, dismay. She let the curtain fall, unable to reconcile them, retreating into the dark, closed space of the palanquin.

No. She was Sand. She was Sand collecting mangoes. That place in her memories wasn't one she'd ever seen. But she could still smell sandalwood and the damp morning mists. Her arms ached.

And then her hand slipped from the branch.

The world slowed as her arms windmilled. Her hand struck the trunk behind her, but she couldn't find anything to grab, and then her foot flung free of its spot between two branches. She was falling. Branches whipped at her, her vision a blur as her head flew back and then ricocheted forward. Each of her injuries registered only as things that might hurt later – building up one on another. The ground. The ground would hurt.

It gave beneath her only a little. The air whooshed out of her lungs and she opened her mouth to suck in more. But the air she breathed made her feel sick. Sand coughed and then retched to the side, her head spinning. She lay there, just gasping for breath.

Her arms were bleeding. The numbness where the branches had struck her gave way to a sharp, stinging pain. Sand rolled onto her side and then pushed herself up slowly, discovering fresh aches with each movement. She was still alive, though the thought didn't comfort her. There was a deep gash on her left forearm. She probed at it, hissing in pain, examining the way it slashed through skin and fat and into the muscle beneath – the layers of her laid bare. That would need stitches.

That thought . . . wasn't hers either.

The world still rocked around her, moving as she moved her eyes. Nothing for it. She had to get up, get back to the village. Thatch could sew up her arm. Her tunic had ripped on the way down. She helped it along, tearing off a strip to wrap the wound with. When she finally got to her feet, the earth didn't feel solid; it was as if she were on a boat, like the one that had brought her here. The one that had brought them all here.

No. She hadn't been on a boat, had she? She wasn't sure what she was thinking, who she was.

The bag of mangoes lay near the tree, half upended. Several mangoes had rolled out, and she collected them, slinging the bag over her shoulder once more and wincing. It felt like a blacksmith had taken up residence behind her eyes, using her skull as an anvil. With every beat of her heart, an answering throb started in her head.

Her bag was still not full.

Sand eyed the tree and then went straight back to the base

of it to climb once more. But something stopped her just as she reached for the first branch.

Why did she need to return with her bag full? What sort of nonsense was that? Her cold, gray heart flushed with color. She could just . . . go back to the village. There were plenty of mangoes for them all, and the others were cultivating or harvesting food as well.

Something had changed between the memory and the fall, and she wasn't sure what. It was as though she'd pulled back the curtain and was finally seeing the palace. The world was not just inside the palanquin.

Halfway back to the village, on the turn in the path that jutted over the ocean, Sand stopped. The spray from the sea kissed her face as she looked out over the horizon. The jagged edges of the reef surrounding Maila broke the water in places, like the ridged backs of some strange animal. Beyond the reef, the Endless Sea waited. A thought struck her, and it knocked out her breath as surely as the fall had.

Why was she on Maila at all? Why didn't any of them leave?

7

Jovis

Somewhere in the Endless Sea

I t was not a kitten.

I watched Alon playing with the creature near the bow. It leapt onto his wriggling fingers, mouthing at them with a gentle jaw. For one, its ears were small and rounded. It didn't have claws on its front paws – which looked closer to digits than to paws, with a fleshy web between. The brown fur on its body was lighter on its belly, and as dense as an otter's fur. I should have noticed when I'd plucked it from the water, but an entire floating island had just sunk right in front of me. One could be forgiven for missing smaller matters.

A vise tightened around my heart. The boy had been busy taking care of creature, but I'd watched the horizon until the island had disappeared beneath it. I might have hoped that the island had stopped sinking, but the smoke that had billowed upward finally disappeared at sunset, and I just knew. All those people. I wanted to scream at the horror of it.

The water would have come up to their ankles, and then their shoulders, and then the land would have ceded completely to the ocean. People who had holed up in their homes would have been trapped in them, cold ocean filling their lungs instead of air as they beat their fists uselessly against their ceilings. Pressure against their ears as the depths claimed them.

I raked a hand through my hair. Both were covered in dust. My lungs still felt scratchy with it.

At the bow, Alon was scratching the beast behind the ears. I didn't know what manner of creature it was. There were so many animals that lived in the Endless Sea, no one could quite keep track. Did it even matter? Something that lived in the water by the look of its webbed feet. It made me feel quite a bit less generous, that I'd likely not saved the beast at all. But it still seemed to be an infant that had somehow been separated from its mother, and it had eaten half my store of fish, ravenous as a shipwrecked sailor.

Chittering, it dashed from the bow to where I sat at the stern. When it saw it had gotten my attention, it sat neatly at my feet, tail curled around its haunches. And then, cautiously, it rose to its hind legs and laid one of its odd paw-hands on my knee. Wide, black eyes stared up at me with a strange solemnity.

"Mephisolou likes you," Alon called. "He knows you saved him."

"Mephisolou?" I scoffed. "You named it?"

"Him," Alon said, stubborn.

I acquiesced. "You named him Mephisolou?" I regarded the animal. He certainly didn't look like the monstrous sea serpent from folklore, ready to devour an entire city if they did not pluck him some cloud juniper berries. "Mighty name for such a small fellow."

The boy shrugged, his gaze going to his feet. He traced a circle on the deck with his toe.

Oh, would it truly hurt me to humor him? "Mephi," I said. "Mephisolou doesn't quite roll of the tongue."

"I think it sort of does," Alon said, a smile returning to his face.

"You call him what you like then. Mephi," I said, offering a hand to the creature. I expected him to sniff my fingers or to bite them, but he only lifted his paw and placed it on my hand – like we were two old friends greeting one another in the street. A shiver went up my arm, raising the hairs up to my shoulder. I pulled my hand away gently and ventured to stroke the fur on his head. All solemnity vanished. Mephi leaned into my touch so hard that he fell over, his body curling on the deck. He murmured like an old woman digging into an especially satisfying stew.

I laughed – and I'd not expected to laugh for a long time after Deerhead Island. As if my laugh had startled him, Mephi jumped to his feet and scrambled back to Alon, rolling into him and grabbing at his fingers again. The boy giggled. And then, quick as a storm rolling in, he began to sob. "Is it gone? Is it really all gone?"

The people. Trapped. I swallowed, aware of Alon's eyes on me. "Aye, I think it is."

He sobbed all the harder. But it would be worse if I'd hidden the truth from him. Reality was a harsh mistress, but it was one that could not be denied.

Mephi curled at the boy's side, patting him with his paws as he cried. And then the creature stared at me.

Was he expecting me to do something? I cleared my throat. "I'm sorry," I said. The wind whipped my words away. If Alon and I were old friends, and he were a young man, I'd take him to a drinking hall and we'd speak all our happy memories of the dead. I'd offer him a sprig of juniper to burn with the body. But Alon was just a boy and I had no juniper sprigs to burn here, nor a body. "Your auntie might have made it out," I said. This felt like a lie. He didn't seem relieved by my words. He might have believed me in the initial shock of the quakes, but now, in the water of the Endless Sea, my words had nothing to hide behind. Mephi still stared at me.

"Your auntie was a fierce woman," I said, raising my voice above the wind. "When I met her, she made me promise to save you. She was afraid for you. She loved you so, so much."

He'd stopped sobbing, though his voice was thick. "She said she would make me dumplings for my feast. If I lived through the Festival."

I nodded. "She was making them when I met her."

Alon dried his tears on his sleeve. "Was it the Alanga? Are they back?"

I didn't know what to say to that. "The Emperor is supposed to be protecting us from them. That's his job." Lies, again. At least they felt that way to me.

Alon's gaze focused on the horizon. East, where his parents lived. "I want to go home."

And I wanted to get him home. Other boats had passed us by. First the Imperial caravels, eating up their supplies of witstone, and then the Imperial traders, and then common folk who had perhaps inherited a small store of the stuff. I'd dumped an entire two boxes overboard. If I'd left the boy behind, I might have been able to get away with keeping one. No. I'd done a good deal of terrible things in the name of finding Emahla; even so, there were lines I didn't cross, even when I'd first been at my most desperate. Otherwise, how could I ever face her again? So I puttered across the ocean with just the wind in my sails to move us along.

I checked my navigational charts. The islands were all migrating north-west and into the wet season, but the ones in the Monkey's Tail moved closer together this time of year. I made some swift calculations, taking into account the islands' movements. If we were headed east, the isle would be slowly traveling toward us at the same time we sailed toward it. "Get some rest," I said. "We'll be there by nightfall."

The boy fell asleep almost instantaneously, as though he were a construct and I'd embedded this command in his bones. Mephi curled into his side. I hoped the boy's parents didn't mind that I'd foisted a pet onto them.

I was as good as my word, though I always was. We docked at nightfall, just as the sun had slid below the horizon. I waved away the biting bugs that seemed to appear once the sun disappeared and moored my boat. The trade construct at the docks didn't give me much trouble. Oftentimes they'd look from me to my boat, to me again when I declared no goods. But if a construct could get tired, this one was tired. It accepted my docking fee with a snap of its beak and told me all was in order.

I had to shake Alon awake. "We're here," I said. "You'll have to tell me how to get to your parents' home." He nodded at me and pried Mephi loose from his side. "Aren't you taking him with you?"

Alon yawned and shook his head. "Mephisolou wants to stay with you."

"Mephi should be with other Mephis," I said. It was fine by me if the boy wanted to keep him as a pet, though I couldn't speak on behalf of his parents. I couldn't keep a pet aboard my ship. Before Alon could protest, I scooped up the creature, strode onto the dock and knelt. I lowered Mephi into the water, making sure he was awake and could swim. He flipped onto his back in the water, watching me. "Go," I said. "Find others of your kind." As if he understood, he flipped back over and dove.

I waved the insects away from Alon as I returned to him. "Let's go," I said.

Alon gave vague directions. His home was a "little ways" up

from the dock and "beside a big tree". I let him lead us in the dark, crickets singing in the brush all around us. It was busier than usual this time of night, other refugees searching for shelter like sea turtles dragging themselves onto shore, hoping to nest. We finally stopped in front of a modest home with a thatched roof next to a towering banana tree. Despite the vague directions, it seemed to be the correct house. I knocked on the door loudly.

A man answered, his face pale. And then he broke into sobs when he saw Alon. He knelt, grabbed the boy and held him. Beyond him, I saw a woman lying across a bed, her face flushed, sweat beading at her forehead. Her eyes met mine briefly. I knew that hollow look. Shard-sick. Somewhere, her bone shard was in use, and it had nearly drained her life. No wonder Danila had been so desperate to save the boy. I couldn't hold her gaze.

Instead, I found myself staring at the bald pate of Alon's father as he buried his head into his boy's shoulder. "We'd heard," he said. "We heard what happened."

I wasn't sure what to say – I'd brought them back their son, but he'd lost a sister, and was soon to lose a wife. When the man finally drew back, he looked up at me from his spot on the stoop.

"Danila asked me to save him," I explained. "I owed her a favor."

"A moment," he said, before retreating back into his house. He came back with ten coins, all silver. A small fortune for a fisherman. He pushed them on me. I took them graciously. I'd just dumped two boxes of witstone into the sea; I couldn't be expected to start turning down money. I wasn't a monk. Even if I were, I doubted the walls of a monastery would save me from the Ioph Carn.

"Join us for a meal? It's the least we can do, and no one will be sleeping tonight, not after the news." Alon was kneeling at his mother's side, stroking her hair with careful fingers.

The hard pallet and blanket on my boat called to me. I might not be able to sleep on it tonight, but I could at least rest my head on something. "I'm setting sail in the morning," I said, "but thank you. I'm searching for someone. They left on a boat – a little smaller than an Imperial caravel – with dark wood and a blue sail."

The man was nodding, and my heart jumped. "I saw such a boat only yesterday. It must have stopped for supplies, but if you're trying to catch it, you'd best hurry. I was out fishing, and the thing skipped right past me, faster than a dolphin sailing the waves. Only one person aboard, as far as I could see. It was headed east. I'd say Nylan."

Emahla. I'd find my answers. I'd find her – I just needed to catch that boat. "Thank you. And one more thing." I beckoned him close. "Your son. I rescued him before the Tithing Festival. The records are gone. Scar him in the right spot and no one need know."

Alon's father pulled away, his eyes wet with tears. Alon's shard would never be used to power a construct; he'd never need fear his life draining away at any given moment. "Who are you?"

The disappearance of the island had shaken me to the core, wiped away my levity. But now, I found a measure of it again. Who was this man going to tell? I'd saved his son. "Jovis. Best smuggler in the Empire." I pulled up my sleeve to show him my navigator's tattoo – I really, really ought to wrap that.

And then I turned and headed back toward the docks, feeling more pleased with myself than I had in days, the silver coins jingling in my pocket.

I felt quite a bit less pleased with myself when I awoke the next morning, gasping for breath, my jaw aching. I must have clenched it in the night – dreaming over and over of the shaking island, the whole of it sinking into the sea. And I dreamt I was with it, my body sinking into that endless depth, the darkness closing in on me, the weight of the water crushing my lungs. But I was still on my ship, the water calm, my pounding heart louder than the gentle knock of boats against the docks.

The docks around me were full, with more ragged boats anchored offshore. Deerhead Island was no small land mass, and though most people had not escaped, some still had. The Emperor would have to send constructs, soldiers, food. The chaos would at least buy me some respite from the Ioph Carn. If I were very, very lucky, they'd assume I was dead.

Though I would have liked to have left at first light, I needed to start making up for the money I'd lost from tossing the two boxes of witstone. So, after wrapping my tattoo with a strip of cloth, I headed to the market.

The market was no grand, sprawling maze of merchants' stalls. It consisted of two alleyways, the smell of refuse mingling with the scent of dried peppers, frying goat meat and baked goods. The cramped alleyways were made even more cramped by the unwilling visitors from Deerhead Island, seeking out supplies as they sought out loved ones on other isles. I ran a few quick calculations in my head and stopped at a merchant selling sweet melons. They were grown mostly on the southern isles during the dry season, and since we were headed into the seven-year span of a wet season, they'd become more valuable. And they'd be even more scarce now that Deerhead Island was gone. I bargained down the merchant with ruthless efficiency, though the price was higher than I would have liked. She'd just finished tying the twine around the boxes, and I'd reached to lift them when a voice sounded from my right.

"They did a good likeness of you in the posters. Clever, paying orphans to take them down. But it seems the Empire truly wants to make an example of you."

A hat. I'd wrapped my tattoo, and had changed from the soldier's uniform, but I had not worn a hat. I felt the way a rabbit must when it feels the noose about its neck. And like a rabbit, I'd keep kicking. "The eyes," I said, turning to face the speaker, my melons in hand. "They never get those right."

Philine leaned against the wall of a building, one foot crossed in front of the other, perfectly relaxed. She wore a sleeveless quilted tunic, showing off the muscled tone of her arms. A short wooden baton hung from her belt, though I knew she hid knives on the rest of her. "I think they made you look more handsome in the posters," she said.

"Truly? I've heard the opposite from most people when I asked."

She had the most interesting way of rolling her eyes without ever seeming to take them away from me. "Yes. They told me you thought you were funny."

It wasn't a good sign that they'd sent Philine after me. She wasn't flashy; I thought if I looked away from her I might mistake her for a piece of the wall. But her ability to track down the people the Ioph Carn were looking for was the sort of thing you saved for drunken fireside storytelling – when your audience might believe you. I held up my free hand, palm facing her. "I was on my way to see Kaphra." I glanced around and leaned in. "I have two full boxes of witstone. That should cover my debt for the boat and then some."

Her hand reached for her baton. "You never should have incurred a debt at all. You were supposed to finish paying it off before you sailed away on it. It's not a debt; it's a theft, and you know how Kaphra feels about those who steal from him."

From the corner of my eye, I saw a man and a woman watching us a little farther down the alleyway, both in quilted tunics, weapons at their sides. More of the Ioph Carn. They weren't as subtle as Philine was. "He always had another task for me. It would have taken half a lifetime to pay that boat off." I wasn't sure why I was arguing with Philine; she had no power to grant me clemency, but it seemed to be buying me time. The woman I'd just purchased the melons from had backed away from the front of her stall at mention of Kaphra, doing her best to blend in with her merchandise. Most merchants paid some dues to the Ioph Carn; perhaps this one didn't. It was a small isle after all.

"Yes," Philine said. "And you agreed to those terms."

"I have my boat moored at the docks," I told her. "This should only take a moment."

She considered. Two full boxes of witstone was a fortune, and no matter how angry Kaphra might be with me, he'd welcome the extra supply. Ioph Carn smugglers used a good deal of it when they had to outrun Imperial ships. She turned to beckon to the other two Ioph Carn, and I took the opportunity to run.

I might not have been as bulky as any of the three of them, but I was quick on my feet and knew how to work around a crowd. The two boxes of melons swayed at my side, the twine digging into my fingers. I'd lost the witstone; I couldn't lose the melons too. The refugees shuffled through the alleyway like ghosts, silent and morose. No one was lively enough to stop me or to mind too much as I wove around them.

Philine would be following, unburdened. And even if she hadn't seen where I'd gone, she would find me.

The way I saw it, I hadn't had much choice. Seven years ago, on the morning Emahla had gone missing, I'd seen in the distance – so faint I'd thought it a dream – the dark boat with the blue sails. A blink and it was gone.

I'd tried to find some semblance of a life without her, but no one had wanted to hire a half-Poyer navigator who came without Academy recommendations. When the Ioph Carn had approached me with their offer, it had seemed the best way to get away, to leave my grief behind.

And then, two years ago, I'd seen the boat with the blue sails again, clearer, but fading into the distance faster than I'd thought possible. I'd failed her for five long years, not knowing where to go or what to look for, instead of trusting my own eyes. So I stopped responding to Kaphra and struck out on my own. Two years I'd spent chasing rumors on my stolen boat, both evading the Ioph Carn and sending them what money I could to pay my debt. And now I was closer than I'd ever been and they wanted to stop me?

No. Not this time. I kept my promises.

I wove through the streets, my breath ragged in my throat, my boxes of melons banging against my thigh with each step. Faces flashed by me – old, young, weathered and smooth, but all of them weary. Some faces were still covered in dust from the collapsing buildings, tear tracks cutting their way from eyes to chins. The docks were just a turn around the corner.

A shout went up behind me, and I glanced back before I could help myself. Philine's lackeys made their way through the crowd far less gracefully than I had. One of them had overturned a bucket of fish, sending a silvered stream into the street.

But where was Philine?

I turned around just in time to see her hurtling out of the corner of my eye. Her shoulder struck mine with an impact that knocked my breath halfway out. The twine around the melon boxes tore from my grasp. It felt like I was watching myself fall from a distance. I struck the ground shoulder first, my hands still trying to get a hold of the melons.

"You don't have witstone," Philine said.

"I have melons," I choked out when I could finally get a breath. "You can sell them for a tidy profit."

"Not interested," she said, her voice flat.

"I've been sending money to Kaphra, plus smuggler's fees. I send a cut of all my profits. I don't want trouble."

She loomed over me, blocking the rising sun. A thin, black tendril of hair had come loose from her plait, swaying against her cheek with the ocean breeze. The other two Ioph Carn pulled up beside her, breathing heavily. Philine lifted her baton free of her belt. "And that's why we're not going to kill you."

A street never clears so quickly as when the Ioph Carn are about to visit a beating on someone.

Even when the first few blows fell, I was thinking about how I could get away, how I could best them. Pain exploded across my shoulders and back, blotting my vision with red. I grabbed for something, anything, that could get me out of this situation. Only the dirt of the street and a few small, loose stones. I threw them at her anyways, and Philine dashed them away with one gloved hand. "I don't enjoy this," she said. "If you stayed still, it would go faster."

I believed her when she said she didn't enjoy it. Her fellows didn't seem to hold the same philosophy as she did. A kick to my ribs sent me sprawling in the dirt, and I caught the glimpse of a grin, white teeth flashing like the underside of a bird's wing.

Pain layered on top of pain – sharp over dull, bright over bruised. I heard the strikes of Philine's baton more than I felt them – beating against my ribs like a drumstick, my body an instrument. A person could dance to the beat had they the inclination. The world around me faded, grew muffled, as though I were perceiving everything through a woolen blanket.

"Stop," Philine said. Her lackeys ceased and took a step back in unison, obedient as any construct. I licked my lips and tasted copper.

"I don't care if you ever had the witstone you promised me.

I don't care if you ever will," she said. "I'm here to take you to Kaphra."

She didn't wait for me to give any sign that I'd heard her; but then again, I couldn't have if I'd tried. Even my tongue hurt. I might have bitten it during the beating. I seemed to discover some new injury with every movement.

I had to get to the docks, had to follow that boat, had to find Emahla. I wasn't caught yet. I wasn't caught until they brought me before Kaphra, both hands and feet bound. Philine reached down to grab me, but I shrugged off her hands. "I'll come with you," I said, staggering to my feet. And then I reached into the pouch at my side, pulled out a few strips of jerky and stuffed them into my mouth. I swallowed and breathed out, straightening my spine and pulling my shoulders back. "Stay back," I said, holding a hand out. "I've no wish to hurt you. Kaphra wouldn't like it."

The three Ioph Carn glanced at one another, confused. "What did he eat?" one of the thugs said to the other. He only shrugged in response.

Philine took a step forward.

I am strong. My ribs aren't digging sharp edges into my lungs. Merciful skies, that hurts. No. *No pain.* I had to believe it or they would not. I let my posture speak for me. *Go on. Try me.* "Or didn't Kaphra tell you about the time he had me hit a monastery?"

Philine's eyes narrowed. "You don't have cloud juniper bark," she said.

That was the key – always make *them* say it.

She realized her mistake as soon as the words came out of her mouth. The two Ioph Carn thugs with her shrank back. No one had seen one of the monks fight in years. And the stories still circulated, growing grander with each telling.

"He's a thrice-cursed liar. How many times do you think

he's pulled this trick before? He doesn't have any," Philine said, though even the step she took forward was hesitant.

I'd pulled this trick once before, but she didn't have to know that.

"How do you know he doesn't?" one of her lackeys said.

She turned to snap at them, taking her gaze from me. "Don't be idiots. The monks steep the bark in tea, they don't take chunks of it and *eat* it. They'd be stuffing their throats full of splinters!"

It was distraction enough. I backed up one more step and pulled down one of the street stalls, blocking the street between us.

Finding Emahla would make this life, these debts, this beating all worth it. I swept up the boxes of melons and made for the docks, shouts following me down the street. I hunched and breathed through the pain, putting one foot in front of me, then another. My knees creaked as I ran, but I was running. When I wiped my face with my sleeve, it came away red. My pulse seemed to vibrate, hot from every bruise. I'd bought myself time, but I wasn't sure if it was enough.

I couldn't hear footsteps from behind me, but I heard shouts as the Ioph Carn pushed people from their path – a cloud I couldn't quite shake. I knelt and unwound the rope mooring my boat as quickly as I could.

A chittering sound greeted me as I leapt aboard. The stern knocked up against the dock as I searched the deck for the noise. Mephi sat near the prow, a fish proffered in his paws. He chittered again and held up the fish, as if asking me to take it. I didn't have time for this.

"I can't keep a pet aboard," I told him. That crack to my ribs must have jolted something loose in my brain because I was talking to him like he was a person. "You need to find your own kind." I pointed at the water.

The chittering, which had been soft and pleasant before, grew louder. He sounded like a squirrel scolding me for getting too close to its tree, only a hundredfold. The wind was already blowing eastward, and the cloth billowed as my ship began to move. Philine appeared from between the buildings, her face red, her baton held at the ready. I wasn't clear yet.

I seized Mephi by the scruff, ready to toss him overboard. Beneath the wet outer layer, my fingers brushed his thick, dry undercoat.

His cry turned plaintive – a piercing, wailing sound. My chest tightened in an almost instinctual panic. He was, after all, just a baby. He was alone in the Endless Sea, and though I'd rescued him, I'd brought him to this other island, wholly unfamiliar. What if he couldn't find others of his kind? What if he couldn't hunt enough for himself? Would I be leaving this creature to die a slow and painful death? What would letting him stay a little longer even cost me?

Disgusted with myself, with my weakness, I dropped him back on the deck. "Fine. Just don't get in my way."

His wailing stopped mid-cry. He didn't run off as I'd expected. With a satisfied *prrreeeeeet*, he deposited the fish at my feet.

I dashed to the sails and wondered again if I'd been imagining him swimming toward my boat, back at Deerhead Island. I sighed – I'd likely never know. "I'm going to regret this, aren't I?"

I just couldn't know how much.

8

Lin

Imperial Island

I held out a nut. "Come on, little spy," I cooed. "You're still following orders. Just one nut. It won't hurt."

The spy construct twitched its cat ears, grooming its face with paws a little too large for its squirrel body. Its tail curled around the rafters, holding it steady. Constructs didn't have much personality, but this one watched the nut with one eye.

The sleeves of the servant uniform scratched my wrists as I reached into my sash and produced another nut, flourishing it next to the first. Now I had the spy construct's full attention. Its tail uncurled and it took a half-step forward.

"That's it. Come on down. The witstone isn't going anywhere." Sunlight filtered through the shutters of the storage shed, bright bars across the weathered wooden floor. Boxes of witstone, standard Imperial-sized, were stacked one on top of the other almost to the ceiling. A cloth was draped over one box; a half-measure sat loose on top of it.

The spy construct took another few steps toward me and then

jumped onto the highest box, its tail and whiskers twitching. I'd seen it creeping around after me as I'd walked the palace halls. My father, keeping an eye on me. But that didn't mean it couldn't enjoy a little treat in the meantime. There were no guards for this fortune of witstone, but spy constructs watched all the servants. And this spy construct, like all spy constructs, reported to Ilith, Construct of Spies. And Ilith preferred to eat thieves slowly rather than imprison them.

Claws scratched against wood as the spy construct scampered closer. I did my best not to move, though my arm ached from holding my hand outstretched. And then it took the first nut from my fingers. An animal would have dashed away with its prize. But the construct just stayed where it was, eating the nut. I'd already noticed it; it had already given up trying to remain hidden. So what was the point? I examined the way its parts all blended into one another like a creature born this way. Father did good work.

The sinking of Deerhead Island had changed things. The Construct of Bureaucracy was worried about the refugees and where they would go. The Construct of Trade wouldn't stop talking about the loss of the witstone mine. The island governors had already started writing to Father – a few offering to take in some refugees in a gesture to try to curry favor, and others had already stated their intentions not to take in any. Whatever instability already existed in the Empire, this event would widen the cracks. And there was still the matter of why the island had sunk at all. I tried not to think – what if all the islands sank? What if this was part of the islands' migratory pattern we knew nothing about, spaced hundreds of years apart? I took in a deep breath. If that were true, I could do nothing to change it. What I needed to focus on were things I could change – and that included staying my father's heir so I could take his place when he died.

I pulled back the rough sleeve of the servant's uniform and offered the second nut to the construct. It sidled even closer this time and took it. Its beady black eyes regarded me. Could a construct ever like someone? This one enjoyed nuts; why not a person? And if it did enjoy someone's company, could that loyalty ever overcome the commands written into its shards? I'd confused constructs before by forcing their commands into contradictions, and the four first-level constructs that helped Father to govern seemed to have some modicum of personality – but what about a third-level construct like this spy?

But I was here for other reasons. I'd seen these spies watching the servants, and I was hopeful that Father hadn't completely altered its original commands. My memories might not have been as good as Bayan's, but I watched the world around me more closely. I'd seen a servant go out into the city on her day off. When she'd draped a coat over her uniform, the spy construct following her had simply stopped.

So I'd taken a servant's tunic from the laundry and disguised myself.

The creature stared at me as I reached out a hand and plucked a piece of witstone from the loose pile. Its nose twitched but the rest of it moved not a bit. I drew the witstone to my breast, and then made a show of stuffing it into my sash pocket.

For a moment, I thought I'd misjudged. The construct sat on its perch on the witstone box, watching me like it was waiting for another nut. Then an ear twitched, its nose twitched, its head twitched. It dashed past me, slipping beneath the gap in the door. It would be making its way to the palace now, to the tunnel in the courtyard that was just big enough to accommodate its little body. It would disappear into that tunnel, making its way to Ilith's lair and reporting to its master on the theft by a servant.

Once I was sure it had gone, I put most of the witstone back, reserving a little in case I ever needed it. Father had never forbade me access to the witstone. If he tried to punish any of the servants, I could tell him I'd asked them to bring me a little for an experiment.

I checked between the slats of the shutters, peered around the crates, looking for any other spy constructs. I found I was well and truly alone.

The key I'd retrieved from the blacksmith two nights ago felt heavy in my sash. The bow was different from the original, but I had the feeling that my father would know if he saw it. Just the knowledge that I carried it made me walk differently, I was certain of it.

The servants performed their work in the mornings and in the early evenings before dinner. Father had taken Bayan behind one of his locked doors so they could practice. The palace was mine.

When I strode back in through the entrance, the whole place felt different. The sunlight streaming in looked brighter and everything seemed to vibrate with my reflected excitement. There was a key in my pocket, and it opened one of the many doors I'd been denied.

I strode up the left set of stairs of the entrance hall. The mural at the top was faded, the only remnant here of the Alanga. My ancestors had built the palace around this wall – a reminder of what we'd fought against.

A row of men and women stood, shoulder to shoulder, their hands clasped and their eyes closed. The Alanga. I wasn't sure which was which – who was Dione and who was Arrimus. I must have known before I'd lost my memories. Despite the fading paint, the richness of their robes was still visible. The cloth still looked soft. I resisted the urge to run my fingers across the mural as I passed.

I started with the largest, most ornate doors first. On two of them, my key hung loose from the door, swallowed by the enormity of the locks. And then I grew a little less ambitious, testing the key on doors that seemed they might fit. The quicker I found it, the more time I would have to explore it. Father and Bayan's training sessions often lasted until dinner, but I couldn't trust it would always be that way. My heartbeat quickened with each new failure.

What if I'd somehow been mistaken? What if this key opened no doors? What if Father had placed it there as a trap? What if he just needed a good excuse to cast me out and to raise Bayan in my place?

I was Lin. I was the Emperor's daughter. I would learn his bone shard magic and would prove to him I was worthy of taking his place. I would prove to him I was not broken. I repeated it to myself in my head like a litany. It was the only thing that mattered.

When the lock turned, it took me a moment to notice. It was a small, nondescript door near the end of a hallway on the first floor, the varnish faded and on the edge of peeling. Sunlight had warmed the brass doorknob. I took one last glance up and down the hallway, and then stepped inside. The door closed behind me with a soft click.

Darkness surrounded me; there were no windows in this room. I should have thought to bring a lamp, but in my flurry of planning it hadn't occurred to me. My imagination supplied beasts in the darkness, perhaps even Ilith, just waiting for me to step closer before claiming me as prey. I swallowed and kept my breathing quiet as my eyes adjusted. A thin bar of light shone at the bottom of the door, and it rendered the room in color-less shapes.

But it was enough for me to find the lamp hanging beneath

the lintel, and the tinder below that. I lit the lamp with trembling fingers, unsure if what I felt was excitement or terror. When I turned the light on the room beyond, I found walls lined with drawers – and no constructs waiting to eat me.

The drawers were labeled. Tiny drawers, like ones meant to store rings or earrings. Several to my right had small pieces of paper with handwritten notes sticking out. I went to them, my footsteps creaking across the floorboards. When I peered closer, I made out Bayan's handwriting.

A–122 – Deceased
83–B–4 – Alive
720–H – Alive

It continued like that, scratches across papers. My hand cramped in sympathy. But when I looked to the labels on the drawers, horror clawed its way up the back of my throat. *Thuy Port – Deerhead – Year 1510*. I knew what I would find when I opened the drawer. I opened it anyway.

Little shards of bone lay inside, cushioned by velvet, white against red – the way they must have looked when they'd been chiseled away from their owners' bodies. Bayan had been here, testing the shards from Deerhead Island, seeing which owners still lived and which ones were dead, and thus had no life with which to power a construct. Their bone shards would be inert.

It had been five days since the news about the island, and this was what my father worked on? No matter how complex his four tier-one constructs were, they couldn't run an Empire. The Empire needed him, and he was cataloging the remains of a disaster, seeing which ones were still useful.

I shut the drawer. I wasn't sure when I'd begun to realize

my father's rule was failing. It might have even begun before I'd fallen ill. But what I did remember was watching my father's hand shake as he turned the pages of a trade agreement, squinting at the pages until he gave up in frustration. "Review it," he'd said, tossing it the Construct of Trade. And then he'd gone into one of his secret rooms and had shut himself away.

His soul might have held strength enough to power ten constructs, but his body was weakening.

I lifted the lamp and walked along the rows of drawers until I found *Imperial* and the year 1508. The shards within were all labeled with letters and numbers. There had to be a catalog somewhere. The drawers went up to nearly the ceiling, ladders placed at intervals along the wall. They went to the floor as well, and when I knelt, I saw the drawers at the bottom were longer and taller. I set the lamp aside and pulled one open.

A book lay within. The cover was of some scaly leather – either green or blue in the dim lamplight. I brushed it, almost expecting dust but finding none. Yellowed pages smelling of ink and old glue ruffled when I opened the book. So many pages, and so many names. The span of the Phoenix Empire never ceased to surprise me whenever I was confronted with evidence of it. I could trace my lineage back to the beginning, to the people who had finally fought and defeated the Alanga.

The pages toward the back were crisper. I found year 1508, and then – *Numeen*, in the neat handwriting of a bureaucracy construct. *03-M-4.* I closed the book and adjusted it until it looked undisturbed. And then I searched for 03-M-4.

There was an empty space in the drawer where his shard would have been. Relief flooded my limbs, and then shame for feeling relief at all. There was something written in tiny letters beneath the label. I peered closer, swinging the lamp over the drawer. *B – for practice.* Bayan. He was using Numeen's shard in his practice constructs.

Better than being in regular use in one of my father's constructs, but not by much. The shard would be in Bayan's room. And judging by the meticulously kept notes, he would notice if I took it. He'd notice, and he'd tell Father, and then I'd have to find a way to explain. I'd sneaked into Bayan's room a couple years ago, just out of spite, and he'd noticed each thing I'd moved and touched. He even kept his shutters locked now. I'd checked. If my father had a key to Bayan's room, I didn't know which one it was.

Numeen might not know his shard was being used, not for quite some time. But then he would start to feel it in the mornings and late at night, a weakening of his limbs, an unnatural exhaustion about his shoulders heavy as a sodden blanket. Weariness would become his constant companion. Eventually, he would die, a little too soon and a little too young.

But the constructs kept us all safe. They were as numerous as any army. My father always said the Alanga would one day come back, and when they did, they'd try to reclaim the Empire. All the Alanga had powers, but their rulers had more than most. When one island's ruler fought with another, the clash of their magics had killed so many hapless bystanders. Enormous walls of water, windstorms that flattened cities. The greatest of them, Dione, could drown a city while saving all the flies, but most Alanga didn't have that level of control.

What could mere mortals do against such power?

I picked up another shard, turning it over in my fingers, noting the identifying numbers and letters inked onto its surface. My ancestors had found a weakness, a way to kill the Alanga – a way my father hadn't yet shared with me. Did he really care about the well-being of the Empire? I wasn't sure.

We need an Emperor who cares about us. I did care. But I couldn't take back Numeen's shard without getting caught.

I set the shard back down and closed the drawer, feeling as though I were trying to hide the shame in my heart.

The lantern swung from my hand as I whirled about. There was more room to explore, and I might find something other than bone shards and catalogs. I went to another column and tested a few more drawers. Just shards.

At the very back of the room, the wall was free of drawers. I pressed a palm against the smooth plaster, wondering what lay on the other side. A dark shape caught my gaze. Another door, wedged nearly into the corner. I hurried to it, my excitement mounting with each step.

This brass knob was cool to the touch, and I tried to turn it before I saw the keyhole beneath. The doorknob rattled in my grip.

Locked. Of course.

I pushed away from the door, frustrated, and then seized the key in my sash pocket. It slid easily enough into the lock, but the tumblers wouldn't turn. I tried pushing on the door, I tried pulling it. I tried jiggling the key in the lock as I turned, hoping that this was the right key, even as I knew it wasn't. It wouldn't be like Father.

He just couldn't make things easy for me, not even once in my life. I jerked the key from the lock. My breathing seemed to echo off the cabinets, off the walls.

The door. I'd been so focused on the lock, I hadn't looked at the door. Something seemed to seize my heart, squeezing hard enough to make me gasp. Two bronze panels were fastened to the door. Engravings of cloud junipers rooting themselves at the bottom, curling upward, their branches filling the top.

The beauty of the engravings weren't what had startled me,

though the door *was* beautiful. I'd not seen this door, not in the five years since I'd been sick. But I knew it, the way I knew the feel of my teeth beneath my tongue. I grasped at a feeling, a smell, an image of this door lit by multiple lanterns. It wisped away from me, never substantial enough to grasp.

I'd been here before.

9

Jovis

A small isle east of Deerhead

If anything can be said about the Ioph Carn, it is this: they are persistent. I was in my ship with the sails hoisted and my lines checked when Philine and her men ran skidding down the road toward the docks. I think Philine called out, "Stop!"

Waste of breath, that. Does anyone actually stop when they're being chased? She'd just beaten me; what did she expect — for me to turn around and thank her for the kind request? No. I did what everyone else who's ever been given that command does — I fled faster.

Mephi chirruped as I ran from one end of my ship to the other trying to get the sails filled with wind and my stern pointed in the right direction. The harbor here was small, the opening barely large enough to fit an Imperial caravel. I wouldn't be scraping my sides against the breakers, but I certainly didn't have the space I had back on Deerhead.

Mephi sat at my feet as I went to the tiller and pointed to the Ioph Carn, running down the docks toward us. "Those people are not good people." He tilted his head to the side, his eyes fixed on mine. I was doing it again. I was talking to an animal. I could blame nerves. I'd always talked too much, too often – except when I was home in the kitchen, or out on the Endless Sea. Other places I was restless, always restless. Emahla had never taken me seriously until she'd seen me silent.

Philine didn't go for any ship they'd sailed in on. She hurried her lackeys into a dinghy, untied it and urged them to row.

They had arms thick as posts and sinewy as salt-soaked ropes. I glanced at my own slender limbs, and then to the sails, billowing but not skipping me across the water. I'd not reach better winds until we left the harbor. There was still the handful of witstone. I could still outrun them. "Don't get underfoot," I said to Mephi, and then shook my head. I'd done it again. Oh, what did it matter if the talking made me feel better? And it did. Made me feel in control.

I lifted the storage hatch, lifted the loose board and felt around for the witstone.

Only smooth wooden boards. A dizzying sensation rushed over me, bringing bile to the back of my throat. The witstone was gone. I swiped my hand across the space. Perhaps a wave had hit my boat in the night and the stone had shifted, rolled into a corner. I tried a third time, my head stuffed with cotton.

It couldn't just be gone.

Something cold patted my other arm. I pushed myself up and saw Mephi, watching me, clutching his paws like a worried auntie. When I looked over his head, I saw the Ioph Carn looming.

Would that I could control the wind or the sea. All I had aboard was a spear I used sometimes for fishing. I grabbed it anyways, set my boat toward the harbor entrance and stood on the port side with my spear. My bruised ribs ached as I breathed, waiting.

Philine's expression was grim, her baton at the ready. She'd not let me get away a second time.

My heartbeat thudded against my ribs, steadier than I thought the situation merited. Sweat slicked my palms as the dinghy grew closer. I could see the veins on the Ioph Carn's arms as they rowed, the tendons straining on Philine's hand as her grip tightened around her baton.

The dinghy knocked against the side of my boat, and in that same moment, Philine grabbed at the side of my ship with one hand and seized the end of my spear with the other hand – just as I tried to jab her off my boat.

She used my spear to help haul herself up, nearly sending me tumbling overboard. I righted myself, barely, just in time for her to put the butt of her baton into my already-bruised ribs.

The pain took my breath away and I hissed it back in through my teeth, trying to focus on something, anything, else. The spear. I still had it. The end of it was still in her grip. I shoved with the spear, trying to put her off balance, trying to send her overboard.

She merely looked annoyed.

I needed her to get off my boat; I *needed* her to. I needed it with the panic of a drowning man. I couldn't go to Kaphra, not now. I would have made any demon's bargain, would have shaken hands with the greatest of the Alanga himself. Just to send Philine over the edge.

She smiled as though the desperation I exuded with every breath were a perfume. With her free hand, she pulled a blade free of her belt, cocking her arm to throw. By her gaze, she was aiming for my eye.

A ball of brown fur hurtled past my feet, launching itself at the woman. Philine's expression shifted all at once, her jaw clenching. "Shit!" She dropped the knife and it tumbled into the ocean behind her.

Mephi locked his jaws around her ankle, a growl rumbling in his throat. She tried to shake him off. I remembered the sharp little teeth he'd used to eviscerate the fish I'd given him. They'd hurt, but they wouldn't put her off for long. Damned woman still had her fingers tight around the end of the spear, and she was more than a match for me in strength.

And then something shifted inside me. It felt like an unlocking, a moving of tumblers, and then a soft and subtle click. I could feel myself quaking, a quiet roar sounding in my ears.

Philine kicked Mephi to the side. I took in another breath and the pain left my ribs. The air seemed to flow into my lungs and then dissipate into my limbs, bringing new strength. I felt it first in my bones, a subtle tremor of power. And then in my legs – now solid and as strong as the corner posts of a house. It flowed upward, into my back and arms, and in the next instance I was no longer grappling with Philine. It was still her in front of me, but it felt like wrestling with a child. I lifted the spear experimentally, and her feet nearly came free of the deck.

I watched the sick realization travel across her face. Was that what I'd looked like when I couldn't find my witstone? And then, before I could think any of this through, I tossed both her and the spear into the water – just before the breakers. It was as easy as tossing a fish back into the ocean.

Just as quickly, the strength left me. I collapsed onto the deck, my breath ragged in my throat, my gaze on the sails as we left the harbor and headed out into the Endless Sea.

Mephi crept over to me. He placed both paws on my knee, his whiskered face solemn, blood marring the fur beneath his mouth. "Not good," he said in a squeaky, guttural voice. He patted my leg. "Not."

A beating at the hands of the Ioph Carn I could handle. Being chased out of the harbor and losing the last of my witstone – that too it appeared was not beyond my abilities. But this?

My brain promptly gave up.

I woke to the sound of the ocean lapping at the hull. Colors and detail filled in like paint soaking into paper. First the sun, high and bright in the sky. And then the wind whipping at the sails. I squinted.

Mephi stood at the prow of the ship, his whiskered face into the wind, fur ruffling. As soon as he heard me stir, he scampered over and chittered, his paws combing through my hair as though he were searching for a meal.

I waved him off and sat up. My whole body felt stiff and sore, like I'd been tumbled and buffeted by waves before being rudely tossed ashore. That was the thing about beatings – they got worse before they got better.

The Ioph Carn.

I jolted up, pain lancing through my body sharp as a knife. The isle was still in view, though getting rapidly smaller. I didn't see any boats following me – not yet. It would have taken them time to fish a sodden Philine from the ocean, and time to ready their boat. Their ship wouldn't be as quick as mine, and I wasn't sure how much precious witstone they'd want to expend in capturing me.

The wind ruffled my hair, sending it into my eyes. I tucked it back behind my ears and made a quick round, checking the lines and the sails. I looked through my charts again, just to be sure. We were headed in the right direction and the wind was good, so there wasn't much to do except sit and wait. The Navigators' Academy always liked to say that patience was the first thing they taught their students, though that hadn't been my first lesson there. My parents had known what I'd be confronted with. They'd tried to tell me as I'd packed my bags for Imperial.

"They won't accept you," my father said, his voice soft. "They won't see you as one of them."

"I know," I said, rolling my eyes as I pulled books from my shelves. "They'll ask me if I've spoken with the ancients, or if my name means 'snowy mountain' in Poyer."

My mother wedged herself between me and my bags, her brows low. "We're trying to tell you something important! Anau is small; everyone knows us here. They don't know you in Imperial. They'll think they know you, and that's very different."

I'd sighed, a youth who thought he knew more of life than his parents did. "I'm half-Poyer and half-Empirean – is that what you wanted to remind me of?"

They'd exchanged a glance, my mother's face exhausted and exasperated, entreating my father to explain. If I'd not been fool enough to deny it, I'd have seen I'd missed their point entirely. "Jovis," my father said, "we wanted to remind you that you are both Poyer and Empirean. And no matter what they say, that doesn't make you any less than them."

I'd nodded and thanked them, though I still hadn't quite understood. I'd passed the entry test, hadn't I? But when I'd arrived at the Academy, the instructors had put me in my place as a half-breed spectacle, and the first thing I'd learned was that a life as an Imperial navigator would be a lonely one.

I sat at the tiller and regarded my new companion. He seemed determined to ensure I was in no danger of loneliness. Maybe I could have ducked Philine's knife-throw. Maybe not. It seemed I'd plucked him from the water and he'd plucked me from a messy death.

"So what are you?"

Mephi only sat on his haunches and scratched at one small ear with a foreleg. His lips drew back into a grimace as he searched for the right spot. He did look something like an otter. The digits on his paws were longer, his ears pointed instead of curved. His face was more angular than round, which is why I must have mistaken him for a cat at first. Despite his kitten size, his body was longer so he could stretch easily up to my knee.

After watching him struggle for a moment, I sighed and reached out to help him scratch. He leaned into my touch. Though his fur was coarse, his undercoat was soft as downy feathers. It felt the way clouds looked – decadently fluffy.

I rubbed a thumb over his head and paused. There were two bony knobs next to his ears. The beginnings of horns? I couldn't think of any sea-dwelling creatures with both horns and fur. Feeling very foolish, I said, "I don't suppose you could tell me who and what you are?"

Mephi only opened his mouth and let out a satisfied chirrup.

Had I imagined him speaking before? I'd been overwrought, having been beaten, narrowly escaped and then narrowly escaped again. But despite the lies I told others, and the lies I sometimes told myself, I didn't think this was something my mind had made up.

"There are parrots," I said to Mephi, "that live on a few of the islands. Some people keep them as pets and they can speak like people do."

I'd stopped petting him. He pawed at the knee where I'd placed my hand, and I obliged, scratching his cheeks.

"Is that what you do? Just repeat what you've heard?"

Mephi crouched, and before I could register what he was doing, leapt into my lap and sprawled across my legs as though he belonged there. I sat still, not daring to breathe, a little afraid this wild creature might bite me. When he didn't, I rested a hesitant hand on the warmth of his shoulder. He let out a grumbling sigh and laid his head between his paws.

I'd once swum to the bottom of a cove at home just to see how long I could stay there. When my lungs were fit to burst and even my brother had splashed at the surface in his worry, I had uncurled my legs and pushed myself toward the surface. It felt like that now, like my heart was uncurling, surging up to some brighter place.

A boat appeared ahead on the horizon – a dark shape against the water. The wind picked up, and my ship cut through the water, bouncing a little on the waves. Mephi didn't stir. Would that I could fall asleep so quickly and without any cares. The boat on the horizon wasn't an Ioph Carn boat, and it wasn't an Imperial ship. Oddly enough, it had no sails at all. The Empire still kept galley boats, but even their galley boats had sails.

But as we drew nearer I realized that the ship did have sails. Only they were the same blue as the sky.

I was on my feet in a flash, spilling Mephi onto the deck. Alon's father had seen the boat heading east, but it must have anchored out of sight, or come back to the isle for some unfinished business – because it was here, now, right in front of me.

I checked the sails. I was only carrying the two boxes of melons; I didn't have a full cargo hold. This was as fast as I could push my ship. The other boat perhaps hadn't seen me or just didn't care, because it looked like I was gaining on it. I went to the prow and squinted before remembering I kept a spyglass. My head was full of wasps, buzzing, disorganized.

I lifted the bench at the prow, pulled it out and snapped it to its full length. With the rocking of the waves and my unsteady hands, it took me more than one try to set it properly against my eye. The horizon came into focus, as did the dark-hulled boat. The blue sails billowed, and near the stern stood a figure.

Only one that I could see, and cloaked in dark gray. The first time I'd seen the boat had been on the morning Emahla had disappeared. In the initial panic, one of my aunties had suggested that perhaps she had drowned herself, and even though I knew she hadn't, I went to the ocean. Mist hung heavy over the beach, waves crashing on shores I couldn't see. I'd gone to the very edge, the water seeping into my shoes, sucking cold at my toes.

Something had moved in the fog. At first I'd thought it the water, or even the fog itself. But then I'd seen a patch of blue. A blue sail. I'd blinked, and it was gone. Even the sand beneath my feet hadn't felt quite solid; how could I be sure in that moment that any of it wasn't just a terrible dream? I'd already begun to miss her, my heart knowing what my head couldn't.

And then I saw it again five years later. Five wasted years. I'd been paying off my own boat – something larger than my father's fishing boat, something that could move from island to island without being capsized in the first storm. The Ioph Carn were the only ones who would let me pay it off by working for them. I hadn't had a choice. But on the anniversary of my brother's death, I'd stopped at an isle east of Imperial and burned a sprig of juniper on a bluff in Onyu's remembrance. Clear skies, sunny. It was there I'd seen it again – the boat with the blue sails, a lone figure at the rails. This time, I knew I wasn't imagining it. I'd cut contact with the Ioph Carn and spent the next two years chasing whispers of blue sails.

Now, as I stood on my boat with the strange ship in my sights, I imagined leaping aboard, seizing the cloaked figure, shaking them. Asking them what they'd done with Emahla, where they'd taken her, where she'd been all these years. I still knew the weight of her head on my shoulder, the creases in her cheeks when she smiled, the warm, callused feel of her palm against mine. The way she always seemed to understand me even when I couldn't find the words.

But these things were fading, no matter how desperately I held them, dissolving like salt into the waves. And that was the worst thing about this grief – not just knowing that she was gone, but knowing that eventually new memories and experiences would layer on top of them, making the distance between us ever wider. The days we'd spent swimming and fishing at the beach, the first time I'd kissed her, the dreams we'd shared – I was now the only keeper of these memories, and that was the truest sort of loneliness. There were so many things I still wanted to tell her, to share with her.

The figure turned toward me. For a moment, I thought they met my gaze through the distance. And then they went to the sails. A moment later, I caught a glimpse of white, wispy smoke. Burning witstone.

I snapped the spyglass shut. I had no witstone, but my boat had been designed to be quick. There might still be a chance, depending on how much witstone the other ship had. I cast my gaze about my boat, suddenly aware that despite my imagination, my certainty that I'd leap onto the other ship and take it by force, I had no weapons. Even the fishing spear was gone, dropped into the harbor with Philine. And, as my body kept reminding me, it wasn't in the best condition at the moment.

"We'll figure something out, won't we?" This talking to Mephi was starting to becoming a habit. He followed at my heels as I paced the length of the ship. I had a small club on board I used to dispatch fish I'd caught. That would help a little. And back there, when I'd been fighting Philine, I'd gotten something of a second wind. Perhaps I'd get a third wind?

It didn't matter. The answers I'd been looking for were aboard that ship, and I would let the Ioph Carn beat me every day of my life before I'd let this chance pass me by. I went to the prow of the ship, fish club in hand, hoping the bruises and the blood made me look intimidating rather than pathetic. And it was there, in the prow of the ship, that I watched the other ship start to pull away. It felt like I was on the beach again, looking for Emahla, realizing that everything I did was useless. My fingers tightened around the fish club until I felt splinters beneath my fingernails. "I can't ... I can't keep doing this." I wasn't even sure what I meant by it.

Mephi murmured at my feet and then rose to his haunches and patted my knee. Before I could look down at him, he'd scampered to the sail and climbed the brazier's legs, his tail wrapping around the metal. He tumbled into the bowl itself, ashes dusting his fur.

"I don't have any witstone left," I said. "It's all been burned."

But Mephi wasn't looking for witstone. He sat in the brazier, faced the sail and *breathed*. Smoke curled from his mouth, wispy as the smoke from burning witstone. The smoke brought a wind with it, and then a full breeze. It caught the sail and filled it, spreading across the surface like oil across water. My boat lurched forward.

"Mephi! Mephi*solou*!" Giddiness filled me, swimming up my neck and making me dizzy. "What are you? What are you doing?" I didn't know what I was saying. Was this a dream? And if so, when had I started dreaming? Before I could question what I'd seen, Mephi breathed in and out again, more smoke wisping from his mouth and wind filling the sail.

I checked the horizon. The ship was still there, and we were moving quickly, skimming across the waves as though borne on wings. I checked through the spyglass again. It could have been my imagination but I thought I saw even more witstone smoke rising into the blue sails. How much witstone did they have? The boat was not marked with any of the Empire's sigils, and even smugglers and thieves never got their hands on much witstone. I'd only been able to the once, and that had been through careful manipulation of the Empire's constructs and its soldiers. Did it matter though? I'd bludgeon the whole Empire with my fish cudgel just to get her back. I stood at the very edge of the bow, the wind and sea spray in my face, ready to leap as soon as we were remotely close enough.

The blue-sailed boat pulled away again, the wind in my face going slack. No. Not now, not when I hadn't seen this ship in years, not when I was so close to getting answers. We'd slowed, and the other ship had sped up. When I glanced back, I saw Mephi in the bowl, breathing out ragged little gasps.

"We have to keep going!" I called to him, and I didn't care that he was an animal. He might not have understood my words, but he had to understand my tone. "We can still catch them." So close, so close. I was a starving man with honey held just beyond his lips.

Mephi blew again, the sails filled and the ship jolted and skipped. He crouched in the brazier, ashes trembling on his whiskers. "Not good," he croaked out.

The shock I felt this time at his words was different. I couldn't care about this creature I'd plucked from the sea. I couldn't care about Alon, or the other children I'd left behind. Emahla might, even now, be on *that boat*. Some part of me knew it couldn't be true, not after so many years, but there was a good deal of me that was still standing on that beach the morning she'd disappeared, hoping that somehow things could be right again. And that part of me *needed* to catch that boat.

Mephi took in another shaky breath. He hadn't lifted himself to his feet; he still crouched in the brazier like a wounded animal protecting its belly. I remembered the way he'd sighed and laid his head in my lap, completely trusting. The way he'd thrown himself at Philine, buying me much-needed time. Guilt and desperation tangled in my chest. How many more breaths would it take for us to reach the other ship? Too many. He'd be dead before we reached it.

I knew this – I *knew* it! – yet I still wanted to at least try. Too many lies I was telling myself, one on top of the other.

"Stop," I said.

Quiet though the command was, Mephi collapsed into the bowl, his breath unspent. The sails calmed; the water beneath us lapped at the wood.

And the ship I wanted so badly to board disappeared over the horizon and into the Endless Sea.

10

Lin

Imperial Island

The cobblestones of the street were slick with rain from the afternoon, lanterns reflecting from its surface. I knew this way now, the way I knew the other parts of this routine. Wait until Father had finished questioning me and sat down to tea, break into his room, take a key. He didn't question me every night, so I'd only stolen two more keys so far.

But it mattered to me, because when I got the copy back, I'd have two more keys than Bayan did.

A few people still lingered on the streets, speaking to neighbors in the lilting accent of Imperial Island. They glanced at me as I passed – I never had time to change out of my embroidered silk tunics – but returned to their gossip. Father rarely let me out of the palace on my own, so no one really knew my face. I'd gone twice in a palanquin, with servants to reach past the curtains to take my coin to the vendors. I never set my slippers on the stones of the street, never felt the air of the city against my skin.

I peered into the closing shops as I passed them. Their

occupants wiped down tables or folded things into drawers. A tailor's shop held a wealth of fabric, bolts stacked one on top of the other, the ends spilling loose, like a multi-hued waterfall. Next to it, a bakery, the air around it still suffused with yeast and steam. And then after that a drinking hall, its shadowed corners still filled with people murmuring to one another. Mugs clinked and smoke wisped from the entryway. It smelled like the sort of place that was always damp, with more than one puddle soaking into the weathered floorboards. A part of me wanted to go inside, to ask for wine, to fit myself in between these people and listen. What would I read on their faces? But I had a key heavy in my sash pocket. If I did not hurry, Father would return to his room and discover what I'd done.

So I strode to the blacksmith's shop and slipped inside. The bell on the doorknob clanged against the old wood and the black-smith looked up from his work. He only let out a little grunt – not satisfied, not displeased, but . . . wary.

"I have another key," I said, reaching into my sash pocket. I pulled out the key. He took a moment before extending his hand and letting me press the key into the valley of his palm. Without a word, he peered at it, taking in the dimensions. He pivoted on his stool and started opening drawers. "The same price for this one as the last," he said. He knew who I was now. He could have asked for more. I had it.

But I only pulled out the two silver coins and set them on the counter, watching as he pressed the key into the wax mold.

His brow furrowed as he worked. He flicked his gaze to my face, and then back at the key. A moment more and then he asked, his attention still on his work, "Did you find my shard?"

The blacksmith affected nonchalance, but he licked his lips, his shoulders tense while he awaited my answer. He'd asked the last time as well, and I found myself dreading the question even more than I had before. Because I knew where his shard was; I just couldn't get to it without getting caught. "No," I said, the lie past my lips before I could stop it. Though I pushed past the unease, it settled like a sickness in my belly. "There are many more rooms to unlock, and I don't know which rooms are which. I'll find it soon, I hope." I took his same nonchalant tone – as though this thing didn't matter.

It mattered to him.

And it mattered to me. It shouldn't have mattered. My father always said I needed to look out for myself, that I couldn't rely on others. But I was relying on Numeen, and he was fulfilling his end of the bargain. Sweat gathered on his brow, shining orange by lamplight. Past him, on a shelf, were a few small trinkets – a wooden carving of a monkey, a bouquet of dried flowers, some incense and a chipped mug. I wondered what they meant to him.

"How many children do you have?" I shouldn't have asked, but like the drinking hall a few doors down, I felt drawn into this world I didn't know.

The furrows in his brow evened out. "Three. A son and two daughters." I watched this broad-backed man, who had spoken so roughly to me when we'd first met, turn from rock into sand. "They're all too young to be helping me here, but they want to. The eldest especially." He laughed at some private memory.

"You must love them very much." Did my father ever speak of me that way to others? Or did he just lament my lost memories and tell them how he might cast me out? I tried to imagine Father's cold facade dissolving as he spoke of me and couldn't.

The warmth in Numeen vanished as soon as the words left my mouth, and I realized too late how they might sound to him. Like a threat. He jerked open another drawer and dug around in the back. "Here's the key you brought me last time. I'll have this one ready in another day or two." He set it and the key I'd brought on the counter, took my two silver coins and turned away from me.

I recognized this at least. It was a dismissal.

So I took both keys, tucked them into my sash pocket and left. The moisture on the cobblestones soaked through my slippers as I ran back to the palace gates. Plaster wedged beneath my fingernails as I climbed the wall and found my way back down.

I made it back to my father's room, breathless, sweat tickling the small of my back. Bing Tai only grumbled a little this time as I tiptoed inside and placed the key back where I'd found it. I didn't wait around to see when Father would be back. I went to my room.

It was a cupboard compared to my father's chambers, but I preferred it that way. It felt like being embraced by walls. Every place in my room felt safe; there were no unknown corners. Just the bed, the desk, a thick rug, a wardrobe and a couch. As soon as I closed the door behind myself, I let out a sigh and shucked off my dirty slippers, shuffling around beneath my bed for another clean pair. Bayan and Father both stayed up late. I'd wait them both out.

I folded my legs beneath me and did what Bayan had recommended. I meditated.

Whatever magic this had worked on Bayan, it didn't work on me. All I could think of was Numeen with his furrowed brow and his laugh as he talked about his children. Surprisingly relaxing fare, but not revelatory by any means. I focused on my breathing and waited until the night felt truly silent.

And then I went to the door and out into the sleeping palace. I didn't light a lamp; the moon shone through the shutters and provided enough light so I didn't run into walls. And I knew these hallways well enough.

I checked Bayan's room, just in case. Father was a creature of habit, but Bayan was like a restless ghost. I was never sure when he'd appear, what his mood would be and whether or not he had arrived in order to do me some mischief. Outside his door, if I held my breath and listened very hard, I could hear his breathing from within – steady as the waves crashing at the shore.

I went back to the shard room first and tested the new key on the cloud juniper door. It jammed before I could get it even halfway inside. Not the right door. So I went from door to door in the palace, my breath echoing off the walls, my footfalls sweeping against the floors like broom bristles. I shivered as I passed the mural of the Alanga, their hands clasped and eyes closed. The hallways felt larger at night, like darkness had broadened them.

The key finally slid into place on the tenth try, in a door across from the questioning room – the one where my father took his tea. The darkness when I opened the door was impenetrable. No moonlight graced the walls or floors. I had to feel around for the lamp hanging by the door frame, and it took me more than one try to light it.

When the lantern flickered to life, I had to suppress a gasp. I'd been lucky. I'd found the library.

In many ways, it was similar to the bone shard room – but instead of tiny drawers lining the walls, there were shelves stacked with books. The room felt softer too, with rugs across the floorboards, couches between shelves, and windows high on the walls. During the day it must look beautiful, light streaming in from above and glimmering off the golden script on some of the covers. At night it felt like walking into a hidden glade.

I set the lantern on a side table and began to sift through the books. A good many of them were historical or philosophical, but I ran my hand over one with an unfamiliar script and pulled it from the shelf. It was nearly long enough to take up the entire depth of the shelf. I flipped the broad pages.

The symbols written on the inside were the same ones my father carved into his bone shards. There were small explanations written beneath the symbols in a neat, tidy script – not my father's hand, but one of his ancestors.

Most were simple commands – to follow, to sound an alarm, to attack – but the further I read, the more complex they grew. Some commands could be combined with others on the same shard to form a different command. Attack could become attack but not kill. There were identifying markers too. I found the one for servants' clothing, with a note that the shard had to be laid across the clothes it was meant to identify while the marker was carved.

I pulled down a few more books with the symbols on the binding. Some were aimed much more specifically – one entire book, for example, was dedicated to building the commands for spy constructs. Another for bureaucrats. Yet another spoke of the commands for attacks – a description of each attack and when it should be used laid out in symbols.

My mind whirled, an ache starting behind my eyes. It wasn't the dim lighting. Learning these symbols and when they should be used would be like learning an entirely new language. It effectively was a new language – with its symbols and its system of organization.

Maybe Bayan wasn't stupid. Maybe he just had too much to learn.

I sifted through the shelves, trying to decide if I could get away with taking any of the books, even just for a day. Nothing too large, of course. And Bayan had moved past beginner skills. He would likely not notice, and neither would my father, if I borrowed a book of beginner commands.

I mounted one of the ladders attached to the shelves and began my search, swinging my lantern over all the titles.

This felt more satisfying than any meditation. The only sounds in the room were my own – the scuff of my feet against wood, my breathing, the crisp *swoosh* of turning pages, the creak of old binding. The library smelled of old paper and the faint scent of burning oil. The library lamp was an intricate thing, enclosed in glass to prevent any unwelcome contact with all this old paper.

On the third rung of the ladder, near the back of the room, I found what I was looking for.

It was the sort of book you might give to a child learning their letters. The symbols within were painted large, the written explanations short and simple and accompanied by illustrations. I wouldn't be making any Empire-toppling constructs with this sort of information, but even the tallest tree starts from one small seed. I tucked the book beneath my arm.

And then something odd surfaced within me – a feeling that I'd been here before. Not just in this library, but here, on the third rung of this ladder, at the back of the room. No, the fourth rung. I took a step up and without knowing exactly why, I slipped my hand into the space above the books and below the shelf. I reached back and behind the books.

I should have felt surprise when my fingers closed around another book. I should have surmised that someone had pushed too many books onto this shelf and one had fallen to the back. Instead, I knew that someone had placed it here deliberately, to hide it.

I fumbled with the lantern and the book beneath my arm, but I managed to keep my grip on it. It was small, with a green cover, unmarked. When I opened it, it didn't smell quite as old as the other books, its pages still white and not yellow. Dates were written at the tops of pages, paragraphs below. The handwriting was loose and flowing and it was like seeing a person on the street who could have been my sister in another life. I knew it the way I knew the shape of my nose. Yes, it looked a little more graceful, the words never cramped at the end of the page the way mine sometimes did – as though I'd never planned how to end each line. But it was my handwriting.

It was my book. I snapped it shut before I could lose my grip on the ladder. This book too I needed to take with me. I hurried down, nearly spilling the books from my grasp. The lantern swung from where I'd hooked it around my arm, the light casting moving shadows across the rugs. I hopped the last rung, relieved to be back on the ground again.

The sound of scratching emanated from behind me – nails against wood. I whirled, my heart sticking in my throat.

A spy construct watched me from the shelf, its tail twitching.

11

Ranami
Nephilanu Island

Ranami sat in the bamboo chair her captors had politely led her to, her hands clasped over a book in her lap. She'd read it through three times already. It was a shame it had to come to this. She didn't want this, despite appearances otherwise.

Gio, the leader of the Shardless Few, sat across from her, head cradled in his palm. He kept his gray hair clipped short to his head, the same length as the stubble on his chin. He regarded her with his good eye while she tried not to stare at his milky one. "You're sure she's coming?" Gio asked.

"She'll be here," Ranami said. Or at least she hoped Phalue would be. They'd had another fight. It seemed to be something they did often nowadays. The first weeks of their courtship had been infused throughout with a golden haze, everything brighter and better. But then Phalue would say something or do something that reminded Ranami of the vast differences between them. Phalue might be beloved because of her common mother, but she lived in a palace. She ate when she was hungry, she slept when she was tired and she wore her simple clothes not because they were all she had but because she disdained the silken ones. Phalue had a wealth of choices.

Ranami had not had the same.

"We had a fight," Ranami admitted to Gio. "But she has always come back." Phalue's temper often sent her careening from Ranami's home, a whirlwind of biting words and slammed doors. Ranami loved how passionate Phalue was, though it made her seem a little foolish at times. Because she'd always return, usually a few minutes later, with sweet apologies and a yearning to start over.

So Ranami was sure, when she'd contacted the rebellion for this false kidnapping, that Phalue would arrive at the Alanga ruins, storming in like a typhoon that very same night. Instead, they'd all slept here, morning fog leaving dewdrops on their eyelashes.

"Perhaps this is the time she does not come back," Gio said. He scratched at his stubble and then laid his hands on the sword in his lap. "Phalue has always cast off lovers the way an unlucky fisherman throws back fish that are too small."

Ranami knew she was not a small fish, not to Phalue. She knew it surely as she knew all the back alleys of the city. "It's been three years," she said. "What fisherman holds on to a fish that long that he does not intend to keep?"

Gio shrugged, acquiescing. "That may be. But she is not here."

"Keep your men and women at the ready," Ranami said. "When she arrives, she's like to knock a few heads on her way in."

This wasn't ideal, but every other tactic she'd tried had fallen on deaf ears. How else could she get Phalue to listen? The island was fractured, its people at cross purposes. The only one who could heal such a wound would be the governor. Ranami couldn't just tell Phalue all the policies that needed to be implemented. Phalue needed to understand the reasoning behind them.

It was a tall order, Ranami thought miserably. She hadn't asked Phalue to change when she'd turned her down. Phalue had come to it herself without any of Ranami's help. Like so many street urchins, Ranami had long admired the governor's daughter from afar, dreaming of finding Phalue's favor, of climbing out of the gutters and into a palace.

But dreams had a way of only making sense while you were having them.

Something rustled outside. Ranami straightened. "I think that's—"

It was all she had time to say before she heard a cry from outside, a thud, the sound of steel against steel. She looked to Gio, who gave her a nod.

Phalue knew how to make an entrance at least. Stupid, reckless Phalue, whom Ranami loved beyond all reason. She leapt from her bamboo chair and ran toward the doorway. The walls of the ruins were covered in moss and vines, but the main walls still stood. It must have been a beautiful sight in its prime. There were still pieces of carved plaster littering the ground. As soon as she reached the outer door, she saw Phalue. Even now, her heart jumped; her stomach swooped – as though she were leaping from a cliff and into the Endless Sea. Phalue stood over an unconscious rebel, her expression thunderous, her jaw so tight Ranami was sure her teeth must be hurting. There was no soft beauty to Phalue's face, no gently curving brows or generous lips. Her cheeks looked carved of jagged coral, her nose a piece that had not been smoothed away. Black, thick brows were like slashes across her forehead. Hers was the beauty of ospreys, of sea serpents, of a wave crashing against rocks.

It was a wonder Ranami had been able to turn her away at all.

"Phalue!" she called out.

When their eyes met, Ranami remembered: they had fought. "I'm safe," she said. "No one's harmed me."

Phalue apparently had not remembered their fight because she sheathed her sword in one smooth movement, took two steps forward and buried her hands in Ranami's hair. Their foreheads pressed together, and Ranami felt Phalue's fingers tremble. "I was afraid," Phalue choked out. "I thought— I should have known someone might want to hurt you. What do they want? Money?"

Phalue kissed her, and Ranami forgot where she was in the softness of her lover's lips.

"It doesn't matter," Phalue said when they broke apart. "We can go now. The guards are unconscious."

Ranami peered around her. "You didn't hurt them, did you?"

Phalue gave her an odd look. "Oh, they'll hurt when they wake up, but what does it matter? I've never killed anyone before; I wasn't about to start now." She let out a shaky laugh. "Can you imagine what my father would say? Killing is not the purview of governors, or something like." Her gaze went beyond Ranami's brow and she stiffened.

Ranami whirled to see Gio.

Right. The entire reason she was here in the first place. "Phalue," she said, putting a hand to her sword arm before she could draw it again. She knew her too well. "I want you to meet Gio. He has some things he wants to say to you."

Phalue's gaze slid back to hers. "Was he held here with you?"

And here was the part she'd been dreading, the reason she'd halfway hoped that Phalue would not come. "Not exactly," Ranami said. "I came of my own free will."

"You ... what?" Phalue seemed more surprised than angry. And then she peered more closely at Gio, running her gaze over his close-cropped hair, the scarred eye, the sword at his hip. She looked to Ranami in disbelief, and then back at Gio again.

"Ranami, that's the leader of the Shardless. My father wants to kill him. The Emperor wants to kill him. He and his people have been causing innumerable problems for the Empire. Did you know they toppled the governor on Khalute? It's a small isle, but sooner or later the Emperor will send his soldiers and his constructs."

"I know," Ranami said, lifting her hands, trying to forestall Phalue's anger. "Some of the rebels are here for a very specific reason – but I found out they were here and I got in touch with them." It had taken more than just a little work to do so. They weren't exactly known for being friendly and open with outsiders. But she'd read Caleen's *Treatises on Fiscal Equality*, and quoting it had apparently impressed the Shardless enough to get her a contact. Arranging this false kidnapping had taken even more convincing. At first they'd hoped she would turn against Phalue, work with them while undermining the governor's rule. But she'd refused. There had to be another way, one that involved installing Phalue as governor.

Phalue's eyes narrowed. "There's a price on his head. I should report this."

Ranami saw, out of the corner of her eye, Gio straightening, his arm moving to his sword.

"Phalue," Ranami said, her voice gentle, "who will you report to?"

Phalue's expression flitted from determination, to confusion, to dismay. Ranami knew her thoughts – they'd shared their worlds with one another, their hopes and disappointments. The only person Phalue could report this to was her father, and he'd use the reward money to throw another lavish party or to build another addition that his palace didn't need. Her lips pressed together. "I could find a spy construct to report to. The money doesn't matter as much as the Empire's safety."

"Just listen to what he has to say. Please." Ranami took Phalue's hands in her own, running her fingers over the calluses.

"We could both be hanged just for talking to him," Phalue said, her gaze still on Gio. "Whatever he has to say, it's not worth your life."

Ranami squeezed her palms. "Remember what you said to me when we fought? You said that you couldn't change the way you'd been raised, that you felt like I was looking down on you for not being born on the street. I know you've worked hard. I'm not asking you to change your past. I'm asking you to consider your future, and the choices you have ahead of you."

"Choices not everyone else has," Gio said. He'd relaxed again, his voice taking on a somber, oratory tone. "I won't mince words with you – we need your help. The caro nuts the farmers grow here are all sent to the heart of the Empire for sale, where they fetch the best prices. The farmers themselves cannot afford to purchase any. The oil in these nuts is an effective cure for the bog cough, and we are entering another wet season. The children of these farmers have already begun to die."

At least Phalue hadn't tried to kill him, or stomped away. But she lifted her shoulders and sighed. "I have an allowance. I can purchase some caro nuts to give to the farmers."

It was a kind gesture. And Phalue was full of kind gestures. It was part of what Ranami loved about her. But that would only help a few farmers; it wouldn't solve the problem. Phalue had never felt that itch in the back of her throat, the aches in her body from long work that couldn't better her status, the helplessness of watching loved ones suffer.

Gio looked her in the eye. "That won't be enough. I want you to help us steal some of the caro nut shipment and let the farmers have them."

Phalue scoffed. "You're mad."

Gio shrugged. "I've never claimed otherwise. I'm not a baker or a net-mender. No empire lasts for ever, and I think this one has been overripe for a long, long time." He began to tick off fingers. "The Emperor is old, and few people have seen this daughter of his – not since she was a baby. He's shut himself away, and rumor has it he's pursuing experiments with the bone shards he's collected. He says we need to keep contributing bone shards to power the constructs, because the Alanga might someday return. It's been hundreds of years. If it weren't for the ruins and the odd artifact, I'd hesitate to believe they ever existed. They are not coming back. The Emperor's sworn duty – to protect us from their magic with his own – is looking more and more like we've set an old dog to guard a pair of unworn slippers.

"The premise of the Empire? The very things it was built upon? They don't exist anymore. But still everything goes to the heart of the Empire to be picked through before the scraps are returned to us. We are tired of picking through scraps, Phalue. We want to build something new. Think of it: a stop to the Tithing Festivals. Wealth distributed more equitably. A Council made up of representatives from each of the islands. You could be a part of this if you wanted. The people would love you more than they already do."

It didn't move her. Ranami had tried such speeches on her, and Phalue had only repeated her father's talking points. Everyone had a job to do in the Empire. Those that worked hard were rewarded. She gave examples of those who had lifted themselves from poverty. And yes, a few had, while the rest reached and scraped and hoped. It was like explaining the concept of a tree to a giant squid.

"You want to help the farmers? Help them meet their quotas."

"They can't always do so," Gio said.

"Some of them do," Phalue said. "If they do, why can't the rest?"

Ranami clenched her jaw. "You would place the lives of children on meeting quotas?"

Phalue pinched the bridge of her nose. "You know it's not about that." She looked to Ranami. "You frightened me half to death. Do you know what it's like to wander into your lover's home and find it overturned and her gone? I don't want to do this anymore – these fights, these partings and then finding my way to you again. We need to find another way to make this work."

Oh, by the depths of the Endless Sea – was she proposing again? Here, in front of the leader of the Shardless Few and the two who still lay unconscious on the floor? This would be the least romantic of all Phalue's proposals. Ranami had told her "no", more than once. It wasn't that she didn't want to marry her. She did, more than anything. But that was in the dream world, where there was only love and the two of them, not here, where their two worlds scraped painfully against one another. She did not want to be a governor's wife. She couldn't sit in that palace and live that life, knowing that she'd been raised in the gutter, that her heart would always hurt every time she saw an urchin on the street. No matter how many times she told Phalue that, she wasn't sure how to explain what that really meant to her. "Phalue . . ." she said, and then stopped, unsure of what else to say. There was too much to feel that she couldn't put into words. Someday, Phalue would get tired of asking. Someday, she would move on. If only she'd stop asking.

But this time, Phalue didn't propose. "I want you to move into the palace with me. It's been long enough. I am respectful of your wishes, and I come to the city to visit you, but you don't need to live in a shack. And sometimes what I want has to matter too."

Was this some strange attempt at compromise? "Are you saying you'll help them?" Ranami asked.

Phalue shook her head, and for a moment, Ranami's heart sank. And then she exhaled, long and slow. "This is the Shardless Few we're talking about, Ranami. You think this is some sort of game? That you can invite them here to stay, to help the farmers, and they'll just leave? I know you think me naive, but I'm not so naive as that."

Gio wisely only crossed his arms and said nothing.

"I know it bothers you," Phalue continued, "but these things are this way for a reason. The farmers receive land from my father; they owe him their fealty. Yes, I think the way he spends the money is stupid, but it is still his right to send the caro nuts to the wealthier islands, where he can fetch the best price for them. He still pays the farmers their fair share. He keeps order and peace, and that deserves payment."

Ranami gritted her teeth. Again, this old argument. They could go around in circles like this for hours. If even the leader of the Shardless couldn't move Phalue, what hope had she? "I don't know how to make you understand," she said. Her eyes felt hot, and to her embarrassment, tears rolled down her cheeks. She'd done everything she could to bridge this gap between them. It felt like an ending, one she didn't quite know how to swallow.

Phalue took her hands in her own. "You went to a lot of trouble and have put us both in danger. And Ranami – I would break mountains for you. This is certainly the strangest thing you've ever done, and the most idiotic, but if it means that much to you, then fine. It's not as though my father will miss a little extra money. Just this once though." She brushed the tears from Ranami's cheeks with her thumbs, then kissed the tracks they'd left. "No more of their children will die from bog cough – not this season. And you –" Phalue turned her attention to Gio. "I'm sending a message to the Emperor that you're here. By the time he receives it, we'll be finished and you should be gone. This island is not ripe for your rebellion. We're fine as we are."

Gio must have nodded his assent because Phalue slipped her arms around Ranami's waist. "There. Can we not fight anymore?" Behind her, one of the unconscious rebels stirred and groaned, putting a hand to his head.

"Thank you," Ranami said – and she wasn't sure if she was talking to Gio or Phalue.

12

Jovis

Somewhere in the Endless Sea

I had ill luck. Soon after I'd told Mephi to stop blowing into the sail, the wind died down completely. We rocked in the waves, gentle as a baby's cradle, the sun baking the deck hot beneath my bare feet. Mephi lay in the shade at the bow of the ship, curled on a blanket I'd laid out for him. Once in a while he turned over in his sleep, murmuring. If I laid a hand on his back, he quieted.

I sifted through my navigational charts and watched him, a hand at my sore ribs. I really had no idea what sort of creature he was. No one truly knew the depths of the Endless Sea or what lived in it. The islands all had a short, shallow shelf before they dropped off, vertical, into the depths. They all moved through the Endless Sea, so there must have been a bottom to each of them. My brother and I had often bragged of diving far enough to feel where the island had begun to narrow again. Every child did.

Mephi looked almost like several creatures. Almost like a kitten. Almost like an otter. Almost like a monkey with his webbed, dexterous paws. What would he look like if the nubs on his head sprouted into horns? Almost an antelope? And what sort of creature could create its own wind and could talk besides?

I rubbed at my forehead and tried to force my scattered thoughts into some sort of order. What I knew was this: I'd given up a chance at finding out more about Emahla's disappearance in order to keep this creature from harm.

My heart pulled me in two different directions. I wanted to care about Mephi. He murmured in his sleep again, and I felt the frown I hadn't known was there dissolving. No, that was a lie I was telling myself. I already cared about him. But Emahla . . .

We'd been children when we'd met, so young that my brother, Onyu, had still been alive, before the Tithing Festival that had taken his life. I'd been digging for clams at the beach, my mother a short distance away, her skirts hiked up and tied about her thighs.

I wish I could say I remembered the first words she spoke to me. I wish I had a grander story, one where I saw her and was struck dumb, or one where I knew that she was special. Her father brought her with him as he went stilt-fishing close to shore, and she watched me for a while. I braced for the usual comments: "Are you from here?" "Do you speak Empirean?" "What are you?" But Emahla only found a stick and began to dig with me too. "Bet you I can find more clams," she said. From then on, we were friends. To me, she was just a girl – all black bushy hair, gangly limbs, fingers and toes that always seemed to be sticky. Sometimes I couldn't wait to see her. Sometimes I hated her with the passion only a child can gather. And after Onyu died, she became my best friend.

I hoped she knew I was looking for her.

Something knocked against the side of the boat. I peered over to see a few loose pieces of wood. Although they were weathered, they looked like broken boards and not driftwood. Either remnants of a shipwreck or remains from Deerhead Island. The horror seemed to wash over me anew, thinking of all those people left on the island, sucked down into a watery grave on what should have been dry land. I wrapped my fingers around my right wrist, the bandage I'd tied about it rough beneath my fingertips. There would be no tattoos on most of their bodies; there would be few bodies to find, if any.

I focused on the charts again. At the end of the dry season, the isles of the Monkey's Tail moved closer together. And they moved north-west this time of year. I made a few quick calculations to find the position of the next isle, adjusting our direction to match.

The wind finally picked up that evening, and Mephi woke up. He chirruped from his spot on the blanket but didn't get up, so I found myself feeding him pieces of a fish I'd caught. His whiskers tickled my fingers as he ate. He smacked his lips, sharp white teeth flashing, his head bobbing. I stroked his forehead absently.

"My mother would tell you to eat quietly," I said. "She would say that people all the way on Imperial could hear you chewing." I waited, holding my breath, hoping he'd speak again.

Mephi looked up at me. "Not . . . good?" His voice creaked out of him like a rusty door hinge.

I laughed. So perhaps he was like a parrot. "Not good," I confirmed. "Not good at all."

He took the next piece of fish from me with his cold paws and ate it as delicately as any governor's son.

"Do you understand what I'm saying?" I said, peering into his black eyes.

Mephi only looked back at me until I again felt foolish for talking to an animal. When I really thought about it, I couldn't believe I'd let the boat go over *this*. I'd worked my fingers to the bone, I'd stolen from the Ioph Carn, but as soon as this little creature seemed to be in pain, I'd thrown it all away.

There was still time. If I stopped at the next island and sold the melons, I could use the profit from that to buy more goods to sell at a markup. I could save the money to buy more witstone. I'd find the blue-sailed boat again.

That night, Mephi crawled beneath the blanket to curl at my side as I slept. I felt him lean his body against mine, his little heartbeat a thrum against my ribs. Strange, that I'd let him out into the ocean only a few nights before, telling him to find his own kind. I shifted, hoping I wouldn't somehow inadvertently crush him at night. "Don't expect this every night," I muttered to him. "It's just because you're not feeling well."

He only sighed and laid his head on my shoulder.

I woke to a cold, whiskered snout in my ear.

It took me shrugging off the blankets and shoving him away with my free arm to notice that the aches from the Ioph Carn beatings were gone. I froze. I stretched to the side, expecting a sharp lance of pain from my ribs. Nothing. And then I was pushing the last of the blankets away, lifting my shirt, checking for bruises. Oh, they were still there. I pushed at one experimentally, just in case. Aye, that hurt. But they didn't look as angry as they had the day before.

A splash sounded behind me. "Mephi!" I was calling out for him before I remembered he knew how to swim. My breath caught in my throat as my mind conjured all the beasts I'd seen during my years smuggling – sharks, giant squids, sea serpents, toothed whales. All of whom would see Mephi as a delicious morsel. But I heard him chittering before I even leaned over the side.

He was abreast of the boat, swimming in the water as though

born to it, making pleased little noises as he ducked and dove and turned over onto his back.

"No, Mephi. Not good!" I said.

As much as he'd seemed to understand me before, now it truly was like I spoke to a cat. He ran his paws over his whiskers and then dove again, deep, out of sight. I sucked in a breath and held it, my heartbeat pounding in my ears. Part of me worried about him being eaten. Another part of me wondered if he'd seen others of his kind, or if he'd decided we'd journeyed far enough together. Maybe that would be best – I wasn't even sure if he was supposed to eat fish, or if he was supposed to be getting milk from his mother.

His head popped up again, near the bow, a fish nearly as big as he was in his mouth.

Relieved, I put the net out to help him back into the boat. I deposited his sopping wet body on my deck, and he deposited the fish at my feet. "Don't do that again," I scolded him. "You're still too small." How big would he grow anyway? He watched me and chirruped.

I looked at the fish and then back at him. "You can have it." Maybe he didn't understand my words, but he took my meaning well enough. At least he was recovered.

We reached the next isle that afternoon. I left the melon boxes on the deck as I tied up my boat, a wary eye on the construct at the docks. It had a hawk's head on an ape's body, with the clawed feet of a small bear. I wished I could say it was grotesque, but the Emperor did good work.

I did better work, though, when it came to pitting my wits against theirs.

Constructs weren't people, even if a few bore human parts. The lives of the shards in their bodies powered them, and the commands written on them gave them purpose. But depending on how tightly those commands were written, well, they could be subverted. And despite the smooth work on this construct, it was a dockworker and would be lower-tier. Fewer commands, more loopholes.

And I could sail through a loophole the way I might a gap in the rocks.

As soon as the construct saw me tying my boat, it hobbled over to me. "State your goods," it said. Its voice was like the buzzing of insects against a lamp.

"I am a soldier of the Empire. Stand aside." I wished I'd held on to the jacket for more authenticity, but I'd fooled these constructs before without.

The construct tilted its head to the side, examining me like prey. "You are not," it said.

"I am, and you are instructed to obey the Emperor's men." I looked down at my clothes. "Oh, it's the lack of uniform, isn't it?" I let out a heavy sigh. "I'm afraid I lost it."

With a duck of its head, the construct peered at my chin as though it could make sense of me from a different angle. "Lost it?"

"In the shipwreck," I said.

"There are no records of recent Imperial shipwrecks."

"But you know what happened with Deerhead Island?" I said. "Allow me to be the first one to report it. We were there for the island's Tithing Festival, but we were caught in the current of the sinking island." It was best to sprinkle in as much truth as possible into lies. "I was able to swim free, but I had to lose everything except my underclothes to do it. I'm the only survivor."

The feathers on its neck ruffled before it shook its head and they smoothed again. "Your Imperial pin—"

"Lost that too," I said. "But I am a soldier, and you must obey the Emperor's men. Step aside and let me pass."

I could almost see the gears working in the creature's head, and I tried not to sweat. Mephi, still on the ship, stayed thankfully silent. I'd run into a couple of upgraded constructs, who had been instructed not to obey anyone without an Imperial pin. This was a small isle though, and a lower priority. And there was only one Emperor. I hoped this was an older, original construct.

It didn't press me for the pin. It stamped in place, its claws clicking against the wood of the dock, its fingers winding about one another.

I didn't wait for further questions. I reached back into the boat, grabbed the melon boxes and swept past the dockworker. When I turned my head to glance back, I found Mephi bounding at my heels. "You shouldn't be here," I hissed at him. "You need to stay on the boat."

Again, his ability to understand me seemed to slip. Instead of turning around, he leapt to my waist, his feet scrabbling for purchase on my belt. Before I could swat him away, he had settled onto my shoulders, his long body draped around my neck. I expected him to feel too warm, like the scarves my father's people wore. But his fur was as cool as mist against my skin.

"Fine," I muttered to the creature curled about my ears. "Just don't get in my way or make a nuisance of yourself." After thinking for a bit, I added, "Or say anything." I was here to sell melons, not to spin lies about what sort of creature Mephi was.

It took me asking a few friendly strangers for directions before I found the market. The market here was larger than on the last isle, though still small. This one wasn't cramped into two narrow streets; it was laid out in an empty square at the center of town.

I did some mental math and tried not to think of the fortune of witstone I'd tossed overboard, possibly still sinking into the Endless Sea. If I could sell the melons at a profit, I could buy a little bit of illegal witstone. The blue-sailed boat was still small, and it wouldn't be braving the vastness of the Endless Sea. It would hop to another island, and there was only one other island nearby. I was out on the Monkey's Tail, a string of isles one after another. Farther east, after the Monkey's Tail, was Hirona's Net, and the blue-sailed ship might lose itself in that cluster of islands. I didn't have much food left, but I could fish from the side of my boat – enough to get by, at least. The other ship would have to make stops to resupply and to rest, and if I made decent time, I'd be able to catch it still on the Monkey's Tail, before the Net.

I bought a hat first, setting it firmly on my head, the straw brim shading my eyes. And then I searched the market for a likely buyer.

When I set my boxes on the table of a nearby farmer, he only looked at me warily. "Melons from Deerhead Island," I said. "The island is gone, as you've no doubt heard, and we're going into a wet season. It will be years before any of these melons are grown again."

The thin man glanced at me sideways, rubbing his palms over his pants before he stood. "It's ill luck, trying to make a profit off of others' misfortune." But he gestured for me to open the boxes anyways.

With his permission, I took his pry bar and lifted the first lid off.

The farmer peered inside and then shrugged. Oh, he was a liar almost as skilled as I was. "I grow these on my farm as well." Both he and I knew that didn't matter. The season was over and he was likely already getting a good price for them.

"And I'll wager if you wait even ten more days, you'll get a better price for them. If you grow them, you know these store for a full year. What more could anyone who is facing a wet season ask for? They'll get tired of their greens and soft-rind fruits, and they'll have a sweet melon to remind them of warmer, drier days.

The supply will be less than it's been in prior years. Deerhead grew a lot of them."

"They're blemished," he said, pointing to a nearly imperceptible scar on one of the melons.

Mephi made a little squeak of protest. I reached up to scratch his head, hoping he would keep quiet. "That doesn't change the taste."

"Those willing to pay a high price prefer their fruit to be as beautiful as their jewels."

And so it went, back and forth, until we both declared a deal could not be made – before he grudgingly acceded that perhaps some sort of accord could be reached.

The silver coins filled my purse with a delightful jangle. Finding someone willing to sell me witstone under the table though, now that would take some doing.

"Jovis?"

I didn't recognize the voice. It was gravelly and low, and didn't belong to anyone I knew, I was certain of it. I kept my head low, my shoulders pulled so tight that my cheeks were hidden in Mephi's fur. The hat covered nearly the full top half of my face. Did they put up posters on as small an island as this?

"Jovis!" the voice said again, more insistent.

Just when I was hoping that there was some other person named Jovis in the marketplace, a hand grabbed my arm, pulling the wrapping of my tattoo just far enough to expose the rabbit's ears.

"I knew I'd find you here."

13

Lin

Imperial Island

I stared at the spy construct on the shelf, my mouth dry, my heart fluttering at my ribs like a caged bird. It must have come in through one of the high windows, sent to skulk around the palace at night, checking for anything gone awry. It had found what it had been looking for.

It would scurry back to the courtyard and beneath the boulder in the center, down into whatever lair the Construct of Spies lurked in, and it would tell her I'd been found where I didn't belong. My father would disown me and the Empire would fall into pieces at his death. It would be broken.

Like I was broken.

No. I gritted my teeth. I could not let this be the end.

We moved at the same time – the construct toward the window, and I toward the construct. It reached the end of the shelf at the same time that I reached out my hand.

I expected to close my fingers around empty air, but I was quicker than Bayan or Father had ever been. I caught the creature by its winding tail. It screeched, a terrible, high-pitched sound that rebounded from the walls and shelves. It rang in my ears. By all the isles and the Endless Sea, it would wake even the servants in their separate quarters! I pulled the creature tight to my chest, curling my hands around it. Its teeth clamped down on my palm.

That smarted. I did my best not to cry out. I jerked my hand away and swaddled the construct in the bottom of my tunic. It shrieked at me until I wrapped its head too. It could still breathe through the cloth. If I killed it, where could I hide the body? I could take it outside the palace walls, leave it somewhere or bury it.

But the shards would no longer take life from their former owners. There'd no longer be a need to suck life away to power the construct. And my father always seemed to know when one of his constructs died.

It would raise too many questions. I had to keep the construct alive for now.

Scenarios ran through my head. If I kept it in the palace, I'd be found out. Father didn't come often to my room, but he did sometimes, and Bayan more often – to fetch me or to bother me. And there were other spy constructs in the palace, always watching.

I could only think of one place to keep the creature.

By the time I reached the blacksmith's shop, the sun was cresting the horizon. I'd cleaned up the mess in the library and had dropped off the journal in my room. I'd taken another tunic to wrap around the construct. This would be cutting things close. My father and Bayan usually both stayed awake into the night and did not rise until well after dawn. I could not say this was an everyday occurrence though.

The bustle of a waking city was so different from the quiet within the palace walls. Doors open and shut, people strode past me in a hurry, baskets beneath their arms or bags slung over their shoulders. No one looked at me – a girl with her own bundle beneath her arm. They all had their own business to keep. Light filtered golden into the streets, chasing away the blue-tinged shadows of the night before. And the night fishermen were filtering in from the docks, their catches in buckets, filling the air with the ocean-water scent of fresh fish and squid. Water slopped from buckets and onto the street; I had to dodge puddles more than once before arriving at my destination. The drinking hall next door was silent, its patrons long since gone. The blacksmith's shop was closed, but I heard the sound of a tiny hammer striking metal.

I knocked at the door hard enough to make my knuckles ache.

Numeen answered the door, and he frowned when he saw me. "You shouldn't be here. You were only just here last night."

"I know," I said, and slipped past him before he could stop me. "I've come to ask a favor."

"I can't do favors." But he closed the door behind himself. Sweat beaded on my scalp as soon as the door swung shut. Numeen had a small fire going, and despite the chimney and the open window, the entire shop felt like a furnace.

"A favor for a favor," I said.

"You found my bone shard?"

"I – no." Again, the pang of guilt. I shook it off. I'd find a way to retrieve his shard when I had the chance. I had larger things to care about. I reached into my sash pocket and pulled out the witstone I'd taken from my father's store.

Numeen's eyes widened when he saw it. The trade of witstone was highly regulated by the Empire. No one was to buy or sell it without the Emperor's knowledge and consent. But I'd heard the reports from the Construct of Trade. The Ioph Carn stole and sold witstone, and a few others did as well. If you got your hands on some witstone, there was always a way to sell it, with or without the Empire. "What are you asking of me?"

The bundle beneath my arm twitched as though it knew we were speaking of it. "I caught a spy construct," I said. "I can't kill it – my father will know. I need a place to keep it until all of this is over. Can you make a cage for it? Keep it somewhere in your shop?"

"If the Emperor finds out, I'm dead. Not just me, but my entire family."

"Then think of your family and what you could do for them if you sold this witstone. It won't be for ever, and I'll be back periodically to check on it."

"And with more keys," he said, his tone resigned. This was the truth of it, and I watched the realization dawn on his face. He couldn't just walk away now. With that first key, he'd tied his fate to my own.

I proffered the bundle with the spy inside. It squirmed, but once in the grip of the blacksmith, the spy quieted. I watched his face, unsure of what to say. My father might have noted all Numeen had to gain in this bargain. He might have simply thanked him. I wondered how good at reading expressions my father really was, or if he just didn't care – because I saw more than resignation in Numeen's face. I saw resentment in his tightened lips and brow, his silence. "I'm sorry," I blurted out before I could stop myself. I was Lin. I was the Emperor's daughter. But still, I was sorry. "If I could do this without help, I would."

"And what is it you intend to do?"

Become Emperor. Earn my father's respect. The words wouldn't come out. I'd been skulking about, stealing keys, trying to unravel my father's secrets so that I could prove to him my worth, broken though I was. I'd always been anxious that he might die without leaving me any of his secrets, with only bitter words for me on his lips. I didn't know how to explain that. So I said instead, "To survive."

Numeen nodded and closed the curtains. The space inside the shop seemed to grow even hotter, firelight casting everything in red and yellow. "Come back when you need another key."

I fled the shop, the bell at the door jangling as I let the door swing shut behind me. The streets were already brighter, the faint orange glow of lanterns in windows giving way to dawn. The servants would already be about their work.

I didn't stop to rest. I ran through the streets, dodging surly, sleepy inhabitants as they prepared for the day ahead, baskets under arms and quick huffs of breath extinguishing lanterns. I was a dancer entering the stage four steps too late – upsetting those already there and unable to find my place.

There wasn't time to take the servants' entrance. When I climbed back to the top of the wall, the constructs there eyed me but did not raise the alarm. I picked my way back to the palace by rooftop, doing my best to keep my footfalls soft against the tiles. Below me, I saw the few servants sweeping the empty pathways of this walled city in miniature, or carrying buckets of water from the well to the palace itself. The periphery buildings all remained empty – free of dust but with cracked and fading paint. Someday they'd be alive again, when I was Emperor.

By the time I'd reached the palace itself, the sun had risen above the harbor. Light glittered off the ocean, making jewels of each cresting wave. The seabirds had begun to call to one another. Here, at the palace, I felt a step removed from the ocean – nestled into the foot of the mountains. But I didn't have time to dwell on that. I found a window at the far end of the palace, swung down from the roof, and slipped inside.

I saw a few constructs on my way back to my room – trade constructs, war constructs, and bureaucrat constructs – here to report to their superiors. I wasn't in their purview, so they paid me no mind. Still, I only breathed easily once I shut the door of my room behind me.

The journal and the beginner's book of commands were where I'd left them, shoved hastily beneath my bed. One held the key to my past; the other to my future. I ran my hands over the covers. Here, in the quiet of my room, Numeen's words turned over in my mind.

What was it that I intended to do?

The spy construct had made it clear: I couldn't just sit around waiting for my father to die, hoping that if I learned enough, he would choose me as heir. Too many variables, too many things that could go wrong. And Father had taught me this much at least. Do not rely on that which you cannot control.

I had to seize control.

I rubbed at the green cloth cover of the journal, yearning to devour the information within. Reluctantly, I set it down and reached for the book of commands. There would be time for both, but I had to prioritize.

My father ruled his Empire by proxy, all his power and commands distributed to his four most complex constructs: Ilith, Construct of Spies; Uphilia, Construct of Trade; Mauga, Construct of Bureaucracy; and Tirang, Construct of War. It occurred to me that this must be why he guarded the secrets to his magic so zealously.

If I were smart enough, if I were clever enough, if I were careful enough, I could rewrite the commands embedded into their shards. I could make them mine. Father didn't think I was enough. My memory was lacking. But I knew who I was now. I was *Lin*. I was the Emperor's daughter.

And I would show him that even broken daughters could wield power.

14

Sand

Maila Isle, at the edge of the Empire

Sand saw to her own stitches that night, after she'd brought her haul of mangoes back to the village. No one commented that she hadn't brought a full bag. She wasn't sure anyone noticed at all. Everyone else was focused on the completion of their own tasks. Once everything was gathered, Grass began to sort through it. That was her task. Sand couldn't remember a time when it hadn't been.

Surely, though, there must have been a time? Grass's face was scarred as a fallen coconut, the brown backs of her hands spotted as a seal's fur. Her hair was still black, and her back straight. She wasn't ancient, but she wasn't young either, and there must have been a time when she'd been young.

The others all lined up for their dinners, waiting patiently for the food to be scooped into bowls at the cookpot. Fish stew by the smell of it, probably with a side of mango and the hard grains Cloud always harvested from seagrasses.

Sand dipped the needle in and out of her forearm, flinching

at the pain and yet relishing it. It seemed to sharpen her senses and her mind – which had felt dulled until she'd fallen from the tree.

She tied it off at the end and gnawed at the string to sever it. And then she went to talk to Grass, whom Sand judged was the eldest among them still living.

"When did you come to Maila?" she asked Grass.

Grass frowned up at Sand, her spotted hands sorting everything into piles – things to eat now, things to eat later, things to save for as long as possible. "Come to Maila?" she repeated. "I've always been here."

"You grew up here?" The words tasted strange on her own tongue. She couldn't imagine a child-Grass, running about the island. With parents, friends, family. The image wouldn't cohere. And then Sand thought of herself here as a child, and found she had no concept of herself as a child at all. There must have been a time she'd been a child. She frowned. She couldn't remember her parents. Surely that was a thing one remembered.

"I've always been here," Grass said.

"Yes, but what about before?"

"Before what?"

"Before Maila. Someone must have come from somewhere . . ." Sand trailed off, suddenly unsure what she was asking. They had always been here. The thought reverberated in her skull, like a chime struck true that wouldn't stop ringing.

No.

It wasn't true. How could it be true? They hadn't sprung up from the rocks like some storied monsters. They were people, and people had parents. People had places they'd come from. Her eyes darted over the people waiting in line.

Glass, Cliff, Coral, Foam ... Coral. There was something about Coral, some memory she couldn't dig up. It was like a word she knew but couldn't quite remember. And then it flashed in her mind once, like lightning.

Coral hadn't been here for ever. The thought tried to wriggle away from her, a fish caught in bare palms. She clamped down on it.

Coral hadn't always been here.

Sand strode to her, her breath coming short, her limp jolting her injuries. "Coral."

Coral barely turned, despite the urgency of Sand's tone. Long eyelashes fluttered against her cheeks. "Yes?"

"When did you get here?"

"I've always been here," Coral said, not meeting Sand's gaze.

The longer Sand held onto that clamped-down thought, the clearer it became. "Four nights ago, what did you bring back to the village?"

"I always bring a bag of clams."

Sand resisted the urge to shake Coral by the shoulders. "You don't. You didn't. Four nights ago, we had no clams. Someone ..." The thought fuzzed again, fogging up like her vision after water had splashed on her eyes. Someone else? She tried to focus on it and then gave up.

It didn't matter. Someone else had done it at some point, though Sand couldn't remember who. "It wasn't always you. Think. How did you get here?"

"A boat," Coral said. Her mouth remained open, as if she were shocked by the words she'd uttered. And then she frowned, twining her hands together. "That can't be right."

"It's right." How long would this clarity last? Sand wondered if she'd be back at the mango trees the next day, struggling to fill her bag, not remembering the day before. She pressed a hand to the wound she'd sewn up, and the feel of the thread beneath her palm helped her focus. Today was different. The day that Coral had arrived had been different. Sand didn't know Coral, not really, but her every movement and gesture said one thing to her: soft. Limpid eyes like tide pools, every word voiced with hesitation. She needed to wring an answer out of her before Coral folded. "What sort of boat?"

"Is it important?"

Sand closed her eyes briefly, and she had some distant memory of praying to old, dead gods, the scent of musky incense thick in the air. She could smell it. She met Coral's gaze. "It's the most important thing in your life. It is more important than collecting clams."

This seemed to have an impact at least. They both shifted forward as the line moved, but Coral pressed her lips together. "It was a small boat, with dark wood, but large enough for passengers. I think I was in the hold. It was dark. I don't know, I'm sorry."

"But you left the boat at some point. You had to get from the boat to Maila. You must have seen more." She wished she could reach into Coral's mind and pluck the memory from her.

"Yes," Coral said slowly. The line moved again, only one person between them and the stewpot.

If they made it to the front, Coral would get her food and then she'd forget all over again, lost in the routines of the day. Sand knew it. She watched another ladleful of stew pour into a bowl with a deepening sense of despair. "What did you see? Tell me now. Please."

Coral bit her lower lip. She raised her bowl, ready to receive her dinner.

Sand seized her wrist. "Think!"

The words fell from Coral's mouth. "The sails. They were blue."

And then a ladleful of soup dropped into Coral's bowl. Her face went blank, as though a hand had brushed across a piece of slate, wiping it clean and leaving only faded marks of chalk behind.

15

Jovis

An island in the Monkey's Tail

If a man could die of stress, I'd have died several hundred times over in the past few days.

"Jovis," the voice said again.

I tried to shrug off the hand on my arm, not looking at its owner. "You are mistaken," I said, making my voice lower, gruffer. "I'm not who you're looking for."

But the hand would not be shrugged away.

Mephi, still curled around my neck, leaned up to whisper in my ear. "Not good?"

"I don't know yet," I said, louder than he had.

So when I turned to see who had accosted me, the man looked startled by my response. "You don't know what yet?"

"Who you are and what you want." Relief made me a little sharper than I'd intended. The man wasn't Ioph Carn. He had no weapons and had the soft outline of a person who enjoyed the small pleasures of life. But it was just as well I'd been sharp; he knew my name, and there was a reward on my head.

"I heard –" And then he lowered his voice so drastically I had to lean in. – "about what you did on Deerhead."

He'd what? I'd been on Deerhead for all of an afternoon. What had I done? Escaped it sinking? And how had he heard? Oh wait – of course. I'd been drifting on the waves like some indolent governor's son, bereft of witstone and wind. Others would have arrived here before me. "I'm not sure what you're talking about." This time, when I jerked my wrist away, he came with it, stumbling and almost falling face first into the street. I caught him and set him on his feet.

I hadn't meant to pull that hard. Had I? I flexed my fingers when I released him. Huh. No more pain. But I couldn't check my bruises right now.

"The boy," he said, his eyes darting about the marketplace. He lifted his hands, his fingers curling as though he wasn't sure if he should form fists. "Please don't lie. I had to pay for this information. I had to pay a lot of people. I've been watching for you."

Alon. The boy Danila had bade me save from the Tithing Festival. The rise of apprehension in me was like a tide; I didn't notice it until I was already wet.

He licked his lips, and I saw sweat beading there. "I have something to ask of you. I have a daughter."

"No." When I'd flippantly dismissed the thought of who Alon's parents might tell, I'd been thinking of the Empire, not other desperate parents. My mistake. I cast my eyes about the marketplace too. How many people had heard my name? I shouldered past the man, trying to find emptier streets.

Mephi shifted on my shoulder, his paws digging into my skin. He made a soft, indignant sound in my ear.

"This is what's not good," I said to him. "I get threatened into freeing one boy from the Tithing, and now everyone wants a turn at it." I turned into an empty alley, refuse pooled in the center of it. Footsteps sounded behind me.

"Wait, please. I'll pay you."

If I were a dog, my ears would have pricked. I had too little money and too little time to catch the blue-sailed boat. And besides that, the Ioph Carn were on my heels. My purse had a healthy weight to it, but my circumstances called for it to be plump. I pivoted so quickly that the man nearly ran into me. "I'm in a hurry."

Mephi curled his tail about my throat and took a step down my arm toward the man, a trill in his throat. The man eyed my shoulder warily. "It wouldn't take much time. I know someone on another island."

I waited for him to elaborate. He wrang his hands like his fingers were a washcloth. I sighed. "Everyone knows someone on another island."

"A friend," he said quickly. "Someone who is part of the Shardless Few. On Unta."

I had no love for the Emperor, but I wasn't keen on the Shardless either. Still, if taking this job could get me closer to Emahla, I needed to chance it. And Unta was on my way and close; only two days' worth of travel. "And you want me to do what? Out with it."

"Take my daughter with you. Smuggle her off this island and take her to my friend. She'll take care of her. I'll pay you to do it."

"The Shardless Few are a bunch of fanatics who are always sticking their necks out so the Empire has an easier time of lopping of their heads. You'd be better off trying to get her to a monastery. She'd be protected from the Empire behind their walls."

He looked affronted. "I'd never see her again. And what if she doesn't want to be a monk?"

I sighed. "Fifty silver phoenixes."

"Done."

I blinked. He didn't look destitute, not with that belly, but his clothes were still simple. A humble man? I'd misjudged before. I should have asked him for more to begin with. Fifty would get me what I needed though. "This will take a little time," I said. "And don't expect me to dig into my own stores to feed your girl. I'll need you to pick up food, blankets, water."

"Forged documents?"

So he'd been expecting to pay for those too? I had asked for too little. "No. No need."

"But how will you get past the trade construct?"

I gave a little flourish with one hand, in considerably better spirits than I'd been just a moment before. "I'll tell it a story. A beautiful, elaborate lie, if you will." I turned the flourish into an outstretched palm. "Half the money now, if you please."

He gave me a dubious look.

"There's a reason the Empire put a price on my head. I'll do what you've asked, and I'll do it well. Do you think they'd spend the money to keep putting out posters of some half-witted smuggler fresh off his mother's breast?"

He counted the money out after that.

"Bring her to the docks at sundown, but don't approach the boats. I'll meet you on land." I stowed the money in my purse and left the alley, pleased with myself.

Mephi evidently was pleased as well. "Good," his creaky voice said in my ear. He rubbed a furry cheek against me.

That was interesting. Did he understand the meaning of what he was saying? There were legends of very old sea serpents that had learned our human tongue, and more stories still of magical creatures living in the depths of the Endless Sea — but those were stories. This was a kitten of a creature, and I could almost cup him in my hands if he curled into a ball.

"No," I said. If he knew what he was saying, I'd teach him right. "The money is good. The task? Not good."

"Good," Mephi insisted again.

I sighed. What was the point? Did I really want a creature on my boat who could talk back to me? Despite the thought, I smiled and reached up to scratch Mephi's head. He chirruped and sank onto my shoulder, his fur tickling my neck. "We should feed you. And I need more information."

The city wasn't a bad size, and I soon found I had two drinking halls to choose from. I chose the one nearest to the docks. The smell of fish mingled with the scent of old smoke as I stepped inside. One breath and a pang of homesickness swept over me. My father regularly met his Poyer friends in a place like this. Onyu and I would sometimes wander inside when we knew my father was done with his fishing, sneaking past the veil of pipe smoke to watch them play a game of cards. If we were lucky, my father would let us play a hand. "Your mother won't like that I'm teaching you two to gamble," he'd say. Half the time that was the end of it, and half the time, if we waited, he would grumble a little and pull out a chair for us to share. The lacquered cards were written in Poyer, and I made sheepish, half-hearted attempts to learn it. Each mistake I made seemed to highlight the sallow color of my skin, my loose curls, my gangly limbs. Onyu's pronunciation was always better, though I knew enough to understand when my father's friends smiled at my brother and said, "Ah, he speaks like he was born to it!"

The same praise was never offered to me.

There were no Poyer playing cards in this drinking hall. It was halfway empty this time of day, but there were still a couple of fishermen at a table, having finished their day's work. I could hear them muttering to one another. "The only thing the Emperor will say is that Deerhead Island sank because of an accident."

"An accident. What sort of accident sinks an entire island?"

"I'll wager it's the Alanga, and he's just too old and weak to stop them. Maybe this island is next. Maybe they all are."

They gave me sharp looks when I slid into a chair at their table. There were, after all, plenty of other tables without occupants.

"I'm intruding, I know," I said, "but I'm looking for someone."

Their expressions did not change until I waved down the owner of the establishment and ordered sweet melon wine for us all. And then they exchanged glances. One of them shrugged. They both eased in their chairs and looked to me, waiting to hear what I'd say next. Drink was an easy way to make friends, and I wasn't looking to make permanent or loyal friends of them. Just afternoon friends. Friends enough to pick their minds clean and leave them with the thought, "He was a nice fellow." Enough to dissuade them from finding any Imperial soldiers stationed here as soon as I left.

"A boat came this way. A dark wood boat with blue sails. Smaller than an Imperial caravel, but large enough to carry some passengers – perhaps ten uncomfortably."

"When?" said the man on the left.

"Recently. In the last few days."

He rubbed at his chin. "No, haven't seen it. Wish I could give you more for your trouble."

The other man only shrugged again, and I wondered if that was all his body was capable of doing. But then he frowned. "You should ask Shuay. Older woman, works just north of the docks selling cooked crab. She knows nearly everyone on the island and keeps a sharp eye on the docks. Sees everyone that comes in and out." The owner set our mugs of melon wine on the table, and he took a drink. He laughed, his gaze on the bottom of his mug. "Probably saw you when you came in."

Mephi crept down my shoulder toward the man on my left, who proffered a hand to him. Mephi sniffed it, and the hair on his back lifted. He backed away, head low, ears flat to his skull. Lips drew back from bright white teeth.

"Hey now," I said, scooping him up and depositing him back on my shoulder. I was half-afraid he might spout off "not good" again, raising far more questions than I knew how to answer.

"What sort of pet do you have there?" the man on my left asked.

A thousand lies ran through my head at once. But these were just fishermen who found Mephi curious, and Mephi hadn't said a thing. "I'm not sure," I said, trying to soothe the creature. The fur on his back eventually smoothed. "He claimed me, I suppose. Lost his mother. Have you seen anything like him before?"

"Can't say I have. I'd be careful though. I know a woman who took in a baby seal. It was an orphan and she thought it was cute. Grew to nearly the size of a fishing boat and bit three of her fingers off before it swam away."

"I'll be careful." I took a small sip of melon wine. One more piece of information. I spoke slowly, gauging their reactions. "I'm heading for the next island in the Monkey's Tail. East. I need to get there quickly."

They exchanged glances.

"You won't find much of that trade here," said the shrugging man, "except through the Ioph Carn."

The Ioph Carn. They were as bad as the Empire sometimes. Either you paid the Empire, you paid the Ioph Carn or you paid them both.

"I've heard that fishermen keep pieces of it sometimes, just in case they need to outrun a storm." I brushed my purse, the coins inside clinking together. "I'm willing to pay a premium."

The man on my left grunted, tapping his fingers on the table. Dirt and fish blood stained his fingernails. And then he reached into his purse and pulled out a sizeable chunk of witstone, showing it to me beneath the table.

Mephi curled tighter around my neck, his whole body going tight until he felt like a snake trying to make a meal of me. I had to untangle his paws from my shirt, loosening his grip. "I'll pay you ten silver phoenixes."

"Not good!" Mephi shrieked. "Not good not good!" He darted down my arm, hung over the edge of the table and swiped the witstone from the man's hand. It clunked onto the floor.

Even a half-full drinking hall had too many eyes. All of them locked onto me and Mephi. Infernal creature! I shot up from the table so quickly that my chair overturned. I should have left him there, screaming, his fur all on end. I could find witstone somewhere else and be rid of both this island and beasts that spoke. Emahla should be all that I cared about. But I'd not even finished the thought before my hand was around the nape of his neck, lifting him, setting him back on my shoulder. "May the winds be favorable," I said to the two fishermen, and made for the door.

"Are you trying to get me killed?" I hissed to Mephi. Outside, the clouds had crept in. The air smelled of damp grass and ocean. Wind brushed through Mephi's fur, and it wasn't until I put a hand on his back that I felt him trembling.

"Not good," he whimpered, miserable.

"How am I supposed to find Emahla if I don't have witstone?"

As if in answer, Mephi took a deep breath and exhaled a wisp of white smoke.

"Well, that might work in a pinch, but it's not as good as witstone. You'll have to find a way to get used to it." I stopped in my stroll down the street, shaking my head. When had I begun thinking he could understand complex sentences? But I could puzzle out the vagaries of chronology later.

I found Shuay near the docks, just as the fishermen had indicated. Steam rose from her stall, mingling with the low-hanging clouds. Wind rattled the fronds that made her roof. "Two pennies for steamed crab legs," she said without looking up. She was a thin, older woman, black hair laced with silver streaks.

I paid her for two, because people are always inclined to be kinder once you've done business with them. She handed over the crab legs on banana leaves, and I proffered one serving to Mephi.

As soon as he smelled it, his trembling ceased. He seized the crab and began to noisily tear shell from flesh, making little sounds of satisfaction as he found the meat within.

Shuay laughed. "Your friend is hungry."

"I think he's always hungry." I fed him another piece of crab leg. He was making a mess of my shirt, but I couldn't bring myself to care that much. I'd not changed it since the beating, and there was still some dirt and blood caught in the fibers. "I was told you know a lot about who comes in and out at the docks. I'm looking for someone."

I didn't even need to pay her. Shuay leaned forward, her elbows on the counter of her stall. She smiled in an invitation to go on, and something about the way her eyes wrinkled reminded me of my mother. A sensation of vertigo swam over me briefly. It seemed only the other day that I was back at home in her kitchen, sitting next to her on the bench, my hip pressed to hers as I chopped scallions.

How old would she be now? Her hair had been all black when I'd left. Did it have silver in it now like Shuay's? Had her shard come into use? Was she sick like Alon's mother? I couldn't even think it.

I breathed in the smell of steamed crab, trying to reorient

myself. "Have you seen a boat come through here? Dark wood with blue sails?"

When she nodded, I thought my throat would close up.

"I didn't just see the boat," she said. "Saw the captain of it too, and his companion. They came by on their way out."

I couldn't speak.

"Tall fellow, long face, big cloak – does that sound right?"

I nodded and choked out, "And his companion?"

"Young lady. Shorter than he was. Big, dark eyes. Thick brows and a thin face." Shuay frowned. "Not pretty but striking, I'd say. Lips that turned a little upward at the corners. But she looked scared. Terrified. Didn't say a word, and neither did he."

Mephi must have sensed my distress because he dropped the crab leg he'd been working on and began to pat my hair with one paw. I couldn't rely on a verbal description, but the face she'd spoken about bloomed in my mind. Emahla's face. No one had ever claimed she was beautiful – except for me. And I'd meant it.

Shuay patted my hand. I was still holding my serving of crab legs, my grip creasing the leaf. "You can sit down if you need to."

The kindness in her voice almost brought me to tears. I knew deep down that this was another piece of information for her to peddle, to feel important, but I'd done my share of using people for my own satisfaction. I couldn't fault her.

I tried to keep my voice steady. "Did she have a mark here?" I pressed a finger below my right eye.

Shuay's expression grew pensive. "Can't say that she did. Not so much as a freckle."

All the hope and panic and fear fled, leaving me dark and hollow. Not her. Just someone who looked like her.

"I should go. Thank you." I handed the rest of the crab to Mephi, my appetite gone. I had things I needed to do.

It took me most of the afternoon to hunt down more witstone, and it took the rest of the afternoon to get Mephi to accept it. Or at least to form some semblance of tolerance. There must have been some smell attached to it, because if I touched it, he shrank from my hands, hissing and spitting, looking more like a pincushion than an animal. I had to run water over my hands before he'd get anywhere close to them, and still he curled his tail around my neck as though he meant to choke me with it.

What choice did I have though? He was an animal I'd plucked from the ocean only days ago. Emahla was the woman I'd pledged my life to. And perhaps Shuay was mistaken. Perhaps the woman she'd seen was Emahla. I had to know for myself. I felt it like a string tied tight around my body, painfully taut, dragging me onward.

I went back to the docks at sundown.

The man who'd paid me to smuggle his daughter was there waiting, a box of supplies at his feet. His right hand rested on the shoulder of a little girl, her hair plaited, her eyes somber. His left hand rested on ... another child. A boy of the same age. I didn't need to look at the man's pleading expression to know what he was going to ask of me.

There should have been a word for this feeling – of surprise, yet not surprise. My mother had scolded me often when I was young: "One foolish choice is like a rat you let go. It will spawn more consequences than you first thought possible."

Mephi chirruped at the sight of them, the first sound he'd made since I'd slipped the witstone into my pocket.

My foolish choices were spawning armies.

16

Lin

Imperial Island

Blood stained my fingers. I wished I had an apron like Father's, or Bayan's. But I made do with a tunic I never wore anymore, wedging the cloth into the space between my fingers and fingernails.

I'd found the room where Father kept the parts. Bird parts, monkey parts, cat parts, parts of animals I'd never seen or even heard of stacked in an insulated icebox. The room itself was dark and cold, carved from the stone below the palace. Even so, it smelled faintly of decay and musk. I'd taken some parts I was sure wouldn't be missed – small ones. A sparrow's wings, the soft little body of a rat, the head of a salamander. I squinted as I crouched over the pieces on my bedroom floor. The stitching was harder with body parts this small, but according to the book I'd read, the bone shard I'd put into its body would mend any mistakes. It was the larger bodies that had to be more delicately put together, for the bone shard magic could only mend small mistakes.

I tried not to be overeager. I was more interested in carving a command onto the fresh shard waiting in my sash pocket, and in using the magic to move my fingers through and inside the construct's body. Would it work for me? Or were there some details from my past that I'd missed? Perhaps I didn't have the ability to work with the shards, and that was why my father kept me from his magic.

A knock sounded at the door, and my heartbeat kicked an echo. I shoved the construct beneath the bed, wiped my hands again, lamenting the blood that had settled and dried in the cracks. I didn't have time.

The knock came again, as if to emphasize that point. I smoothed my hands over my tunic and went to the door.

I pulled open the door so quickly it stirred a breeze. With the breeze came the scent of sandalwood.

Father stood at the door, hands wrapped around the head of his cane. He leaned on it and peered into my room. Not for the first time, I wondered what accident had removed his toes. And then I remembered what I'd been doing.

If I looked back now, he'd notice. So I kept my gaze on him, hoping he couldn't see my pulse fluttering at my neck, trying to form a mental picture of my room. Had I left anything out I shouldn't have? It was too late to do anything except wait.

His gaze trailed back to me. "I haven't seen much of you lately," he said. "I've been busy, of course. The constructs are in constant disrepair and the soldiers are always bringing them back to me to be mended. But you've not come to dinner."

I'd been expecting Bayan. "I've been meditating," I said, remembering the advice he'd given me. "Bayan said it helped him to regain his memories." I let my gaze fall from his, feigning embarrassment to be caught in the middle of it.

Father nodded. "It's a good idea. I'm glad you're trying to

remember. There is much that you've lost. The young woman you were before — she's still there, I'm sure of it." He focused somewhere past my shoulder.

And what was wrong with the young woman I was *now*? I cleared my throat, shifted from foot to foot. I wanted him to leave. If he thought I was desperate to return to meditating, to remembering, so much the better. It wasn't that I didn't want to remember. I did. But in the beginning I'd spent days and nights scraping through my thoughts, trying to find who I'd been before. I'd grasped for it until it felt my head was squeezed tight by bands of iron. All I had was who I was now.

Father noticed — how could he not? "I admire your dedication," he said, his voice low and gruff, "but I'd like you to join Bayan and me for dinner tonight. We've things to discuss and I'd like you there."

I hesitated. The half-formed construct was still beneath my bed, together with the journal and the beginner's bone shard book. But when Father said he'd like for me to join, what he really meant was that I had to. He kept a veneer of politeness over his commands, but it was thin, and easily scratched away by disobedience. So I nodded before he could read too far into my hesitation, stepped into the hall and closed the door behind me.

For a moment, Father didn't move. We stood there next to one another. Even stooped and aged he was slightly taller than me, his cane lending his thin frame some weight. Heat radiated from his robes like a candle burning too hot and too quickly. The sandalwood smell of him filled my nostrils, mingled with the bitter-tea scent of his breath.

A quick glance at me, appraising, and then he limped down the hall. His robes swirled behind him like waves crashing ashore.

I followed, wary.

The dining hall was next to the questioning room. Bayan

was already inside, seated at the right-hand side of my father's place. A place had been set for me across from them. There was a message in this – but there was a message in all the small things Father did. I was the outsider here.

Servants flitted in and out as I took my place at the table. Father was still lowering himself into his cushion, his cane set on the floor beside him, one hand on the table, another hand on the cushion itself. I almost expected to hear his bones creaking and grinding against one another as he sat.

A cup of jasmine tea steamed at my right hand; a small stuffed chicken with golden, crisped skin graced the center of my plate surrounded by a pile of glistening vegetables and white rice. I'd nearly forgotten what a formal meal was like. I didn't often go to the dining hall for dinner, and Father rarely asked me to join them. Many times I just ate what the servants brought me in my room.

I honestly preferred it that way. Between Bayan and Father, eating in the opulence of the dining hall was like being invited to an elegant dinner among sharks. Was I here to eat the meal, or was I to be the main attraction?

Four more seats were at the end of the long table, no plates set at them. My spine stiffened as Father's four highest constructs entered the room. The servants sped up in their work, and I knew they wanted to leave as much as I did. I envied that they could.

Tirang, Construct of War, an ape with clawed feet and a long, wolf-like snout. He sat nearest to my father, his claws clicking against the floor. Ilith, Construct of Spies, who took up twice the space of the other constructs, her many hands folding in front of her on the table. Mauga, Construct of Bureaucracy, a sloth's large head on the body of a bear. He lumbered in like a bear just out of hibernation, and rolled into his seat. He rocked back and forth until he settled. And finally, Uphilia, Construct of Trade, a fox with two pairs of raven's wings. She glided in on silent footfalls, her four wings folded at her sides. She sat on her cushion and started to clean her face with one front paw.

These were the four constructs I needed to gain control of. If I had them, I would have my father's respect.

Father began to eat with trembling hands. I was afraid each bite wouldn't make it to his lips. But when he spoke, his voice was strong. "News?"

Tirang spoke first, his voice like sand ground against stone. "Your soldiers are stretched thin. In addition to the governor they overthrew, the rebels are gaining a foothold in other islands among the Monkey's Tail. A little over a hundred of your war constructs have been dismantled. I'd like to request a replacement."

Father cast his spoon aside. "If Mauga's bureaucracy constructs cannot repair them, then you're short a hundred war constructs. There will be no replacements."

Bayan leaned forward. "Perhaps I could—"

Father silenced him with a contemptuous glance. He looked to Ilith, and I held my breath.

Ilith's mandibles clicked. "The Shardless Few is expanding its influence. People are unhappy with your taxes, and the recent destruction of Deerhead Island has stirred up more unrest. They don't trust you to keep them safe – which brings me to my next report. Your people are ill content with the Tithing Festival. Even some governors are muttering about the necessity of it. It's been a long time since the Alanga were driven out of the Empire, and people have been less inclined to think them a threat."

"I work every day to maintain this Empire," Father growled, his hand closing into a fist. "And these ungrateful brats think they'd be better off without me. The Tithing is a small price to pay for the protection I give them. I spend days of my life making constructs, keeping ever vigilant. In the days of my grandfather, the people were grateful. It was an honor to give up a shard. Now they mewl about how the Tithing kills some of their children, how it drains days of their lives — when I have drained my entire life."

Both Bayan and I sat silent, knowing that if we spoke the wrong word, his anger would refocus on us. We could feel it like a living thing, a blind snake waiting for a mouse to move.

Finally, he sighed and waved a hand. "Mauga, have the old tales circulated again. Pay a troupe to travel the isles and have them put on a production of *Phoenix Rise*. Everyone likes the story, and it will remind people of what my ancestors have done for them. What we are still doing for them. Keeping them safe."

Mauga grumbled a little to himself, claws clicking on the table as he shifted.

Ilith looked to me and Bayan, and then back to my father. "The tales may not be necessary. I've had some reports about Alanga artifacts . . . awakening."

Father clenched his hands. "Artifacts are not the Alanga themselves. We'll speak on that later."

I looked to Bayan and found him looking back at me. Father might not have seemed concerned, but Bayan was.

"Very well. But another thing you should know," Ilith said. "My spies have brought me a rumor. It could be nothing but the spawn of some wild dreams, but there may be someone stealing your citizens away from the Tithing Festivals before they are complete. His name is Jovis."

The trade construct's wings twitched, and Mauga lifted his sloth head. "I know that name," Mauga said. "And so does Uphilia. We had posters made."

My father leaned on the table, lacing his fingers together, his head bowed. "A fugitive?"

"A smuggler," Mauga said, his voice a rumble in his throat. He snuffled. "He has been ... hmmm ... a problem. Two missing boxes of witstone from the mine at Tos. He does not pay any relevant fees."

"Of course he doesn't." Uphilia's tail lashed. "He's a smuggler."

"He pays his fees to the Ioph Carn. No one escapes both the Empire and them," Ilith said.

"Ilith, keep your spies listening for more word of this Jovis," my father said. "But he is a smaller problem next to the Shardless. Tirang, organize a strike against the rebellion on the Monkey's Tail. Send some war constructs. Gather information first."

And then he returned to eating his dinner, as though that took care of things. What about reaching out to the governors? What about the island that had sunk? It could have been my imagination, but I thought I felt a tremble beneath me, a tremor.

No one else even so much as glanced downward. Just my mind playing tricks on me.

"Eminence," Bayan said.

My focus turned to him and I picked up on details I hadn't noticed before. He'd eaten not even half of his plate. The fingers of one hand curled around his napkin. He was nervous.

Bayan straightened. "The last construct I made – I changed the command out to the one you recommended. But is it possible to keep the original command and modify it to work the same way?"

And that was all that was said about politics. Constructs, my father could talk animatedly about for hours.

Father tilted his head to the side. "It's possible," he said, tapping his chopsticks against his plate, "although not necessarily advisable. A command, once written, cannot be erased or overwritten. It can be modified, but you run the danger of a less effective command. If you're not careful, you can even run the risk of altering the command in a way you didn't intend. A missed mark, or an unintended one, can change a meaning completely. It's best to use a fresh shard and carve a new command."

"But what if you run low on shards?"

Father snorted. "The Shardless Few and this smuggler aside, we will not run out of shards."

"Nothing lasts for ever. Not even the reign of the Alanga."

"The Shardless have no plan. They know what they don't want, but they don't know what they do want. No movement survives without a vision of the future, because without it, there is nothing to strive for. The rebels aren't a real threat, and you don't need to start hoarding shards."

They spoke not just like teacher and student, but like father and son. In the soft lighting of the dining room, Bayan looked like a younger reflection of my father. No wonder he had chosen to foster him. No wonder he was considering replacing me with him.

I felt my brows furrow as I watched Bayan, and I smoothed the expression away before anyone could notice. His expression was calm, but his fingers still curled into his napkin. He hadn't asked just out of curiosity. He'd asked because the asking had made Father comfortable. The question that made him twist his fingers was yet to come.

If I were Bayan, I would have been patient. I would have let the mood in the room relax further. But Bayan's ambition was not a patient thing.

"Will you give me the key to the door with the cloud junipers on it? I'm ready."

The cloud juniper door – the one I recognized from a past I no longer knew. I tried not to appear interested but I needn't have bothered. Father's attention was fully on Bayan. "I give you keys when I deem you ready. If I have not given you a key, you are not ready."

Father said it calmly, but I watched the way he set his chopsticks to the side even though he wasn't done eating. There was a warning in such calm. It was the retreat of the ocean from the shore, just before a tsunami.

Bayan didn't notice. "I've done everything you've asked of me, and I've done things you've not even asked. Every time you go through that door, you come back invigorated. I want to know what's behind it."

Father's hand lashed out far quicker than I'd thought possible for his age.

The blow couldn't have hurt that much, but Bayan cowered, holding a hand to his cheek. And then Father grasped his cane. He started to lift it, and then, thinking better of the action, let it rest back on the floor. The constructs sat on their cushions like statues, watching with disinterested eyes.

He'd beaten Bayan before. It hadn't occurred to me until now, but Bayan never knew his place, and Father was fond of reminding others of theirs. It must have hurt more, years ago, when my father had been stronger.

"You wait," Father hissed, his breathing heavy. "And you keep covetous thoughts to yourself. If you ask for things you cannot understand, you're more imprudent than I thought you were."

Bayan wiped the spot where Father had struck him. The blow hadn't been hard, but one of the rings Father wore had left an angry red mark. "If I was your true-born son, would you have shown me?"

So he was jealous of me. I wasn't sure what to make of that. I'd been so jealous of Bayan I hadn't thought of how he might feel about my station.

Before I could puzzle out my feelings, Father raised his left hand. "Tirang."

The Construct of War rose. Father had only to crook one finger and the construct pulled a dagger from his belt and started toward Bayan.

No matter what little power remained in Father's limbs, his mind was still sharp. And with that came the control of all the constructs on all the islands of the Empire.

Now Bayan was afraid, as he should have been before. I should have relished this victory. I should have gloated, the way Bayan had so many times over his keys.

Ah. I couldn't. The idea of watching Tirang carve up Bayan just made me queasy, not glad. It swirled in my belly, spurring me to action.

"I have a question as well," I blurted out. All four constructs looked to me, and Father's crooked finger relaxed. Tirang stopped in the middle of the dining hall. "Is imprudence an inherited trait, or is it learned?"

By the Endless Sea and the great cloud junipers – I'm not sure what prompted me to speak except for pity. It worked, in a manner of speaking. Father stopped paying attention to Bayan. He seemed to have forgotten he was there. Tirang went to sit back at his seat by the table. Bayan slumped on his cushion, terror washing away like dust after a wet season rain.

And my father, with all the vast power of an Empire waiting at his beck and call, turned his attention to me.

17

Jovis

An island in the Monkey's Tail

He offered me five more coins to take the boy too. The boy was the son of a family friend, and his daughter hadn't wanted to leave without him. It was a pittance in comparison to what the man had given for his daughter, but wasn't I going that way already? And what was two stolen children if I was already going to be executed for one? The Empire couldn't very well chop my head off twice. Not that they wouldn't try, but I'd not heard of the Emperor bringing anyone back from the dead just yet.

These were the lies I told myself, because I didn't want to admit that it seemed to make Mephi happy, and that mattered to me.

As soon as I'd agreed, the beast had climbed back down my shirt, curling his way around the children's ankles and begging to be scratched about the ears – delighting and charming them both. I supposed it was just as well. If we all had to share my boat for a couple of days, at least one of us should be good with children.

I watched the man say goodbye to his daughter, both trying to hold back the tears. They'd not see one another again for a long time. He could report her as dead to the Empire. But Ilith's spies were everywhere, and if he tried to follow they'd put the puzzle pieces together. I missed my own family more than I could say, so I let them have their moment. I hadn't thought in a long time about how it must be for my mother and father – one son dead at eight years old, and the other gone for years, his face on reward posters from the Empire. I'd not written to them, not wanting to draw attention to the fact that I had a family at all. I didn't think about it because it hurt to, like lifting the bandage on a wound that had never quite healed.

When they were done, I beckoned to the children. "Come on," I said to them. "Keep close and don't say anything."

"What about the construct?" the girl asked.

I pivoted and lifted a finger. "That. That was saying something."

"But—"

"If you say the wrong thing, we'll all be caught, and the Empire will chop my head off."

They both sucked their lips into their mouths, eyes wide. Mephi rose to his haunches and patted their arms with his paws. I let him comfort them, but there was no point in trying to shield them from this reality. Children understood life and death, though adults liked to think they didn't. And I wanted to get out of this alive.

"Good? Good. Let's go."

I heard the tap of their footsteps as they followed me onto the docks. The construct saw me coming and hurried toward me. I ignored its approach, making a beeline for my boat. Mephi leapt aboard as soon as we were close enough, and I knelt to unwind the rope keeping us moored. Rain began to fall in large, splattering droplets, darkening the wood beneath me. I didn't stop, even when the construct stopped in front of me.

"The Tithing is five days away," the construct said. "You are not authorized to remove children from the island this close to the Festival."

"That's fine," I said smoothly. "But I'm a soldier, and I have orders to take these children east."

"You are *not* a soldier." The construct spoke with a note of triumph, as though it had spent all day puzzling out my earlier words.

"I am," I said. "I was shipwrecked, and I lost my uniform and my pin."

"The Empire would have reissued them to you," the construct said, still smug.

"They would have – if I'd the time to request them. But I'm on an urgent mission, and requesting a new uniform and pin would delay the purpose of that mission."

The construct peered at me with narrowed eyes, the feathers on its head ruffling. "What urgent mission?"

I laughed, rose to my feet and tossed the end of the rope aboard. My boat drifted a little from the dock. The children behind me remained mercifully silent. "Are you trying to trick me? I'm not to speak of the mission objectives. The Emperor himself handed down the order."

"The Emperor himself?"

"Yes." I stared into the construct's face, letting nothing crack. I *was* a soldier. I could tell this lie to myself and make it feel true. "Now stand aside and let me be on my way."

"I cannot allow smugglers free passage in and out of the harbor."

"I'm an Imperial soldier."

"You have not shown me proof. You could be a smuggler." The construct's voice rose to a whine on the last words.

"You also don't have proof that I'm a smuggler," I said, reaching behind me to seize one of the children by the shirt. "I've got places to be." I gave the girl a little heave to help her jump onto the boat, and took hold of the boy. The boy, having seen what I'd already done, jumped with my helping hands.

The construct muttered to itself on the dock, its voice like the whine of a boiling teapot.

I didn't wait to see what conclusion it would reach. I leapt aboard my ship and set to work on the sails. Mephi followed me, chattering at my feet. If I still had bruises from the Ioph Carn's beating, I couldn't feel them. The sails hoisted easily, the rope pricking my palms. The rain began to fall in earnest, a gray gauzy curtain between us and the rest of the world. I lifted the cargo hatch as we began to move out of the harbor. "Go in here," I told the children. "It's dark and a little wet, and I'm sorry for that, but once we're out on the ocean and away from other boats, I'll let you up."

I think they had a little more confidence in me after what I'd done with the construct. They lowered themselves into the cargo hold with no complaints – not even when I swung the hatch shut over them. Mephi ran from the bow to the stern and back again, trying to bite at the rain. I laughed at his antics. Of course, the creature hadn't seen rain before. It had been a dry season, and this was the first rain of the wet season. I wondered if, when the dry season came back seven years later, Mephi would even remember what that was like.

"Yes," I said to him as he dashed past me. "Water from the sky can be an amazing thing."

He stopped biting at the rain to look at me, and then lifted his head to the sky again. "Water," he said in his rusty hinge voice. "Water!"

"Rain, actually – it's just made of—" I stopped and shook my head. I don't know why I thought it made a difference. "Yes," I said instead. "Water."

Mephi let out a little warbling cry, and then ran to me, slamming his tiny body into my shins. "Water. Good!"

"I suppose it is." I sat at the tiller and let the rain soak my clothes.

It had been a long time since it had rained like this. I was thirteen when the last wet season had begun, at the beach with Emahla. We'd made a little game of seeing what sort of bounty we could pluck from the ocean and from the sand. I'd just captured an enormous rainbow crab, and crowing with delight had nearly shoved it in her face. "What have you got? A few clams and a sea urchin? I've got –" I seized the claws of the crab, waving them about. "the biggest and most delicious of crabs. He's Korlo the Crab and he's happy to meet you. He sinks boats in his spare time. So, you see, I'm not just bringing back food to fill the pot. By capturing this crab, I've made myself a hero. They'll sing songs about me. Jovis, conqueror of crabs! Savior of the seas!"

Emahla only rolled her eyes. "Telling stories again? You're such a liar."

The crab twisted in my grip and pinched the meaty flesh between my thumb and forefinger with a claw. "Ow! Dammit!" I shook it loose, and Emahla had laughed.

The rain had started then, all at once. Clouds had been threatening it for days, but had chosen that moment to follow through. We'd both been born in a wet season, though it had been a long time since. It still rained in a dry season, but not like this. This was as though heaven held an ocean, and the dam keeping it there had finally burst. Water rained from the sky like a waterfall. Emahla had laughed again, throwing her arms and her head back, letting her bucket of clams fall to the sand. Just like that – with the rain sticking her hair to her skull, gathering like glass beads on her eyelashes, running like tears down flushed cheeks – I knew.

"You're beautiful," I'd blurted out, and had changed our friendship for ever.

All the joy had rushed out of her. "You're such a liar," she said again, but this time, she didn't sound sure. And then she'd turned and run from the beach, leaving her bucket behind.

She hadn't spoken to me again for fourteen days, which to me had seemed like a lifetime. I'd knocked on her door several times, only to be turned away kindly by her mother or father. The one time her younger sister had opened the door, she'd bluntly said, "She doesn't want to see you," and had shut the door before I'd had a chance to ask for anything.

I'd forgotten what life was like before we'd been friends. I tried to find other boys and girls to play with, and while they accepted me into their groups with little protest, they asked first if I spoke any Poyer, if it was true the Poyer had bears for pets and what did my name mean? Surely it had to mean something. They didn't laugh at the same jokes Emahla did. They had their own language, and I floundered when I tried to adapt, because I did not want to. I wanted the comfort of Emahla's presence, the way we understood one another.

When finally she'd knocked on my door again, I'd been breathless with relief. She didn't try to pretend it had never happened, or even try to slip into our old conversations first. She stood in my doorway, her black hair streaming in satin ribbons about a solemn face. Eyes so dark I thought they could swallow me. "We can be friends," she said simply. "Nothing more."

I was little more than a boy, and had all the clumsy eagerness of a pup. "I was only joking. Come on, don't scare me like that. I didn't mean it."

She stared at me, and my lies were like wet sheets of paper, disintegrating at the slightest touch. I wilted beneath her gaze. She sighed, probably out of pity more than anything. "Do you want to go pick coconuts?"

I'd nodded and slipped on my shoes.

It was never the same again after that, though we both tried. I'd noticed that I liked women, and Emahla was fast growing into one, and I liked her more than any of all the others combined.

Later, on nights where we'd sit on the beach and gaze at the stars, she told me that she fell in love with me on a rainy day in my mother's kitchen. "You were helping your mother make dumplings," she'd said, her head pillowed on my shoulder. "You were quiet. For once in your life, you were quiet. And when I sat next to you to help, shoulder to shoulder, I could feel a future in that silence. You always say so many things. Always, always talking. So many stories! But it wasn't until you were silent that I could feel the truth of you beneath all the words, all the stories. I always knew we could laugh together, that we could do fun things. But I never thought I could tell you what was in my heart, to share pain and disappointment and to have you cup that in your hands. To breathe back your own sorrows. I always thought you'd just make a joke or tell me a funny story about a fisherman who accidentally hooked the moon."

She'd kissed me the day after the dumplings, solemn as the day she'd told me we could only be friends. And then she'd laughed when it was done, and I'd laughed, and then I'd kissed her again and again, as if the world was the ocean and she the only air I could breathe.

Sitting in my boat, remembering this, I couldn't tell if I was crying. The rain was warm against my cheeks. Mephi crept over to my feet. He stared at my face and then leapt into my lap. He rose onto his haunches and placed his paws on my chest. "Not good?" he said, looking into my eyes.

"No." I cleared my throat. "It's the sort of good that you get sad about because you no longer have it. A very good."

He pressed his head to my chin, his whiskers tickling my neck. "A very good," he cooed.

I rubbed the little nubs on his head. I thought of what Emahla would make of this creature. "Someday. Someday we'll find it again."

He leaned against my chest and sighed.

18

Lin

Imperial Island

I could feel the pulse of my heart at my neck, throbbing beneath my ear. My father locked his gaze with mine. I wanted very much to avert my eyes, to look away, to make some apology. Why had I drawn his attention to me instead of Bayan? Would he send Tirang to cut me down? But I kept my head high and I studied each movement in his face. Anger, hot as the blacksmith's forge, then dismay. Fear, so quick I almost missed it. He settled finally into embarrassment. "Perhaps imprudence can be a learned trait," he said grudgingly. "I do my best not to teach it." He lowered his hand to the table.

Tirang strode back to his cushioned seat, as if he'd not been about to wreak violence at all.

I let out a breath. Bayan looked sick with relief.

But I'd not escaped all consequence. Father's gaze still rested on me. "Do you claim more prudence, that you should lecture me on the lack of it?"

"No, of course not," I said, and this time I did lower my eyes.

"May I remind you that you only have six keys."

Nine, I corrected in my head. "That is true."

I heard him shifting on his cushion, the brush of fingers against the table. When I looked at him again, he'd moved his plate to the side, his hands clasped in front of him. "You said you've been meditating on your past. I think it's good that you're finally putting in some effort, and effort does not go unnoticed." He reached into his sash pocket and produced a key. It clicked against the wood as he laid it on the table. "I have some questions for you."

For the first time I didn't feel weak with wanting. Anger roared in my belly. He laid the key on the table like I was a dog and the key a treat. He'd give the treat to me, yes, but only if I performed first. So many times I'd been denied satisfaction. But this time I'd read some of the journal. My journal. "Ask," I said.

I must have given some hint of my anger, for Father looked a little taken aback. Bayan, next to him, shrank into his seat as though he wished he could sink into the floor. But soon Father gathered himself. "What was the name of your best childhood friend?"

I let the first two questions pass – he always asked three – though I hemmed and hawed as if I were truly struggling to find an answer. "Perhaps I need to meditate more," I said after the second.

Father only looked displeased and asked me his third question. "What was your favorite flower?"

A sprig of jasmine blossoms had been pressed into the front pages of the book, the scent of it mingling with old paper. "Jasmine," I said. I paused and closed my eyes, taking in a deep breath. "I think I used to keep some of it even when it was out of season. I'd press it and smell it, even long after the petals had dried out."

Father's face went slack. Amazement and something else. Hope? Did he truly hope for me to regain my memories? If he did, why didn't he tell me my old memories, all the times we'd interacted? Surely that would jog loose memories more swiftly than this. "Yes," he said softly. "You loved jasmine, even more than all the exotic lilies in the garden." His gaze went far and away.

I let him have whatever memory paraded in his skull, though I really just wanted to shake him and ask what he saw in his mind. Instead, I waited and then cleared my throat. "The key?"

Father shook himself, appearing more like the old man he truly was. "Yes." He slid the key across the table to me.

I waited until his hand was back at his side before I took it. It was bronze and small and still warm to the touch, a simple bamboo pattern stamped onto its bow. Certainly a less elaborate key than others I'd seen upon my father's chain, but I was beginning to find out that the intricacy of the key had little to do with the value of the secrets I'd find behind its door. "Which door does it go to?"

Father waved a dismissive hand. "You can find out yourself. The both of you may go."

Bayan started as though expecting another blow. I'd barely touched my meal but I rose to my feet and watched as Bayan did the same. He seemed to regain some of his dignity as he straightened, running his hands over his tunic and wiping at the corner of his mouth. He gave my father a wide berth as he made his way to the door, and gave the four constructs an even wider berth. I followed him into the hall.

The door clicked shut behind me, and I heard Uphilia's voice as she spoke to my father about taxes and licence fees.

Bayan didn't leave straight away; he lingered in a restless way, shifting from foot to foot like he knew he had to be somewhere but wasn't sure where.

I made as if to pass him.

"Thank you," he blurted out. "You didn't have to come to my aid. It would have been better for you if you hadn't."

I gave him a considering look. "If I hadn't, I would have had to watch Tirang wash the floors with your blood. Not my idea of dinnertime entertainment."

Bayan barked out a short, nervous laugh. All the grace and cleverness had washed out of him. "You didn't have to do it." He pressed his lips together, and the wild look in his eyes faded, though sweat still beaded on his brow. "Thank you," he said again.

"I should thank you for telling me to meditate," I said. "It obviously helped."

He shrugged. "I didn't tell you to help you. I didn't have good intentions."

"I know." But he didn't hate me. Strangely enough, I was feeling grateful for that.

We both stared at one another for a moment, Bayan's gaze considering, as though he were weighing something. Then he thrust his hands into his pocket and nodded at my hand. "The key. I know where it leads."

I was still holding it, the metal cool in my grasp. "Where?"

"I'll show you."

I would have rather he just told me, but I didn't want to risk losing this small kindness from a rival. So I followed him through the twists and turns of the palace. He never turned around even once to check if I was still there, not even as we passed servants and climbed stairs to the smaller third floor. We ended at a place I'd not passed through often near the back of the palace, where it nestled into the mountains. The door we stopped at was brown and small, so that Bayan would have to stoop to get through it. The wood was worn, the varnish peeling toward the bottom.

"Here?"

Bayan nodded.

Feeling a little odd, I fit the key into the lock and turned.

It opened to the sky. Walls on either side of the door sheltered the path from wind and intruders. These walls were better kept than the ones surrounding the palace, the plaster smooth and unbroken. Stairs led up a mountainside, the setting sun outlining each step in gold.

Bayan slipped in after me before I closed the door. I gave him a questioning look but he said nothing, only waiting until I'd locked the door. I brushed past him as I made for the stairs. He had the same sandalwood smell as Father did. I wondered if it was a thing done with calculation, like an orphaned pup trying to absorb an adult's scent so the adult would claim it. Or perhaps he was more alike to my father than I was, even choosing the same perfumes.

The stairs were uneven, some so tall I had to brace myself against the wall to climb them. Others were barely the height of two of my fingers pressed together. I was more than a little jealous of Bayan's long legs. But he didn't stride past me. He waited as I struggled, though I heard him laugh more than once when I struggled with a particularly difficult step. I gritted my teeth. Once, I glanced back to see how far I'd come, squinting against the sun. The array of steps below was dizzying; the tiled rooftops of the palace buildings spread beneath me. I felt like I could land on them if only I jumped hard enough.

When I finally reached the top, I had more than the climb to take my breath away.

The stairs leveled out into a round courtyard, bound on all sides by the same wall. Mountains rose beyond the courtyard, jagged edges framing the stone. In the middle of the courtyard, its branches curling out over nearly the entire space, was a cloud juniper.

If I'd seen one before, I didn't remember. All I did remember were paintings of them, or carvings. They grew mostly in the mountains, with enormous taproots that reached to the very depths of the islands. Most of the living cloud junipers were either inaccessible or walled off in monasteries, where they were cared for and worshiped. Their berries and their leaves and their bark were managed by the monks and doled out sparingly.

I took a few hesitant steps toward it, still unsure if it was real. And then I lifted a hand to cup a branch in my fingers. The sharp, evergreen scent of it filled my nostrils, the short needles pricking my palm. A few dark berries dotted the ends. I wanted to bury my face in it and breathe it all in.

"Be careful not to take anything," Bayan said. "You can't take any of it without the Emperor's permission."

"Who cares for it?"

"I do," Bayan said, "though I expect your father will ask you to take on some of those duties as well."

"Is that why you showed it to me?" I said, amused. "So you'd have someone else to help?" I peered into the branches and saw one of Ilith's little spies, its tail curled around the needles. It squeaked when it saw me, climbed higher, and then turned to rebuke me again. How like Father to not even trust his own foster-son.

"Can you blame me?" Bayan said. "The Emperor has me learning all the commands – it's like learning an entirely new language – putting together constructs, taking care of the cloud juniper and learning politics. I have hardly a moment to myself before he summons me again for one task or another." Bayan looked to the spy construct. "Go on, report all that too. I don't care." It only twitched its tail and watched us. "At least he leaves you alone."

I huffed out a breath, and it tasted of bitterness. "Yes, he leaves me alone because to him I am broken."

"But mending a little," Bayan said.

I looked at him — with his black, shining eyes, his full lips, his angular jaw — and wondered if I could ever trust him. I couldn't read the expression on his face. It wasn't blank, but it didn't divulge its secrets either. I didn't really know Bayan, except as a rival. Almost as soon as I'd recovered from my illness, even as I searched my mind for some memories of my prior life, he'd been there — a constant threat. Father had made it clear from the very beginning what I was up against. "Do you want to be Emperor?"

"Of course I do," he said.

"Why?"

"Because if you're made Emperor, then what happens to me? Will you be content to have another person living in this palace who knows all your secret magic? Your family has always guarded the bone shard magic zealously. And now your father fosters me, teaches me everything he knows. I'm not a fool. I know what happens to me. I'm a liability if left alive."

He was right, though the thought of ordering Bayan's death made me ill. There had to be another way. "Is that the only reason?"

He leaned against the trunk of the cloud juniper. He looked as tired as my father did, and Bayan a fraction of his age. "What does it matter? I do this to survive. You too do this to survive. And now look. We both have seven keys."

"We are rivals."

"Yes. And here, that's the only thing that matters." He swept away from me, back down the steps so quickly I could not follow.

The sun slipped below the horizon, casting everything in a wan, blue light. And I was alone in the darkening courtyard, the wind rattling through the cloud juniper branches.

19

Phalue
Nephilanu Island

Phalue lifted the mug to her lips and pretended to drink. Her father, at the head of the table, cast her an approving glance, and she did her best not to roll her eyes. "You should try to relax sometimes," he'd said to her more than once. Other than his broad shoulders and his height, she wasn't sure what she'd inherited from him. He sat upon his cushion with indolent gracelessness, his black hair tied back, his lanky limbs hidden behind various brocaded fabrics. Phalue hated brocade. It was hot, itchy, and heavy. She preferred her clothes simple and functional. Phalue liked to spar; her father abhorred physical exertion. She enjoyed walking in the city, among its citizens. He remained in his palace like a turtle inside his shell.

And Ranami had the nerve to tell Phalue she didn't know enough outside her sphere? She knew plenty. Her *mother* was a commoner. Yes, her mother's house was quite a bit nicer than Ranami's tiny abode, and she had more money after marrying a governor – but she'd grown up with two brothers all squeezed into the same room. Her mother had known hardship. And Phalue often spent time with the people of the city. She'd tempted more than one to her bed, back before she'd met Ranami. What didn't she know about the people her father ruled over? Why did Ranami keep insisting that she didn't understand? Was this a contest – who had suffered more? And if she lost such a contest, was it even *her* fault?

When her mother had been governor's wife, she'd convinced her father to lower the quotas. And he had seen, with his very own eyes, one of the farmers lazing about, his trees untrimmed. What did Ranami propose to do about that? Steal caro nuts for the farmers, apparently.

"Dearest, you're scowling again," her father said. A pretty young woman leaned into his side, her hand resting in the crook of his arm. Phalue couldn't remember her name. Taila? Shiran? She supposed she had that in common with her father: a love of beautiful women. But Ranami was more than just beautiful.

Again, that rising tide of love mingled with a wave of frustration. Phalue smoothed her expression. "I was just thinking about the caro nut shipment."

Her father raised an eyebrow. "Is my gallivanting daughter suddenly interested in trade and bureaucracy?"

"Are you?"

He gave a shrug. "I wouldn't say I'm interested, but it's a responsibility of my position."

"Nephilanu is migrating into the wet season. What if we surprised the farmers this year? Don't lower the quotas until after the harvest is complete, but once it is, let everyone who's met the lower quota have their share of caro nuts. They are more likely to suffer the bog sickness working in the fields than any of the nobility at the heart of the Empire."

Her father set down his mug. "You've an overly soft heart,

Phalue. You'll need to work on that before you take over the governorship.

"I've given them that land, and they need to repay me somehow. It's a fair bargain. The trees don't take up all of the land, and they can grow crops on the rest. I didn't force them to it; they took the bargain of their own volition. Any failure is laziness on their parts." He shook his head and took another drink. "You sound like one of the Shardless. Save your pity for the unfortunate without choices."

It was the same argument she'd parroted to Ranami. Phalue frowned. But she wasn't sure if she'd describe the farmers as lazy, despite her father's convictions.

"Again with the scowling," her father said.

She changed the subject. "The fountain in the courtyard. You should destroy it. People are talking about the Alanga returning. You know it's not just a fountain now. It's an artifact that might be used against you should they return."

The woman on her father's arm paled.

"You're not the governor yet," he said lightly. "The eyes closed. Nothing has happened. It's been part of the courtyard for generations. It's the Emperor's job to keep the Alanga away, and the Sukais have done a fair job of that for hundreds of years. I'm not sure why we should stop trusting them now."

Where she would have normally shrugged off her father's complacency, now it bothered her, like an itch she couldn't scratch. "I should go," Phalue said, pushing herself to her feet.

"Already? You've barely eaten."

"I'm meeting Ranami in the city. We're visiting the countryside." The truth, yet not the truth. They weren't visiting. They were stealing caro nuts. The thought made her belly churn and swoop, a wave crashing over rocky ground.

"I'm so glad you've made amends with her," her father said,

reaching for a banana. "I'd rather you married another noble, but I suppose urging you to that would be a bit hypocritical of me." He pressed his lips together as he focused on peeling the fruit. "But you should get married, foster some children, choose an heir. I won't live for ever."

With the way he drank and hid in his palace, it would be a fair bit shorter than "for ever." Phalue shook her head. "I'm not having this conversation again. I'll get married in my own time." Which apparently was when Ranami was ready. If she ever was ready. "I'll try to be back for dinner."

"If you see your mother," her father said, "tell her to come visit."

Phalue only shrugged at the suggestion and strode out the door. Her mother hated to visit.

Ranami was waiting for her at the door of her home; Phalue barely had to knock before she answered.

"You're late," she said, her cheeks flushed. She stepped out and shut the door. It was quietly done, but sharply, in a way that made Phalue very aware that she'd angered Ranami.

"I was held up at lunch with my father."

"You're not taking this seriously." Ranami looked to the sky, peering at the clouds in a vain effort to find the sun. "We need to hurry. It will take time to get to the farms, and we need to avoid being seen by any of the overseers." She shoved a rough brown cloak into Phalue's hands. "Do you have to wear the sword? It's going to stick out."

The cloak was a little small for someone of Phalue's size, brushing just below mid-calf when she put it on. And the sword did stick out. "I can strap it to my back." She unbuckled her belt and refastened it around her shoulders like a bandolier. "There."

Ranami only gave her an exasperated, skeptical look, and then grabbed her hand. "It'll have to do."

They walked out of the city together, and despite Ranami's irritation, she didn't let go of Phalue's hand. Stone streets turned to dirt and mud; tiled roofs turned to thatch. The buildings diminished into the trees and brush of the forest.

It was an adventure of sorts, or at least as close to one as Phalue would ever get. She'd agreed to help the Shardless reluctantly, but what harm would stealing a few nuts do? And what could possibly happen to her if she got caught?

They paid an ox cart for a ride out to the farms. The cart swayed and creaked at each pit in the road, and Phalue watched Ranami stare into the trees. A breeze caught at her long, dark hair, and the backdrop of cloudy sky made Ranami look like a storm goddess. Even wrapped in a rough brown cloak, she was beautiful. It was the determination in her jaw and the set of her lips, the slight bit of worry at her brow, her dark and solemn eyes. "I'll read those books you wanted me to. When we get back," Phalue said.

"You always *say* that," Ranami said, her voice distant.

Phalue reached out for her, putting an arm about her shoulders, pulling her in close, kissing the crease between her brows. *I'm sorry.* She willed Ranami to understand. This was important to Ranami so Phalue would have to make it important to her. Ranami let out a little sigh and leaned in. They fit together like two sides of the same nut. At times like this, everything felt so right between them.

It began to rain just before they got to the farms. Phalue didn't remember what a wet season was like; it had been seven years since the last one. Somewhere in the closet back at home was an oilskin coat that no longer fit her. The rough cloak did a fair job of keeping the moisture out, and the rain would only help them avoid being seen. As soon as the orchard appeared ahead, Ranami rapped her knuckles against the cart. "We'll get off here, thank you."

Phalue took Ranami's hand and helped her from the cart. Rain weighed down the hood of Phalue's cloak, the cloth sticking to her forehead. Back in the city, the children would be running about in the streets, amazed that so much water could fall from the sky. As the years wore on, they'd begin to long for sunny, clear skies. For now, though, the rain was something to be welcomed.

Mud squelched below their feet as they ran for the nearest hut, where Gio said he'd meet them. Phalue had to knock twice at the stoop before the door swung open with a creak.

"You're late," Gio said when he opened the door.

Phalue did her best not to roll her eyes. "I'm here, and this place isn't exactly close to the city. I agreed to help, so let's get this done."

Ranami and Gio exchanged glances.

"Come in," Gio said finally. "You're getting soaked to the bone out there."

As they strode inside, Ranami loosed her hand from Phalue's grip and took a step away. Phalue had the odd sense that Ranami was somewhat ashamed of her. But she couldn't address that now.

The hut turned out to be only marginally drier. The floor was of rough-hewn boards, with gaps in places wide enough to fit mice through. The thatch leaked in a few spots, and a man was in the middle of putting bowls down to catch the falling water. The droplets tinked against the clay, creating a strange symphony.

In the room just off the main one, Phalue saw a young woman with a baby cradled in her arms. She swayed back and forth and cooed to the child, the floorboards creaking with each shift of her weight.

The only lavishness in all the hut was a thick rug. Worn and faded in places, but with an intricate vining pattern.

Ranami nodded to Gio, and then went to the man setting the

bowls down. His hair was streaked with silver, his dark eyes almost as large as Ranami's. He had a gentle slope for a nose, generous lips and a strong, pointed chin. He stood up and opened his arms to her.

When they'd finished embracing, Ranami turned to Phalue. "Phalue, this is my brother, Halong."

Phalue felt the world go still. Ranami hadn't mentioned any family. As far as she knew, Ranami had grown up alone on the streets.

"Not by blood," Halong said, a fond smile on his lips. "But when you're scrounging for meals in the gutters, if you find someone you can trust, you've found something more valuable than gold."

"It's good to meet you," Phalue said. She pressed her hand over her heart in greeting, and Halong did the same. His smile faded when he did so, though.

For the first time in a long time, Phalue felt out of place. What was she doing here, with the leader of the Shardless Few and a caro nut farmer? Was this really what Ranami wanted? She was the daughter of the island's governor – didn't that mean anything? When she let her hand fall back to her side, she felt it curl into a fist. To them she must seem a gilded brute, fed from her father's generous table, her simple clothes still sporting embroidery at the cuffs and collar. She tugged the rough cloak tighter around herself, heedless of the rain that still clung to it. "My name is Phalue," she said.

"I know who you are, Sai." Halong raked her over with his gaze.

Ranami placed a hand on his elbow. "She's here to help."

Gio stepped forward, his thumbs hooked into his belt. "The plan is simple, and only needs a few people. Phalue, you distract the overseer and his underlings when he counts the boxes for shipment. Halong works at the warehouse. He'll trade three out for dummy boxes while you're distracting everyone. Ranami will take the real boxes and give them to one of the farmers."

Phalue was shaking her head before Gio had finished. "I don't like it. It risks Ranami too much. Everyone expects to see this man at the warehouse, but if they catch her with the boxes, she'll be in trouble that even I don't think I can save her from. And who is this farmer she's taking the boxes to? Can we even trust him?" The introduction of these people that Ranami knew that Phalue had never even known about – it put her off balance. She was fumbling, trying to find her way back to solid ground.

"I know this isn't a game," Ranami said, her voice clear, her chin raised. "If there are consequences, so be it."

"Are we doing this now? Do I at least have the chance to meet this farmer who is holding your life in his hands?"

Ranami's lips pressed into a line. "Come on," she said, seizing Phalue's hand. "If this doesn't get through to you, I don't know what will." She led her back out into the rain.

"Why are you so insistent that I need to be 'gotten through to'?" The rain slicked Phalue's hair to her cheeks, running in cold rivulets to the base of her throat. "I'll admit, this Halong has a small house – though not as small as yours – and owns little enough. But he seems well fed, and he has a family. He grew up as a gutter orphan, but he did well for himself. He worked hard."

Ranami wheeled on her, wrenching her hand from Phalue's. "Is that what you see? A simple life but well enough? Yes, Halong has worked hard and does well for himself. He does better than well by the standard of gutter orphans. Most of the children I knew died. I did things I'm not proud of just to get a bite to eat. So did Halong. And though Halong does have a wife and a family, his firstborn died of bog cough. And yes, he still does *well* for himself! He farms and he works in the warehouse. He gets up before dawn to work the fields he purchased from your father with his promise of giving all the crops over. And because that's still not enough, he works in the warehouse too so his family can live in a hut that has more than one room.

"Is *well* what you see when you look at him? I have to wonder, then, what you see when you look at me."

"And this is why I always bring coin with me when I go into the city. To give to the gutter orphans. Someday, I hope to adopt one or two. But there will always be suffering. I can't fix everything!"

But Ranami had already turned and was marching off through the trees toward a larger building down the slope. Phalue wanted to call after her, to tell her what she saw. She saw a stubborn woman. She saw a soft and gentle heart wrapped around an indomitable will. She saw the woman that she loved, forged by terrible experiences – experiences she'd never bothered to tell Phalue about. Instead, she merely gritted her teeth. "You're impossible." The wind and rain ate her words. If Ranami heard them at all, she gave no sign.

Phalue had to rush to keep up with her.

At the bottom of the slope, Ranami wrenched open the door to the building and stalked inside.

It looked larger close up. Phalue paused to crane her neck up to the thatch roof. All the windows had been shuttered against the rain. It didn't look like someone's house. It looked more like . . . a barn. Phalue ducked inside.

Only two lamps lit the entire space, so it took time for Phalue's eyes to adjust. She smelled the people before she could see them. It smelled like dried sweat, made damp by the rain again, like breath gone bad, like old soup kept too long on the fire. The dark outlines of them became clear. Beds, piled on top of one another, and people piled into the beds. Someone coughed in the darkness.

Phalue stumbled forward, trying to find Ranami. It was like swimming in a dark ocean filled with seaweed. "Ranami."

And then she was there, in front of her, smelling sweet and clean. Phalue wrapped her fingers around the hem of Ranami's shirt, clinging to her the way she would a buoy.

"This is where most of the farmers live," Ranami said. "This is the living your father provides for them. If they want to grow enough nuts, most of the land must be used for the caro trees."

Phalue had seen the conditions some of the gutter orphans lived in from a distance. She knew intellectually that their conditions were grim. Yet the press of these bodies, all this life crowded under one roof was a world she'd not experienced. She'd never been in the midst of it, asked to do more than to toss a few coins in charity. She glanced to the side and saw a father and son on a bed, all their worldly belongings on a shelf behind them. "Can we speak outside?"

"No," Ranami said. She was a torch of anger, a burning spot in a sea of gray. "This is what your father does. He builds extensions onto his palace with his money and doesn't spare anything to provide a better living for the farmers. You think this is much different than how I grew up? But they are not on the streets. They do well enough for themselves."

Phalue heard the twist in Ranami's voice when she said "well enough", and she wished she'd never said it in the first place. There would be no reasoning with her at the moment. She sidled closer to her. She couldn't be sure in the darkness but she felt gazes lingering on her, tendrils tickling at the back of her neck. "Which farmer is the one you trust?" she whispered.

Ranami looked at her as though she had peeled a banana, thrown it away and then consumed the peel. "All of them, Phalue. I'm bringing the boxes back to all of them."

"How can you be sure——?"

"Because I'm just like them. I got lucky, if you could call it that, taking an apprenticeship with a bookseller who taught me to read because it made me more valuable to him. Treating me just like one of his books, putting his hands all over me in places I couldn't grab back fast enough. But without that, I would have taken your father's stupid bargain just to get off the streets. These people here have all lost people they love. The bog cough, other sicknesses, falling from trees while harvesting. How long will it be until you are governor?"

Guilt trickled into Phalue's chest. "When my father is ready to retire."

"And as long as he decides he's not ready to pass on his title, you wait, patient and comfortable, while these people die," Ranami said, her face thrust into Phalue's own.

Phalue couldn't hold her gaze. She couldn't bear to be here, stifled among the beds and the coughing. She whirled, striding to the door like she was coming up for air. The rain hit her face, and even the chill of it couldn't wash away the shame. But these people had chosen this. They'd made a bargain with her father. The land and a small cut of the profits for the caro nuts and the work. No one had forced them to it.

And then she remembered the meal she'd had before leaving her father's palace. The cold noodles in peanut sauce, the rich and spicy goat curry, the greens cooked to the translucent shade of jade. Everything festooned with flowers, artfully painted on the side with sauces. The wooden beams above her head painted in gold and red.

If not for the apprenticeship with a bookseller, Ranami could have been one of them. Perhaps she would have worked her way into a position like Halong's.

Perhaps not. She couldn't believe that every one of these people crammed into this space were lazy.

So either her father dealt with these people unfairly, or they were simply worth less. And knowing Ranami, loving her, Phalue couldn't wrap her mind around the latter.

Yes, she helped the orphans when she went into the city. Perhaps there would always be orphans. Phalue did what she could with her allowance, but it would never be enough. What would be enough when she was governor?

Ranami's righteousness made her vulnerable. Phalue had sat in her father's court. She knew the vagaries of human nature. Being leader of the Shardless and spouting ideals did not make Gio virtuous. Being poor did not make these people trustworthy.

But none of this changed the fact that Ranami was right: what Phalue was doing now was woefully inadequate. If she was to rule these people, she had to truly fight for them. And she'd never backed down from a fight.

She took in a few deep breaths, the air cooling the heat in her chest. She'd rather have faced a thousand swords. Nonetheless, she pivoted and plunged back into the darkness of the farmers' home. It took her a moment to find Ranami, who was speaking to a farmer sitting at one of the few tables in the building. The dim light cast them in faded shades, like a rug that had seen too much sun.

In two quick strides, Phalue was at Ranami's side. She took her hand. If Ranami would not protect herself, then Phalue would have to do it for her.

Ranami let out an exasperated sigh. "Are you trying to propose to me *again*? Every fight we have doesn't mean I'm about to leave you. And if I were about to leave you, I'd just leave."

"No." All the words she wanted to say were tight in her throat. She swallowed and tried again. "I want to help. I really want to help."

Ranami brushed the wet hair back from Phalue's cheeks, her

touch a caress. "I know." She squeezed Phalue's hand. "This has to happen soon. We'll need a distraction."

Phalue coughed in an attempt to hide the tears in the back of her throat. "Yes. I'll give you one. A large enough one for you to steal a hundred boxes of caro nuts."

Ranami laughed and seized Phalue's ears, bringing her face down to eye level. "Just the few, love. That's well enough."

20

Jovis

Somewhere in the Endless Sea

I dropped the children off on Unta, with the woman from the Shardless Few. She glanced at my tattoo, more than a little awe in her gaze. "How did you do it?" she asked. "How many did you have to fight?"

"A dozen," I told her glibly before turning to leave. It hadn't occurred to me until the island was out of view that she might not have known I wasn't serious. I made good time, gliding through the Monkey's Tail like a feather in a stream, even without witstone. Everything seemed to come easier – hoisting the sails, trimming and hauling up the anchor after we'd made port. Mephi took his turn at the sail a couple of times, though he seemed to tire quickly. The isolation on the ocean gave me time – perhaps too much – to think things through.

I'd found Mephi near Deerhead, which was close to the end of the Monkey's Tail. I'd never seen a creature like him. He had to come from somewhere, so there had to be others of his kind. But what kind of creature could blow clouds of white smoke?

Mephi, for his part, didn't seem to notice my brooding. He dove overboard whenever I gave him permission, asking "not good?" and "very good?" in equal measure, until I began to sit him down in the evenings in an effort to teach him something else. Anything else. The word "good" was starting to lose all meaning to me. But he was a fair bit better at catching fish than I was, and I was soon glad I'd kept him with me, if for no other reason than this.

At night, he curled up by my cheek, his nose nuzzled in the space between my ear and shoulder, murmuring until he fell asleep.

I kept an eye out for the blue-sailed boat, but I fell into the sort of haze that routine brings. So it was more than a little startling when I stopped in a small harbor and heard the first stirrings of the song.

Mephi had grown to cat-sized in the interim, but still small enough to ride on my shoulders. I had stopped at a drinking hall to see if I could buy some supplies from the owner. A musician in the corner played with a set of bells and a small drum at his belt.

"Just the barrel of fresh water, if you have it," I said to the woman behind the counter. She had the same staid attitude as Danila. I stopped her as she started to turn around. "Actually, a sack of rice too?"

"That's an extra two silvers," she said.

"Two?" I had the money, but I did enjoy a good bargain.

The tune sneaked up on me from behind, like a thief taking your purse. It wormed its way into my head before I'd realized it, my foot tapping in time to the beat. Catchy, no matter that I didn't dance.

"Aye, two," the woman said, scowling. "If you haven't been living in a cave, you'll know about Deerhead. More people wanting rice. Less rice."

And then I heard my name. A shock ran through me, my heart freezing and then kicking at my ribs like a horse trying to get free. It was my name. In a song.

> He steals your children, sets them free
> The constructs' power source they'll never be
> He's a star in the sky, the twinkle in your eye
> He's Jovis.

Mephi chirruped right in my ear, his tail winding around my throat. He *definitely* knew more words than not good and very good.

"We need to get out of here," I muttered to him. "Yes, I'll pay the two silvers," I said to the woman. I fumbled for my purse, missing twice before I found it, my wrist catching against my belt. "Here." The coins clinked on the countertop.

She looked to the coins, and then her eyes looked a little higher.

I felt the air against my wrist before I realized that the bandage had slipped. There was my rabbit tattoo, in all its glory. If I knew what was good for me, I'd have scarred it over.

"Jovis?" she said.

Just the posters were bad enough when I'd been running from the Empire and the Ioph Carn. Now I was trying to hide from people who thought I was some sort of hero.

"They paid me to do it. Steal the children, that is," I explained to her. I could have opened my mouth and vomited frogs, and she would have treated me with the same cursed reverence. "I've only saved three."

"Take the rice," she said, reaching beneath the counter and putting a sack on it. She pushed my coins back to me. Other people were starting to notice.

I seized my coins and whirled, looking for the door.

The music had stopped.

"Jovis," an old woman said from my right. The lamp above her turned, casting moving shadows across her stricken face. "I have a grandson turning eight."

"My niece," another woman said. "Her father died of shard sickness two years ago."

And then they were standing from their seats in the drinking hall, moving around the wooden pillars so they could make eye contact with me. Clamoring, begging. So many voices. So many wants and fears. So many children.

A tremor started in my bones, a humming that shook me from the tips of my ears to the end of my toes. It asked to be released somehow. "Stop!" I stamped my foot on the ground, expecting just to sway the floorboards a little.

The foundation shook. Dishes rattled on their shelves. The beams creaked, a little dust coming loose. This was more than just the result of strength. This was something else.

Everyone, with Deerhead Island so recent, stilled. All the bells on the musician's bandolier chimed with the fading vibration, the only sound left in the hall. I glanced from face to face and saw fear writ there. So much for my quick, quiet stop at a harbor to restock supplies. I went for the door and everyone moved out of my way.

The breeze was warm and wet, ruffling Mephi's fur. I could still feel my pulse pounding at my neck.

The time I'd picked up Philine. The man in the alleyway I'd almost toppled. The ease with which I'd done my work on the ship. My fast-healing wounds. They weren't just coincidences, some trick of my mind. Now, with the shaking of the drinking hall, I had to admit it. Something had changed, was changing with me. I'd always been different; the people around me couldn't stop reminding me of it. But my differences had always meant I had less power. I could shout into a room and be ignored in favor of other voices. Now, I could make the same room tremble. I should have felt excited; who could ignore me now? But I couldn't seem to stop my hands from trembling.

"Is it you?" I said to Mephi.

"Perhaps," he said in his squeaky little voice. As though he knew what thoughts turned in my head.

I nearly jumped out of my skin. "Perhaps? After bombarding me with 'not good' and 'very good' for days, now you give me 'perhaps'?"

"Still learning. Don't know. Many things don't know," Mephi said, nuzzling my ear with his cold nose. I shivered, and only half from the chill. I'd thought him like a parrot, and here he was, speaking fully formed thoughts like a child. I couldn't gain my bearings. It felt like I stood at the edge of a dark sinkhole and I was catching glimpses of movement far, far below.

Looking about, I found a large branch fallen from the recent storms. I picked it up and tried to break it. The bark merely roughed up my palms.

Mephi crawled halfway down my arm, patting my elbow with his little paws. "Try harder."

When I'd made the foundation of the drinking hall tremble, I'd been panicking a little, just wanting everyone to stop, to leave me alone. This branch – I needed to want it to break. A part of me wanted it to, and a part of me didn't want it to. Because this sort of change, I knew, was the sort a person didn't come back from. I would be plunging into that sinkhole, unsure of what lay at the bottom and with no one to guide my next steps. "I'm afraid."

Mephi merely scrambled back up to my shoulders, paws combing through my hair. "Is fine. Me too."

I could run from this, the way I'd been running from the

Empire and from the Ioph Carn. But I'd rather be running *to* something, and not inadvertently causing havoc as I went. I pushed away the fear and concentrated. The humming began in my bones again. I could almost hear it if I held my breath and listened.

When I bent the branch again, it broke beneath my hands as easily as if it were a twig. "How is this possible?"

"Don't know," Mephi said. "Neat though."

I laughed and let the two pieces of the branch fall to the ground. "I suppose, in a manner of speaking. But what are you, Mephi? Are you a sea serpent like Mephisolou?" In the stories, the ancient sea serpents had magical powers and could speak like people did.

I said it jokingly, but Mephi only wrapped his tail around my neck and shivered. "Don't know."

That made the both of us.

The noise within the drinking hall had begun to reassert itself, the musician playing another song with his bells and his drums. No one, it seemed, had the courage to chase me down. "Should we still get our rice and water?"

"Rice!" Mephi said with satisfaction. I wasn't sure if I was feeding a creature sometimes, or some sort of bottomless pit in the shape of an animal. How was I going to keep him if he kept growing?

Steeling myself, I strode back inside the drinking hall.

The whole room went silent again; the only noise was the creak of the lamps swinging from the breeze that came with me in the door. "I'm just here to buy some food and water," I said to the patrons. "I'm not here to rescue anyone, or to cause any trouble. Just food." I lifted my hands as one would when approaching a wounded animal.

They watched me as I went back to the counter and pulled

four silver coins from my purse. "And I'll pay for what I take," I said to the owner.

She took my coins grudgingly.

"Jovis," a voice said from behind me.

I was getting very, very tired of hearing my name on others' lips. I turned and found my way out of the hall blocked by my least favorite member of the Ioph Carn.

Philine.

I almost expected to see her wet and bedraggled, as if she'd just emerged from the bay I'd dumped her in. Instead she was back in her leathers — new ones, by the looks of them, with various sharp implements planted in various places on her body. Her baton was out and in her hand. "How long did you think you could run for?" she asked me. "The Ioph Carn has more resources than you do, and our ships are nearly as fast."

"I don't want trouble," I said. "There are a lot of people here that could get hurt. Yourself included."

She rolled her eyes. "What, more cloud juniper bark? Please. I don't fall for the same stupid trick twice. You're coming with me. Back to Kaphra."

I just wanted my thrice-bedamned rice and water. I curled my hands into fists and felt the strength in them. "I don't want to hurt you," I said, and was surprised to find that I meant it. All I'd ever wanted was just to be left alone to find the woman who had been my wife — years ago.

"Oh, you're very funny. Keep trying me, though, and I'm going to start to feel insulted. Besides, you think it's just me here for you?" she said, scorn in her voice. "I've five more with me, all of them trained by my hand."

"Let me pass," I said. "I'll get you your money, and I won't hurt any of you." Mephi, on my shoulder, crouched and shoved his nose behind my ear.

Five more men and women filtered in behind Philine, all wearing the same leathers. Philine laughed. "What are you going to do this time? Summon the Alanga Dione back from the dead? Call a sea serpent to eat us? How many more stories does Jovis have up his sleeve? You were lucky last time. There are more of us now. And we all know you're a liar."

"Let everyone here leave," I said, eyeing the nervous patrons.

Philine looked to the ceiling as though she found the wood pattern there particularly interesting. "And then what, Jovis? What do you think is going to happen here?"

I nodded to the owner behind the bar, and she walked swiftly around it. "You can settle your debts later," she said. She gathered the other people inside the hall and ushered them out. The Ioph Carn didn't move to allow them to pass, but neither did they stop them.

"What about your pet?" Philine said, her voice mocking. "Aren't you afraid he's going to get hurt too?"

"I just want to go," I said. I took a step toward the door. All six of the Ioph Carn took a step forward.

"Ah ah ah," Philine said. "No farther."

"Or what? You'll kill me? Isn't Kaphra planning on that anyways? To make an example?"

They all stepped toward me again, and Philine raised her baton.

I lifted a hand. "Don't."

"Well, now I *am* feeling insulted." Philine's mouth twisted on the words, the look in her eye sharp as the daggers at her belt.

I felt a thrumming deep within me, tremors like the shaking of Deerhead, vibrating outward to the tips of my fingers. I drew myself up and made for the door. "Don't stop me."

A smile quirked at the corner of Philine's mouth. She'd wanted me to try because she wanted to hurt me. The baton came down swiftly, right toward my shoulders.

I caught it.

Despite what I'd done outside with the branch, I was still surprised. Philine seemed more surprised still. Her eyes widened in disbelief, and then she gritted her teeth, trying to force the baton down.

No. Not ever again. I seized the baton with both hands and this time I was not afraid. I broke it cleanly in two. The *snap* reverberated from the walls of the drinking hall, and Philine let go. I tossed the two broken ends of it to the side. "Let me pass."

Philine studied me for a moment, puzzled, as though I were a freshwater fish she'd found in the ocean. And then she shook her head slowly. "No." With steady fingers, she pulled two daggers from her belt.

The Ioph Carn behind her didn't waver at all. They were with her to the end.

I took a deep breath. I hoped I wasn't wrong about this. "Go, Mephi," I said. He hopped from my shoulders and ran beneath a table.

Not one of the Ioph Carn shouted, not one grimaced; they only darted in, quick as swallows.

I ducked to the left of Philine's swing and gave her a push. Not even all my strength, and she flew back. Mugs shattered as her body wiped a table. Another woman swiped at me with a sword. I caught her hand and gave her a kick to the ribs. I felt the bone give way and break beneath my foot. She crumpled.

The next two came at me quickly, and I hopped back, trying to give myself more space. The Ioph Carn weren't mere brawlers, and Philine was a good teacher. The two hung back, waiting for the other two, and together, the four of them spread out, trying to surround me.

Me? I avoided a fight whenever I could. I had no training. Only my wits and what gifts Mephi had given me. Wits had to count for something, didn't they? I grabbed chairs from my left and right and flung them at the men and women approaching, hard as I could.

The chairs splintered on two of the Ioph Carn, sending shards of wood into the air. They both collapsed, one with a splinter of wood through his shoulder. Had I really thrown that hard?

The other two, both men, rushed me, not even checking on their fallen companions. I'd spent too long awed by my own strength. I wasn't ready.

A flash of pain burst across my ribs, and then a warm, burning sensation. I kicked back again and felt something crack beneath my foot. I didn't have time to check the wound or how bad it was. I caught the other man's wrist before he could bring his blade down on my arm. Quick as I could, I squeezed until his grip opened, and then cast the offending blade away. I didn't *want* to hurt or kill anyone. The man merely frowned when I let him go and pulled a dagger from his boot.

"There's one of you and one of me," I said. "Do you really want to do this?"

He had the scowling countenance of a barracuda, with a raised scar across his cheek. He said nothing, only flitted his gaze up and down my body as if searching for some weakness. Behind him, Philine groaned. She began to push herself to her feet.

The thrum inside me grew into a roar. "Just . . . stop!" I picked up the table to my right and broke off a leg, wielding it like a club.

The scarred man advanced.

I caught his slash on the table leg and then let it go. His dagger, embedded in the wood, carried his arm down, unbalancing him. I seized him by the back of his leather jerkin and helped him along to the floor. His face crashed into the wooden floorboards and he lay there, still.

When I looked up again, Philine was standing just beyond, two daggers in her hands. She regarded me with a mixture of fear and annoyance. "What *are* you?"

It was the very same question I'd asked of Mephi. A man in search of his wife. A smuggler. A thief of children. They swirled together in my mind. "I don't know."

Philine considered, her head tilted to the side. And then she nodded to herself almost imperceptibly. "Come back with me to Kaphra. We can find a way to use your talents. He'll forgive your debt."

I almost laughed in disbelief. "Do you think that's what I want?"

She shrugged. "Don't all men seek power?"

I could feel that thrumming inside me, the hum in the air before a lightning bolt struck. "I just want to be left alone!" I stamped my foot again, and the entire building shook. It creaked and groaned like an old man with an ailment.

Philine remembered Deerhead. The color drained from her face, her gaze going to the ceiling beams. Her men and women were slowly drawing themselves up, clutching their injuries, but even they froze when the drinking hall trembled.

"Get out," I said.

They fled, half-running, half-limping. Even Philine.

I had no illusions. This was the Ioph Carn and no one crossed the Ioph Carn. They'd be back after me again with more of their kind. Exhausted, I sank into a chair and poured myself a mug of wine from the pitcher at the table, heedless of who had drunk from it just moments before. The wine slid down my throat and cooled the fire in my belly.

Mephi, from the other side of the drinking hall, chirruped.

He crept out from beneath the table. I held out my hand to him and he scampered over, dodging the leftover remains of the two chairs. I helped him into my lap, and he pressed his furry head to my chest. "Very good," he said as I scratched his ears. "I still can't decide if you're more trouble than you're worth."

I was halfway through my mug of wine when the drinking hall owner pushed open the door. She eyed the damage.

"I'll pay for it," I said. It would pinch my purse, but I wasn't a cyclone or a monsoon, heedless of the wreckage I left in my wake.

"The others," she said, looking behind her, "can they come back in too?"

I waved a hand. "They're your patrons, not mine. It's not my business to say who can frequent your establishment."

They trickled in behind her, hesitant as feral cats still hungering for a meal. I watched them in dismay as they took in the destruction, and their eyes widened in awe. I groaned inwardly. First the song, and now this. If I'd wanted to just be left alone, I wasn't doing such a great job of lying low.

And then they began to approach me. I leaned on my elbows and debated draining the entire mug. I knew what they were going to say.

"Jovis." A young woman sat in the chair opposite me, her hands wringing together. Still, she held my gaze despite her fear. "What could I give you to save my son?"

21

Lin

Imperial Island

The steady beat of hammer against anvil soothed me as I worked. The spy construct was small and required more concentration than I thought possible. I hadn't tried this part before tonight – reaching into a construct's body to manipulate any shards within. I'd returned the pieces of the small construct I'd built to the storeroom; this spy construct was a more pressing issue. And now that I needed to reach inside a construct, I felt the frustration building. I concentrated, held my breath and tried again.

My fingers met only fur and flesh, and the spy construct squeaked.

"By Dione's balls!" I wiped the sweat gathering on my forehead. I had time, at least. I wasn't rushing back to beat my father to his rooms. No keys, just the beginner's book beneath one arm. I could stay out all night before he noticed I was gone.

I wasn't concentrating hard enough; I was angling my fingers the wrong way . . . I wasn't even sure what I was doing wrong.

My father and Bayan had locked themselves into a room to practice the bone shard commands, so I had time. I looked to Numeen. He'd be packing up soon, heading back to his family for a well-deserved meal. I should hurry. I shook out my fingers, closed my eyes, breathed deeply. What had the book said? To imagine I was dipping my fingers below the surface of a lake.

But I hadn't been to a lake before, not that I could remember. So I thought about dipping my hands into the pond by the Hall of Good Fortune, feeling blindly for the koi fish beneath. My breathing steadied, my heartbeat slowing.

I lowered my fingers.

It was more like a warm bath than the pond at home. I still felt the creature's fur tickling my palm, but beneath it the flesh was liquid between my fingertips. Something small and jagged met my touch. A bone shard. I had to tug a little to free it, but it came loose. The hammer stopped striking the anvil.

When I opened my eyes, I held the bone shard between my fingers, and Numeen was looking at me with a mixture of fear and awe. The spy construct lay frozen in place beneath my hand. "Do you have an etching tool?" I asked.

After a moment's hesitation, he reached into a drawer, pulled out a thin metal tool and tossed it to me. I caught it in my free hand and turned the shard over. There was a gray smudge on it, which I wiped clean. I squinted at the commands etched onto the tiny shard and set to work.

Amunet – to observe. *Pilona* – servant. Beneath that, in subtext, was written *remal* – clothing – with what looked like a star etched next to it. Next to *pilona* was written *essenlaut* – within these walls – with another star etched next to it. On a new line, *oren asul* – report and obey – and then *Ilith*, with one more star etched next to it. I stuffed the construct back into its iron birdcage and studied the words for a moment. *Amunet pilona essenlaut.*

Oren asul Ilith. The answer came to me, quick as a minnow darting from the shallows. The construct was to observe servants within the palace walls, and report to and obey Ilith.

I couldn't change much. The shard had already been bound to the palace, to the servant's clothing and to Ilith. But I had a clean shard in my sash pocket.

I pulled out the fresh shard, took the etching tool and created my own command, trying not to think too much on whose shard this might be. *Oren asul Lin.* And then I pressed the shard to my breast, and while doing so, carved a little star next to my name.

The construct inside the cage hadn't moved. With a deep breath, I closed my eyes again, held my breath and lowered my fingers to its body. Again I felt the warmth, the strange sensation of moving my fingers through liquefied flesh. I lodged the shard inside and drew my fingers away.

As soon as my fingers left the construct's body, I felt it leap to its feet again.

"You're mine now too, little one," I whispered to it. I gave it a little pat on the head and pulled a nut from my sash. "Your name is Hao. When I call your name, you must do as I say."

The little thing whisked it from my fingers, turning it over in its paws, devouring it. When it was done, it groomed its whiskers and then leapt to Numeen's shelves. It scampered along, leapt to another one and then absconded out the open window above Numeen's head.

I was safe.

I held out the etching tool to Numeen, but he shook his head. "Keep it. Looks like you need it." He turned back to putting away his tools and extinguishing the fire in the forge. And then, falsely casual: "Did you happen to find my shard yet?"

The question was always like a knife, twisting in my ribs. I'd checked more than once, but Bayan still kept Numeen's shard. "Not yet." I kept my tone neutral. "I'm still looking for the room where my father keeps the shards for Imperial."

He nodded like that made sense. "It will be difficult, taking your place as Emperor," he observed, "if you do not have the key to all the shard storerooms."

"There are many rooms in the palace, and most of them locked." I didn't have to feign any bitterness. "I can steal maybe two keys at a time, but if I didn't make it back in time, my father would notice. One key he might pass off as some other accident. I wish I could do this faster, I really do. But there is much he doesn't wish me to know."

Numeen frowned. I knew the way of it on most islands. Children often learned their trade from one of their parents, or at times from a close and trusted friend. But knowledge was meant to be shared, one generation to the next. Instead, my father locked it away from me, guarding it more jealously than he did the piles of witstone in his storeroom. I shook my head. "I should go. You need to get back to your family." A warm home, a warm meal, a warm bed.

He rubbed his big hands over his face and let out a sigh. "What do you do for meals most nights?" He asked like he wasn't sure he wanted the answer.

"Sometimes Father requests my presence at dinner. Otherwise, I call a servant to bring food to my room."

Numeen pushed himself up from his workbench, wiping his palms on his apron and then hanging the apron on a hook over the anvil. "Come on. If you don't need to be back right away, you can come have a meal with my family."

Out in the city, among its people. The idea of it called to me, pulsed in my blood like the sweet strains of a violin. "Are you sure?"

"Or you could go back to the palace and eat a rapidly cooling meal in your room alone," Numeen said, his voice a grumble. "I made the offer. Take it or leave."

"I'll go," I said before he could rescind.

He only nodded and went to the door. I hurried behind him and waited as he locked it. The air outside had the petrichor smell of rain after a long dry season. The eaves of the nearby buildings still dripped from the afternoon's storm and lamplight reflected off the cobbles of the street. The dry season had broken in a spectacular way.

My spy construct hadn't gone far. I could feel its presence, a tickle in the back of my mind. It followed us as we moved, as though expecting something. I pulled another nut from my sash pocket and offered it. The creature scampered down, took it and then climbed back to the rooftop to eat it.

"Don't tell them who you are," Numeen said as I fell into step behind him. "And don't let that construct follow you inside."

"I'm not stupid."

He gave me a sidelong glance over his shoulder.

"I'm doing the best I can with what I have. Tell them I'm a visitor who frequents your shop."

Numeen shook his head. "You are the daughter of a wealthy patron, but the steward of your household forgot to check your roof before the rains. Your dining hall is a wet ruin and since you were at my shop to pick up a lock and key; I invited you to dinner. Lin is a common enough name."

"Very well."

We picked our way through the streets of the city, farther from the palace walls and toward the ocean down below. The moon had risen, and it cast a silver glow across the water. I thought I could hear, even from here, the knock of ships against the docks, the creak of rope as docking lines were pulled taut.

I kept in silent step behind Numeen, my mind wandering. I'd been reading from the green-covered journal, trying to glean what useful information I could. Most of it was the dithering, excitable words of a young girl. Had I truly been so carefree at some point? Younger me had delighted in koi ponds, in mountain bamboo, in the goats she'd seen one sunny afternoon in the countryside, climbing a tree. Present-day me cared only for the keys and for establishing myself in the palace. "What did you know about my mother?" I said.

He took a moment to answer. I couldn't read much from his back. A slight tilt to his head, which could have read as either confusion or digging deep into old memories. "I only know stories, rumors, gossip."

"What sort of gossip?"

"Just that she was more clever than she was beautiful, a governor's daughter and that it was an advantageous political marriage. But they said your father could do better if he'd chosen to. He was always too immersed in his books and his constructs. So handsome as to be beautiful, but wasted within the confines of his library. Keeping us safe, they said, so they admired him."

"They. Who is 'they'?"

"Most people," Numeen said.

But not him. "And you?"

He shoved soot-blackened hands into his pockets. "How honest do you expect me to be? You are seeking the Emperor's throne, to take over the Sukai Dynasty. You could become the most powerful woman in all the known islands, and you ask me to speak ill of your family?"

"Please." There was so little I knew. I grasped the whispers from the servants the way one might grasp spiderwebs in their hands. I could not weave a tapestry from these threads. "I won't get angry."

"What are you hoping to gain?" he asked, rolling his shoulders in what could have been a half-hearted shrug.

Everything. Knowledge. A past. A connection to a father who treated me more as a pet than a daughter. I couldn't tell him the truth about my memory. "I want to know what people say about my mother and father. What everyone says."

"It's not pretty, and it's not romantic. If you're looking for beautiful stories, I have none. From what I heard, your father didn't like your mother much at first either. And then something changed, maybe a year into their marriage. I don't know what it was; no one does. But after that, the Emperor heaped both affection and praise on her. He brought her into the city and paraded her about. So I suppose it was romantic in the end."

They could have fallen in love – it happened often with these political marriages. At first both parties were indifferent, but familiarity bred comfort and comfort bred closeness and the end result of all this was love. But such a thing seemed too simple for Father. There was something about him, the way he disappeared into locked rooms, the way he dealt with both Bayan and me, that spoke of secrets even darker and deeper than Ilith's lair.

"Nearly there," Numeen said. His broad back was like a mountain in front of me. We turned into a narrow alleyway, and then he stopped to unlock the front door of a fairly large house. A rush of warm air hit my face as soon as it opened. The smells of cooking fish and steamed vegetables assailed my nostrils, making me remember I hadn't eaten since late morning. I followed him inside and left my shoes and construct at the door.

Past a short, narrow hallway, the home opened into a large room, the kitchen and dining area merged into one. Several people were in the kitchen, gossiping with one another as they chopped vegetables or fried fish in a pan. The sizzle of oil sounded as the man at the stove flipped a fish. He was built like an anvil – short and broad – just like Numeen. If I looked at them from the corner of my eye, I might have trouble telling them apart. I judged the rest of them. Two families in the one household, with a treasured grandparent between them all. That was why the house was larger than I'd expected.

Four children sat at the table, peeling garlic and shelling nuts. They looked up as I approached and stared, but said nothing, though I could nearly see them bursting with it.

Numeen stepped into the kitchen. "I brought a guest. She's the daughter of a patron of mine, and their servants didn't prepare for the rain. Their dining area is wet through and through. I offered her a dry place to eat."

"Next you'll be telling the birds to roost in your room with you and your wife," Numeen's brother said. "No offense meant."

A smile tugged at the corner of my lips. "None taken. My name is Lin."

Numeen's brother only grunted and tilted the pan. The two men were more similar than probably either of them cared to admit.

I stepped into the kitchen. "Can I help?"

"Oh, of course not." A woman turned from the vegetables she was chopping. She was slender and taller than Numeen, built like bamboo – all narrow and flat and graceful. By her fairer skin and curling hair, I guessed her to be half Poyer. The timing was right. The migration patterns of the Poyer isles only brought them close to the Empire's curving archipelago once every thirty years or so. She aimed an affectionate gaze at Numeen. This must be the wife he spoke of.

"Please," I said. "I prefer to keep myself busy." It wasn't a memory, not exactly, but I felt I knew this dance in my bones.

"You're a guest," Numeen's wife said, now chopping onions. She wiped at her watering eyes with an elbow. "You should just sit down."

So I went to her side, picked up another onion and began peeling it. The pungent scent stung my eyes and my nostrils.

She gave me an approving glance but said nothing.

When the meal was ready, we all sat at the table together. It was so different than dining in my father's palace, with the constructs lined up on one side of the long table, the quiet servants, the wind whispering through the shutters and my father's ever-present disapproval. Here, I couldn't hear any wind at all. Perhaps it was because the building was nestled between two others. Or perhaps it was because, even if there had been wind, it would have been difficult to hear above the din.

Two children sat to my left and Numeen sat to my right. Numeen's brother sat with another man I judged to be his husband. Everyone spoke, several conversations going on at once. The little girl to my left patted my arm. She couldn't have been more than five.

"That's Thrana," Numeen said. "My youngest."

"Look." Thrana held up a folded paper bird. "I made this today."

I took it from her, the paper soft beneath my fingertips, refolded and crinkled in a hundred different ways. Black ink marks slashed across its wings. Something about peas and peppers. A piece of scrap paper, handed down to her and remade into something new. I could see the hope in her eyes as she watched me. "It's lovely."

A smile burst across her face. "Lin says it's pretty," she said to her brother. "You can have it," she said to me.

"Oh, I couldn't take it." I handed it back to her. "Surely such things should be treasured by the ones who've made them."

Thrana smiled shyly as she took it back.

Numeen shrugged. "She's been trying to make one for a few days," he said, spooning rice onto his plate. He passed the bowl to me. "She's a stubborn girl, just like her father."

"Not a trait I'd brag about," his wife said.

I took a heaping spoonful of rice, the steam caressing my hand. "How long have you been married?"

"Fifteen years," Numeen said at the same time she said, "Too long." And then they both laughed, and he kissed her cheek.

It made me wonder what sort of marriage I could look forward to. One of power and secrets, and possible love – like between my father and mother? The only man I knew close to my age was Bayan, and we'd been at one another's throats since I'd recovered. I couldn't imagine – or thought I couldn't – what it would be like to hold the hand of someone like Bayan, to lean into his side, to have him kiss my cheek. I felt the heat of a blush traveling up my neck as I thought of his hands at my waist, the fullness of his lips against my skin.

I stuffed the thought away and focused on the meal in front of me.

"Lin." The elderly woman who looked like Numeen's mother called to me from the other side of the table. "We're not poor. Take more rice. You're too skinny."

Again, I felt I knew this dance. I took another spoonful and settled it on my plate before passing it on. I *was* hungry. "Thank you, auntie," I said to her. It was as if my old memories were pushing against a thin sheet, and though I could make out the shape of them, I could not grasp them completely. But I'd never grown up in a household like this. I knew my mother had died when I was young, and my father had few relatives. I must have at some point met my mother's family. Now I couldn't even remember enough to write to them, and my father hosted very few guests.

"Do you live nearby?" Numeen's wife asked.

"Not far," I said. "Closer to the palace."

She nodded. Most of the wealthier men and women in Imperial

City lived close to the palace. It must have served some function years ago, under the rule of prior Emperors, when the palace gates were open, and people could seek an audience. "Your home is very beautiful," I said to her. It was modest, but large, and someone had painted the beams.

"Very crowded, I think you mean." A glint of amusement in her eye. She looked pointedly at the clutter in the kitchen, and the two wooden toys splayed out where someone might trip on them. "There are nine of us here, and we all share a room except Grandmama."

I wasn't afraid of offending her by letting the assumption stand, but I corrected her nonetheless. "No. I meant it the way I said it." I tried to think of how to put into words the feeling of being walled in by Numeen on one side and his daughter on the other, elbowing me accidentally each time she took a bite. There was something comforting in that closeness, in the smiles around the table, in the regard they held for one another. "It's the people who fill it that make it beautiful."

Her cheeks reddened, though she seemed pleased. "Well, see?" she said to Numeen. "It's not messy. It's beautiful."

"Not as beautiful as you." He brushed his fingers against her jaw.

It was odd to see him in this environment. In his shop he was gruff and silent, and I'd never seen him smile. Here he relaxed, and even the admonishments to his children were soft. He was like a snake with a freshly shed skin – brighter and more polished, made anew.

I'd lifted a bite to my lips, my head low over my bowl, when my gaze trailed to an open window. A spy construct sat on the lip of it, watching us with black, shiny eyes.

It wasn't my construct.

What had it seen? What had it heard? I shot to my feet before

I realized I'd done so, the presence of my construct a buzz in the back of my mind. "Hao! Capture the spy!" I cried out.

The scrabble of little footsteps sounded, and the spy construct stiffened, its ears swiveling. It darted *into* Numeen's house. His brother leapt up, alarmed, and all four children screamed.

Hao appeared in the window, looked for the other construct and dashed for it. They leapt over the pots in the kitchen, unseating one and sending it crashing to the floor. Numeen's wife seized a spatula and began to chase the creatures, trying to beat them with it.

"Not the one chasing!" I said, but no one seemed to hear me.

Finally, Hao cornered the other spy near the table. Hao jumped, scuffled with it and then pinned it to the ground. Before Numeen's wife could beat either of them to death, I strode over, the etching tool still heavy in my sash. I knelt, seized the other spy and reached into its body. The shard came free easier this time. And then I took the spy in my hands, went to the window and pushed the shard back into its body. It lay there for a moment and then came back to life, leaping to its feet and scampering away, its mission forgotten.

The room behind me had gone silent.

"Lin is a common name," Numeen's wife said. "But it's also the name of the Emperor's daughter."

I turned to find them all looking at me. The house, that had seemed so warm a moment before, now felt frigid as snowmelt. Numeen's wife took a step toward the children, putting her arms over their shoulders, pulling them in just a little. It was a subtle movement, but one I understood. And Numeen's brother reached for the soft spot on his skull, the place where his scar was.

I was Lin. I was the Emperor's daughter.

And I had worked bone shard magic in their home. A place where they could at least pretend, for a little while, that they were safe.

"I'm sorry," I blurted.

I fled.

22

Jovis

Nephilanu Island

We were already late. I crept through an alleyway toward the city's marketplace, where the Tithing Festival was being held. According to the locals, they cleared the marketplace of stalls for the Festival every year.

Mephi, now as tall as my knee, pressed his body against my leg. "We do a very good," he said in a stage whisper.

For what felt like the thousandth time, I made a lowering gesture with my hand.

"A very good," he said, only a little more quietly.

This was becoming a habit. And people always talked about habits like they were a thing that would kill you one day. "Jovis has a habit of gambling" or "Jovis has a habit of drinking too much melon wine" or "Jovis has a habit of steering his ship into storms". It seemed, apparently, that what Jovis had actually developed a habit of was rescuing children from the Tithing Festival, and thus getting his face painted onto more stupid posters. It was probably the most foolhardy way to get a lot of portraits done for free.

But how was I to turn all those people away? They hadn't come empty-handed. I needed the money. Back in that drinking hall, among the ruin I'd made of the Ioph Carn, and their awed faces, I'd felt larger than I actually was. A sparrow who'd mistook himself for an eagle.

And they'd written a bedamned song about me. A song.

So many justifications. So many little lies I kept telling myself. I'd even once told myself that Mephi would be disappointed if I didn't cave to those people's pleas. So a habit was best to describe it. Habits were things done with little reason, over and over, until momentum made them more difficult to stop than to keep going. *Click click click*. I looked around for the source of the noise. Oh. There was the tip of my steel staff, clicking against the stones as I walked. Very stealthy of me. I'd commissioned it at the last island, because hands weren't great at stopping blades. And now I'd formed yet another habit – tapping it against the ground when I was nervous. I stopped, leaned on it and took a deep breath.

Rescuing children before they reached the Festival was one thing. Rescuing them *at* the Festival was quite another. But the parents had been desperate. And generous.

"Keep out of trouble," I said to Mephi. "You're still too small."

He only waggled his head and clacked his teeth at me, like a dog tasting something bitter, but I didn't have time to admonish him. I peered around the corner.

The square was hung with multicolored flags, someone softly playing a flute in a corner. Distractions for the children. Several of them had started to cry, even in spite of the lulling effects of opium. The sound of it chilled me, reminded me of my brother sobbing that day before he'd gone to the ritual. Five soldiers that I could see, two of them in front of me at the alleyway's mouth. Three others in the square. One was keeping the children in line.

One consulted the census taker's notes. One stood in the center of the square, chisel already in hand.

And then I caught sight of the child facing the crowd, kneeling in front of that soldier. My mouth went dry. The boy looked like my brother at that age. I still remembered my mother's hand tight in mine at the Festival, the smell of sweat thick in the air. She'd been squeezing my fingers harder than she'd intended, I think. I hadn't understood back then. I couldn't.

Onyu's gaze had met mine as the soldier numbed the spot behind his ear and peeled back the skin. Blood trickled down his neck, pooling a little at his collarbone. I'd glanced at the soldier's sweaty face, his lips pressed together as he'd placed the chisel against my brother's skull, wondering why he was taking so long.

"Little brother, you worry too much. My friends said only one of twenty-five die in the Festival," he said. He'd always been braver than me.

When the soldier finally hit the chisel, Onyu had been looking at me, his mouth curved in a slight smile. I think he meant to be reassuring. But I watched the life go out of his eyes as the chisel went too far, as it dug into his brain. One moment there, the next gone, surely as a flame snuffed out by the wind.

I didn't *know*. Not until my mother held his limp body in her arms and started wailing.

One in twenty-five. And I'd done nothing to stop it.

I'd only been six then, and too small to make any real difference. Now, here, I had the power to push back. I should have waited to attack, gathered more information. But I found my feet moving forward before I could stop them. Habit.

I struck both soldiers in front of me at the same time, aiming for the same spot on the back of the skull. Both crumpled. My hands ached, only briefly. The injuries I'd sustained from my drinking-hall brawl with the Ioph Carn had faded quickly. I wasn't sure what Mephi was, and I wasn't sure what this bond between us had done to me, but the precipice had been the day I'd let Mephi back onto my boat. I'd careened past that and now all I could do was see where this led.

Right now it was leading me to pull the soldiers' unconscious bodies into the alleyway. The milling children and parents in the square were so caught up in their own fears that none of them seemed to notice the soldiers' absence. When they did, I doubted they'd raise an alarm. That was the problem with ruling a populace that didn't love you. Few people cared when you got hurt.

Five children, all of them friends and neighbors. The parents had pooled together money to pay me.

I leaned over to whisper in one woman's ear. "My name is Jovis. I'm here to help the children. When I say 'stop', get everyone out of the way. Tell your friends."

The woman stiffened a little at the sound of my voice, but then nodded and tapped on a man's shoulder.

I felt something rub against my knee. Mephi, trotting along beside me like some sort of strange dog. People started to notice. When he'd been kitten-sized, he'd been easy to pass over. Now, his odd features couldn't escape attention. His webbed paws smoothly navigated the uneven streets. His legs had grown only marginally, but his neck had lengthened a little. The nubs atop his head were now prominent, the fur there rubbed bare, though the horns beneath had not broken past skin. And he'd begun to shed. Not fur, but a soft and pale dandruff that shook loose like flour whenever he was dry.

One of the soldiers by the group of children followed a villager's gaze. His eyes widened.

"Stop!" I cried out.

The square erupted into chaos. People moved toward the alleys. The soldiers all turned to find the source of the shout.

Children tumbled toward me, past me, moving like molasses in their drugged states. Mephi, disobedient as ever, darted out to help round them up. "Mephi!" It was useless, it always was.

The soldiers reached for their swords. I lifted my staff and braced it between my hands, ready to meet them.

And then I heard the creak of bending wood from above. On the rooftops, four archers crept to the peak of the roofs and crouched, reaching for arrows. This bond with Mephi gave me speed and strength; what it hadn't given me was better hearing. Or a bigger brain. I should have known this would happen. One of the parents had told the Empire, and the Empire had set a trap for me. I was oddly flattered – they'd never tried to set a trap for me when I'd been a smuggler, which was probably why I'd been able to get away with that shipment of witstone.

Two more soldiers emerged from an alley. Nine against one.

I took in a breath and the thrumming began in my bones, like the cavernous breathing of some enormous animal. I tightened my grip on the staff.

"Jovis," called the soldier who had been consulting with the census taker. She looked battle-worn, her armor scored in places, her face weary. The square had nearly cleared, though a few children without their parents lingered at the edges, stupefied by opium. "By the order of Emperor Shiyen Sukai, I am authorized to bring you in for questioning."

"And the executioner's block, I've no doubt," I said.

"So you won't come quietly?" She took a step forward, and her soldiers stepped with her.

"If you know who I am, then you know I've fought off fifteen of the Ioph Carn and won. What makes you think you will have any better luck?" I threw up my chin, giving the lie some weight. Truth was, these were the worst odds I'd faced. I noticed a couple of the soldiers shoot one another sidelong glances.

She opened her mouth to speak, but I didn't let her.

I stamped on the cobbles with my right foot, and the thrumming within me sank into the earth. The stones beneath me trembled, the buildings shaking. My little quake only had a radius of perhaps thirty feet, but the soldiers didn't know it. Nor did the people of the town. Someone screamed, and the archers dropped their bows to brace themselves on the roof. Everything else faded from my awareness.

I went to work.

I took out their leader before anyone had recovered, striking her sword from her hand with my staff, kicking it to the side. I brought the other end of the staff around to strike her across the shoulders. She went down.

The next two had the presence of mind to attack me, and I laid them out before they could even land a blow.

The *clink* of an arrow skittering across cobbles sounded. The archers had recovered. I took a breath and stamped again. The one who'd fired the arrow hadn't had time to brace. I heard a yelp as he fell from the rooftop to hit the ground with a thud. The last three soldiers on foot tried to give me space, tried to circle around so they could surround me. But my staff was long, and I could wield it with force even when holding the end of it. I pulled the end of it up to my shoulder, the metal cool against my ear, and swung. Two soldiers jumped back. The last tripped on a stone and my staff caught her in the chest.

I heard the impact of the arrow before I felt it. A ripping, wrenching sound. I faltered, barely catching myself before I could fall. And then a fiery gout of pain from my shoulder. Grimacing, I stamped again, but this time, the archer was ready for it. I heard no more archers falling from the roof. I had to end this quickly, lest I become a pincushion. I took two swift steps toward the remaining two soldiers on the ground, punching one in the gut with the end of my staff, bringing the end of it around to clobber the last one in the head. Vicious moves, but they worked.

When I whirled, I saw a familiar figure running across the rooftops.

"Mephi, you idiot!" I didn't have time to say anything else.

He sank his sharp little teeth into the calf of one of the archers. He was a fair bit larger than when he'd attacked Philine, so I wasn't surprised when the archer let out a scream and dropped her bow, trying to dislodge this creature from her leg. Two more archers, and one was aiming at Mephi.

I didn't think. I threw the staff, hard as I could, at his head.

He tried to get his hands up to protect his face, but they were tangled up in the bow and arrow. The staff hit him, and he rolled off the roof. He hit the ground with a thud and did not rise.

The last archer made a run for it.

"Shit." My staff hit the cobblestones with a clatter, and I went to pick it up. The other archer was still wrestling on the rooftop with Mephi. I needed to learn how to throw knives or something. I had only my staff – and I could help Mephi or stop the other soldier from raising an alarm. Something in the thrumming shifted. I became aware of how *wet* the square was. The water puddled on the cobblestones, gathered in the gutters, in clay jugs in the building to my right. Even in the bucket someone had left in an alleyway at the edge of the square. They felt almost like . . . pieces of myself. And then, just as quickly, the sensation vanished.

I didn't have a choice, not really. I threw the staff at the soldier trying to dislodge Mephi. It went just a little wide, clattering against the tiles. But her grip slipped from Mephi at the noise, and he opened his jaws. The slick tiles provided no purchase as she overbalanced. She rolled to the edge of the roof, falling to the ground with a yelp. She lay there, still.

I was surrounded by blood and bodies, a few of which were still groggily coughing up yet more blood.

A squeak sounded from behind me. Right. The children. The whole reason I'd gotten into this mess in the first place. Some of them had escaped with their parents, but some had come from smaller, neighboring islands and were relying on the soldiers to get them home.

"We're leaving," I said to them. "Now."

The arrow still jutted from my shoulder, aching every time I moved. I reached back and, bracing myself, snapped off the end. Pain radiated from the wound in a burst, setting my teeth and making my breathing come short. I'd have to see to it later. Right now, I had to keep moving.

One of these children's mother or father had betrayed me, had betrayed all of them. But I still had their money jangling in my purse, and besides, it wasn't the child's fault. I'd get them away from the ritual and into safe hands. More easily done on this island, where the Shardless Few had dug in a small foothold in the countryside, away from the cities.

I herded the children through an alley and they went, docile as little lambs. Mephi scampered down from the roof, clinging to a gutter pipe. It protested at his weight. And then he was jaunting beside me, overtly pleased with himself. "Did a very good," he said.

"No. You would say, 'I did well.'"

"Did well?"

"I did well." And then I sighed. Was I really teaching the basics of grammar to this creature? "And you didn't. I asked you to stay out of it."

Mephi let out a snort that told me exactly what he thought of that command.

"Aren't pets supposed to do what their masters say?"

He gave me a long look, and despite the pain in my shoulder I laughed. So he wasn't exactly a pet. A friend maybe. I hadn't had a friend since I'd left home to search for Emahla, years ago. Even now I worried at my frayed focus. We'd lost the blue-sailed ship, much as I'd tried to convince myself that we hadn't. I lied to myself each time I woke – *Today I will find it again*. It had been weeks.

Each time I confronted the truth, my loyalties clashed painfully. Didn't I care about Emahla? Didn't I want to help her? But Mephi couldn't stand the smell of witstone, and he couldn't explain why. I'd tried to burn it in his vicinity once, and he'd vomited until he could only heave up bile. I'd stolen things I shouldn't have, had driven hard bargains, had ignored the pleas of those asking for help. But I couldn't cross this line. I hated myself for it.

But I couldn't hate him.

At the docks, the dockworker construct tried to stop me, with my five children huddled behind me. "Please state your goods." I knocked it into the water with a sweep of my staff. I'd long since gone past elegance and lies.

It took half a day to sail around to the other end of the island, and the opium began to wear off almost as soon as we'd left the harbor. The children cried and huddled together like a mass of lost puppies. Mephi did his best to calm them, but they really wanted their mothers and fathers. I knew better than to even try. I never knew what to say to children. Instead, I sat away from them, worked the arrowhead loose from my flesh and stitched shut both my skin and my torn shirt.

I had to drop anchor in the shallows, and I urged the children into the water. It looked about to rain anyway and the rest of them would soon be wet. I waded to shore with them, my pants heavy with seawater. The wound in my shoulder was sore, but it had already begun to heal.

A woman sat on the sand, watching me. She was dressed simply, a rough-woven tunic and a wraparound skirt. Before Emahla, I might have said she was beautiful. Her long black hair was plaited behind her, framing a face with wide, expressive eyes and a pointed chin. She rose to her feet when I approached. "Jovis, I presume?" she said. "I was told that's who would be bringing the children."

I rubbed at my chin. "What? The face doesn't look familiar? I've had a hundred portraits of myself scattered across the Empire. I've been paying gutter orphans to collect them for me."

She gave me a sidelong look. "Nearly as vain as the Emperor. Will you clamor next to have your face stamped onto coins?"

"With as big a head I'm growing, it wouldn't fit."

She placed a hand over her heart in greeting, and I returned the gesture. "My name is Ranami. I've heard about you."

"Good things, I hope."

"It depends on who you're asking." She bent down to greet one of the children. They wandered up the beach like lost ghosts. "A friend of mine is coming to take you someplace warm where you can get washed up and put on dry clothes. We'll let your parents know that you're safe. And we've got food too. Would you like that?"

The girl nodded.

A man stepped out of the trees, grizzled, with a scar over his milky left eye. I felt my eyebrows lift. I knew the man. But then, damn well everyone in the Empire knew him, because he'd had more posters spread about than I had. Gio, the leader of the Shardless. The stories said he'd killed the governor of Khalute with his own two hands. He placed his hand over his heart to greet me, and then beckoned to the children.

They went, leaving me alone on the beach with Ranami, my boat anchored behind.

"So this is where the leader of the Shardless Few is hiding?"

Ranami's mouth quirked. "And who would you tell?"

I lifted my hands, palms up in a helpless gesture. No one would ever believe me. I'd made sure of that. "Fair enough."

Mephi had taken the chance to go for a swim. He rolled in the waves, chattering to himself. I could feel the pull of the Endless Sea from behind me. Somewhere out there were the answers I sought to Emahla's disappearance. I turned to go.

"I have an offer to make you," Ranami said.

I knew what she would say before I faced her. Everyone now thought they could buy me, even the Ioph Carn. They hadn't cared much when I'd been a smuggler of goods, when they *could* have bought me. First people were afraid when they saw what I could do. And then, once the fear had passed, they started making me offers. The only ones I'd taken so far were to rescue the children.

"Join the Shardless Few," she said. "Help us overthrow the Emperor."

I shook my head. "No. And you're not the first to offer me some sort of loose employment. Oh. Except you wouldn't pay me, would you?"

She pursed her lips.

"I'm not a hero. I never set out to be a hero in the first place. Those children? Their parents paid me to rescue them."

"But you can do things others can't. Unless people exaggerate, you have the strength of ten men and can even make the ground tremble. Think of all the good you could do with that. You could give the people their voices back."

I looked to the sky and sighed. "The Empire was established to save those people from the Alanga. The Shardless Few is trying to save those people from the Empire. Who, after, will save the people from the Shardless?"

"The Alanga are not coming back, no matter what the Emperor might say. His constructs are more like toys than an army. He's a tinkerer, not some benevolent protector. And ours are the lives he's tinkering with."

I was young, but she was a little younger by my guess. She still had the vigor to believe in ideals. "What does the rebellion plan to do with the people once it's saved them? If there is no Emperor, who will rule us?"

She lifted her chin. "We will rule ourselves. A Council, formed from island representatives."

I didn't ask any further questions. I knew an invitation to pros-elytization when I heard one. I ran a hand over my face. Endless Sea, I was tired! The dry clothes and hot food promised to the children sounded like heaven to me now. My feet squelched in my shoes each time I shifted my weight, my wet pants clinging to my thighs, my shoulder a dull ache. "Sounds like a messy process." I strode toward the water. "I'm not what you're looking for."

"Wait!" she called after me. "I know what *you* are looking for."

I stopped.

"A boat of dark wood and blue sails, heading toward the greater islands. I know where it's going."

I had no idea where the boat was anymore, and I'd never known its destination. "What do you know about it?"

She wasn't going to tell me just because I'd asked. Of course she wasn't. "I'll tell you what you want to know, but you must help us first."

I pivoted back to her, helpless as a puppet being jerked about by its strings. Emahla – always for her.

"What would you have me do?"

23

Jovis

Nephilanu Island

"And that's all you want from me, I suppose?"

When a shark offers up a pearl, be wary of its teeth. My father liked to tell me that when we were sailing, though I found this lesson most often applied on land.

Ranami uncrossed her arms. "Ten days of your time is not much to ask."

"And I expect I can just sit myself down here, wait for ten days and you'll give me the information I want." Internally, I was screaming. Ten days. Ten days of letting that boat get farther and farther away, grasping for answers that were slipping through my fingers.

"No," Ranami admitted.

"Tell me what it is exactly that you want me to do, and then we'll talk."

"Come back with me; let Gio and the others explain."

"The others," I said flatly. How many of the Shardless Few were gathered on this island? If the Emperor had his spies out and about, they'd find out soon enough. And who needed to trust people when you had constructs as small as squirrels who could do your work? Yet the promise she dangled in front of me – of knowing where that boat was going – flashed like a fishing lure on a sunny day. I was guessing at this point, following a trail that had long since grown cold. If I knew its end destination, I could find the quickest route there, catch the boat while it was still docked. I thought of Emahla's wine-dark eyes, what it would be like to see them again, and I felt like my throat was being pressed by the weight of all the islands atop one another. "Do you know if she's still alive?" I said in a low voice.

Ranami's eyelashes fluttered, her gaze going to the sand. "I'm sorry," she said and she sounded genuinely remorseful. "All I know is that you were looking for the blue-sailed boat. I didn't know—"

I swept past her and heard Mephi splashing out of the sea to follow me. Of course she didn't know. No one seemed to know what happened to these young men and women, why they were taken. But she knew where they went, and that was something. "It doesn't matter." I had to take this chance. I had to stop lying to myself, telling myself I'd find it again on my own. I wasn't a child, hoping for glimpses of sea serpents from shore.

She hurried to keep up with me and I didn't wait. "You don't know where you're going," she said in a firm voice before stepping in front of me. And she was right: I didn't. Where did one hide the rebellion's leader from the Empire?

The forest floor was damp beneath my feet. Most people were glad to see the rains come after seven years of a dry season. Yes, the winds picked up and made the sailing quicker. But the rain made the sailing a fair bit more miserable, and the ever-present moisture in the air made me feel like my fingertips had grown permanently wrinkled. Mephi scampered ahead and around us both, pouncing on dew, snapping at a butterfly, clambering halfway up a tree before jumping down again. He didn't say anything, for which I was eternally grateful. All I needed now was to be explaining to this woman why my pet *talked*.

Ranami led me to a cliff covered in vines and vegetation. Birds and monkeys called in the trees above, their voices layering on top of one another. The skies had cleared, though I knew that wouldn't last. There were no roads out here, no villages, not even the hint of rooftops in the distance. That would help with the spies, I supposed. And then Ranami drew aside some vines to reveal a crack in the cliff's face. A crack barely large enough for a person to shove themselves through. She looked to me, her gaze cool.

I balked. "You can't be—"

She lifted her arms, sucked in a breath and disappeared into the rock.

Mephi chittered excitedly. I lifted a finger to my lips. "Don't," I said. He quieted and only headbutted my knee. I scratched his ears and approached the crack. I lifted the vines like a curtain and peered into the darkness. I thought, when I looked at it, I could see some faint glow from within.

"Will you follow?" Ranami's voice emanated from the darkness as though she'd become only shadows.

Mephi sat on his haunches, black eyes staring up at me.

"You don't have to come," I said to him. "You can wait for me back on the ship."

He shook his head, chirruped and slid through the crack as if his bones were liquid.

I clenched my fingers, unclenched them, feeling sweat gather on my palms. I'd never been fond of enclosed spaces – which was perhaps another reason I didn't like the wet season. So much waiting around indoors for the storms to pass. I couldn't see how far this crack went, how long I'd have to squeeze for. What if there were spiders?

Emahla would do it if our positions were reversed.

With a quick breath, I stepped sideways into the crack, my head facing the light of day. One step. Two. The stone on either side pressed on my chest and on my back. I felt caught between two mountains, with another mountain bearing down on top of me. Was this how an insect felt right before it was crushed underfoot? Three steps. Four. My shirt caught on an outcropping. It wouldn't tear away when I tugged. I was trapped.

I stopped, trying to quell the panic. One step back, and then forward again. My shirt fell free.

One more step, and I felt the crack widen. A warm body brushed against my legs. Mephi. Just the feel of him relaxed me, knowing he was there and he wasn't scared. He was much smaller than I was. If he wasn't scared, I shouldn't be either.

Finally, I was able to turn my head. A few more steps and I couldn't feel either wall against me anymore. A lamp flashed in front of my face. When it was lowered and my eyes adjusted, I could see Ranami's face, grim but satisfied. "We're farther in."

The cavern was barely wide enough to accommodate my shoulders, but now it was merely an uncomfortably small hallway and not what felt like a death-trap. If this was where the Shardless were hiding, I understood how they hadn't been found yet. I had to watch my footing – the floor of the cavern was uneven, though someone had made an effort to clear the jagged rocks away.

Ranami and the lamp disappeared around a corner, and I hurried to keep the light in view. I almost stumbled when I rounded the corner.

The floor here was smooth, the walls widening into a proper hallway. Lamps hung at regular intervals on hooks from the walls, illuminating symbols carved into the rock. I had to look both left and right before I saw Ranami again, walking down the hall.

"What is this place?" I said when I'd caught up.

"We're not sure," she said, "but we're almost certain they made it. That they might have lived here."

They. One of the Alanga. I'd known that Nephilanu had been the place where Dione, the last of the Alanga, had made his stand against the Empire. It made sense they would have had a hideout here.

"They must have had a lot of oil," I said.

"Yes," she said, her voice dry. "It's quite dark. I see you've noticed."

Lovely. I was glad we were getting along so well already. As long as what they wanted me to do didn't involve working closely with this woman. "Or they might have lit the place with magic."

Her shoulders stiffened. The idea hadn't occurred to her. It was odd to me – that there was evidence of magic all around us in the form of the Emperor's constructs, yet no one seemed to think any other sort of magic existed. It clearly had in the form of the Alanga. And if folklore was to be believed, cloud junipers had some magic as well, though it was zealously guarded by the monasteries.

When I concentrated, I could feel the thrumming in my bones, the power waiting to be unleashed. The ground beneath me seemed to hold its breath, waiting for me to send that thrumming through the soles of my feet and into the rock. There was something of magic living in me too, either put there or awakened by Mephi. Where he'd gotten it, I didn't know. I found myself tapping the end of my staff against the wall. When I tightened my grip, sweat made my fingers slip. Sometimes I wondered if magic was like a parasite, a thing that lived in me, but wasn't a part of me. The thought had kept me awake on more than one night. But I trusted Mephi, and the bond we'd formed hadn't harmed me. When I was using the magic, when I felt the strength in my limbs and the thrumming in my eardrums, I couldn't feel fear. All I could feel was a fierce joy. Was it good or not good? I wasn't sure.

The hallway ended in a room large enough to be a palace's dining hall. Lamps lined the walls, and though they made the place almost bright, I still felt as if I'd already forgotten what the sky looked like. A group of people sat at the far end of the room at a table of stone. One of the tallest women I'd ever seen stood leaning against the wall, though there was room enough for her at the table. She was dressed in a leather jerkin, a sword strapped to her side. Not quite the bearing of a soldier – no uniform, no brass pins – but she had her hand on the hilt of her weapon and I didn't doubt she knew how to use it. Black hair fell to her shoulders in waves, framing a chin that was stronger than mine.

Ranami hung the lamp by the door and went to the woman. They embraced, though there was something awkward in the gesture, as though neither quite had their heart in it. "I'm back," Ranami said. "And I brought the other part of our plan as I promised."

The tall woman looked me over like I was a stray dog brought in from the storm. "Him," she said, her voice flat.

I was the one who didn't want to be here. "Why don't you tell me what it is you want me to do and I'll tell you if I can do it before you go judging my abilities." I could hear the voices of the children from the room beyond, and the thick smell of a rich curry stew. My stomach growled.

Gio rose from his spot at the table. "Jovis," he said, "I'm glad you decided to join us. You understand, bringing you here, telling you this – it puts us at risk."

Mephi leaned against my knee. I rubbed his ears, taking

comfort from his presence. "As Ranami so kindly pointed out to me: who would I tell? Everyone wants me dead, it seems, including the Empire."

"You could bargain for your life," Gio said.

"We both know the Empire would not keep their end of that bargain. Will you tell me or not?"

He exchanged a glance with Ranami. I wasn't stupid. This verbal game we'd played was pointless. If he told me and I didn't agree to their plan, he would kill me. If I did, and I succeeded, he'd likely still try to kill me. Ranami was a believer – she would never pose a threat to Gio. He could smell it on her, like a wolf searching for a dog among the sheep. Me? I was a survivor. I'd bargained with the Ioph Carn and then stolen from them. I would do what I needed to do. He could smell it on me too, I was sure. So we circled one another, wary and snapping, knowing that this might very well end in bloodshed.

"The governor here is a strong supporter of the Emperor," Gio said. "Much of his commerce comes from sending caro nuts to the inner Empire. It's made him rich. We overthrow him. Cut off the supply of caro nuts and weaken the Emperor's support at the beginning of the wet season. Just as the bog cough hits the main islands, the governors will be clamoring for caro nut oil that the Emperor does not have. If we control the supply, we'll be able to leverage that to gain new allies and to turn some of the governors against the Empire."

My gaze flicked to Ranami. She stood leaning against the wall with the tall woman, their fingers entwined. While she didn't look at me, she didn't look at her partner either. Rebellions could tear the bonds between people as surely as they could form them.

"And my role in this?"

"If the stories are even halfway true, you're a powerful fighter. We need someone to assassinate the governor's personal guard. Someone who can take them all out, if needed. This will be coordinated with a frontal assault."

I could still feel the thrum of the power within me, now fluttering against the louder beating of my heart. "I'm a smuggler. I'm not an assassin."

"I've been told you took out six of the Ioph Carn's best fighters and nearly knocked a drinking hall off its foundation in the doing of it."

"I didn't knock it off its foundation. I did shake it just a little, but that was more to keep them off balance and frightened than to destroy anything. And I didn't kill the Ioph Carn." But I couldn't deny there'd been six.

Gio only watched me as I blathered, his dark eyes calm. "Six trained fighters against one smuggler," he said, as though that settled it. Perhaps it did. He lowered himself back into his seat, though he'd turned it to face me. "I have no qualms about your abilities in a fight. But we have other pieces falling into place, and you'll be working with me. We'll need the ten days."

I'd heard about Khalute, Gio's assassination of the governor there, his takeover of the island for the Shardless Few. Some stories said he'd done it alone. Some stories said that was where he'd lost the eye. Well, I'd had my fill of stories and songs, and I knew how they could be built more of dreams than truth. I glanced around the cavern, the carved pillars, the empty sconces. "I'll be working with you in what way? You want to know how I do it?"

The grim set of his face shifted, his lips pressing together like two cliffs in a quake. "Yes. But you won't tell me that." He shook his head. "No. I'll be going with you."

24

Ranami
Nephilanu Island

The theft of the caro nuts had gone well. The next step – telling Phalue what the rebels had truly planned – that hadn't gone nearly as well. Ranami sat by the ocean, a book in hand, waiting for Phalue to arrive. She dipped a toe into the water and watched the fish dart away from the ripples.

It could have gone worse, though Ranami wasn't sure what worse would have meant. Once Phalue had truly understood what it was like for the farmers, she'd done her part with gusto. She'd run out to the guards, claiming she'd been attacked in the woods. She'd led them on a merry chase, leaving Ranami to gather as many boxes of nuts as she could carry.

But Phalue never could do anything halfway. Once she'd made her mind up, she threw herself into the task at hand.

Once she'd made her mind up.

Ranami supposed it was a big leap – asking a person to steal caro nuts and then asking them to keep quiet as you overthrew their father. She breathed in the ocean air, heavy with the scent of rain, and tried again to read. After finding herself reading the same paragraph three times, she snapped the cover shut. History couldn't compare to the present, not with such turmoil ahead.

"You wanted to meet me?" Phalue's voice emanated from above.

Ranami set the book aside, rose and threw her arms around Phalue's neck. She smelled faintly of floral soap and sweat. She must have hurried here.

Phalue's arms tightened briefly around Ranami's waist and then she stepped away. Their embraces had been like this lately, the brief visit of a bee to a flower and nothing more.

"I have something to ask of you," Ranami said.

Phalue crossed her arms. "Don't you think you've asked enough?"

Ranami knew that tone. They were about to have a fight. Phalue was heading breakneck in that direction, and once she got going there was little that could slow her down.

Ranami tried anyway. "Have I done something to make you angry?"

"It's not that simple. It's not about what you've done and haven't done. Yes, I'm angry, but try to see this from my viewpoint. I love you. I would move mountains for you. And, apparently, I would betray the Empire for you."

"You were doing the right thing."

"It's lovely that it's that simple for you. You take me to the farms, you show me how terribly these people live and how little they ask for – so I try to make amends. And then you take me into the very heart of the stronghold of the Shardless Few. Remember how I said I would send a letter to the Emperor telling him the Shardless Few were here? Gio told me that they intercepted my letter. I knew it wouldn't be so simple: one task and they'd leave. Do you think he'll be content to let me walk away from this freely? I know too much now. You've brought me to the den of hungry tigers."

Ranami was speechless. She hadn't thought of that – she'd only thought of how much she'd wanted to bring Phalue into the fold, to show the trust in her that she'd bestowed upon Ranami. "You won't tell your father?"

Phalue pursed her lips. "No, I won't. But you've split my loyalties. You're asking me to choose. Do I choose my father, or do I choose the Shardless? And there's you, standing very clearly with them. You know all their secrets. I love you, Ranami, but you never told me you were in this deep."

The hurt in her voice stung more than all the kicks Ranami had received as a gutter orphan. She hadn't been in so deep in the beginning, but when she'd gone to them for help, they'd answered. It was more than she could say for most people. And the more they'd given, the more she'd owed them in return.

"There could have been other ways. I could have convinced my father to step down. Now, if I choose my father, I lose you. If I choose you, I lose everything else. I've never been overly fond of my father's rule, and I don't agree with him, but he's not a cruel man. He's indulgent and lazy, and could probably use the sort of whipping my mother dispensed upon me once in a while. I've read a few of the books you asked me to. I know revolutions aren't bloodless and calm. And I won't see him hurt."

"Help us then. Help us make this a peaceful coup."

Phalue closed her eyes as though summoning the patience to deal with an unruly child. Then she wrapped her arms around Ranami again, and this time it felt like a true embrace. "Tell me what happens afterward." Her breath tickled Ranami's hair.

Ranami tried to push away but found Phalue's grip too tight. "After?"

"Yes. After my father is deposed. Build me a dream, Ranami.

Am I governor then? Do you come to the palace to live with me? Would you be a governor's wife under these sorts of circumstances? Would the rebels allow you to? Would they allow *me* to?"

"I don't think it would happen that way."

Phalue let go. "Then what are you doing this for?"

Them together – it had never been Ranami's end goal, not the way it was for Phalue. Ranami loved Phalue – she felt it to her very bones – but there were other things to consider. And this wasn't something she could explain without hurting her. She knew, when she looked at Phalue, that it wasn't the same for her. "I have to think of everyone else," Ranami said.

"I trust you," Phalue said, "but I don't trust the Shardless."

"We could use your help," Ranami blurted out, "infiltrating the palace. We've set people to learn this information, but informants are not always reliable. Knowing when the guards change shift, the weaknesses in the walls—"

Phalue threw up her hands. "Think about what you're asking of me. That's all I want."

Ranami drew in a deep breath, steadying her voice and her hands. This was like that crack that led to the ancient tunnels. If she wavered too long in the middle, she'd only find herself trapped. She had to either retreat or push forward. She pushed forward. "Please just trust me."

Phalue cupped her cheeks in her hands, and Ranami felt the calluses on her palms as Phalue kissed her forehead.

"I knew you'd be trouble from the first moment I saw you," Phalue said. But she said it with fondness, not scorn. Her fingers trailed down over Ranami's neck, caressing her shoulders. Ranami leaned into her touch, thinking of all the nights together, curled in one another's arms. "But this is something you'll have to do alone. I can't help you. I love you enough not to stop you.

I see how important this is to you. Just don't hurt my father. Promise me you won't."

They could do it without Phalue, but it would be a fair bit harder. Her gaze focused beyond Phalue, to the road. Five of the governor's soldiers marched toward them. Ranami clutched at Phalue's jerkin. She'd stolen four boxes of caro nuts for the farmers. "They're here for me," Ranami gasped out. "They're coming."

Phalue's hand went immediately to the sword at her belt.

"Sai," one of the soldiers called.

A cold cell, damp as the gutters she'd slept in as a child. No light, no fresh air, grasping at scraps of food. "Please don't let them put me in a cell. I can't go to a place like that." Her fingers curled in Phalue's shirt; she couldn't have let go if she'd tried. The panic that writhed inside her was an animal thing, wide-eyed and kicking, a mouse in the claws of a cat. "Don't let them take me."

Phalue used her free hand to gently disentangle Ranami's fingers. "Don't worry." Her voice soothed. "You're not going anywhere except back home." She turned to face the approaching men. "Tythus," Phalue said to the guard at their head as they halted in front of her. "Does my father need something?"

Ranami had a vague memory of meeting the young man at some point. He'd been smiling then though.

"Unfortunately he does," Tythus said. He looked uncomfortable, as though he were about to tell a struggling cart driver that his last ox had died. "He heard of your trip to one of the caro nut farms. Four boxes of nuts went missing."

Ranami couldn't speak. Couldn't breathe. Phalue would defend her, but at what cost?

"Your father has sent me to bring you in."

You. He was looking at Phalue.

For a moment, Ranami couldn't process the words. She

should have felt relieved that it wasn't her. But Phalue? She didn't dare grab on to Phalue again, but she needed something to steady herself.

Phalue's shoulders tightened. "He thinks I've stolen boxes of caro nuts? Don't be ridiculous, Tythus."

Tythus's throat bobbed as he swallowed. He hesitated before gripping the hilt of his sword. "It's your father's order. He wasn't in a good mood."

For a moment, they just stared at one another. And then Phalue let go of her sword. "I'll come peaceably. No need for any worry. Whatever he's gotten into his head, I'll sort it out."

Tythus nodded and let out a breath. He stood to the side. "After you."

Phalue glanced back at Ranami, and she could see the glint of fear in Phalue's eyes. And then she turned her head, and let them lead her away.

25

Lin

Imperial Island

The tabletop was smooth and cool beneath my fingertips, and I tried not to sweat. Father had called me in for questioning again, but this time I thought I knew the answers.

"Where did you go on your fifteenth birthday?"

I'd nearly finished reading the green-bound journal. I wished I'd written more specifically about my immediate world, the way things had smelled and tasted. Mostly I'd written about the way I'd felt about things. I'd written a little about my father, and strangely, even my mother – whom I knew had died when I was just a little girl. The father I'd written of was firm but kind, and that was all I could glean. I'd written like I'd known who I was and would never have cause to doubt it.

Father was watching me. My thoughts had flown away, though my gaze had remained locked on his. I was so tired. So much studying.

My fifteenth birthday.

I thought back to the journal, trying to organize my scattered thoughts. Oh yes. I'd written of that day with a good deal of excitement. "A lake, up in the mountains. We spent the day there." I smiled, as if remembering something pleasant. And if I thought about it, I could almost see the lake I'd written about. The sunlight glittering off its surface, the wind rustling through the trees. "We took a picnic lunch and ate on the shore, throwing crumbs to the birds."

Father nodded. He let out a long breath; he'd been holding it. "You said it was one of the happiest days of your life."

How could I have known that? I'd only been fifteen. That was eight years ago. But I held my tongue and watched as he slid a key across the table to me. I waited, not daring to touch it.

"The library," he said. "It's down the hall from here if you take a left, four doors down on the left, near my rooms. It's time you started learning how to create a construct, and how to write its commands." He pulled a folded sheet of paper from his sash pocket and slid it across the table to me. "Here is a list of titles you should start with. Finish reading them and come back to me so I can test your knowledge."

I glanced at the titles, recognizing them as books I'd already stolen and subsequently replaced, devouring the contents as if the words were fish and I a starving cat.

"You may go."

I rose to my feet but was held fast by the question rising in my throat. It was important to have this unfettered access to the library, but I still felt the absence of my memories like a hollowed-out portion of my chest. "If the lake was one of the happiest days of my life," I said, hesitating, unsure if I should continue, "why did we not ever go there again?"

Father's eyes narrowed. "Who says we didn't?"

My heart jolted. Of course. We might have. But I didn't let

it show on my face. I held my ground, hoping he was bluffing, hoping I was calling his bluff.

Father thumbed absently at his robe at the spot where he usually kept his long chain of keys. His gaze went to the window, to the lights in the city below and the stars above. "I'm not sure. We had other things to do. Always other things."

"We could still go."

The look he shot me carried with it a tidal wave of pain and remorse. "Don't you think I've thought of that?" he said, his voice soft. And then he shook his head and waved his hand. He cleared his throat. "Go. Read the books. Tell me when you're done."

I left the questioning room, more baffled than I'd been all those times I couldn't answer his questions. The library key – the real one – lay heavy in my pocket. I could have hoped for a new key, a new room, but at least this way I could study day or night in the library without being spied upon.

But the library was not empty when I arrived, and spies were not always constructs.

Bayan sat on the rug, his back to the wall and a book in his hands. He looked up when I entered. The light from the lamps seemed to gild him, turning his taupe skin golden. He looked even more beautiful by lamplight, an ethereal being of light and shadows. "You got another key," he said, his voice flat.

I brandished it, taking a little delight in the fact that I now officially had more keys than he did. "I did. And well earned, too."

He only nodded back at me, his face solemn. And then he reached into his sash pocket and produced another key – this one with a golden bow. "So did I." The solemn look on his face burst open, cleanly as a cracked egg, revealing the smile beneath. "Poor Lin, always playing catch-up." The words didn't bite the way they usually did. I couldn't tell if it was his tone, or if it was because I had a few more keys Bayan knew nothing about.

I shrugged. "What are you reading?" I strode toward him and leaned over his shoulder to look.

He twisted away from me, cradling the book as though it were an infant and I'd just jeered at it. "It's none of your business."

"Does it matter? I'm allowed to read it now too."

"You wouldn't understand it," he spat back at me.

Oh, a fair bit more defensive than he should have been. I made as if to turn around, and then as soon as he'd relaxed, whirled and bent my head to the side.

" '*Era of the Alanga*'?" I read aloud. "Aren't you supposed to be studying?"

He glared at me, sullen. "Aren't you?"

Well, he had me there. I couldn't look for the books I needed to reprogram Mauga, the Construct of Bureaucracy, not while Bayan was here. So I lingered. "Is it interesting?"

He seemed to weigh whether my words mocked him or not. When he couldn't dig out even a grain of contempt or derision, he sighed. "Yes, it's interesting. It's about the time before the Sukai Empire was even a thought in someone's mind. Before the Alanga began fighting one another."

"What does the book say it was like?" I should have been needling him, trying to get him to leave, but I couldn't help my curiosity. Father's entire justification for the bone shard collecting, for the constructs, was to keep the Alanga from rising again.

"They could make the wind rise up when they called it, they lived for thousands of years and no one dared to challenge them. Each one ruled an island. It could be a dream or it could be a nightmare, depending on who you asked. If you didn't agree with the way they ran things, it wasn't like you could disagree. But things didn't get really bad until they went to war against one another. Their capacity for destruction was immense."

I thought of Deerhead Island, the way it had been wiped from the map. Father had put out a statement saying the sinking had been caused by a mining accident, which, if the servants' gossip was anything to judge by, had been less than reassuring. "Did the Alanga sink islands?"

"It doesn't say."

"But the Sukais found a way to kill them."

"Yes, well, we know all about that." He snapped the book shut. "Unless you don't remember lessons?"

I wasn't a lackwit; I still knew my numbers. "It's not like that. You know it's not like that. You *gave* me this illness in the first place."

He ran a hand over the binding of the book. "It could be that you had forgotten through ordinary means."

"What, like old age?"

He looked at me, startled, and then we both burst out laughing again. I really should have hated him. I'd strongly disliked him for the past five years. And now it seemed that was fading. The sharp edges of him looked different, now that I understood why he disliked me. We diminished into giggles, and then into silence once more. "Does it say how the Sukais killed the Alanga? I know *Rise of the Phoenix* likes to pretend it was a special sword. Father said that isn't true: it just plays well with commoners."

"A special sword that gets handed from one Sukai to another so they can kill the Alanga? Why wouldn't the Alanga just take the sword from them then? They certainly were powerful enough to."

"I didn't say that *I* believed it."

Our words were combative, but they didn't hold the bite they'd had before.

"Of course it doesn't say," Bayan said. "That knowledge is passed from Emperor to Emperor. They didn't write it down."

He rose and put the book back on the shelf. His sleeve fell to his elbow, exposing bruises on his arm.

Four bruises, four straight dark lines. All the mirth went out of me. My father's cane, marked across Bayan's flesh. "How often does he hit you?" The words spilled out of me. I put a hand up to stop them, but it was too late.

Bayan stiffened. He was back to the old Bayan again – cold and distant, mocking and cruel. "Only when I make mistakes. Not often."

"He shouldn't hit you at all."

Bayan pushed the book into the shelf until it knocked against the back of the bookcase. "I lied," he said, holding my gaze with his. "He hits me more now. Ever since you started getting your memory back. You skulk around and feed spy constructs – oh yes, I've seen you doing that – and act as though you aren't the favored one. As though you might be cast onto the streets at any moment."

"He threw me out once four years ago—"

"And you didn't even leave the palace walls before he called you back. You know how he is. He did it to scare you, to light a fire in your belly. He watched your face for what it did to you and knew it was working. But has he ever hit *you*?" His eyes searched mine, his chin out, head tilted, waiting for a response.

I didn't know what to say. All the little diplomacies I'd learned fell away. I couldn't give Bayan an answer that would satisfy him, that would make him my friend, that would soothe him. "I'm sorry."

Bayan seized the ends of several books, pulling them onto the floor. "I don't want your pity! He doesn't hit you because you are the favorite. You are the one he wants to win. You think he doesn't care, but if he didn't care, he'd hit you twice as hard. You don't need all your memories back to see what he's doing."

He stood there for a moment, his chest heaving. And then he swept for the door, the dark blue hem of his flowing pants like a retreating wave.

He slammed it, and the dust rose from a few shelves by the door. It was what I'd wanted, I supposed.

I took my time searching the shelves and finally pulled down a few more complex books on the bone shard language. One on building constructs that obeyed someone other than its maker, another on effective ways to write over existing commands and another simply on higher-level commands.

I'd have to rewrite Mauga's commands at night when my father slept. Mauga spent much of his time in the palace, in a room he'd reshaped into a lair. I'd have to study quickly.

Bayan's words wormed their way back into my mind. Was it true? Was I the favorite? Was I somehow playing into my father's hands? I couldn't imagine why he might want me to reprogram his constructs and to overthrow him. And what *would* I do with Bayan once I was Emperor? A cold trickle of guilt bled into my chest. I wondered if there was a way I could keep him here in the palace alive, or a way I could force his fealty to me. I didn't want to kill him.

Other days for other problems.

First was the matter of rewriting Mauga's commands in a way my father wouldn't know.

And I had no guarantee I would live through that.

26

Sand

Maila Isle, at the edge of the Empire

A boat with blue sails. Every time Sand's memory threatened to go hazy, she thought of the blue sails. They hadn't all been here on Maila for ever; perhaps none of them had. A boat had brought them. It followed that a boat could take them away.

Sand worked at the problem the way a child might worry at a loose tooth with her tongue. Coral had arrived later, and there had been someone before Coral that Sand could not remember. So the next night, when everyone lined up to receive their bowl of food, Sand went to a nearby coconut palm and scratched out a tally. Two hundred and seventeen. That's how many of them were here right now. If she'd had the time, she would have written out all the names she could remember, but a sense of urgency drove her forward. What if whatever happened to her during her fall from the mango tree just disappeared? What if she became like the rest of them again?

She searched for another person she couldn't recall being

here for ever. It came to her a little easier this time, like she was exercising a muscle she hadn't known existed. "Leaf," she said, approaching a frail-looking young man. He sat near one of the bonfires in the center of town, eating his stew, his glassy eyes reflecting the fire. He didn't wear a shirt, and his ribs pressed against his skin like fingers across a taut piece of leather. He nearly dropped his spoon when she spoke to him.

"Yes?" he said.

Sand didn't bother trying to coax the memories from him the way she had with Coral. She needed to push farther. "You came here on a dark, blue-sailed boat. You were placed in the hold. But when you came onto deck, when you arrived on this island, where on the island were you put ashore?"

"I've been here for ever," Leaf said. He held his bowl tight to his chest as though it could protect him.

"No," Sand said, and he trembled. She stalked closer. "You were somewhere else before you were here. Tell me where you disembarked."

His eyes grew wide. "I don't remember."

But her words were starting to make sense to him, Sand could tell. "Did you see any landmarks? Where was the sun?"

"A cove." He looked startled to hear the words coming out of his mouth, like he'd suddenly realized he was spitting up butterflies. "The sun was behind us."

A cove on either the east or the west side of the island. Maila wasn't small, but it wasn't very large either. If only she'd spent her time exploring instead of going back to the same bedamned mango grove over and over. "Anything else?"

He shook his head. "No." Then he frowned. "Wait! There was someone aboard who was not like us. He wore a gray cloak."

Not anything that would help with the location, but Sand

stored the information away for later use. Leaf went back to his bowl of soup, though he now wore a troubled expression. But Sand didn't have time to waste on comforting him. If Coral was any measure, he'd forget again soon enough. She looked around at her fellows until she found another who'd arrived more recently.

When the evening was done, she'd questioned five of them and had more specifics. The cove they were all brought to was on the east or the west side of the island, it was small – large enough to fit the boat and no other vessels – and the beach was rocky, littered with bits of coral. One tall banana tree stood just off the beach. She rubbed a hand over the wound she'd stitched on her arm, feeling the roughness of the threads against her palm. They could find it if they looked for it. She'd spend every day looking, and she was sure no one would notice that they no longer had mangoes.

A hand tapped her on the shoulder. Sand whirled. It was Coral, eyes large and brown as hulled coconuts. She held a bowl of stew out to Sand. "You forgot to get your dinner," she said. "Here."

Sand took it, a little mystified. No one had ever brought someone else food. You went to the cook pot or you went hungry. "Thank you."

"I heard what you've been asking the others," Coral said. "You're trying to find out where we came from."

Sand looked to the bonfires, warming her hands on the sides of the bowl. "No. I'm trying to find out how to get away from here." She thought Coral might react with alarm or consternation, the way she had when Sand had questioned her the night before.

Instead, she nodded. "If we came here somehow, then there must be a way off the island. Even with the reefs."

Last night it had been as though Coral had been wiped clean; now she spoke like Sand's plans were her own.

She caught Sand looking at her. "It came back to me tonight when I sat down to eat, and then more when I heard you asking questions and you didn't get in line. Before that I was foggy again. But I'm clear now."

Sand's hands shook. She didn't need to search alone if she could bring the rest out of this fog. She started to set her bowl down, but Coral stopped her.

"Eat. I'll start asking the others how they came to be here. You need to eat."

"But what if it goes away?"

"It won't."

Still, Sand devoured the stew, burning the top of her mouth. She was making progress, and that meant they could get off the island.

Even with the both of them, it still took two more nights before any others seemed to find their way out from the fog. Grass found his way first, when he went to Sand and asked her why they were all on this island in the first place. Leaf was soon after, along with Frond and Shell. As they began to clarify their thoughts, Sand began to plan.

"We need to scour the island for the cove we arrived at," she told them over dinner. "We've been arriving in waves, yet we don't seem to remember when it happened. The boat doesn't sound big enough for all of us. If the boat brought us here in groups, then it is possible it will come again. If we prepare, if we bring others out of this mind-fog, then when the boat comes again, we can seize it." The words felt wrong in her mouth somehow, though she couldn't place it. "We can find this one on the boat who is not one of us, and we k—" *We kill them.* She could barely even think the words. It was like trying to see through clouded water. She just couldn't work her way to the bottom. She looked to Coral. "What would you do to the one sailing the boat?"

"I would—" Coral stopped and frowned. She tried again. "Obviously, we have to—"

Sand held up a hand to forestall any further effort. "There's something stopping us from violence." It was as though she wore a collar and each time her thoughts went in that direction, someone pulled on the leash.

"Direct violence," Coral said, her large black eyes focused on the tree line.

Sand felt a little ashamed that she'd ever thought Coral soft and weak. "An accident might have to suffice." She could say "accident". She could think about it too.

"I can start looking for the cove on the east side of Maila," Leaf said.

"The west side of Maila is larger," Frond said. "Shell and I can look on that side."

Sand looked to Coral. "Talk to more people. See who we can lead out of the fog. The more of us there are, the easier this will be." She stood, her bowl still in her hands. Something about the movement triggered a memory. Sand wasn't here by the bonfires — she was rising to her feet in the dining hall of a palace. The beams above her were painted in red and gold; the wall panels were murals of cloud junipers and leaping deer. The air smelled faintly of fish sauce and green tea.

Across from her, at the table, a man watched her. Straight-backed and handsome, dark eyes regarding her with wariness. His blue silk robes spilled about him like a waterfall. "What is it exactly that you want to know?"

Sand found her mouth opening, and a voice that wasn't hers emanating from her throat. "Everything."

A blink, and she was back on Maila once more, her empty bowl in hand, Coral's hand at her elbow. "Are you all right?"

These memories that weren't hers — whose were they? She knew instinctively that she wouldn't find her answers here on Maila. "Fine," Sand said. "But the sooner we find the cove, the better."

27

Lin

Imperial Island

I waited by my window, watching the sun set over the city. I ran my hands over the green-covered journal, trying to calm my racing heartbeat. Tonight, I would reprogram Mauga. Numeen's engraving tool pulled on one side of my sash, its weight a constant reminder. I had to do this now, before I was caught.

I'd rewritten the spy guarding the cloud juniper in much the way I'd done with the first one. Two of the tree's berries nestled against the engraving tool in my sash pocket. If I ate them, they'd give me strength and speed, but I wasn't a cloudtree monk. I didn't know how long that would last. Still, I might need the advantage.

The journal entries hadn't at all been as enlightening as I had hoped. I sounded like a younger, much more carefree version of myself, excitable at small things, like seeing dolphins in the Endless Sea.

The sun was lowering itself to the horizon, slow and steady as an old man into a too-hot bath.

I flipped the journal open again, finding a random entry. "I went to Imperial City today. It was beautiful – all the roofs here are tiled, and the streets narrow. So many food vendors!"

I frowned. I'd written as though I'd never been to Imperial City.

The previous entries had all been small highlights. Little experiences that any young woman would write about, but with few identifiers on the specific place or even the people I'd been with.

"It's much larger than back home."

Back home? The palace? I flipped pages, scanning, trying to glean something useful. Just the mundane activities of a girl.

The light from the window dimmed. I looked up to find the city bathed in the pale light of a fading sunset. By the clouds on the horizon, it would rain tonight or tomorrow.

I snapped the journal shut. It was time. If I didn't move now, I'd never move, frozen by indecision.

I'd read the books on advanced commands and overwriting commands over and over, and had pulled several more off the shelf for good measure. I'd had to return twice to the storerooms for more oil for my lamps. My mind felt stuffed with the strange, smooth tones of the command language; I couldn't fit anything else into the tired recesses of my head. I wasn't sure it was enough.

I wished I'd had years to study it.

Mauga would be in the dining room, reporting to my father. Mauga wasn't my father. He had no reason to lock his room when he was away.

My spy construct appeared on my windowsill, ready to report.

"Later," I said, holding up my hand. "Check the halls on the way to Mauga's room. Tell me if there's anyone there."

The construct squeaked. Sighing, I fished around in my drawers for a nut, which I handed over. "Did you ask Ilith for nuts too?"

It only chattered and scampered away.

"I'll bet you don't," I said to the empty room. "I'll bet my very bones."

I went to my door and cracked it open. No one, not even a servant.

I watched the end of the hall until my construct appeared there, running toward me. I stepped back to let it pass.

Its tiny chest heaved. "Nothing," it said in a quiet, high-pitched voice.

Hearing it speak still unnerved me. It was too much like a person, even though I knew it wasn't. Somehow it felt different for the higher constructs, which behaved more like servants than animals.

"Give me your report tomorrow." I left my room and stalked down the halls. No one had lit the lamps yet; the sunlight hadn't completely faded.

For once, I was grateful Father didn't keep enough servants.

I smelled Mauga's room before I saw it – a musky, earthy scent. I came abreast of Bayan's room. Perhaps he was right that I was the favorite. My nose wrinkled. I certainly had a better room.

For a moment, I stopped, overcome by curiosity. What did Bayan do when he had hours to himself? He'd brought the sickness with him – at least I could always be sure I didn't have buried memories of him. The relationship we had was the one we'd always had. In the quiet of the hallway, I could hear him moving within his room. The floorboards squeaked as he stepped. If I put my ear to the door, I might even be able to hear him breathing.

I shook my head and stepped away. What did it matter what Bayan was doing? Why did I even care? Just because he'd been kind to me once or twice didn't mean we were friends.

Mauga's door was still three doors down. I held a sleeve to my mouth and nose and focused on my goal.

The hinges creaked as I slipped inside Mauga's room. Darkness shrouded me; only a sliver of light peeked in through the heavy curtains.

Mauga didn't need a bed or a desk. Straw had been spread across the floor, likely in an attempt to contain the smell. A pile of blankets had been shoved into a corner next to a bowl of water and an empty bowl that smelled like raw meat left too long in the sun. I felt I was exploring an animal's den, not a room.

When Mauga was done with his reports and Father has dismissed him, he'd return. I wasn't sure what Mauga did at night. Sleep? Meditate? The thought of Mauga sitting in a meditation pose made me want to laugh. Exhaustion could make even the most solemn of occasions silly. I closed my eyes and breathed. I needed to focus.

There had to be a place to hide. I'd need to take him unawares.

What was I supposed to do – bury myself in the blankets?

It took me another moment before I realized: yes, that was exactly what I had to do. Feeling a little ill, I went to the blankets and picked one up between thumb and forefinger, my other hand still holding my sleeve to my nose.

It was covered in Mauga's coarse, dark hair. I'd never thought I was squeamish, but then I'd not truly had the chance to test my stomach. Blood and flesh from the constructs was one thing; filth was another.

A scratching, scrabbling sound came from the door. Father must have dismissed Mauga early. I took a deep breath and then ducked beneath the blanket, leaving a corner tilted up so I could see out of it. Could a smell smother a person until they could no longer draw breath? I supposed I was about to find out. Mauga lumbered into the room, heaving out a sigh as he closed the door behind him with his great claws. He shuffled about, his path meandering, his sloth nose near to the ground.

He froze. Slowly, he lifted his head and sniffed the air.

I let the corner of the blanket fall, my palms sweaty. Could he smell me even through his own stink? I didn't see how, but then, I was human, with a far less sensitive nose. I waited in the dark, my breath heating the pocket of air below the blanket. I could feel the moisture of my breath gathering on the cloth, making it damp. Retching would give me away, so I took in a breath and held it, listening carefully for any sounds.

Mauga must have deemed the room safe because I heard his claws scrape along the floor. He groaned a little as he settled into the blankets, and a small portion of his weight pressed me into the wall. A small portion of Mauga's bear body was still a significant weight. The breath I'd held burst from my lips. This would be a fine way to die – crushed by my father's bureaucratic construct, my face frozen into an expression of disgust.

If I moved my arm, he'd feel it. But I had to move if I was to reach into Mauga's body and procure one of his shards. Mentally, I began to fortify myself. I wasn't always able to reach into the constructs right away. I still failed a good two out of ten attempts. My wits were sharp but my skills were not yet as practiced as Father's or Bayan's. And I was tired, so tired that my bones ached. I'd have only the one chance. I took in a breath quietly and thought of how pleased Father would be when I finally showed him I was his daughter. I was the only one who could be his heir. I was a force to be reckoned with. I pulled my arm up.

Mauga shifted, feeling the movement beneath him. Before he could move away, I concentrated and plunged my hand into his body.

Or I tried.

My fingers met only coarse black fur. Not now. No. Not this time.

Mauga rose. "What? Who's there?" he said. He always

sounded like a person on the verge of falling asleep. But he could move quickly when he wanted to, and his claws were long and very sharp. He might kill me before even recognizing who I was.

My heartbeat galloping, I threw off the blanket. The breath of air I took in felt cold and fresh. "I am Lin," I cried out, before he could lift his claws.

Mauga regarded me with his soft brown eyes. "You are not supposed to be here." He lifted his claws regardless.

Horror clutched its fingers around my throat. I could run, but where would I run to? I'd committed to this as soon as I'd walked into his room. I'd known I might die. I pushed past the fear, let it slide away from me.

I held my breath, leaned forward and pushed my hand into Mauga's body.

This time, it slid in. I watched, fascinated, as my fingers disappeared. Mauga's claws halted in their descent; his eyes went glassy. I searched for a shard and found more than I could easily count. It was like reaching into the ocean to feel one of the posts at the dock and finding only barnacles beneath one's fingertips instead of wood. I wasn't sure where to begin.

The book on complex constructs with more than one shard had assumed three shards, maybe up to ten. Mauga contained at least a hundred. It was a lot of lives to drain for one construct. A hundred men could easily do the work that Mauga did – though I knew Father would not trust those hundred men. The book had said commands for obedience should be placed higher, closer to a construct's brain. Less urgent commands could be placed lower, where they'd cede precedence to higher commands if they contradicted.

I grasped a shard higher up and pulled it free. I had to squint to see what was written on it.

Esun Shiyen lao – obey Shiyen always. The star identifier was engraved next to my father's name.

Always was not a word I could easily convert. "Until" and "when" were obvious replacements, but neither word contained "lao" in it, nor were they shaped in such a way I could add a few strokes to change the meaning. I should have taken another shard from the bone shard room and dealt with any consequences later. Then I might have replaced a command instead of seeking to alter it. What else had my father written into the shards? I replaced the one I'd taken out and reached for another, lower down.

This one was not a command shard but simply a reference shard engraved with the tax formulas for witstone.

Another shard dealt with the constructs that reported to Mauga. There were general shards about behavior and temperament. Mauga should be "slow to anger" but "ready to use his claws in defense of the Empire".

Other shards related to the system of island governors, and the management of the Empire's mines. One, near the bottom, was a command to never reopen the mine on Imperial Island. That one I considered for a while before replacing. I hadn't known there had ever been a witstone mine on Imperial.

The light was fading. I dared to open the curtain wider. I needed to come up with a command that would allow me to assume control of Mauga when the time came.

Obey Shiyen always. "Always" was the sticking point.

Time ticked past until I almost thought I could hear the knocking of the water clock in the entrance hall. Sweat trickled down my shoulders and tickled at the small of my back. I wished I'd brought parchment and ink with me so I could scratch out possible solutions. Instead, I turned the words over in my head, trying to find a weakness in them.

I replaced it several times, pulling out other shards and

puzzling over their meanings. But I always came back to the first one. This one took precedence, and if I moved too much, Mauga wouldn't function properly and Father would find me out. I needed to be subtle.

The moon rose and an ache started behind my eyes.

I was Lin. I was the Emperor's daughter. It was my place to succeed him and my place to make him proud. It was my identity.

Identity.

The identifying mark. With trembling fingers, I reached into Mauga and seized the highest command again.

The star next to Shiyen. Mauga didn't have an independent concept of who or what Shiyen was. My father had held the bone to his bare chest and engraved the mark.

I could do the same. I could be Mauga's Shiyen.

I moved aside the collar of my tunic, held the shard to my chest, and took up the engraving tool. I carved over the star, carefully, and felt the change take place in the command.

I placed the shard back inside Mauga and began removing others.

If I let Mauga go, my Shiyen would contradict my father's Shiyen. Mauga wouldn't function properly, if he functioned at all.

So I sifted through the other shards for mentions of my father's name. And when I found them, I added one more stroke, changing Shiyen to Shiyun.

It was close enough to my father's actual name, and the constructs so rarely ever used his actual name, calling him "Eminence" or "Emperor" instead. It could work – at least until I'd finished rewriting all four of my father's highest constructs.

As I sifted through them, I searched for one I could modify to replace the highest command. Mauga would still need to obey my father, at least until I was ready.

At last, near the bottom, I found one I could use. *Ey Shiyen ome nelone vasa* – tell Shiyen about unusual things. A catch-all.

I thought for a moment and then put my engraver to the bone, modifying the command to *Esun Shiyun ome nelone bosa* – obey Shiyun about most things.

Sloppy, but it just might work. I put it back into Mauga's body, just below the command to obey me always.

And then I backed away from the construct just as he began to come back to life. I left, swiftly, before he could notice I was there. I blinked in the light of the hallway; the servants had lit the lamps while I'd been working.

I'd done what I could. If it worked, it worked. If it didn't, I'd have to face the consequences.

I hurried back to my room, trying to run the scent of Mauga off of me. My door, when I returned, was ajar.

My heart pounded in my ears; my mouth went dry.

I pushed the door open, nudging it a little at a time. Someone was sitting on my bed, shrouded in the darkness of the room. Whoever it was sat still, as still as Mauga had when I'd removed shards from his body.

I wanted to run, to go anywhere but into my room where that dark figure waited. But it was my room, and the journal was in there, hidden beneath the bed. If I fled, I'd be leaving my room to be ransacked.

I took a lamp down from its hook on the hallway wall and thrust it before me, trying not to tremble. "Hello?"

No reply. And then, soft and rasping as a cat's tongue: "I need your help."

Bayan. The fear left me in a rush, like a wave eroding the sand beneath my feet. It left my knees weak and my step unsteady. "What are you doing here? It's the middle of the night."

"I couldn't think of where else to go." His head jerked to the side.

There was something wrong with him. I could tell by the way he moved and by the way he didn't move. I caught my breath and strode into my room, a little bit annoyed. "Father is probably better equipped to help you, no matter what the problem is."

"No!" he cried out.

I stopped in my tracks, the lamp held high. This close, I could see him shaking, as though he'd caught a chill. "Bayan?"

He turned his face to me.

I opened my mouth but couldn't speak. Dread dropped a weight in my belly. Bayan's high-boned cheeks sagged. His lower eyelids fell away from his eyes, leaving red pockets of flesh gaping like two extra mouths. It was as if he were made of wax and someone had held a flame to his flesh. "Do you know what he does? He's growing things down there, Lin. He's growing . . . people. His experiments."

"You're not making sense. What do I do?" I reached out and then stopped, my hand hovering above his shoulder. I wasn't sure if touching him would make things worse. I wasn't sure what was happening at all.

He gripped my shirt with weak fingers. "Hide me. Please."

Why had he come to me? Was I truly the only person he felt he could trust? I swept my gaze over the room. A wardrobe stood in the corner, and there was under the bed – though I'd hidden the journal there. "The wardrobe," I said. I'd have to figure everything out once he felt safe.

He sagged with relief, his hand still gripping my shirt. "Thank you. I'm sorry for all the times I was cruel to you, I really am."

"Don't." Every word seemed to cost him. I put an arm around him and let him lean on me as he stood. Beneath my hand, I could feel his ribs. He gasped a little as he stood, and his ribs gave beneath my fingers as though they were sponges and not bones. He was disintegrating before my eyes and beneath my touch.

Was he ill again? And why didn't he want my father to help him? "Bayan, maybe we should—"

"There you are." Father stood in the open doorway, his sleeves rolled up past his elbows, his fingers grasping his cane. His arms were rough and thin as the dried-out husks of dead branches. A construct stood behind him, a hulking leathery-skinned creature with an ape's face and fingers. "Bayan is sick," he said. "I'm taking him with me."

Bayan sagged in my grasp and said nothing. I felt my father's gaze on me, waiting for me to let Bayan go, to step away. I should have. Instead, I cleared my throat. "He said he doesn't want to go with you."

"He doesn't know what he's saying. He has a fever and it's making him delirious. Ipo, gather the boy."

Though his skin felt soft as uncooked dough, Bayan did not feel warm to the touch. The leathery-skinned creature strode into my room, its arms outstretched. What could I do? If I denied my father now, I had no way to fight him.

"Please no," Bayan rasped out. "The memory machine."

The memory machine? But I couldn't ask questions with my father standing there. "I'm sorry," I whispered.

I let Ipo take him from my arms, a vise about my heart. "Don't hurt him," I said to my father.

He looked at me as though I'd grown another eye. "He's my foster-son. Why would I hurt him?"

But the incredulity in his face was cold. There was something about the way he looked at Bayan, the way he looked at me . . . I couldn't place it. It wasn't fondness or hate, or any emotion I knew. "Just be kind to him."

Father limped to me and before I could move away he had taken my chin in his free hand. "Who are you to tell me what to do?" He sounded angry; he sounded hopeful. The heat from his hand suffused my cheeks. His gaze roved over my face, from my forehead to my eyes to my mouth.

I parted my lips to speak and felt him lean in closer. "I am Lin."

He let go of me abruptly. Father turned and strode away, Ipo following behind with Bayan in its arms. "I'll let him know of your concern when he wakes up."

The door shut behind them, and I curled my fingers into fists. I wasn't sure what about my answer had displeased him. This time, though, I wasn't sure how much I cared. I went to my bed and found the keys I'd stolen and replicated, slipped between the mattress and the frame. I grasped the one for the bone shard room.

I'd rewritten one of my father's highest constructs. Now for the last three.

28

Jovis

Nephilanu Island

I tapped the end of my staff against the cavern floor, wondering if it would hold. The power thrummed in my bones, waiting to be unleashed. Would the walls cave in, the stone and earth fall upon our heads? Should I risk it?

And Gio, that smug bastard, just waited. He held his sword at the ready, and I'd felt the flat of that blade more than once. The man was old, but surprisingly spry. He smiled. "The point of this exercise is not to hurt me or anyone else by accident. Take me to the ground, but don't hurt me."

I huffed out a breath. "If I can't hurt you, what am I supposed to do? Dance with you?"

Gio stepped to the side, giving me the narrow view of his body. "In a manner of speaking, yes. Don't raise an alarm. Keep your actions quiet."

I swung the end of my staff at Gio's legs and he parried. He gave me a reproachful look. "Now everyone has heard the clash of steel against steel. I know you're a threat. I shout for help. You've failed."

I wasn't sure what he was expecting me to do. In the corner of the hall, Mephi sat by the hearth and watched, his chin against the floor. He met my gaze when I looked to him, but offered nothing more than a yawn. I'd asked him not to speak in front of the Shardless, an order that he obviously found onerous.

"Try again." Gio turned his back to me. "I'm a guard in the halls of the governor's palace. How do you get past me?"

I tapped my staff against the floor.

He looked over his shoulder. "You get my attention?"

"I bribe you," I said.

He cracked a smile. "Bribing a guard when you're in the middle of the governor's palace? A bold move."

"I'm fond of bold moves."

"Bold moves get you killed." The corner of his mouth twisted, his face gone suddenly grim as though struck by a memory that had left him bitter. "The guards in the palace will be loyal. Everyone has a price, but you wouldn't be able to pay it. Be smarter." And then he turned again.

I stepped lightly toward him, my footfalls soft against the cavern floor.

And then Mephi dashed across the cavern floor, slamming into my knees. He leaned into my calf, gazing up at me with wide black eyes. I bent to scratch the nubs behind his ears. "Did you eat enough?"

Gio, his back still turned, let out a heavy sigh.

"I can be quiet when I want to be," I said. "And why do we need this sort of practice? You said you're going with me. I won't be doing this alone."

"Maybe because I'm not ready to die just yet," he said drily.

I tapped my staff against the cavern floor. The lamps sent

my shadow flickering across the ground. "Show me then. Stop giving me vague directions – I never learned well from that." I pivoted and faced the wall.

I'd barely settled my stance when a breeze stirred the hairs on the back of my head. An arm settled around my neck; a hand pressed over my mouth. I dropped my staff, startled. The man's sinewy elbow clamped tight. Very quickly, my vision dimmed.

Something screeched, and Gio swore. He let me go.

Mephi had sunk his teeth into Gio's boot and was doing his best to unbalance him. I thought Gio might kick at him, or pull away. Instead, he knelt and looked Mephi straight in the eyes, his demeanor flowing from surprise into calm. "I mean him no harm." He held both hands upright, palms out. "I'm not hurting him, I promise."

It seemed I wasn't the only one who'd fallen into the trap of addressing Mephi like he was a person.

Mephi, for his part, unhinged his jaw and let the boot go, though he stayed crouched on the floor, all the hair on his back on end.

"Your pet doesn't like me much," Gio said.

"He's particular." I rubbed at my throat. I'd not seen Gio move before he'd attacked me. And he was deceptively strong. It seemed the leader of the Shardless Few had earned his legends. "Give him a fish though, and he'd forgive you for murdering me. Fickle beast."

Mephi turned narrowed eyes on me. Did he understand "fickle" now too? I hoped not.

I glanced around the cavern we'd been practicing in. This hideout the Shardless had acquired was vast – larger on the inside than I'd thought possible. In a few places, light filtered in through vines, tinted green. I scooped my staff from the ground. "How did you know this place was here?"

"We were lucky. When we came to Nephilanu, one of my scouts found it."

Lie.

I pressed him on it. "One of your scouts saw the crack in the cliff face and decided to go for a pleasure outing into its depths? Whoever this scout is, they have a death wish."

He smiled. "Don't all of the Shardless Few? Those of us who escaped the Tithing Festival live in constant fear of discovery."

I let the change of subject pass. "And the rest of you?"

His grin faded into his usual grim expression. He picked up a lamp, beckoned to me and strode from the room. I followed, Mephi on my heels.

Faded murals adorned the walls of the hallway, remnants of silver paint catching the lamp's light. I could make out some of the scenes, though some of the walls had been damaged, leaving chunks of the paintings missing. Men and women in flowing, high-necked robes, their hands upraised. Waves crashing against a cliff. Wind bending trees. And then a series of paintings that took me a moment to process. Four islands, each one lower in the water.

Not four islands. One. Sinking.

I put a hand to the wall, feeling suddenly dizzy. The ground beneath me shaking, dust clogging my nostrils. Men and women and children screaming. Animals swimming away, trying to escape. Hands clawing at thatch and tile as water rushed into homes, as the Endless Sea claimed city after city, life after life.

I wanted to vomit. It had happened before – somewhere in the long history of the islands. Back in the time of the Alanga or before.

The brightness of a lantern struck my eyes. Gio had stopped and turned. "Are you all right?"

Mephi rose to his haunches and patted my leg, little worried sounds in the back of his throat.

"Fine." What was I to say? I would never be all right again.

He didn't believe me, but he didn't pry.

He led me into another cavern, this one with a hole in the ceiling that let in some light. Pallets were set up near the light. "I wanted to show you," Gio said, setting the lamp down. "We don't all escape. The rest of us live in fear of the day our shards are pressed into dead flesh."

Several men and women lay on the pallets, their thin limbs held tight to their bodies, curled like the legs of dead spiders. Three of them craned their necks at the sound of Gio's voice. The last one lay still, perhaps no longer able to hear anything at all.

"Their shards must have been in use for some time," Gio said. "But the sickness and the weakness don't often strike until the end. It's so gradual, most of us don't notice. A twinge here, a bout of exhaustion there. By the time it's noticeable, the decline is quick." He approached the pallets and knelt, checking in with a woman who hovered over them with a pitcher of water and a damp rag.

"Lenau passed last night," she said to him. "We buried her in the jungle."

I kept my distance, though Mephi did not share my hesitation. He bounded forward and slipped his head beneath the hand of the man closest to the light. The man laughed and obliged, stretching out his gnarled fingers, rubbing Mephi's ears.

"It's been happening to more of us," Gio said. His voice echoed across the cavern. "This is the fate that awaits many of the Empire's citizens. Not death at the hands of the Alanga, but death at the hands of the man sworn to protect us."

I'd seen the shard-sick, cloistered in the corners of houses, cast aside in alleyways. Sometimes, it had been a person I knew.

I stood there, unsure of what he wanted me to say, unsure of what *I* wanted to say. But I knew what he would say next.

"You can help us."

Everyone – always grasping, always wanting more, always needing more. I didn't have it to give. My fingers slipped on my staff, my hand grown slick with sweat. I was a liar, but I kept my promises. And I'd promised Emahla I would find her. "The blue-sailed boat," I managed.

Gio nodded. "Yes, I know you're looking for it."

"You've set spies on me?"

"I didn't need spies. Only ears. You've not made a secret of your search."

One of the men coughed. His eyes were sunken, his skin stretched over his cheekbones like tanning leather. I tried not to stare. The man was withering away. My fingers itched. I wanted to touch the scar behind my ear – the scar where the soldier had struck me with his chisel. I'd told my mother and father and no one else. "I didn't take bone," the soldier had whispered, his breath hot against my ear. "I know what happened to your brother and I'm sorry." He'd held a shard of bone in his hand – not mine. "They'll find out someday, but today isn't that day." And then he'd pushed me toward the other children, weeping and bleeding, waiting for their mothers or fathers to bandage them.

No one had saved my brother. Even if he hadn't died, he might have been one of those bodies on the pallets, wasting away as his shard was used.

"Care to tell me your thoughts?" Gio's voice broke through the memory.

"No, not really."

He sighed. "So you don't want to join the cause. But tell me this: what happens after you find the blue-sailed boat?"

I'd find Emahla. I'd go home. "It doesn't matter."

"A person who can't see a future doesn't have a future," Gio said.

"Is that a proverb? One of Ningsu's?" I turned away from the sick men and women, gesturing for Mephi to follow. But Gio followed me too.

"No," he said. "Someone I knew once said that. She was right."

I looked at him sidelong, studying his face. A scar ran over the milky left eye, interrupting the line of his brow. Despite the gray hair and the lines of his face, he somehow didn't strike me as old. Not as old as he looked anyway. "What's your story? You apparently know mine."

He reached down to scratch Mephi's head absentmindedly. Mephi chirped and bumped his knee. Oh, so they were friends now? "It's long," Gio said, "and mostly uninteresting. Suffice to say, I thought I knew my destiny. I thought I knew what was right. But I made mistakes. A good many of them. I'm just trying to set things right, and to find people who will help me do that."

I held my hands out, as if to show a beggar I had no coin. "You're asking the wrong person."

Gio nodded. "It seems perhaps I am. But what will you do, Jovis, when the shards of your family are put into use? The shards of those you care about?"

My heart felt like a stone, sinking into the depths of the Endless Sea. "Who says I care about anyone?" I was a good liar, but this lie sounded hollow even to me.

"Gio," one of the women called from her pallet.

He turned to tend to her, lifting her head to help her drink. Who would help my parents if they both fell ill? Maybe the Shardless Few would serve that duty since I was absent, chasing Emahla across the Endless Sea. They would be better family than I was. I pushed the bitter thoughts aside and slipped away. Mephi padded silently at my side. He said nothing as I took a lamp from the wall and strode back down the passageway we'd come. I knew he was bursting with questions, just as I was, but I didn't trust the room they'd assigned me as a place to speak. So I crept through darkened corridors, the echoing voices fading behind me.

The lamplight disappeared down the ends of hallways, receding into emptiness and silence. Gio's questions drifted from my mind, replaced by my own. "There aren't any doors that I can see. How far do you think these go? How deep?"

Mephi wove around my legs, stopping me in my tracks. "Don't know."

Of course he didn't. "I was just thinking aloud," I said. "His scouts didn't just find this place. He knew about it some other way."

I swung the lamp around the corridor. Faintly, in the distance, I could hear voices, though I could not hear what they said. The air here smelled like earth and ice.

"Like him," Mephi said.

"Of course you do. He talks about saving everyone, about making everything better. But do you know how often that works? Setting up a Council with representatives from each island? People want simple solutions. When this all began, people thought the Sukais would save us. Instead, they've enslaved us all. I need to look after me and mine. And that means finding my wife. If bringing in a new world order means so much to you, why don't you stay here with him?" It was a stupid thing to say, petty, and even saying the words aloud felt like tearing my heart into two. I didn't know how to take them back.

"Never leave you." He wove through my legs again, nearly making me trip and forcing me to halt. I hated to admit how much his assurance eased the tightness in my chest. Mephi sat on his haunches in front of me. "But, Jovis," he said, and the sound of my name in his raspy voice made my spine tingle, "the people here – also your people."

I thought of the long hours I'd spent at the Academy at Imperial, the sidelong glances at my skin and features, the way I'd had to always work harder and longer just to prove myself. Who among them had cared about me? I'd spent two lonely years there, watching my back and earning their grudging respect – until I could claim my Navigator's tattoo. They'd wanted me to fail, and had been disappointed when I hadn't. "They are *not* my people!"

I slammed a hand against the wall and felt, almost too late, the thrumming in my bones. I pulled the blow, sucked in the tremor before it could shake the tunnels around us.

Mephi had lowered himself to a crouch, his ears flat against his head, his eyes on the ceiling above us.

I let out my breath slowly, afraid that letting it out quickly might shake the foundations of this place. "I'm sorry. I need to be careful."

His gaze still on the ceiling, Mephi crept forward and patted my foot. "We stay together. We leave together."

Relief swelled in my veins like a tide. I put out a hand to lean against the wall – and stumbled. The lamp swung wildly from my hand, threatening to slip from my grasp. I tightened my fingers around it, focused on putting my feet beneath me. The wall I'd slammed my hand against was no longer there. "What is this?" I lifted the lamp once I'd caught myself, my heartbeat thundering in my ears.

Mephi slipped past me before I could stop him.

"Wait, you don't—" I cut myself off, shook my head. Mephi's tail disappeared into the dark room. It wasn't any use. He wasn't a pet, no matter what the Shardless assumed. He was a friend. A very foolish friend.

I stepped in after him, keeping the lamp held high. I needn't have worried. The room was small, no monsters hidden in its corners. I checked behind me and found a slab of stone for a door. I ran my fingers along the edge. Back out there, in the hallway, I could have sworn the walls had been smooth – no doors or doorways to speak of. Where had this come from then? Had the light just been too dim for me to see the outline of it?

Mephi had opened a chest and was rifling through it, dust filling the air around him. "Stop it," I called to him. "You don't know what's in there." But it was as though I hadn't spoken at all. He tested his teeth on a stone bracelet, and then tossed it aside when it proved not to be edible. His furred form was swathed in bolts of elaborately embroidered cloth – half of which he'd emptied onto the floor.

I sighed and checked the rest of the room.

A sinking bed lay in the middle of the room, and in a corner a deep tub had been carved into the floor. It must have been a lovely place to relax a long time ago. Stone shelves lined the walls. They were mostly empty, but when I held the lamp up to them, I could see impressions in the dust where items had once lain. My spine prickled. Someone had been in here, and judging by the dust, it had even perhaps been in the past year. "Mephi," I hissed to him. Even my whisper seemed too loud. "Get out of there."

A couple of scraps of wood lay on the shelves, but there in the corner I saw something else. A book.

Mephi scrambled from the chest and darted to me just as I pulled the book down. "Food?" he asked. I couldn't tell what time of day it was, but it must have been close to sunset. Past dinnertime. He'd been eating even more than usual lately, and had been more sluggish in the mornings.

"No," I said. A brief longing hit me – to be free of this place, of this darkness, to be out on the water again. "We'll get some food in a moment." The cover of the book was unmarked, the binding decorated with only a few lines of flaking gold paint. When I opened the pages, they crackled. An earthy scent wafted from the paper. I brought the lamp in close so I could read it.

I didn't recognize the script.

I knew Empirean; I even knew some Poyer. But this was neither of those things. The script was tight and small, words nearly running into one another. I flipped through the pages, looking for something I recognized.

And then I stopped. Flipped a few pages back.

This word. I knew this word. It was written differently from what I was accustomed to, but it was the same word.

Alanga.

29

Lin

Imperial Island

Uphilia moved like a ghost through the palace. I didn't know where she lived so I'd had to send my little spy construct out to find her lair. It took my spy three days to report on its location. Three days I spent poring over books, trying to study as my mind filled with images of Bayan *melting*. I couldn't figure out what had happened to him. Each time I saw Father in the hallways, he didn't look at me. I'd dared only once to ask him where Bayan was, and Father had only said "resting", a warning in his tone. I knew better than to press the issue. Still, I'd gone to Bayan's room the next night and had found it locked. When I'd placed my ear to the door, I'd heard nothing, not even the sound of his breathing.

Why hadn't he wanted to see Father? Why had he wanted to hide from him? The only conclusion that made sense was that Father had done this to him.

The night air breathed down the back of my neck, bringing with it a few small drops of rain. Of course Uphilia couldn't live someplace easy to reach. Foxes liked snug little dens, and ravens could fly. I clung to the tiles of the palace roof, slippery with rain. My engraving tool was in my sash pocket along with an extra two shards of bone from the bone shard storeroom. I'd have to be careful what commands I added to Uphilia, lest I upset the balance of existing commands, but this would give me more room to work with than I'd had with Mauga. And I knew Father cared more about trade than bureaucracy. I had the suspicion she'd be a more sophisticated construct than Mauga.

I stepped across the curved roof, going slowly, doing my best to keep my footing. The rain and wind threatened to topple me from the tiles. The palace was several stories high; I'd break more than just a rib if I fell. My foot slipped a little. My heart jumped into my throat. I windmilled my arms, trying to keep my balance.

I didn't want to die like this.

My hands broke my tumble, and I slid only a little way down the roof. My palms were raw, and from the fiery feeling, I guessed one of my fingernails bled. I hated Uphilia and her stupid lair. She nested near the peak of the roof in a hollow my father had made for her just beneath the gable. It would be foolish of me to try walking again. So I crept across the roof on my hands and knees, cursing the rain that fell faster and ran into my eyes.

The edge of the roof came into view. I made my way to the edge, lowered myself to my stomach and peered over.

Loose straw peeked out of a hole carved into the wall below the gable. I caught the glimpse of black feathers, the white-tipped end of a red tail. Uphilia had returned to her roost. By how still she sat, she was likely sleeping. Even so, how could I sneak up on a winged fox? I'd never be as quick as she was, I couldn't fly and getting into her lair would be difficult enough. I needed to find a way to do so quickly and block her escape at the same time. I could lower myself from the edge of the roof but the tiles were slippery, and I'd need to drop into her lair right away.

There was a decorative piece at the gable, curling iron nailed to the beams. I edged to the peak of the roof and probed it with my hands. It was nailed securely to the beams, and there was a horizontal piece I could fit both my hands around. It wouldn't be easy, but if I lay on my back, put my hands around this piece and kicked off of the roof – I could get enough momentum to swing around and into Uphilia's lair.

I wasn't an acrobat but I was short and light. However, the piece still might not hold my weight. I didn't see much choice though.

The cloud juniper berries were still in my sash pocket. I took one and popped it into my mouth. It tasted musty and sharp, a slight bit of juice escaping between my teeth. Ignoring the taste, I chewed and swallowed it. I wasn't a cloudtree monk, but I knew the stories. No one had ever assailed a monastery – not even my father – and succeeded.

It took only a few beats of my heart before I felt the effects. My heartbeat quickened, strength flowing into my arms and to the tips of my fingers. If I'd been in my rooms, I would have tested my strength on something benign. But I didn't have the luxury. The rain on the roof tiles soaked through the back of my shirt. Above me, clouds obscured the moon, a dim halo shining through them. When I looked at it, I could see the raindrops falling just before they hit my eyes. It was a dizzying, disorienting feeling.

I reached around the edge of the roof, flailing, searching for the horizontal metal bar. I had to walk my fingers down to it, but I found it.

It was this or being disowned. It was this or disappointing my father. It was this or perhaps even ending up like Bayan, my flesh melting from my bones. *The memory machine.* Had my father taken my memories? Or was it something he was building to try to give them back? Is that what had happened with Bayan? Had it malfunctioned? How long until he tried the machine on me? Later. I could think about it later. I tamped down the horror and pushed myself into an upside-down bridge.

Taking a deep breath, I shoved off of the roof and felt the world tilt.

The iron of the gable piece was slippery in my fingers. It creaked as my full weight fell upon it. I was facing the ground when one side tore from the beams. Everything seemed to move more slowly, each beat of my heart feeling like it might be my last. I swung my legs to my chest and saw the opening of Uphilia's lair before me.

I might not make it. But with a burst of enhanced strength, I kicked my legs out hard. I let go.

For a moment, there was only me and the air and the whites of Uphilia's eyes. She woke to find me hurtling toward her in the dark, in a place she thought no one but she could reach.

I tumbled into her soft body, my arms outstretched, and caught her. She snapped at me, and her teeth sank into the soft flesh of my side just below my ribs. Even though I knew by now that my father's highest constructs would still attack me, the pain of it surprised me. I tried twice to get my hands inside her body, and only succeeded in tangling my fingers in her fur. She shook her head, her teeth still nestled into my side. Warm blood soaked into my shirt. My whole side burned.

If I didn't get myself together, if I didn't end this, I would fail.

I was Lin. I was the Emperor's daughter. I would not fail. The words burned in me, molten iron forged into a blade. A deep breath in, and then I tried once more, moving my hand slowly, with purpose.

Uphilia's body gave beneath my touch. She froze as I searched inside her for the bone shards, her teeth still embedded in my skin. I found the shards stacked one on top of the other, and it felt like there were more than there were even in Mauga. At the top of the chain, I pulled a shard free. I had to wiggle it like a loose tooth before it disengaged.

When it was safely in my palm and outside Uphilia's body, I took a moment to pry her jaw open. It was like levering open an oyster. Blood soaked my shirt and the wounds burned, but I adjusted my sash around the bite to stop the bleeding. I'd have to tend to it later.

Lamplight glowed from between the cracks in the floorboards of Uphilia's den, and I held the shard over the light. I'd expected the same command I'd seen on Mauga's shard: obey Shiyen always. But my father had different ideas for his Construct of Trade.

Esun Shiyen uvarn: nelusun 1, 2, 3.

Obey Shiyen unless: conditions 1, 2, 3. It took me a while to decipher the words. This was more complex than what I'd encountered inside Mauga. Uphilia had the option to disobey Father under certain conditions. The numbers would match reference shards within Uphilia's body, though I wasn't sure where I'd find them. They'd be marked with those same numbers.

I bled as I worked, each move sending a twinge of pain into my ribs and hip. Uphilia's feathers tickled my cheeks each time I leaned in close. She didn't stink like Mauga did. Hers was a light and almost sweet musky scent; she smelled less like a dog and more like hay. I checked each shard for a number in the corner. Commands flashed in the dim light from below:

- *Purchase boxes of caro nuts when: condition 9.*
- *When tithes of tuna fall below twenty fish per year, report to Shiyen.*

— *Gather reports on stolen goods from Tier Two constructs daily.*

Finally, I found a shard engraved with a "1" in the upper left side. The engraved words on it were tiny; I had to squint and hold it just above the floorboards to make out the words:

— *If Shiyen does not have all the information Uphilia has, and Uphilia's experience dictates a different decision for betterment of the Empire.*

So my father trusted her enough, or at least trusted her sophisticated commands enough, to let her override him when she thought the occasion called for it. I replaced it, noted its location and searched for the next two.

They were located directly below the first, so I didn't have to search far.

On "2": if Shiyen's decision will result in a total or partial collapse of the Empire's economy. And on "3": if Shiyen is asking for something that cannot be reasonably achieved.

I sat back on my heels, the last reference shard cradled in my palm. I couldn't rewrite the shards the same way I had rewritten Mauga's. I hadn't done the cleanest job, and though he seemed to be behaving as normal, Uphilia was more complex. I couldn't count on the same solution to work with her. I had to find another way.

This time, though, I'd brought more resources with me. I dug inside my sash pocket and brought out one of the shards from the storeroom. This might be an even easier and more elegant solution than with Mauga. I could add another condition to the topmost command. "If Lin asks Uphilia to obey her instead, Uphilia will thereafter obey Lin." I couldn't replace my father with myself in all Uphilia's commands, but this would provide a stopgap measure until I could fully rewrite Uphilia's shards.

I found the topmost command again and used the engraving tool to carve a "4" into the corner of it. And then I held the tool poised over the corner of my fresh, blank bone. I'd made certain, when I'd gone back to the storeroom, to choose an island far away from the inner Empire, one where I didn't know the occupants and never could have met them. One where I might never know the occupants.

I'd avoided looking at the drawer where the blacksmith's shard had once lain.

But the moment I pressed this tool into the bone, I was writing on the life of someone, no matter that they were half a world away. When I placed the shard into Uphilia's body, the shard's original owner might have a day where they felt a little unwell. The thought might cross their mind, but they wouldn't know that their shard was in use. It wouldn't be until they were older that their life would seem to flow more swiftly from their bones. They'd age faster, feel weaker. Eventually, they'd die years before their time, and Father would have to replace the old, dead bone inside Uphilia with a fresh one.

This is what I would do if I engraved the new reference into the bone. I would shorten someone's life.

Several days ago, I might have done so without a second thought. But meeting Numeen's family, getting to know his daughter Thrana – I knew however far away the person was whose skull this bone had been chiseled from, they *were* a person. A person with hopes, dreams and people who loved them.

Was there another way?

I went through the rest of the shards, sifting through the commands, searching for a pearl in the Endless Sea. All I found were grains of sand. I went through them again, desperate. The rain clinked against the tile roof above, a staccato accompaniment to the frantic beating of my heart.

The sky outside turned blue, and then gray. I couldn't delay any longer. I'd come too far to make a different choice. Steeling myself, I engraved the command onto the bone. It felt like I was digging the end of the tool into my soul, scratching irreversible words into its surface.

But it was done.

I shifted Uphilia's body beneath me so I could have better access to the reference shards. I'd need to shift them a little in order to fit this new one between them. But when I slid my hands under her ribs, I felt something across the backs of my hands — not the floorboards, or straw. She was lying on something hard and square. A book?

I moved her to the side. The book she'd been sleeping on was broad and wrapped in brown leather, the cover unmarked. I opened it, shuffling through the pages. It took me only a moment to understand the contents. Names were written inside, and dates. The top of each page was labeled: "Imperial Island".

Birth records. And deaths, by the end dates next to some names. Why did Uphilia have this and not Mauga? Mauga kept track of such bureaucratic matters. It wasn't in Uphilia's purview.

Out of curiosity, I flipped through the birth dates, searching for my own. I found it closer to the end, written in a neat and orderly script.

Lin Sukai, 1522–1525.

My gut turned, a cold mass of writhing serpents. *1525.* I scanned the page again, and then the next page, and the page before. This was the only Lin Sukai listed in the year I was born. I'd been born in the year 1522, but I was also still alive. It was 1545 now, and I was still alive.

I ran my hands over my chest and belly, feeling somehow

less solid than I'd felt just a moment before. Why was it written in this book that I was dead? My hands trembling, I placed the book back on the floor and covered it with straw. I couldn't ask my father. I couldn't ask Bayan. The numbers written on the page fluttered in my mind, a bird's wings beating against a cage.

The sun was rising, and I was out of time.

I shoved the shard into Uphilia, just below the other three reference shards. Before she could awaken, I lowered myself to an overhang below. I had to let go to fall the rest of the way, but the strength of the cloud juniper was still in me. My knees bent only a little on impact. I could make it into a window from here, though I'd need to hurry before the servants began their chores.

I was dead. According to the birth records, I was dead at three years old. Perhaps this was tied somehow to my memory, to why I couldn't remember anything beyond three years ago. But then what were the memories in the journal, written in my handwriting?

And why did my father think these memories should be mine?

30

Jovis

Nephilanu Island

I found Gio in the main hall with the others the next morning, pacing in front of the fire. It seemed he'd had an even more restless night than I had. I'd searched through the book into the late hours, finding other words I recognized. Whoever had written in it had taken some time to practice Empirean. They were crude replications, but the author had been learning. I'd realized I could work backward from these writings, figure out some of the words of this language.

Alanga. I'd seen their monuments, some of their artifacts, but I'd never seen one of their books. I should try to sell it. I could use the money to pay down more debts, to buy more supplies. What did I care for these mysteries? Yet I couldn't deny its discovery had awoken something within me – reminding me of my nights of study at the Academy, the satisfaction of solving a problem.

I was a smuggler. Not a navigator.

Did Gio know about the secret room?

He stopped abruptly in front of the fire, his back to me. Mephi bounded ahead to beg for fish scraps from the cook. He'd already had an enormous breakfast, but I let him go. Gio turned when he saw Mephi, and our gazes met. "You're awake. Good."

I spread my arms. "So it seems. Although this could be a dream."

"Not a dream. A nightmare."

"Yours or mine?"

Gio rubbed his brow, squinting into the fire with his one good eye. "I sent one of my scouts out last night to gather some information on the palace and the best routes to the governor's rooms. She hasn't returned. We need this information if we're to accomplish our aims without being caught."

Before I could form another thought, Mephi was at my feet, crunching on a fish head. He watched me with bright black eyes.

"Send someone else after her," I suggested.

"You saw the shard-sick. We don't have an unlimited supply of spies."

Mephi turned the fish head over in his paws. "Help."

I shot him a dagger-filled look. Of all the times—

"What?" Gio turned, his eye narrowed. He looked to me, and then Mephi, and then back to me.

The last thing I needed was anyone finding out Mephi could speak. They'd run me off the island. The only creatures that spoke in stories were the bad kind. "I said I'll help."

Gio looked me up and down. "You'll help?"

Inwardly, I sighed. This was how it began – agree to help fix someone's roof; the next thing you knew you were building them a new house. "Tell me where you sent her and the information you wanted her to uncover. I'll look for her and gather the information. This doesn't mean I want to join the Shardless. I just want to be on my way as soon as possible."

He considered for a moment and then sighed. "I don't have

much choice. She had a contact in the city. A soldier who's on our side. He gets off his shift late afternoon. You should be able to find him at the drinking hall near the docks. Tell him that the fish were jumpy today, use those exact words. They serve fried squid at this hall – you can smell it before you see it."

"And how do I know who this man is?"

"He sits at the corner table. Middle-aged fellow."

I raised my eyebrows. "Does he have a name?"

"None that he's felt safe to give us."

Stealing things was more straightforward. Go in without a thing, leave with a thing. I nodded. "I'll leave now."

I turned to go, but Gio's voice stopped me. "You can't take him with you."

It took me a moment to understand what he meant. Mephi. I'd grown so used to having him at my side that it had never occurred to me that he wouldn't always just be there. That he couldn't always be there.

"People will notice," Gio said when I pivoted back to him. "You've garnered a reputation. And your pet is unusual. They don't mention your pet in the songs perhaps, but the gossip is a different matter. I'll meet you by the entrance. Cutting your hair after the Empire painted your portraits was a good move, but we can disguise you a little more in case anyone's seen the posters. There are fewer here."

He was right, though I didn't much like it.

The rebels had set me up in a room near the main cavern. It was carved so neatly it could have been formed from a mold. A relief was carved into the ceiling of a woman in flowing robes, a swirling ball hovering over her left hand and water dripping from her right in a flow heavy as a waterfall. A mountain stood behind her. The artist had carved the mountain to be almost as imposing as the woman – a tall and jagged thing, capped at the top with what looked to be a cloud juniper. The tiny lamp in the corner cast angry shadows across the woman's face.

It was a fearsome thing to be stared down by when one was trying to sleep.

Mephi nudged my hand with his head. His head was now nearly to my waist, which made sense when I saw how much he ate every day. He'd be the size of a small pony a few months into the wet season if he kept this up. The fur on his horn numbs had rubbed completely clean, leaving dark, shiny patches of skin. "I should go with you," he said.

I stared down at him, astonished. "Are you speaking in complete sentences now?"

"Sometimes?" He leaned against my leg and peered up at me, his black eyes like river-polished stones. "I should be with you."

"Just nine more days and we'll be gone again." I scratched at his cheeks. "We'll be out on the Endless Sea and you can go fishing off the side of the boat."

He let out a heavy sigh – the sort a husband might when his wife said she was well and truly done sailing in storms, after she just sailed into this next one. He shook his head and began to dig at the blankets. "You are doing a good, but you are alone. Alone is bad. Alone is not good." He made a hollow in the blankets and settled into it, his tail curling about his nose. We'd just woken up. Was he tired again already? "I am alone."

The creature sounded so dejected, I couldn't help but feel sorry for him. I knelt and cupped his head in my hands. His head was now as heavy as a dog's, his jaw wider and heavy with muscle. The bite he'd left on that Imperial soldier must have hurt. Pride filled my chest. He'd come a long way since the ragged little kitten-thing I'd plucked from the ocean. "Don't bother the cook, and I'll be back tonight."

I gave him a last pat on the head and left before he could entreat me again to stay. Ranami hovered outside the door, a sheet of parchment in her hands. Had she heard me talking to Mephi? The doors here were all stone – she certainly didn't look at me as though she'd heard Mephi talk.

"Here," she said, shoving the piece of parchment at me. "It's a map. You'll need to know how to get to the city from here. Take the long way – don't lead anyone back to us. Gio is waiting for you." She seemed agitated, her hands smoothing the front of her dress as soon as I'd taken the map.

I hesitated. "Is something wrong?" I shouldn't have asked. Asking meant I might feel sorry for her, and then I might offer to help. I'd done enough helping. Emahla was out there, and it had been seven years.

She closed her eyes for a moment and shook her head. "It's fine. It will *be* fine, as long as you do what you've promised to. Better men and women than you have fallen to spies or constructs. Watch your back."

"Wait," I said before she could leave. "My pet, Mephi. Can you watch him while I'm gone? Make sure he eats enough? He's been more hungry than usual lately."

Her expression softened. She might not have liked me, but there were few who didn't like Mephi. "He seems very attached to you. I'll do my best."

Gio waited for me near the entrance, his cloak wrapped around his shoulders, his beard nearly hidden in it, a leather bag at his side. He looked like only one dark eye and a scar. "Good luck," he told me.

"I don't need luck," I said with a dismissive wave. "I need skill."

"Good skill doesn't have quite the same ring," Gio said. "And it's not something I can wish upon you."

I stopped and waited as he applied putty to my face to hide the shape of my nose. "This rebellion. You're playing a game with long odds," I said. "Are you planning on winning, or are you only planning on making your opponent miserable before you reach the end?"

"I only play to win." Gio's gaze focused on the bridge of my nose, his thumb pressing near my eye. "And we will win. The Emperor isolates himself. He is dying and no one really knows his daughter. What do you think will happen when he dies? What will happen to all the constructs spread across the islands? They will no longer have any direction. And the rebellion will be there to pick up the pieces."

"But will you remake what's broken?"

"We will build something new. No more Tithing Festivals, no more Emperor. Free trade and movement between the islands," Gio said. "No governors, but a Council made up of representatives from all the known islands." He pulled out a couple of jars, looked at my face, mixed some colors from them and then dabbed them on my nose.

"And what happens to you when all this is done?"

"I build a farm somewhere, live out the rest of my days. I don't want to be Emperor if that's what you're wondering. I'm just the midwife for something new."

His words sounded practiced, like he'd said them a thousand times. I knew a liar when I met one. I recognized one each time I saw my own reflection. And now, looking into Gio's remaining eye, I felt as though I looked upon the glassy surface of a lake on a windless day.

He met my gaze. "What does it matter to you? You're a smuggler. You're not invested in this society. You live outside it."

He was redirecting my question, trying to put me on the defensive. I knew these tricks. "And how will we choose this Council, Gio? All these people who hate the Empire, who hate everyone who has been involved in it – how do we get everyone to join into a common purpose? Will you be the one to heal these wounds? How will you do that from your quiet farm? The Sukais once thought they would heal the wounds left by the Alanga."

He straightened my leather jerkin and checked his work. He nodded, evidently satisfied. "Here." He drew a straw hat from the bag at his side and handed it to me. He apparently thought a little farther ahead than I did. "You do what you said you would. I can tell you what I will do, I can make pretty speeches, but it's the doing that counts. Go."

The best of intentions could be subverted by greed. And beneath the practiced speeches, Gio was the same as most men I'd ever known. He had a wanting heart. They all did. I just didn't know what he wanted. But I went. This wasn't my fight. I wasn't one of them, swallowing their lies the way a drowning sailor swallowed seawater.

Emahla, for you. I would drink a thousand lies just to see your face again.

I used the map to trace my way through the trees and toward the road, looking for the landmarks I'd seen on my way in. Even so, everything appeared different than it had a few days before. A jaguar yowled somewhere in the forest, making me jump. When I scratched an itch at my forehead, my hand came away damp with sweat. Much as I hated to admit it, Mephi was right.

Alone was bad.

But I made it to the road and to the city before noon. Children scampered across the streets, searching for food in the kitchen scraps thrown from windows the night before. They were ragged and desperate as hungry rats. A few of them eyed me, as though they might find something worth taking on my person if only they all attacked me at once. Back home on our small island, we hadn't had cities large enough for gutter children. Any unwanted babes were quickly fostered by families who desired children.

I'd seen them huddled in alleys before, but I didn't think it was a sight I could ever become accustomed to. Gio helped the shard-sick. Would Gio do something for the orphans, too? I dropped a few coins onto the street for them and increased my pace. I was more afraid of hurting them than the other way around.

I heard a scrape behind me – an orphan stooping to gather coins? – and remembered Ranami's words. When I glanced over my shoulder, I saw only the cobblestones of the street. If someone had been there, they'd moved quickly. I tightened my grip around my staff and felt the thrum in my bones. I did not need to fear, even if Mephi was not with me. The woman Gio had sent had walked this same path, but she hadn't had the strength I did.

Still, I'd not lived so long as a smuggler by denying my instincts. I ducked onto a side street, found a crowd of fishermen heading to the market from the docks and slipped into their midst.

"At least we have boats," a woman said to the man next to her. "If it happens here, we'll have the chance to escape."

It took me a moment to realize they were talking about Deerhead.

"Do you think that matters?" the man replied. "You could be crushed in your bed, or not get your boat unmoored in time. I wish we knew why it happened. How could a mining accident sink an entire island?"

The smell of them reminded me of my father, and the one next to me even looked to have some Poyer blood. He was shorter and ruddier than his fellows, and just the feel of him at my side reminded me of my father. I almost expected him to start muttering random facts about fish or sails or seawater. My father had been born outside the reach of the Empire, up in the mountains of the Poyer isles. He'd not had a shard taken from him. But the

Endless Sea called to him when the Poyer isles had ventured close
to the Empire, and he liked to say that when he met my mother,
he knew he'd never go back to the mountains. The man shifted
away from me, breaking the illusion.

I'd have to double back to the drinking hall.

I should have hurried but I took my time, relishing being out
in the open again, away from the dark corridors of the Shardless
hideout. An ocean breeze tickled my scalp; the calls of seabirds
sounded in the distance. Mephi, had he been here, would have
been weaving between my feet, begging me to buy him some
treat he could smell on the wind. I stopped in a couple of places
to take a look behind me. If someone had followed me, they
were gone.

Finally, I wound my way back to the drinking hall. It was
nestled into the cobblestones, a set of steps leading to a narrow
door. Water dripped onto the stoop from the floor above. As Gio
had promised, the air wafting from the door smelled strongly of
salt, oil, and the sharp scent of cooked squid. I placed my hand
on the door and then something prompted me to look to my left.

A construct sat on the street, watching me.

I'd seen spy constructs before – small things with watchful
eyes and an ability to climb. This one looked to be made of
mouse and bird pieces with little claws that scratched the stone
as it scampered away.

The putty disguising my nose was still in place, though that
didn't stop me from checking again. I ducked into the drinking
hall before I could second-guess myself. The man at the counter
barely glanced at me as I ordered a plate of the fried squid. I surveyed the tables. There were three corners with tables in them.
Two of them had single occupants. Both were middle-aged men
in uniforms.

I couldn't think of enough curses to attach to Gio's name.

As I waited, I studied each of the men. Both were full-blooded Empirean men, their straight black hair streaked with gray. As I watched, they both lifted their mugs to their lips, nearly at the same time. Not helpful. I searched for other details. The uniform of the one on the left was slightly rumpled, his boots scuffed. The one on the right looked like he'd gotten a little more sun.

"Here you are." The man at the counter handed me a plate piled high with battered and fried squid. I checked the price and handed over some coins.

I had to choose a seat unless I wanted to stand out.

I adjusted the hat Gio had given me, the brim scratching my forehead. It bought me only a little time. What did I know? Our informant knew the best way to the governor's rooms. He was sympathetic to the cause. If the man on the right had gotten more sun, he probably spent more time outdoors. A wall guard then? Or the doors? The rumpled uniform and the scuffed boots of the man on the left spoke of less wealth, more struggling.

If I were wrong, I might be making a fatal mistake. Not for me – I could fight my way out of this – but for all the Shardless back in their cavern. I took a deep breath, walked to the corner and sat at the table of the man on the left. He glanced at me over his mug and frowned. "The fish were jumpy today," I said, as though that explained anything.

His brow furrowed along familiar lines; he didn't seem the friendly type. The plate of squid no longer smelled appetizing.

And then he reached over and took a piece of squid. "I told you before, you're using garbage for bait. How's your sister?"

I know what you're here for, his feigned familiarity said.

Relief weakened my spine and I slumped a little in my chair. I knew this sort of dance. So I played along. "She barely speaks to me," I said. "How would I know? Have you seen her lately?"

"Fickle woman," the guard said. "You know how I feel about

her. Asked her to have a drink with me in this very spot. She said she would, but never showed."

My chest tightened, but I grabbed a few pieces of squid to hide anything that might be plain on my face. The spy Gio had sent had never even arrived. I didn't dare look across the room to see if the other guard was watching us, though I did check the ceiling beams for spy constructs as I tipped the squid into my mouth. Nothing.

We made small talk for longer than I would have liked, but I supposed we had to keep up the proper appearances. Finally, he pulled a piece of folded parchment from his pocket. "I thought you'd be needing this from last time we talked. As promised – my mother's bait recipe. It never fails. You'll have fish jumping into your ship tomorrow morning."

"My thanks," I said, taking it and sliding it into my purse. I wasn't fool enough to look at it now.

"Just tell your sister I'd still like to have that drink with her if you see her again."

I rose. "I will." And I made for the door. The air outside felt fresher and I filled my lungs with it. I could manage as a smuggler when it was only my life on the line. Always cared more than I should have.

I'd taken two steps when something seized me by the arm. Before I could react, it dragged me out of the stairwell and into the alley next to the hall. My knees cracked against the stone; my head whipped to the side. It took me a moment to register – it was not a human hand.

Claws dug into my arm, and the pain told me they'd pierced skin.

Glimpses filtered through my rattled mind: yellowed teeth, yellowed eyes, patchy dark fur. A whiff of musky animal scent. A low, guttural growl. A construct.

I reached for the thrum in my bones, the strength to throw the creature off of me. The will to make the ground shake. My heartbeat roared in my ears, but my bones stayed silent.

Nothing.

I was alone.

31

Lin

Imperial Island

I balanced on the palace roof, staring down into the courtyard and wishing I could see through the paving stones. Ilith's lair lay somewhere beneath the very bowels of the palace. It had taken me a fair bit of time to puzzle things out. I'd gone to the courtyard first, watching the little spy constructs, one after another, leap into the little hole beneath the boulder. I went to that boulder, stared into the hole, listened at it, even shone a lamp down it at night when I could be sure no one watched me. Each of these exercises was fruitless. I couldn't shrink myself to follow the spy constructs to their master. And Father wouldn't let Ilith be completely inaccessible. There were times he disappeared, and even Bayan didn't seem to know where he was. If I found out where he went during these times, I would find Ilith's lair, I was certain of it.

So I'd sent out my own little spy.

It took five days to find out which door he went to, and another few days to find out which key he used in it. A few days after that, and I had the key in hand, and then heavy in my sash pocket. It was an ugly iron thing. I'd never have paired it with the cloud juniper door.

But my construct couldn't lie.

I made my way around the courtyard toward the palace gates. Somewhere below me was Bayan's room. I still wasn't sure if he was dead or alive, and Father had said nothing. Each time I ran into Father in the halls, I wondered if I was next, if he'd drag me away and melt my flesh. The sooner I finished rewriting the constructs, the better. I bit my lip as I crept forward. The roofs were slippery, as they seemed to always be during the wet season. The way back, when I was tired, would be treacherous.

But I dropped into the city street outside without incident. Businesses were winding down, the people in the streets hurrying about, eager to get home. No one paid me any mind. I made my way to Numeen's workshop as quickly as I could.

His shop was still open when I got there, and he was tending to a customer, writing down their order. Propriety bade me wait, but I had the key to Ilith's lair and little time left. "I need a key," I blurted out. The woman in front of me eyed me but continued her recitation of requirements.

"I'm sorry, can you come back tomorrow? I need to take this order," Numeen said to her.

She frowned and left the shop in a huff.

"This key," I said, pulling it out of my sash pocket. "Can you make a copy now, while I wait? How long will it take?"

He studied my face for a long moment until I felt as pinned beneath his gaze as I did my father's. Just as I felt the heat rising to my face, he relented and plucked the key from my grasp. "I could, but how much time do you have? This shouldn't take long. The key itself is quite simple."

"Not much time. Maybe a little longer than usual."

"I can do it." He turned around and gathered his tools.

The last time I'd seen him, I'd dashed from his house. I wasn't sure what to say about it. I couldn't apologize for who I was or what I had to do. They'd seen me practicing bone shard magic. They'd realized who I was. But Father had said nothing to me. He hadn't even looked at me differently. Whatever they'd said to one another after I'd left, they'd kept my secrets. So I tried something else instead. "Thank you," I said as Numeen pulled a mold from one of his drawers, "for dinner, for the time I spent with your family. It's not like that for me." I wasn't sure how to explain. Dinner with my family was like shutting myself in the palace icebox. Dinner at Numeen's home was the hearth of a fire on a rainy day.

He gave me a long, inscrutable look. "You frightened them."

I wanted to melt, to sink into the floor. "I didn't have much choice."

He turned his broad back to me. The back of his scalp folded as he pressed the key into the mold, like dough in the midst of kneading. "I know. It had to be done." He worked in silence, and I waited, thinking about the mural of silent Alanga in the palace entrance hall, a reminder of what the Sukais had done to their enemies. I couldn't imagine anymore what Father might do if he caught me. I'd thought before he would throw me out – and now, having moved among the citizens, having been to Numeen's home for dinner, that prospect didn't seem so frightening. But after seeing what had happened to Bayan, I wasn't sure if that would be my sole punishment.

Whatever dark experiments my father worked on in the depths of the palace, I might find myself subject to them. *The memory machine*. I wondered if I'd been subject to them already.

Numeen worked the bellows, sparks flying from the fire like bright motes of dust. He poured the white-hot metal into the mold. He waited as it cooled, then removed the fresh key with a pair of tongs. The sizzle as it hit the water in his bucket nearly obscured his next words. Steam rose from his feet, making him look like a demon summoned to do someone's bidding. "Did you find my bone shard?"

I'd known it was coming, yet there was a part of me that always hoped he'd forgotten. "I haven't." The words felt thick and heavy on my tongue. I swallowed past the hollow in my chest.

Numeen took the key between his fingers, examining it, comparing it to the original. "Try not to take my family's fear to heart. Your father says he keeps us all safe, and maybe it takes an unkind person to keep us all safe. But my mother died when I was just a boy, drained by a construct under your father's command. My cousin too died when he was still a young man. Some constructs burn their fuel faster than others. All of us –" He set the original key on the counter and touched the scar on his scalp. " –we wonder when it will happen to us. If it will happen to us. If we will leave behind our families, our spouses, our children.

"Be better than him please, when you are Emperor." He slid the new key next to the old one. "Could be a bit rough, but if you shift it a little as you turn, the tumblers should fall into place. Best I can do on such short notice."

I took both keys and tucked them into my sash. I had to leave, had to get back to the palace before my father returned to his room. But my feet felt rooted to the stone floor of Numeen's workshop. Father spoke often of what was necessary, what was needful. Everything he did he labeled as needful.

I was doing it too. I'd used a shard to power the command I'd placed in Uphilia. I'd left Numeen's shard in Bayan's keeping. I'd failed to do anything to help Bayan when he'd needed it the most. I hadn't had a choice – or I'd thought I hadn't. Numeen was risking everything to help me, including his family. And I hadn't been willing to take Numeen's shard from Bayan and risk discovery.

Perhaps it wasn't Bayan who was so like Father, but me.

"I was afraid," I blurted out before I could stop myself. "Your shard. It's in the keeping of my father's foster-son. If he found I'd taken it, he could tell my father."

Numeen looked at me in the way he might a child who'd disappointed him. "But you know where it is."

"Yes." I dropped my gaze to the floor and felt my heart follow. What would he do to me now?

He didn't admonish me or shout. His sandaled feet shifted on the floor of his workshop. "You should go before your father finds his key missing."

My father, whom they all feared. It kept me in line. It kept Bayan in line. It kept all the citizens of the Empire in line.

I remembered the fear I saw in his eyes each time we sat alone in the dining room together and he questioned me. All the time he spent on his experiments, isolated from the other islands. The servants he constantly watched.

He ruled by fear, and was ruled by it.

As desperately as I yearned for his approval, as desperately as I yearned for a kind word from him, I didn't want to be like him. I wouldn't be ruled by fear.

"The lie I told you ... it's something my father would have done." I shook my head as though I could shake myself free of the guilt. But guilt was there to remind me of when I misstepped. The only thing I could do now was to make amends. I met Numeen's gaze. "I won't be like him. The next time I come here, I will bring your shard, and the shards of all your family — no matter the risk to myself. I'll find other ways to protect the people of the Empire. I swear it, upon the sky, the stars and the Endless Sea itself."

Behind him, the fire crackled, as if sealing my promise with its heat. Numeen only put a hand to his chest and then bowed. "Wind in your sails, Emperor."

I ran back to the walls of the palace, my feet as light as my heart.

I'd made it back in time. Bing Tai only glanced at me from his spot on my father's rug, and I was able to slip out the door without anyone noticing. I took the long way back to my room, walking by Bayan's room as I'd done several times over the past days.

Father wouldn't answer questions about Bayan except to say he was resting. But there were no signs of Bayan in the palace, and his door remained locked.

I could hear Mauga in his room, grunting as he settled down for the night. A few doors down, I stopped outside of Bayan's room. I stepped softly to the door and pressed my ear to it, just to check one more time.

Nothing.

"Are you spying on me?"

My heart leapt into my throat. I whirled to see Bayan – whole and well, standing outside his room with arms crossed.

He wasn't dead, and somehow this surprised me. I threw my arms around his neck, relief making me reckless. "You've recovered!"

Bayan stiffened. He held his arms out to the side as if unsure what to do with them. "I had a fever," he said. "It was hardly the bog cough. What's wrong with you?"

I drew back, all the hairs on my arms prickling. "I thought you were dead. Bayan ..." I trailed off, unsure if I should keep calling him that. Was this even still Bayan?

He rolled his eyes. "A little bit dramatic, don't you think?"

Well, he still had the attitude. "It wasn't just a fever, and you can't convince me that it was. You were practically melting. Bayan; your skin was peeling away from your eyes!"

He stared at me, eyes narrowed. "Is this some sort of trick? Are you trying to spy on me or not?"

I stared back at him. It was like seeing a ghost – because this wasn't the Bayan I knew from a few days earlier. That Bayan had softened to me, had come to me for help. This was the Bayan where nothing had changed between us. "You don't remember."

He huffed out a derisive breath. "I'm not the one who can't remember, remember? I recovered my memories. You're the one still bereft."

"I've remembered some things. I earned another key. Do you remember that?"

Bayan merely rolled his eyes. Part of me remembered why I'd hated him for so long, but another part knew that this was merely the crust of Bayan, a brittle shell that covered dark insecurities. "One more key – such an accomplishment! Will you move? You're in my way."

"What did he do to you?" I wasn't sure what else to say. "Was it ... was it the memory machine?"

For the first time since I'd seen him again, Bayan's sneer faded away. "What do you mean?"

I wasn't sure how much to tell him or what to say. If this was Bayan from earlier – I couldn't trust him. He'd take whatever I said to Father, just to curry more favor. But he couldn't be that different from the Bayan who had shown me the cloud juniper. I took a chance. "You came to my room a few nights ago. You were ... sick. Very sick. You wanted me to hide you, but my father came and took you away. I haven't seen you since."

He frowned as though searching for a tree through a thick fog. His lips pressed together; his black hair shadowed his face. But he snapped out of the mood as quickly as it had fallen. He might not remember, and I might be smarter, but Bayan was not stupid. His eyes locked to mine. "What day is it?"

"We're three weeks into the wet season. It's Sing's Day."

A flash of fear made his face pale. Bayan had always stridden about the palace, clothed in arrogance. He'd not truly known what I knew — what it felt like to not trust your own mind. "I think Father did something to you. I don't know what, or why." The earliest memory I had, that I was sure about, was the chrysanthemum ceiling. A hazy blur from when I'd woken up. Later, I'd woken again in my bed, and Father had explained what had happened, I thought perhaps I'd dreamt the ceiling. Only as time went on, instead of the dream fading, I grew more and more certain it had been real.

I hesitated but forged forward. "Have you seen a ceiling? Painted in golden chrysanthemum blossoms?"

His face, already pale, went blank. It was the sort of stillness I'd seen in rabbits when predators were close — hoping they hadn't been seen. And then he moved again, shouldering past me and into his room.

The door shut in my face.

I didn't need to ask again to know: he'd seen it.

32

Jovis

Nephilanu Island

The claws on my arm detached, only to be replaced by teeth. I struggled to clear my head. I hadn't been this outmatched since I'd been face down in the street, Philine and her lackeys standing over me. I reached again desperately for the power in my bones. Again no strength surged in my limbs, no tremor radiated from the ground. I'd forgotten what it was like to be without it, afraid of very little. Now fear surged in my throat, choking me.

I kept my arm in front of my face, keeping the construct from lunging for my throat. Behind the mass of its body, I caught a glimpse of torn clothing and a few scraps of bone against the wall. It could have been refuse, but I knew better. I'd found the Shardless Few's missing spy.

And if I didn't do something soon, I'd be joining her.

I didn't have my staff or my strength, but I'd gotten by before without either. I formed a knuckle into a point and jammed it into the construct's eye. It roared and released my arm. I jumped back. Blood stained my shirtsleeve, and the glimpse of torn flesh beneath flipped my stomach.

The construct was between me and the alley entryway. I couldn't call for help; if I was rescued, I'd be hard-pressed to explain why a construct had attacked me. I darted for the remains of the spy, hoping she'd carried a weapon. The construct moved at nearly the same time.

Sticky, dark blood met my fingers. Errant bits of dead flesh. Cracked bones where marrow had been sucked out. Terror made my hands shake.

My fingers closed around a leather hilt.

I spun before even seeing what I held. The construct stopped just short of me, a growl in its throat. It was a sinuous beast with oversized jaws and patchy black fur. It had not been constructed with care; its bones pressed against its hide like the struts of a tent. It reminded me of the fish I'd seen washed ashore once, remnants from the depth, flat and dark and full of teeth.

Its yellowed eyes took in the knife I'd seized. Wasn't much of a weapon, really. More like the kind of thing to eat with or to take fishing. And here I was, brandishing it like I held a sword. Confidence had won me more than one encounter, no matter how little I'd earned it.

The construct, however, was convinced only briefly.

It darted for me, teeth bared. I jumped back, slashing at its face with the knife. By the look of the scars across its muzzle, I hadn't been the first to try this tactic. And the beast had learned. It ducked beneath my clumsy attack and snapped at my torso. My shirt ripped. I didn't look to see if teeth had broken skin. I was still alive, and fast running out of time.

Use your brain, *Jovis!* I'd been the best smuggler in all the Empire before I'd met Mephi. Had a taste of physical prowess diminished my wits? I'd survived the Ioph Carn without Mephi.

I could survive this. I couldn't out-fight this creature with a knife. I had to find some other weapon or run, and it was standing, growling, between me and the alleyway entrance. There was nothing else among the cold cobblestones I could use. I waved my knife again, trying to square my shoulders and appear as large as possible. The construct's bony shoulders rolled as it stalked closer.

My foot slid as I backed into the pile that once was the Shardless spy.

I'd been lying to myself. There was still something I could use. I tightened my fingers around the leather hilt of the knife, my palm damp with sweat. I took one more step back and threw it right at the construct's face.

The knife bounced from its head, but I hadn't been meaning to kill it. I used the distraction to reach down and seize the dead spy's ripped robe. And then, as the construct leapt for me, I threw the cloak over its head and wrapped it about its sinewy neck.

There are tales in the Empire that the Poyer wrestle bears. Would that those stories were true and that I'd had some acumen in such sport. Instead, I held tight to the fur at its shoulders, the cloth bunched in my fingers, trying to get behind it, to gain some control. It bucked and writhed, the meat-rot scent of it filling my nostrils. The knife was there on the ground, just out of reach. My injured arm burned. Blood ran to my fingers. My grip slipped. As if sensing my weakness, the construct stilled like a cat just before a pounce.

No. Not like this. Not this far from home.

I gritted my teeth and wrenched my shoulder to the left, pulling the construct with me. It stumbled, and I loosed my grip long enough to seize the knife. Before it could bite me again, I plunged the knife where I judged the eye to be.

It sagged, the muscles slackening as the blade entered its brain.

I let it go, wanting to slump to the ground with it. I was a mess. My hair was wild, my clothes filthy, my arm bleeding out like a gutted fish. Somewhere along the way, I'd lost the nosepiece Gio had applied.

Something had happened to Mephi. The thought pounded at the inside of my skull, echoing my pounding heart. I had to get back. Now. I ripped the torn sleeve from my shirt, using the cloth to bind the wound. My bag still hung from my shoulder, the information Gio had asked for within. But I remembered his interest in Mephi. Had it been a ploy, a way to get me to leave? Mephi hadn't wanted to be left alone. He hadn't wanted me to leave. Had they done something to him?

I stepped out of the alley and into the sunlight, feeling like I'd stepped from a nightmare world into the daytime one. A few people down the street glanced at me but then hurried away. At least I could count on fewer people peering at my face, thinking they recognized me from somewhere. I ran nearly the entire way to the edge of the city, dodging fishermen and irritated denizens. The day was clear, but I felt in a haze, faces rotating around me like stars in the night sky. My arm throbbed.

If Mephi was hurt, if he was injured, I'd kill the lot of them. I'd find a way.

I threw money at a cart driver heading to another city and rode with him, ignoring the way he looked at me when I jumped off partway there. And then I plunged into the forest, feeling my way back by memory. Every so often I stopped to close my eyes, to reach for that thrum in my bones. Each time I hoped I would find it. When silence answered, I had to choke down a breath. My throat was too tight to even swallow.

The cliff face loomed in front of me. The crack – where was the crack? I stumbled from side to side, brushing past vines to search for it. There. Without hesitation, I turned to the side, breathed out and lunged into the gap. My nose scraped against the stone; my breath warmed my face. The only light I could see filtered green through the vines.

The space opened up, but I couldn't see anything. They must have left. Taken Mephi and cleared out. I didn't know what they wanted with him. It hadn't occurred to me before that someone might take him from me. I put a hand to the wall, trying to steady myself.

Who would I chase after: Emahla or Mephi? My heart threatened to kick free of my ribs. It was too cruel a choice. I'd die making it.

A hand touched my arm. "We put out the lamp in the entrance," Ranami's voice emanated from the darkness. "We've seen the Emperor's spies about so we need to be cautious."

I couldn't put words to the relief I felt. I sucked in a breath of cool, damp air, my head spinning. I hadn't realized I'd been holding my breath. "Mephi?"

For a moment, she didn't say anything. Panic fluttered up my throat.

"He's sick," she said finally. A thousand painful possibilities flashed through my head before she spoke again. "You should see him." She took my hand and guided me through the passageway.

She let go once we reached the main hall, the fire roaring in the middle. Mephi was curled on his side by the fire.

I tossed the bag aside and went to him. He didn't respond when I touched him. His cheeks were warm to the touch, and not only from the fire. He sighed a little as I stroked the nubs of his horns, the skin there worn bare of fur. He'd been hungry and tired lately – had I just not noticed the signs of illness?

"You're hurt," Gio said from behind me. I hadn't heard him walking up.

My arm began to throb again as if the reminder had prompted

my wound to reassert itself. It didn't seem to be healing the way my wounds usually did. I gritted my teeth and shook my head. "What happened to him?"

"He collapsed," Ranami said from behind him. "Was doing fine this morning, started to look a little unwell and then just collapsed by the fire. I've been able to feed him a little broth but that's it. Feels like he has a fever."

Gio knelt next to me. "It's nothing that we did," he said as though he knew the thoughts that had been swirling in my mind. "He could have just fallen ill. Animals do sometimes." His voice was calm, even. "Now tell me what happened to you."

"He needs a doctor."

"I'll have one of our Shardless medics look at him. Now tell me what happened to you."

I told him — the rolled sheet of parchment I'd obtained, the construct, the spy's remains in the alley. "I killed the construct and came back here as quickly as I could."

Gio stood. "We need to get into the palace. Tonight."

I couldn't think straight enough to even get my legs beneath me. And he wanted me to infiltrate a palace? "Fool" and "rebel" sometimes meant the same thing. "What do you want me to fight with?" I lifted my injured arm. "This?"

"I'll have a medic see to you, and you'll have some rest before dark, but we can't waste any more time. The Emperor's spies have discovered our informant — which means when the construct doesn't report back, its master will find out. Eventually that means Ilith or Tirang ... and then the Emperor himself. Regardless, the second-tier construct in charge of this region will know our plans. We need to move while the information we've received is still good."

Fanatics were all alike, cut from the same cloth and dyed different colors. "I can't. Not tonight. Not until Mephi is better."

Gio pursed his lips, his brow shadowing his eyes. His gaze focused somewhere over my shoulder. And then he refocused, nodding his head. For a moment I thought he'd agreed with me. But then he spoke. "We go tonight or you'll get nothing from us."

I wanted to break his bones. "I'm not leaving him." Not again.

"What good will you be to him here? He has a fever, Jovis, but he's still eating. As far as I can tell, he's in no danger of dying. But everyone here, him included, will be in danger if we don't use this information now and overthrow the governor."

"Not if I take him back to my ship. Or would you stop me?" I matched his glare and was surprised to find Gio stood taller than I did, his shoulders broad despite his age. Tension hummed in the air between us. He was old and missing an eye and my arm was torn, yet there was danger in what we were doing. It felt as though we both stood at a precipice. But I wouldn't be bullied into leaving my friend.

A quick intake of breath from behind me, the scramble of feet against stone. "Catch it!" Ranami cried out. She brushed past me, hand outstretched. I followed the length of her arm and caught a glimpse of brown fur as something scampered around the corner.

All of the Shardless seemed to move at once, like ants after a foot has pressed into their anthill. Ranami's shout echoed down the hall, vibrating off the walls. Even as I darted after the creature, I could hear others taking up the call.

A construct spy, here in the Shardless hideout. I'd not waited until that cart had gone out of view; I'd not checked behind me. I couldn't be sure, but some deep part of me knew: I'd brought this ruin upon them. I didn't have the speed or strength that my bond with Mephi gave me, but desperation made me quick. I surged past Ranami, following the construct into the dimly lit hall. It darted away from me, even as I strained to reach it.

I leapt for it, reaching. My hand grasped empty air.

And then the construct was squirming through the gap in the rocks, out of the cliff face, into the forest.

Gio and Ranami came up beside me, both of them breathless.

Gio raked me with his gaze. "You were supposed to take the long way. You've led them to us."

I hadn't done it intentionally, but saying so would be cold comfort at a time like this.

"We can't wait until tonight anymore," Gio said. "We have to leave now."

Ranami proffered a hand to help me up. "I'll watch Mephi. Make sure he gets some food in him and rests. I won't let him come to harm. Please go. We will give you what we promised," she said. She swallowed. "We all have people we care about who are in danger."

I reached again for the thrum in my bones. Nothing. There was the matter of my skills – the ones they'd wanted me on board for in the first place – now vanished. But I thought of Emahla and my mother, and at the corners of these thoughts crept the faces of the shard-sick. *I do not care about them. They are nothing to me.* I'd opened my heart a crack for Mephi, and now it seemed the whole world came flooding in. And this was my fault. The guilt lay thick over my heart.

One breath in, one breath out. "I'll go," I said. And the weight of the words felt like an anchor into the Endless Sea.

"Get him bandaged," Gio said to Ranami. "I'll get the supplies and get everyone together."

The medic cleaned the wound – did it look any less angry than it had a moment before? – and wrapped it tightly. "I'd tell you to rest it," she said, "but you won't. If you come back ... *when* you come back, I'll change the bandage."

Now that I'd made the decision, calm had settled over me like a morning mist.

Gio arrived back at the entrance a moment later, my steel staff in his hands, a pack strapped to his back, knives strapped to his sides. "The Shardless will create a distraction at the gates," he told me as we walked into the forest. Rain pattered against the leaves, my feet squelching with each step. "We'll have to climb, but there's a hidden entrance to the palace, built by the Alanga. The governor kept it in case he ever had need of a speedy escape. There are guards but we have their locations and when they rotate out. We take the governor while the Shardless are working the main gate."

"How do they plan to take the main gate?" I hadn't seen that many Shardless in the hideout – not enough to storm a palace.

Gio's mouth settled into a grim line. "We start another riot. Conditions in the farms here have been getting worse. Even people living in the cities have family working the farms."

"So no special weapon then?"

He halted in his tracks, turned and glared at me. "What makes you say that?"

"You're holed up in an Alanga stronghold."

Gio snorted and strode into the trees. "These rumors of old Alanga weapons are ridiculous. The place was empty when we arrived, except for bats, animals who'd made their dens in the caves and the odd cobweb."

I thought of the book, still nestled among my things. "You didn't find anything? Seems hard to believe."

"It's been hundreds of years. The only things standing from their time are the ruins."

"And the stories," I said.

He shook his head and pushed past a branch. "Who knows what's true and what's not? The Emperor propagates most stories, and his forebears too. Those are his words and the words of his ancestors. You should know more than most that stories stretch the truth. Every time he feels insecure in his rule, he sends out those stupid troupes to act out the defeat of the Alanga."

There is truth in lies. "So the tale of Arrimus, who loved her people and defended them against the sea serpent Mephisolou, is a fiction of the Empire? Seems a bright fiction to be told by an Emperor who claims the Alanga are dangerous. And what of Dione, the greatest of the Alanga, who wept and begged for death when the first Emperor found him?"

Gio's shoulders stiffened. "Only fools believe everything they hear."

Interesting. I'd raised his hackles in some way. I prodded him further. "And only fools discount everything they hear."

"What fish do you have in this net, Jovis?" Gio asked with a sigh. "Are you one of those who worship the memory of the Alanga, who hope for their return? Or are you just an ass?"

Despite my unease, I couldn't help but smile. "I've been told I'm the latter more times than I'd like to admit." We trudged in silence for a while before I cleared my throat. "I don't know you, Gio. I've heard of you. But if we're to wade into this side by side, I want to know a little more of who you are." What I wanted to know was how they found the Alanga stronghold, and what the book meant. Were there more hidden doors? How had I opened the one I'd found? But I couldn't ask.

"*I* don't even know who I am; how can you?"

He sounded so weary when he said it that my usual smart responses died on my lips. I held my injured arm close to my chest, put my head down and focused on following him through the forest. Rain splashed at the back of my neck and slicked my hair to my head. We'd both had stories told about us and we both knew these stories held only grains of truth.

We reached the hillside leading up to the palace near sunset. Gio studied the scroll again. "The entrance is hidden, on the southern side." He pulled a couple of lightweight green cloaks from his bag. "We climb and we hide among the bushes. I'd planned to make this ascent at night, but the rain will provide cover, and it will be dark by the time we reach the top. That's when the riot will begin."

If I'd still had the thrum in my bones, I would have reached the top with daylight to spare. But I said nothing, only draped the cloak around my shoulders and followed him up the slope. We ducked beneath branches each time the guard on the walls looked our way, and grasped at rocks. It was slow going.

"So what happens next after you overthrow this governor?" I said when we were halfway up. I'd asked him this before, I knew, but I'd never been good at keeping silences.

For a while, he said nothing, and I thought he'd chosen to ignore me. "I'm not a fool, if that's what you think. With the caro nuts, we can force some of the nobility over to our side. We'll have Khalute and Nephilanu by then, and more are joining the Shardless Few every day. It will be the start of a true rebellion. We strengthen our foothold here, and then strike out at other islands."

"And will the new governor be amenable to this plan?" I asked. I knew where this was going. A coup did not end with the usual line of succession.

"You don't trust me," Gio said, "and that's fine. I wouldn't trust me either. But I do care for the people of the Empire, and I do believe the Sukai Dynasty needs to come to an end. You don't need to see me as a leader. You don't need to believe the stories. But if you care at all for those children you've saved, if it was *ever* about more than the money, then you'd stay. I don't know why you're searching for that boat, or why it haunts you. But if you haven't caught it yet – you never will. Better to stand with the Shardless Few. Time is waning, Jovis. It always is. You can spend your life chasing and running, living half a life."

I waited, a dark, sick feeling writhing in my chest – because I knew it wasn't him I was angry with. But he didn't say anything more. "Or what?" I spat out the words, rain trickling into my eyes.

"That," he said, finding his grip on another rock and pulling himself upward, "is entirely up to you."

The gloom of the day had faded into the gloom of nightfall by the time we reached the top, and the rain had slowed to a drizzle. "Here," Gio said. He drew aside some foliage to expose a door painted the same colors as the wall. He pulled a key from his bag. "We've been working on this plan for a long time."

I adjusted my grip on my staff. I had to tell him I didn't have my abilities. Now, before it was too late. I didn't trust him, but I didn't have a choice.

But then he was opening the door and it *was* too late. Beyond stood two guards in a small room, one facing us and one away, both looking bored. I stared at the one facing the door for a moment.

He moved first, drawing his sword. The other guard turned.

My injured arm throbbed and burned. This was it – the moment I couldn't avoid.

"Jovis . . ." Gio's voice.

I rushed into the room, my staff held at the ready. And then I reached again for the thrum in my bones.

Nothing.

Ah well. This seemed to be my luck lately. I swung my staff at the first soldier. I connected before he could bring his sword to bear. But then something happened with his legs. His face went wide with shock and his feet went out from under him. He tumbled down the hillside. It looked like he was being *carried*.

Gio appeared beside me, a dagger in hand. He engaged the second guard, spinning out of the way of a blow. The man's blade caught in Gio's cloak, and Gio used his momentum to spin the cloth around the weapon. He pulled, wrenching the blade from the guard. Before the man could do anything else, Gio struck him across the face with the hilt of his dagger.

The man fell to the floor.

"It appears the stories were true about you," Gio said, his breathing heavy.

I opened my mouth. Shut it. I reached for the thrum, as though I could have done some magic without realizing it. My bones were silent. A prickle raised all the hairs on my arms.

Whatever had happened, it hadn't been me.

33

Lin

Imperial Island

"I am sick," I said to the spy construct. "Say it back to me in my voice."

The little construct rose onto its hind legs, its nose quivering. "I am sick," Hao said. Its voice was a little bit higher than mine despite its efforts, but it was a fair enough approximation.

"Good." I plumped the pillows beneath my covers and guided the construct beneath the blanket. "Stay here until I return. If someone knocks at the door, say 'I am sick' in my voice." Hao's tail twitched like it understood. And even though I knew I didn't have to give it anything and that it would follow my orders regardless, I took a nut out from my sash pocket and gave it to the little beast.

It devoured it in moments, leaving behind crumbs on the bedsheet that it sniffed out to find and devour. I let the covers fall.

I'd rewritten Mauga and Uphilia. Ilith, the Construct of Spies, was next. The door to her lair lay within the shard storeroom — the small door at the back. I wondered if Ilith left and entered through this way, or if, like the spy constructs, she had some hole that she crawled in and out of, dirt clinging to the underside of her carapace. I shuddered.

Night had long since fallen, but I wasn't sure how long this journey would take me. I'd known exactly where Mauga's and Uphilia's lairs were. Ilith's was more of a mystery to me. That it was through that door, I knew. How far I'd go after that, I had no idea. I tucked my engraving tool into my sash pocket. This time, I'd not brought any extra shards. I'd do this the right way, without hurting anyone.

I slipped out into the silent hallway. The palace was like a shrine at night, lit by the odd lamp here or there, the wooden floorboards creaking a little beneath my weight. When everyone was asleep, I felt alone in the world. There was a comfort in that loneliness, the soft touch of black silk wrapped around me, hiding me away. My father might have ruled the Empire, but when he was asleep, when Bayan and all the servants were asleep, this palace was my kingdom. I held the keys to its doors and plied its secrets from its rooms.

The bone shard storeroom hadn't changed since I'd last left it. I lit the lamp by the door, illuminating the rows of shelves and drawers, all neatly tucked away. So many lives contained in those drawers, so much power for my father.

It didn't take me long to find the shards of Numeen's family, searching by their ages and their names. They felt odd in my hands, now that I knew their owners. These little pieces of them, these bones. They clicked together like lacquered cards in my hands. I didn't have Numeen's but I had his family's. That would mean something.

Tucking all the shards into my sash, I made my way to the door at the back of the room and to the cloud juniper door. With a deep breath, I drew out the key Numeen had made for me and inserted it into the lock. He underestimated his work. It turned smoothly, without the hint of give. The door swung open noiselessly, revealing only darkness beyond. The air inside was cooler, damp with moisture. It smelled like rain and decay.

There were no lanterns on the inside of this door. I had to take the lantern by the first door and bring it with me. The hallway I illuminated only continued a short distance before a set of steps descended into the earth. My insides quaked as I approached the steps. Of all the places I'd been inside the palace, this felt the darkest, like the bowels of some enormous beast, long since dead. The walls around me turned to dirt and stone. I remembered what I'd read – that there had once been a witstone mine on Imperial and my father had shut it down. Was this the remains of it? It certainly felt like the sort of place Ilith would make into her lair.

I came to a fork in the path.

This I hadn't expected. Both passageways looked the same when I held my lamp into their mouths. What if I got lost? All I could imagine was being trapped in these passages, the weight of the earth above me. I'd gone willingly into my own tomb.

I swallowed the fear. This wasn't a maze. Not yet. I could easily find my way out by tracing back my steps. If I panicked here, how much more would I panic when facing down Ilith herself with her eight limbs and eight hands? I breathed in deep and then out, and chose the left passage. The darkness seemed to swallow the sound of my footsteps.

A smell hit me when I'd gone ten paces in. It smelled like Mauga – musky, like old dried urine, hay and dung. I swung my lantern in front of me, my hand trembling. A growl. The flash of yellow eyes. And then something slammed into me, a wall of coarse fur, the wet warmth of a slathering mouth.

Ilith would have sentries, of course. The thought seemed

to exist in the eye of a storm, a calm spot in the turmoil of my mind.

The beast pushed against me, its maw trying to reach my shoulder. The lamp dropped from my hand and hit the mineshaft floor, the flame mercifully staying lit. Its light showed me a beast like a bear, its eyes flashing. I scrambled with my hands, trying to keep it from biting me – shoving, pressing, my arms a weak counterpoint to the creature's strength. I wouldn't be able to stave it off for long. It would tear me to pieces in this passageway. Sweat gathered in the small of my back as I fought for some measure of relief.

Wait. It was a construct.

Its teeth seized my shoulder. I only had one chance at this. I stopped resisting, took in a breath and plunged my right hand into its body.

I felt coarse fur, and then my fingers were inside the creature. It froze, its teeth still digging into my flesh. I winced as I searched inside of it for the bone shards, each movement aching. I found the column of shards near the creature's spine and pulled the top one off the stack. I had to pry the beast's jaws from my shoulder before I could move. It had barely broken the skin, though I knew my whole shoulder would be bruised by tomorrow morning. I lifted the lamp to the shard.

"Attack anyone except Ilith, Shiyen and spy constructs."

That was easy enough to fix. With my engraving tool, I added "and Lin," and held it over my breast as I carved the identifying star. I pushed it back into the construct and continued on my way before it could awaken. The passage seemed to get darker after that, the path leading ever downward.

I caught the next construct before I rounded the corner where it lived, plunging my hand inside it before it could even react to my presence. Again, I rewrote its attack command. The walls down here shone with a vein of chalky, white witstone. It nearly made up the entire left wall. A wealth of witstone, right beneath the palace. Why had my father shut down these mines? Was it for fear that these passages riddling the rock would destabilize the palace? My father wasn't a greedy man, but he was practical. If the mine was still producing, he wouldn't have shut it without good reason.

A little way from the next construct, I found another door.

It looked strange here in the rough passageway, a little brown door with a brass knob. It sat in a round alcove, and the sides had been plastered and bricked off. I tried the doorknob even though I knew already it would be locked. It rattled but didn't turn. Father didn't like to leave many doors unlocked. I supposed I was lucky he at least left the latrines unlocked. I pressed my ear to the lacquered wood. It was cool against my cheek. I couldn't hear anything except my own breathing.

Whatever lay behind that door, it would have to wait until I could find the key and again make my way into these tunnels. Ilith's lair still lay ahead, if I'd chosen the correct fork.

The passage sloped down again, so steep in some places that I had to use my hands to help lower myself lest I slip. I grew disoriented in the dark, sure but not sure that I'd doubled back somewhere, that there were now tunnels above me in addition to the palace. I felt the weight of so many layers pressing down on me, making it difficult to breathe.

When I first saw the glow ahead of me, I thought it some trick of the light. But when I tucked the lantern below an arm and could still see the glow outlining the passage ahead, I knew – I was close to Ilith's lair. I knelt and quietly set the lamp on the passageway floor, careful not to let it click against the stone. I drew the engraving tool from my sash and held it in front of me even though I couldn't do much damage with it. But the weight of it felt better in my hand than nothing.

I crept around the corner.

Something skittered past my feet. I nearly jumped out of my skin. A flash of red fur disappeared around the corner.

My heartbeat pulsed at my throat; my mouth went dry. I froze just like Bayan had the night before, like a rabbit sighting prey. It had been a spy construct. It was here to report to Ilith and it had just passed me on my way into her lair. I wanted to run. My legs were poised to carry me away from here, back up the tunnel, to the safety of my room where I'd spent most of the past five years, under the covers, my breath warming the space beneath the sheets.

But if I went, Ilith would still know. The incontrovertible truth of it made my insides wither. I didn't have another choice. If I stayed here frozen, I'd lose any chance I had. My chances were already dwindling.

Courage. I crept into the glow of Ilith's lair.

Three lamps were scattered across the walls, their light dim as tiny moons. Ilith didn't line her den with fresh hay, not like Mauga or Uphilia. Thick strands of webbing obscured two of the walls. White lines of it were strung across the floor, glittering in the lamplight. I stepped over them, not wanting to test their stickiness. Ilith sat in the center of the room, her back to me. Her hands were busy at work. She wrote missives with two of them. Two others moved over her hair and body, as though they could somehow improve her appearance. The little spy who'd brushed past me sat on its haunches in front of the Construct of Spies and gave its report.

"While they did laundry, two of the servants gossiped about Jovis, the smuggler who has been stealing away children. One of them wondered if he was handsome . . ."

I let out a breath slowly. These rudimentary spy constructs were not people. They did not lead with the most interesting information first. It was going through the day in chronological order. It would take some time before it reported its sighting of me in the corridor.

Ilith's back was turned. I could make it there and start working with her shards before I was given away. I took a few rapid steps forward while the spy construct droned on. Just a little farther.

"Another servant spoke about the rebellion, and wondered how long it would take them to get to Imperial . . ."

Another few steps. I caught a foot on the sticky web and had to bend to extricate it. Despite the cold of the cavern, sweat trickled down my scalp and behind my ears. I didn't dare wipe it away. I was close to Ilith now, so close I could touch her. She smelled earthy and faintly of mold. Her carapace was thick and shiny. I hovered a hand over it. Would it give the way the other constructs' flesh had? Or would my fingers just bounce against it?

"And on my way here, I saw Lin Sukai in the passages."

Ilith stopped writing. She set down her pens and rose, her body rising from the floor. "Lin Sukai? How far into the passages?"

I didn't wait for the spy construct's answer. I reached for Ilith's body. Her slick carapace met my fingertips. I pushed against it and found no give.

Ilith screeched – a sound halfway between man and beast. She whirled, her abdomen knocking me to the ground, the nails from her eight hands clicking against the stone floor. I tried to rise but couldn't; I'd fallen on a piece of web and it clung to my tunic. She was over me in a flash, her old woman's face next to mine, her body blocking the light. "Lin Sukai," she said. Her breath smelled of old blood. "Did you think to sneak up on the master of spies in her own lair?"

"I nearly did," I spat back at her.

She grabbed me by the front of my tunic with two of her arms.

Another two seized my ankles. "I could tear you limb from limb right here."

"Is that what my father commanded you do?"

She laughed. "You have no idea what sort of commands live inside my flesh. You think you can move about this palace and maybe even use bone shard magic, but there are complexities you could never understand."

In answer, I wriggled free of one of her hands and pushed my fingers into her face. She stiffened. The carapace hadn't given when I'd tried, but flesh was flesh. The sight of my hand submerged into her face made me feel a bit ill, but I had to rewrite her commands. I felt around for the shards.

I was elbow-deep in Ilith's face before I found them. They weren't in a thin column like in Mauga or even Uphilia. They were crowded into clusters. They felt like pine cones. I pulled one at random, trying to imprint in my memory where I'd pulled it from.

When I pulled it out and held it to the light, my courage failed. Ilith was right. I didn't understand what was written there. There were some formulas, a few words I didn't know. Frightened, I pushed it back inside and pulled another one. This one had a few words I knew: "when", "never" and "look out". I blinked, hoping I just wasn't seeing the words correctly. I'd read so many books in the library – had I thought those would be enough? I must have just gotten lucky with Mauga and Uphilia. Ilith was a strange, solitary creature, and Father trusted her counsel. He'd made a construct that was nearly as complex as he was.

I pulled shard after shard from Ilith, examining them, trying to discern a pattern to the commands. Of the ones I could decipher, I could see that my father had given her much of her own judgment, marked by parameters I didn't understand.

At last, I found a shard that spoke of obedience to Shiyen.

"Obey Shiyen unless it runs counter to your wisdom and intelligence." Both "wisdom" and "intelligence" had numbers written above them. I searched for the reference shards and only found shards that each held at least five more references.

I wanted to tear out my own hair. How could I rewrite something I didn't fully understand? This would be an even messier job than I'd done on Mauga and Uphilia. But while both of those had been sloppy, they seemed to have held up. My father had called them both to the dining room since I'd rewritten their commands, and he hadn't seemed to notice a difference.

I puzzled out the obedience command again. I bit my lip. I could still change this in a way to work to my advantage. The number "11" was written next to wisdom. I could change that. I held the shard against my breast and went over the "11" with an engraving tool, molding it into a identification star. Ilith would now obey my father unless it ran counter to me and her intelligence. And I could give her another command. I reached inside her and removed the original intelligence reference shards. This would work. It would have to.

The last construct I had to rewrite was the Construct of War. His lair wasn't difficult to find. It was a suite of rooms across from my father's.

I pocketed the reference shards and stepped away from Ilith. She'd awaken soon, and I'd need to get away. Like the other constructs, she wouldn't remember the moments just before I'd rewritten her.

I stepped carefully over the floor, avoiding the webs. The lighting here was dim, and the webs were difficult to see. My foot caught in a web despite my best efforts. I pulled and shook my foot, trying to dislodge it. A scraping sounded from behind me, and I glanced back to see if Ilith was awake yet.

She writhed on the floor, her eight limbs kicking out to the sides as though she'd fallen onto a patch of ice and could not rise from it. A moan emerged from her mouth. "What happened?" she said. I shrank back, wishing there was something I could hide behind. Ilith managed to get two of her feet beneath her. She pulled herself toward me, dragging her abdomen across the floor. "You. You did something to me."

I couldn't move, my throat too tight to breathe through, my heart drumming against my ribs. I pulled my foot free of the web and stumbled, my gaze still on Ilith's face. The flesh there began to sag and wrinkle. I took two steps toward the exit.

There could be no running from this problem. It would follow me into the palace hallways above, back to my bed, to haunt me in the dining hall where I sat across from my father. He would notice if something were wrong with Ilith. I wished things could be different, but wishing so was like throwing coins into the Endless Sea and hoping for some return. Turning around felt harder than anything I'd done in my life. But I turned to face Ilith.

And then I ran at her.

I'd always been quick, and running on the rooftops and scaling the walls had refined my strength. She batted at me with her many hands and I flung them away. It was like pushing aside the branches of a fir tree to find the trunk beneath. Her face emerged from within the flurry of her hands. I plunged my fingers into her flesh. Ilith went still, all her brittle upraised hands framing her face. The warmth of her body cocooned my arm. I reached for the clusters of shards, the rough edges like eggshells. I pulled out a shard, and then another, examining my work, trying to find out where I'd gone wrong. The command I'd rewritten should be fine, but I was missing something among the reference shards.

A sick feeling seized my throat, blossomed out until I could taste bitterness on the back of my tongue. I couldn't stop moving, shifting shards in and out, searching for the mistake I'd made, my fingers trembling.

I couldn't find it.

I sagged onto the stone floor and felt her webs stick to my shins. I'd dealt with Mauga and Uphilia. I should have gone for Tirang before Ilith, gotten more practice in first. Because here I was, faced with my father's most powerful construct – and I was at a loss. I gritted my teeth until I felt my jaw would crack. I had to keep trying. I shoved myself to my feet, ready to try once more.

Soft laughter echoed from the cavern walls. Ilith's sides heaved. "You little idiot. You think this is how you show your father you are worthy? That this is how you earn his love?"

I sucked in a breath, my chest aching. "I don't want his love." But a small part of me did. Why couldn't we go back to the beginning when I had my memories? I was different then; maybe he was too.

"You think he doesn't know?"

"That I don't want his love?" The ache turned into a roiling unease. It wasn't that. There was something else. Something I'd missed.

Ilith's melting face smiled, and my stomach clenched.

"Your keys, your trips outside the city. Your blacksmith friend. Your blacksmith friend's family. He knows, Lin. And he's never loved a fool."

34

Jovis

Nephilanu Island

I examined the floor, trying to find the spot the man had tripped over. He'd looked so startled, like something invisible had slammed into his knees. The floor remained unremarkable.

Gio pulled out the scroll again. "If we take the correct hallways, we can almost entirely avoid guards at all. The riots should be starting any moment now – I told them at nightfall – and that will thin out their resources further. We just need to time this right."

I pushed back the hood of my cloak, tasting rain on my lips. I didn't think I could push people about with my mind. At least, I'd never done it before. It wouldn't have even been something I'd thought to do. "Gio," I said, my voice low, "that wasn't me."

He glanced at me and then back at the scroll. "What do you mean?"

"Whatever knocked the guard over. It wasn't me." A liar through and through, but sometimes the truth was the best route. "I don't have my abilities right now. I don't know why –" *a lie*

"— but I don't. I've tried. I tried when that construct in the city attacked me."

"Well, I certainly didn't do anything," Gio said with a frown. "It could have been you. Maybe something new you've not done before. Maybe it just feels different. Or maybe the man tripped over his own feet." He shook his head. "We don't have time for this."

And then he slipped into the hallway without waiting for my response.

What if it's someone else? I'd never considered that someone else might have similar strange abilities to mine. Would they have a friend like Mephi, or were they like the cloudtree monks, who drank the cloud juniper tea and ate the berries for unnatural strength? The Empire was vast, and there were islands beyond even its reach. I clenched my jaw to keep my teeth from chattering.

I could leave. Leave Gio to his mad quest. Find some way to get Mephi through the crack of an entrance and back to my boat.

Gio was waiting for me. I could hear his breathing from the hall. "You're a good man," my mother had said to me days before I'd left without so much as a note. "Your brother would never have lamented the fact that he died and you didn't. Even if you do."

If I'd been a good man, I would have died a long time ago. "Fine," I snarled to no one in particular. I stepped into the hall and shut the door behind me.

Gio was already silently lifting a chair from a nearby table. He wedged it beneath the door's handle. "For our friend within," he whispered. "Though we should be done before he wakes. Let's go."

Somewhere above us, I heard someone shout. Footsteps creaked against the floors over my head. Gio's Shardless and unwitting accomplices at the gate.

"Those were the only guards in this section," Gio said as I caught up to him. Lanterns hung from the stone walls, placed at long intervals, leaving the spaces between dark. "There will be more when we get to the main floor. Once we go up the stairs, we'll take a right, then the second left, straight through the dining hall, and the governor's suites are just beyond that."

The sound from the gate grew to a dull roar. "Quite the riot your Shardless have started," I said.

"It's been brewing for some time. You'll understand once we reach the main level. Now quiet."

I held my tongue as we crept around the corner and up a set of stairs. Gio checked the landing before gesturing for me to follow. I obeyed, and walked into something from the opulent dreams of the Ioph Carn. Gold trim and paint accentuated the murals on the walls. The tiles inlaid into the ceiling were stamped in curving patterns, then glazed a cerulean blue. They glinted in the lamplight, and for a moment I had the odd impression I'd found an underwater cave, rife with treasures gathered from sinking ships.

I'd seen the gutter orphans in the streets of the city, hungry for any scrap of food. I'd seen the shard-sick, withering away. And here was enough wealth to feed a hundred orphans and care for all the shard-sick. "It's too much," I whispered. Gio shot me a glare and I snapped my mouth shut. But it *was* too much. I wished I hadn't seen it.

We made it to the second left before we ran into more guards. We stopped at the corner. Another pair of them, a man and a woman. Both had their gazes fixated toward the front gate, listening to the sounds of the riot.

"Should someone tell the governor?" the man asked.

"He can hear it," the woman said. "They'll take him out the back way if the rioters breach the walls. You heard our orders. They don't need us at the walls just yet."

Gio patted my arm to get my attention. He motioned – you take right, I'll take left. And then a countdown with his fingers.

At his nod, we both burst into the next hallway. I could see now that there must have been some truth to the stories. Gio moved with a light, silent step, his twin daggers like extensions of his arms. Despite his graying hair, there was strength in his limbs. I was louder, but we still took both guards by surprise. No inexplicable tripping this time, only two guards lying at our feet. It took me longer than it took Gio, and I received a shallow slice to my ribs. The pain in my arm had lessened, though it hadn't healed yet. I was going to have a veritable litany of injuries by the time I lived through this. If I lived through this.

"His personal guard will be with him. Six of them, all well trained," Gio said, his breathing heavy. He gave me a sidelong glance, his gaze dropping to the guard on the floor.

I'd learned a thing or two when I'd rescued the children from the Tithing Festival, but without Mephi I was weak. I hadn't realized how much that power had compensated for my lack of skill. Always had been more of a talker than a fighter. "My arm," I said. "I'm slower than I usually am." Did I sound nervous? Did I sound like I was lying? I shouldn't have said anything. Never could just let a silence sit.

"There will be more difficulties ahead. Take a breather if you must."

I could see the doubt in his eyes. I wondered how long it would take until he figured out that my strength had left me just as Mephi had grown ill. If anyone made that connection, they would try to take Mephi from me. And I'd left him in the midst of the Shardless Few, asking him to disguise himself as a harmless pet. Damn that construct for finding me, damn this whole ill-begotten plot, damn my involvement. "I'm fine," I managed. Best get this over with – find out my fate, one way or another. I needed more rest than I would get.

"A bit of that magic you used earlier might help us in the next fight," he said. Before I could bite back – again! – that I'd not done anything to fling the soldier down the hillside, he opened the door to the dining hall and slipped inside. I followed.

The dining hall was an ostentatious room of turquoise and gold, painted peacocks with bright yellow eyes adorning the walls. Even the goblets were sculpted, the bowls rimmed in gold. I was surprised the Ioph Carn hadn't already found a way to plunder this palace, smuggling out pieces of it a little at a time. It was the sort of task Kaphra might have set me to.

Above us, I heard the toll of a bell.

"The rioters have breached the walls. The guards will try to take the governor out the secret passage." Gio opened the door on the other side of the dining hall and peered through. "They're in disarray. We can take them by surprise. I'll go left. You go right." And then, without waiting for a response, he was gone.

Did he not want to hear me? I didn't have my powers. I tightened my sweat-slick palms around my staff. The muscles of my injured arm protested; the skin there burned and stretched. But I'd backed myself into this corner. Me, Mephi, Gio. Emahla.

The door to the governor's suite was open, a guard halfway in and halfway out, shouting into the room. "We need to leave now. Forget the armor – he won't need it if we hurry."

Gio ducked and ran the length of the hall, swift and silent as a snake in the water. He thrust one of his daggers into the guard's back. The man let out a little gasp before crumpling. I dashed down the hallway, sounding like an elephant compared to Gio's mouse. But the element of surprise was gone and stealth no longer mattered.

Gio had already engaged the next guard. I stepped to his side, bringing my staff down on the woman's head. Her helmet took the force of my blow, though I saw her teeth grit with the pain. It distracted her enough for Gio to bat her sword to the side. I swung the other end of my staff about and jabbed her in the throat. She went down choking.

Battles were never pretty.

Four guards left. They formed a line between us and the governor. I could see a flash of his frightened eyes by the lamplight, his robe wrapped loosely about broad shoulders. He had a full head of disheveled gray hair and a thin beard. Something about his face reminded me of the goats I used to see on the mountain slopes at home. He wasn't young, but he wasn't old. Doubtless he'd expected to rule for many more years.

He still might. The line of guards advanced, their swords held at the ready. I reached for the power in my bones again and felt nothing but weariness in them. I'd told Emahla once that I would fight off a thousand armies just to be at her side. She'd laughed and had kissed my cheek. "Jovis, you're not a fighter."

"I would be for you."

Back then I'd thought hopes and willpower could make a thing be so. Now I knew the limitations of body, mind and heart.

Above us, I heard shouts, a few clangs of metal against metal. Another step toward us. I wondered if they recognized me from the posters, or if they recognized Gio. They might hesitate, but this wouldn't go well for me. Without Mephi's strength, I had only a rudimentary understanding of weapons. They would cut me down like I was a patch of overgrown grass. I couldn't blame them for just doing their job.

I brought my staff up to block as one of the guards swiped at me. The clash rang out, reverberating down the hallway much as the impact reverberated down my arm. My very bones vibrated. Before I could react, the man took another step, inside my guard, and seized my staff. He wrenched it from my grasp and sent it skittering across the floorboards. His great big hand seized the neck of my shirt. I wriggled to free myself but found his grip unyielding.

The other three guards converged on Gio. He fought like a whirlwind, his blades flashing, blocking a blow here, nicking an arm there. But the three guards were relentless. They wore at him until sweat dripped from his brow.

What were the Shardless doing right now? Were they on their way to help?

I'd never had anyone else to rely on as a smuggler. Don't know why I was hoping for that now. I clenched my jaw and kicked back at the man holding me, hard as I could. He grunted as the blow landed. But instead of letting me go, he wrapped an arm about my throat, tightening it until the edges of my vision went dark.

It was through this haze that I saw Gio kill one guard, his knife dancing across her throat. And then I watched, helpless, my hands clawing for purchase, as one of the remaining two guards knocked Gio's cheek with the hilt of her blade. Gio stumbled but didn't fall. Not until the other guard buried his foot in Gio's stomach.

The room went silent. The governor straightened, pulling the two halves of his robes tighter together, refastening the belt. Failure, even though it had seemed inevitable, was still a shock. *Mephi* ... No answering power swelled in my flesh.

The man holding me cleared his throat. "Should we question them?"

The governor shook his head. "There's no time. We need to leave before the rebels get here. Kill them."

35

Lin

Imperial Island

He knows. I bit my lip until it bled, clutching at my sides with clawed fingers. Something I'd done, something I'd said, a spy construct I hadn't seen. Something had tipped him off, and now everything was *wrong*. I wanted to weep. To scream.

Ilith's body deflated in front of me, her face sagging, her legs curling beneath her. She'd not said anything since, I wasn't sure she could still speak. Her body was turning soft, malleable, even her exoskeleton losing cohesion. There was something both terrible and familiar about the way she was falling apart.

That night Bayan had come to me. I remembered the give of his ribs beneath my fingers as he gasped at me for help, as his flesh fell away from his eyes.

Had Father done the same thing to Ilith as he'd done to Bayan? No – Father hadn't done anything to make Ilith fall apart. I'd done this to Ilith. I'd failed in rewriting her commands. I dug my nails into my palms, unable to breathe. The way Father had failed in rewriting Bayan's.

Bayan was a construct.

I could barely wrap my mind around the thought. He was real; he wasn't a thing cobbled together from animal parts. But he must have been sewn together from human parts, the seams smoothed over with bone shard magic, the commands written into his bones.

I didn't live in a palace. I lived in a dollhouse of my father's making, a living graveyard. Despite the fact that Ilith's lair was the size of the dining hall, I felt I was being crushed by the weight of the surrounding stone. If he knew, why let me continue? Was this all some sort of test? And if the sickness hadn't come from Bayan, where had I gotten it from? Tears gathered in my eyes, though I didn't know why. Were they for Bayan, or for myself?

Ilith didn't move. I didn't know how to bring her back, and I wasn't sure I could figure it out before daybreak.

Think, I had to think. Push down the horror, accept the truth, move to the next action. Stealing the keys was pointless. Bringing them to Numeen to copy was pointless.

Numeen.

Even if this was a test, and I'd passed it, my actions had revealed a traitor among his citizens. Perhaps Bayan was right and Father would not beat me for my insolence, for my over-reaching. But Numeen would not fare so easily. I sucked in a breath. Or his family.

I reached for Ilith's face. If I figured out how to fix her before dawn, I could move forward with my plan, could still pretend—

The flesh of her face was cold to my fingertips. I stopped. What was I doing? If I failed, I wouldn't be the only one paying the price. Even if I succeeded, there was no telling I'd have the chance to see Numeen again. I knew now, and Father might read it on my face. I'd been moving forward with only one goal in mind: prove to my father that I was fit to be his heir. Prove I could be an Emperor like him. A hollow ache started in my chest. Everything I'd done, and I still couldn't earn his love or his approval. What did my memories matter? I was still his daughter. I'd nearly forced Numeen into helping me, I'd never fulfilled my end of the bargain and he'd brought me to his family. They'd shown me kindness.

I should have broken into Bayan's room, given Numeen and his family their shards when I'd had the chance, the Endless Sea swallow the risks. They could have been gone from here, escaped to an island on the fringe of the Empire or found shelter with the Shardless Few. I'd made too many false promises, had told too many lies.

I didn't know how to make it right, but I had to try. How could I be the Emperor they needed if I was always trying to be some past version of myself?

Father would still be asleep. There was time. I left Ilith's body on the floor and dashed for the door. My heart pounded in time with each step – up, up, out of the old mines and back to the shard storeroom. The palace was calm, undisturbed. My world had shattered, but the world around me remained unchanged. I tried to keep my breathing steady as I closed and locked both doors behind me.

One more task before I left. I put one foot in front of another, darting down the hallways until I came to Bayan's room. I pounded on it fit to wake the dead.

He opened the door, bleary-eyed, and my ribs were like a vise around my heart. I still couldn't quite believe it. But I didn't have time to waste. I pushed past him.

"Why are you—?"

His room was neat and organized – had my father written that into his bones? It was easy to find the unused shards laid out in rows on the desk. I shuffled through them.

"Hey," Bayan said from behind me. "I'm using those. What are you doing?"

"Nothing," I said as I grabbed Numeen's shard and stuffed it into my sash. "Go back to sleep."

Bayan grabbed my arm. "You wake me up, rifle through my room and tell me to go back to sleep?"

He didn't remember. As far as he was concerned, we were still rivals. So I looked him in the eye and thought about what to say. "I'm sorry my father beats you. He shouldn't. I'm so sorry."

His eyes went wide, his fingers going slack. "How did you . . . ?"

But I was gone already, out the door, closing it gently behind me. I could only hope he wouldn't tell my father. I made my way to the palace's main entrance – because what did it matter now that the spy constructs had no one to report to?

The streets of the city were silent, washed gray by moonlight. It wasn't raining, but a light drizzle laced my eyelashes with silver. I tried to remember the twists and turns to Numeen's house, my heart leaping into my throat. Maybe, if I were lucky, I could get there and back and still fix Ilith.

I found the blacksmith shop first. The door and shutters were closed and locked, the lights out. I struggled to orient myself. When Numeen had taken me to his house, it hadn't been so late. The streets had still been lit, the sounds and smells of dinner cooking wafting from the surrounding buildings. We'd taken a right down the street, that much I remembered. Each of my steps felt hesitant, the darkness a shroud I had to push past.

But I recognized the corner of a house with decorated gutters, another street with uneven cobblestones, a building with a recessed doorway. And all the while my heart beat like I was running, my breath raw. The cold damp of the air met the warm damp of my sweat, mingled into a swampy mixture at the back of my neck.

There.

I wasn't sure how late it was by the time I found Numeen's house. Without thinking, I grasped the doorknob and found it locked. Of course.

I knocked.

Nothing but silence greeted me. I knocked again, louder, and waited. Something creaked above me, a dim light shining through the shutters. Shuffling of feet against wood. Light peeked out from below the door.

What if it was one of my father's constructs? If Bayan wasn't real, I couldn't be sure what was real anymore and what was not. I squeezed my eyes tightly shut, shook my head, trying to dislodge the fear. I took a chance. "Numeen, it's me."

A long exhalation, and then the doorknob rattled. Numeen opened the door, his expression mixed, a lamp held upraised in his left hand. His brow had furrowed somewhere between annoyance and confusion; his lips pressed together and twisted to one side. He was not happy to see me. Still, he stepped to the side to let me in. "You shouldn't come to my house. Only the shop."

I didn't enter. Was my face as bloodless as it felt? "Here." I reached into my sash pocket, pulled out the paper packet I'd tucked the shards into. "Your shard and your family's. You need to leave Imperial now. Get as far away from here as possible. Beyond the reach of the Empire."

He didn't need to know how to read faces to read mine. "Something has happened," he said.

I nodded confirmation. "My father. He knows."

And just like that, Numeen's expression settled on grim. His gaze went to the side of the door. He reached, picking up something heavy. A hammer. Not the sort used for blacksmithing. He handed the packet of shards back to me. "Get my family up," he said. "Tell them to pack essentials." He shut the door, locked it and wedged a chair beneath the knob.

Was it possible to die of guilt? "I'm sorry," I said. It seemed I only came to this house to bring danger and to issue apologies.

He had no reply for me.

I clenched my jaw. Selfish of me to seek absolution. Words wouldn't help them now. I dashed up the stairs, knocking on doors and walls, calling softly to the occupants. "You need to get up. Now. Get your things."

The adults roused first, then the children and Numeen's mother last. I felt like a dog, nipping at the heels of sheep, warning them of wolves. I'd brought this wolf to their doorstep. Foolish Lin, who thought she could have secrets in her father's palace. They moved slowly at first, and then more quickly, packing bags, shushing the children. Numeen's daughter Thrana held her paper crane in her hands, her eyes wide, a small bag slung over one shoulder.

"Down the stairs," I told them. "Numeen is by the door."

I'd taken the first step when the house shook.

Wood cracked, loud as thunder. I froze by the stairs, my muscles curled so tightly they hurt. Numeen shouted – I couldn't tell the words. And then I was turning, dizzy, stretching my arms out as though I could protect these people. They stared back at me. "The window," I said, my words almost lost in my throat. I tried again. "You need to leave through the window." They turned to the window.

I'd not been quick enough. Always too slow, always a step behind.

No. Not this time. Before I could second-guess my actions, I flung myself down the stairs, taking them two at a time. When I whirled at the bottom, I had to remind myself to breathe.

Tirang stood in the ruined doorway, his claws wet with blood.

The lamp had been knocked over during the fight, the flames licking at the wall, the light shining from Numeen's bald pate. He'd been bloodied, but he stood with his hammer at the ready, his feet planted. He wasn't a fighter, though he had the strength of one. Despite his size, Tirang was at least twice his weight.

The Construct of War raised an arm.

"No!" I might as well have been a songbird, crying uselessly into the night.

Tirang's claws fell. Numeen stepped to the side, swinging the hammer and catching the construct in his ribs. Tirang grunted but seized the head of the hammer in his free hand. He shoved the weapon out of the way and buried his teeth into the blacksmith's shoulder.

The man let out a gargling cry of agony.

There were too many members of Numeen's family. They had four children and one old woman. They'd still be crawling out the window, sliding down the roof tiles, finding a way to climb the gutter to the ground.

"Hey!" I picked up a shard of wood from the ground and hurled it as hard as I could at Tirang's head. It bounced from his skull. He growled, letting Numeen go. I just had to buy them enough time.

"Lin," he said.

I'd never been the focus of attention for Tirang, not even at the times I'd most disappointed my father. It took everything I had to stand my ground as he stomped toward me, drawing his sword from his belt. I could still rewrite Tirang's commands if I moved quickly enough.

"You are not supposed to be here."

As soon as he was close, I moved, ducking beneath his sword and plunging my hand toward his torso. He dropped his sword, catching my wrists. Claws pricked my skin as I tried to wriggle free. "You are in my way." His gaze searched the ceiling as his commands sorted themselves, determining the course of action.

Numeen dragged himself to his feet, took a few trembling steps to the street. Blood fountained from his shoulder.

The breath left me as Tirang flung me to the side. Hard enough to hurt. Hard enough to bruise.

But his wrath, it seemed, was not for me.

"Stop!" My voice was not my father's. Tirang did not heed it. He picked up his sword again.

Numeen heard him coming. He swung the hammer. It went wide.

Tirang thrust his sword into the blacksmith's body, quick and efficient. He pulled the blade free without even giving Numeen a second glance, already moving out the door and on to his next task.

My fault. My tongue was numb and tingling. I tasted blood. "Wait." I had to try twice to get myself to my feet. Everything hurt.

I stumbled to the doorway, but Tirang had already disappeared.

"Please!" I wasn't sure who I was begging. I tripped over a cobblestone, catching myself on the wall of the house. I spat a mouthful of blood onto the ground. My ears rang. Someone screamed.

There had to be a way. There still had to be a way. I turned the corner of the house.

I believed it until I saw the blood. Until I saw the broken bodies.

Numeen's wife. His brother and his brother's husband. His mother. His nephew. His sons. I knelt by Thrana's small body.

She still held the paper crane in her hand, the blood from her slit throat spattering the wings with red. I picked it up. My need had always felt desperate. It had always felt greater than theirs. Bile crept up my throat, a bitter taste on the back of my tongue.

I'd been lying to myself.

"You couldn't have saved them."

Father. The sick in my throat turned to frozen slush.

Did I dare turn around? Did I even dare to face him? Somehow, I gathered the shreds of my courage. He didn't look angry, or even disappointed.

"Your work with Mauga and Uphilia was good. You almost succeeded with Ilith. But her commands are complicated, and although you studied hard, I have studied for a lifetime. Ilith is one of my finest creations."

Hot tears rolled down my cheeks, and I couldn't find the strength to dash them away. "You didn't have to kill them."

"I did. They were traitors to the Empire."

It was as simple as that to him.

"Ilith isn't my finest creation though." He watched my face as though looking for something. When he didn't find it, he gave a short nod and held out his hands. "If you rewrite the commands in a construct, the commands must still all remain in harmony. They still have to make sense together. Having a command out of balance is like removing a block of bricks at the bottom of a tower. The tower begins to teeter and sometimes to fall. Likewise, a construct will fall apart if its commands are out of balance."

"Bayan." I picked up the paper crane and stood to face my father. I was going to tear him apart with my own two hands if I had to. He'd have to make Tirang kill me.

"Yes," Father said. He strode forward with his cane, his limp pronounced. One, two, *three* – the pattern echoed from the walls of Numeen's house. He stood before me, and even leaning on his cane he towered over me. He must have been fearsome in his youth. "But even Bayan was not my greatest creation."

The sickness. No one had brought the sickness with them because it hadn't been real. My memories. The ones I didn't have.

He's growing things down there, Lin. He's growing . . . people.

I fought against the horror clawing its way out of my belly. It curdled in my throat as a scream, but I didn't scream. I was Lin. I was the Emperor's daughter. I didn't want it to be true.

"You're still not quite perfect."

And then something struck the back of my head.

36

Phalue

Nephilanu Island

The cell was cold and damp, though not as bad as Ranami had seemed to think it would be. Phalue shifted on the cot and drummed her fingers against the wood. She hadn't "sorted things out" with her father as she'd thought she might. Her father, who had always seemed as warm and indolent as a dry season afternoon, had been cold when the guards had brought her before him.

"What's this I've heard about you showing up at one of my caro nut farms? You didn't say you wanted to visit." He'd sat at the end of the dining-hall table, hands clasped in front of him, no food or drink upon its surface. "You said you were going out for the afternoon with Ranami. Did she go with you?"

Phalue shook her head. She wasn't going to implicate Ranami in this as well, no matter how angry with her she might be. Despite Ranami's protestations that Phalue just didn't understand, she understood that Ranami would suffer far worse consequences. "It was only me."

Her father had only frowned. "Four boxes of nuts were stolen on the farm the day you showed up. Nothing else changed. And though the foreman was reluctant to tell me, he said you led them on a fruitless chase into the forest after nonexistent bandits. What am I to think?"

"Are you accusing me of having stolen from you?" It wasn't hard to sound incredulous. "Why would I do that?"

"I don't know," he'd said in a tone that let Phalue know he was indeed accusing her. "I can't figure it out. I've let you run about freely for too long – going out into the city to see your mother, learning how to spar and now running around the caro nut farms. You're not the governor yet, Phalue."

She hadn't been able to help herself. She'd laughed. Perhaps if she'd kept her mouth shut, if she'd just continued to act bewildered, she wouldn't be in this mess. But she'd laughed. "Father, you don't do any of those things, and you are the governor."

He'd nodded to the guards. "Think things over, sweet. Just not here."

And now she was sitting in the bowels of the palace, just a left turn from the wine cellar, bored and angry with herself. She wasn't even sure what she was angry with herself about – whether it was for falling in with the rebels and Ranami's schemes, or if it was for getting caught, or if it was for just being who she was. She'd never asked to be heir. Phalue wondered if her mother had heard. Her mother would be furious with her father, but after the divorce she was only a commoner. There wouldn't be much she could do.

Footsteps sounded from beyond the cell. There weren't any windows down here; just the dim light of a lantern hanging by the door, so Phalue couldn't be sure of the time. Time for break-fast? Or was it lunch? It didn't really matter, she supposed.

Tythus opened the door, carrying with him a large, steaming bowl.

Phalue sat up. "Breakfast?" she hazarded a guess.

"Lunch," Tythus said. He eyed the tiny slot at the bottom of the cell door, sighed and pulled the ring of keys from his belt. He unlocked the cell and handed the bowl to Phalue.

Noodles swimming in a seafood broth topped with steamed vegetables. The smell brought back aching memories of being a child, drinking soup with her mother while the rain pattered on the roof. She'd forgotten what a wet season was like. "What, no ginger?" Phalue said, her expression wry.

Tythus snorted out a short laugh, but his face quickly sobered. The air down here was oppressive. Phalue studied his face as he left the cell and locked the bars behind him again. No. It wasn't the damp and the chill. Scratches marked the stone beneath the slot at the bottom of the cell door as though someone had slid food along that path over and over. "I'm not the first prisoner you've attended to, am I?"

"You're the most lavishly treated," he said. And then he shook his head. "Forget I said that. You're the heir. It's your right."

The soup no longer smelled appetizing. Of course the cell wasn't as bad as Ranami had feared – because this cell wasn't for Ranami. Phalue glanced around and noticed things she hadn't before. The straw on the floor of the cell was freshly laid. The sheets on the cot were soft beneath her fingers. Even the cot itself felt like someone had added an extra layer of padding. She had the odd, dizzying feel of being back in that warehouse of people, beds fastened one on top of the other, the smells of human bodies packed too closely. The cell was spacious in comparison. Always, always – things were better for her. Even when she'd been born. Her mother had been a commoner, but no matter how fiercely she'd held to that part of her origins, she'd still been born to nobility. Her sparring, her relationship with Ranami, her jaunts into the city had all fooled her into thinking she was worldly, that she was not like her father.

Yet here she sat, accused of thievery, upon fine linen sheets and with a bowl of soup from the palace kitchens. It was as though she were playacting at being a prisoner. And wasn't she? What would her father do to her, his only heir? This was merely a thing meant to frighten her, to bring her in line. When he felt she'd spent enough time here, he would bring her back into the light with an admonishment not to do it again.

Tythus had turned to the door.

"Wait," Phalue said. She set the bowl on the floor.

Even this command, from a prisoner, he obeyed.

"Tell me about the others you've attended. Who were they?" No, that wasn't the right question. They hadn't wandered into these cells of their own accord. She tried again before Tythus could answer. "What did my father do to them?"

"Mostly they tried to steal from him. Like you." He leaned against the wall, putting a cheek to the bars. He let out a sigh. "Are you sure you want to know?"

"Please."

So he told her about the ragged men and women brought here and kept in these cells. People who thought the governor's rules over land ownership were unfair. People who'd tried to make things a little more fair for themselves and their families. Of course they weren't given linens; they weren't given cots at all. They slept on the straw and were given small trays of old, cracking rice. It didn't matter what they ate really, because if their families couldn't pay restitution, they were hanged. Tythus had helped to throw the bodies into a ditch in the forest at night, so as not to disturb her father's guests.

"How often does this happen?" Phalue asked. It must have been raining again outside, because behind her the ceiling had begun to drip.

"Often enough. Very few of them can pay. That's why they stole in the first place."

Phalue shifted in her seat, feeling her bones creak as she moved. The soup on the floor still steamed. It felt like an age had passed, not little enough time that her food would still be warm. "You don't agree with the way my father does things, but you still carry out his orders."

"I'm not proud of myself," Tythus said, and Phalue had never seen his expression so strained. "I have family too though. If I stopped doing my job, they would suffer. My father was a caro nut farmer, and I told myself I wouldn't follow that path. So I worked hard and became a palace guard instead. There aren't a lot of choices for those of us not lucky enough to be born into other families. Yes, sometimes the merchants and craftsmen are without children and adopt others to carry on their trade. But this is such a slim chance. The guard seemed a more sure thing for me."

It startled Phalue to realize that she'd never known about Tythus's father. In fact, she knew nothing about Tythus's family. She searched her memories. Despite all the times they'd sparred, Tythus had always been the one to ask after her relationships, what new woman she was chasing, the troubles she was having with Ranami. She'd not thought to ask him the same questions in return. Her stomach turned. This was his job – sparring with her, listening to her. "I didn't know," Phalue said, her voice quiet. "About your father. Or your family."

He gave her a lopsided, rueful smile. "It's not your place to know."

She squeezed her eyes shut, wishing she could go back, that she could do things differently. "I don't care what my *place* is. I'm supposed to be your friend. Friends know these things about each other. I just didn't care enough to find out. I mean, I cared. I just didn't care *enough*."

"I know you help the orphans when you go out into the city. You're a good woman. Don't be too hard on yourself."

Phalue curled her fingers into the soft linens of her cot. "If I'm not hard on myself, who will be? You? My father?"

Tythus shrugged, his lips pursed, his gaze on the leaking ceiling. "Ranami."

She laughed. Yes, Ranami had been pushing the issue for almost as long as they'd been together. Urging her to see the others around her, to open her eyes to the suffering of the farmers here. "Yes, well there's her if no one else."

"Did you patch things up with her?" Tythus asked, as though they were still sparring in the courtyard.

"Not enough. I was good enough to get her. I don't know if I'm good enough yet to keep her. I'm trying, but the way she wants me to go is muddy and full of thorns. I'm not used to it." It would be easier to go back to the way she'd been, to forget what she'd seen at the farms, to use all the same justifications her father did. She'd told herself that her life had been hard. That she'd worked for what she had. That she'd earned it. But this would be the hardest thing she'd ever done. She swung her legs around on the edge of the bed to face Tythus. She forced down the voice in the back of her mind that screamed at her to leave everything be, to continue on as if nothing had happened. She took the way of thorns. "If it came down to me and my father, which of us would you choose?"

"You." He said it seriously, with no hesitation.

"And the others?"

"I can't say with one hundred per cent certainty, but I'd wager you as well, Phalue."

She would start making things right – with Ranami, with the world. "Unlock the door."

37

Lin

Imperial Island

My room was a prison. The balcony doors were locked. The door: locked. A little light shone in between cracks in the shutters and the doors, but for the most part the room was dark. Only two lamps, burning low. I lay in bed, my gaze on the ceiling. Something had happened down there in Ilith's lair. The last thing I knew was Ilith's face melting, and me trying to fix her. I strained to remember, but it was like trying to get a fishing line free from the rocks. Each tug only served to lodge the memory deeper from my reach.

No. There had been more. I looked to my hand, still clenched, hoping somehow that it had been a dream. But when I opened my fingers, Thrana's bloody crane stared back at me. I didn't know what hurt more – the guilt or the loss. Father had killed them, but I'd led him there.

And then the gasping realization returned to me: I was something he'd *made*.

It explained so much: how I didn't remember before five years ago, my memories of the chrysanthemum-ceilinged room upon waking. I lifted my hands in front of my eyes, wondering how he'd accomplished this. Bayan had said he was growing people. Not just a person. Was I not the first?

I pressed my palm into my forehead. Bayan was a construct. My father had tried to change something within him the way I'd tried to change something in Ilith. Only it had gone all wrong. And then Bayan had shown up in my room, begging me to help him and to hide him.

We were both my father's creations.

But up in Uphilia's nest, there was a record of my birth. Then again, there was also a record of my death. If I was not Lin Sukai, if I was not the Emperor's daughter, then what was I? I curled in on myself in the blankets, my belly a dark, rotting hollow. Did I have a will of my own? My father had made me for some purpose. Whatever his purpose was for me, I knew this: I did not wish to know it. I needed to get out.

I rose from the bed, though it was an effort. A heaviness lay in my chest as if I'd been weighed down with stones. Perhaps I had – what did I know of what I was? A mad laughter bubbled within me. I shoved it down, took a few deep breaths in and out. Think. Father might have made me, but I was not some halfwit. I went to the door, tried the handle again.

It was locked.

For the first time in my memory, I wished Bayan were here. We were more similar than I would have ever guessed. We could have helped one another. Perhaps I could have pried away at the shards inside of him, released him from my father's service, found a way to unlock the memories my father had erased.

The memory machine. The growing people. I needed to know the rest.

I went to the balcony door, to the shutters. Locked. All of

them. And each time I touched my hand to a door or a shutter, I could feel the weight of failure pressing in on me. I sat back on the bed, tempted to shrug off the jacket, the slippers, and to lie down again.

Maybe I'd already done this once before. I couldn't be sure.

My heel touched something. I reached down and pulled the green-bound journal from beneath the bed. I'd hidden it carelessly, but my father rarely came to my room. Unsure of what to do and too frightened to try and fix myself, I flipped through it again.

This time, new details seemed to jump out at me. The trip to the lake in the mountains. The weather had been unseasonably good, I'd written. But if I'd been sixteen, then it would have been the dry season. The weather was nearly always good in the dry season. The sea snake that had bitten me. I'd written that I'd been swimming in the bay. The first time I'd read it, I'd assumed I'd meant the harbor – but why would I write the bay when everyone referred to Imperial harbor as a harbor? And I'd made some reference to the fish my mother cooked. Why would my mother, the Emperor's consort, cook fish when she had servants to do it? I'd thought when I'd first read it that perhaps my mother enjoyed cooking and so went to the kitchen sometimes to indulge herself. All these assumptions I'd made because I'd read this journal wanting it to be some record of past memories. There hadn't been a sickness; I hadn't lost my memories. I'd only begun to form them five years ago, which was when my father must have made me.

This journal, though in my handwriting, wasn't mine. I wanted it to be mine; I wished for it with all the fierce longing of a thwarted child. Without it, I had even less an idea of who I was. But then my father had been pleased when I'd responded with the answers I'd found inside the journal. Who had written it? Who was it that my father hoped I'd be? I wanted to find out . . . but the door was locked.

I hugged the journal to my chest, hunching over the edge of the bed. My slippers and jacket felt suddenly pointless. I wasn't going anywhere.

A knock sounded at the door and then it creaked open. I shoved the journal back beneath the bed. Father hobbled into the room on his cane, a bowl of steamed rice with chicken and mustard greens in his other hand. I watched him as he went to the desk and set the food upon it. And then he looked at me and sighed. "I'm sorry it must be this way."

I kept my expression carefully neutral. "What way?"

"You must understand, by the time I figured out what to do, my wife – she was too long gone. I'd burned her body, sent her soul to the heavens. So I had to make do with what I could find. I'll find a way to fix it," he said, as though I'd said nothing at all. "My memory machine will fix you."

I wanted to scream at him. What was he talking about? Was *making* me something he'd discussed with his late wife? The only thing that needed fixing was what he'd broken within me back in Imperial's streets. I tried another question. "Why won't you let me go?"

A flicker passed across his face like the shadowy wings of a moth. "You shouldn't have done that – rewriting my constructs. You did well. I didn't notice until after Uphilia. That was when I knew you'd go for Ilith. But Ilith is complicated. You still almost managed it. It will take me some time to fix her properly." He looked me in the eye and even in that moment I couldn't hate him.

He'd broken other things in me before he'd killed Numeen and his family. This time I didn't care if he saw the sorrow on my face. "I wanted you to be proud of me. The way a father would be proud of his daughter. I have done everything you've asked. I've done more than you've asked. And still you favored Bayan over me."

He turned my desk chair around and lowered himself into it. The woven reeds of the seat creaked at his weight. He waved a dismissive hand as though all my years of grief were a thing to be wafted away like smoke. "You always did better with competition. And you see, I was right. You found a way to steal from me. You found a way to learn the things I'd forbidden you. You learned them better than Bayan."

He'd known. All the times I'd thought I'd been clever, that I'd found a way around his rules, he had been watching me, silently approving. My stomach dropped.

He was watching me, nodding as though he knew what I was thinking. "You, I can forgive, as long as we get your memories fixed and get the proper ones in there. You've gotten better, but you're not quite there yet. But those who helped you had to pay the price."

My head ached and my eyes burned. All of my resolve to give him nothing, to show him none of my feelings, drowned in the tide of my anger. "And Bayan? Have you killed him too?"

"Why would I do that? He's not the final version, but he's useful." He rose abruptly and strode over to me, his cane tapping against the floor.

I clenched my hands into fists. I should have punched him, I should have wrapped my small hands around his neck. But I couldn't. I sat on the bed and just watched him, hoping he read the anger in my eyes.

"Lin," he said, and he reached out a hand to touch my cheek.

I hated myself for leaning into his touch. All I'd wanted was his approval, his love. I'd wanted to feel like a daughter, like part of a family. But there was something strange in his touch, the way his fingers trailed across my cheek.

"I'm so sorry it has to be this way."

"Why did you have to kill them? They never hurt you." I thought of Numeen's hesitation to help me, his quick hands at the forge, the way he'd brought me into his home and let me eat dinner with the people he cared about the most. All of that was gone because of me. Because of my father. "I hate you." The words were like fire on my tongue, roiling out from the furnace that was my belly.

"No, you don't, little one." The tenderness in his voice confused me, extinguishing the other words I might have said and leaving my tongue only tasting ash.

He turned to leave, and I let him. I couldn't reconcile my feelings with my inability to move, to do anything. I was like a doll who laments the way a child moved her limbs. And then the door shut, and I was up from the bed. I was running to the door; I was pounding my fists against it. The skin on my hands numbed and the bones beneath ached. I should have hit him. I should have killed him.

At last I sagged, cradling my fists in my lap. The right memories? What to my father were the right memories?

The journal. The memories in there from what I'd thought was my younger self. Someone had hidden the journal in the library, and it hadn't been my father. Not many people would have had access to the library. My father, Bayan, the constructs. I thought back farther to a time before I existed.

I went for the journal again, my fingers trembling so hard I could barely open it. Somewhere, there had to be another clue; I just hadn't bothered to look closely enough. I peeled through every page. And then I noticed, on the back cover, the edge of paper glued to it. The corner was curled up a little, loose. I tugged at it, peering beneath.

Someone had tucked another piece of paper there. I pulled it free and unfolded it.

*They look at me and all they see is a young
girl of unremarkable beauty. But they're all
wrong about me. Someday I will be more than
this. Someday, the world will know me. Nisong
will rise.*

I dropped the secret note. I knew the name, though I knew it in conjunction with another. Nisong. Nisong Sukai.

My mother.

Bile mixed into the taste of my tears. I remembered the sad condition of my father's room, how he wouldn't let the servants touch any of her things. He never wanted to talk to me about my mother. He'd had all the portraits of her destroyed. I'd thought him fueled by grief, but now I could glean other motives. They explained his experiments, the way he'd shut out human advisers and most of his staff.

He hadn't discussed the making of me with his wife; he was trying to make me *into* his wife. He must have used that memory machine on me, hoping somehow to instill me with my mother's memories. I wasn't his daughter. She'd died, just as the records said. Of course he'd never loved me. I was a vessel for someone else – a secret, an experiment.

I curled into a ball and wept.

38

Jovis

Nephilanu Island

I'd never thought this would be my end: confined on all four sides by wood and stone. I'd always thought my end would come to me on the open ocean, by a storm, the arrows of Imperial soldiers or a knife between the shoulder-blades from the Ioph Carn. But I suppose death, like life, often doesn't meet expectations.

I couldn't seem to stop staring at the governor's face, feeling that there was something familiar about it. His broad cheek-bones, generous lips, even his deep-set eyes. He looked bleary and worn, his chin dappled with stubble. And then I wondered if his face would be the last thing I saw before I died. Gio wasn't much better – glaring at me as though I'd somehow betrayed him. I looked to the floorboards. Even the grain of wood was a more welcome sight. The guard holding me shifted as he drew a dagger from his belt.

And then I felt a tremor within my bones.

It was like being slapped in the chest with the force of a storm gale. My limbs vibrated with the energy. A moment ago I'd felt weak, helpless. Now I knew I could throw off this man as easily as I might discard a cloak.

And again, I felt a sharp awareness of all the water in the room, down to the sweat on the guards' faces.

Mephi – he must have awoken.

I ducked forward, and the hands holding me ripped away. I heard a *thunk* as his dagger dropped, embedding itself into the floorboards behind me. In one fluid movement, I bent a knee, sweeping my staff up from the floor. I didn't stop, turning the staff in my hands, smashing an end of it into the guard that was holding Gio. I used more force than I'd intended. Her feet lifted from the ground, and Gio went with her.

No time to worry about him.

I felt the air move as the third guard rushed to stop me. I ducked beneath his swing and heard the blade sink into the wood pillar behind me. He yanked at the hilt, trying to pull it free. He'd swung hard enough to part my head from my shoulders. My head was stubborn. He was right to think freeing it would take a good deal of force.

As soon as the guard who'd been holding me recovered, he drew his sword. I sidestepped his slash, stepped within his guard and took his blade from his hand. Just a strike to the wrist with one hand – a tap, really – and his fingers opened. It was like plucking overripe fruit from a branch.

I kicked at the guard still trying to get his sword free, sending him flying to the other side of the room. He went down and didn't get up.

The governor still stood in the doorway, his fingers tight around the doorknob. The whites of his eyes shown clear around his irises. His chest heaved, straining against the ties of his robe. "What are you?"

"A smuggler," I said. "The Empire made posters of me."

Apparently my answer set him not at all at ease because he opened the door to run.

I hesitated, feeling like a dog who'd caught the cart he'd been barking after. I must have looked to him like some avenging monster, my trimmed hair still curling in the heat and humidity, frizzing about my face. "Don't move," I said to him. What did Gio want me to do with the man? He'd said we were to assassinate the governor's guards. He hadn't said what came after that. Gio was still lying on the ground, struggling to free himself from the unconscious embrace of the guard. He straightened, and I watched as he picked up one of his daggers.

The governor froze.

Of course. No coup was bloodless. In the silence, I heard one of the governor's personal guards groan. One, at least, was still alive. And then there were footsteps, fast approaching.

A woman appeared in the doorway, alone. I recognized her by the broadness of her shoulders if nothing else. Ranami's lover. What was she doing here?

Her gaze lowered to the governor. Before I could say anything, she was rushing forward. I thought at first that she meant to kill him, but she knelt at his side. "Father, are you hurt?"

Father? Ranami's lover was the governor's daughter? Now what Ranami had said earlier about having heard the governor's heir was a good woman made sense. She hadn't heard such – she'd felt such. Whether or not her feelings were a reflection of the truth remained to be seen.

"That man is trying to kill me, Phalue," he said, his voice hysterical.

I said nothing, only lowered my staff, hoping Phalue would take my meaning. She glanced at me and then back to her father.

"Protect me," he said, grasping at her tunic.

She smoothed his hair from his forehead with the tenderness of a mother with her child. "I'll protect you. Don't worry. No one will hurt you."

"Then . . ." He looked from me to his daughter and back again. "Then why aren't you doing anything?"

"I am doing something. I'm letting the Shardless Few depose you."

His face went pale. "You're my daughter," he sputtered. "Are you betraying me?"

"I'm sorry." She didn't seem to know what else to say.

The beat of many approaching footsteps sounded. I stepped to the side, out of the way. I was an observer in this, nothing else. More than anything, I wanted to get back to the caves to see what had happened with Mephi.

A horde of men and women appeared in the doorway. Some wore armor but most were in only their clothes, with knives and staves in hand. It was a ragged army. What they lacked in finesse, they made up for in numbers.

Ranami pushed past them. When she saw Phalue, she hesitated.

"I'm taking over the governorship," Phalue said to her father. "It's time."

While everyone was focused on the governor and his daughter, I watched Gio. He'd slipped his knife back into its sheath but I could see the line between his brows. This hadn't been his plan. Phalue wasn't supposed to be here. She was supposed to be imprisoned. A prickle ran up my spine, settling in at the back of my neck. I'd wager anything that one of Gio's rebels was heading to the palace prison right at this moment, a dagger in hand.

Before I could stop myself, I was taking a step toward Phalue and her father, my hand on my staff, setting myself between them and the rebels. It was only one step, but Gio noticed. "It appears Nephilanu has a new governor," I said, because both Ranami and Phalue seemed distracted. Someone had to force the issue before Gio could find a way to spin this. The people behind Gio cheered.

"Round up the survivors," Gio told them. He fixed me with a glare before turning to help them. Oh, the rebel leader would try again, I was sure, but for now he had no choice.

"Take my father to the prison," Phalue said to the soldier standing in the doorway. "Treat him as well as I was treated."

I hazarded a guess that was well indeed, but any prison would be a vast downgrade for this man. Even the bed in this room was elaborately carved, the windows hung with richly embroidered curtains. He was used to his comforts.

As soon as he'd been led from the room, Ranami went to her. "I thought you were imprisoned."

Phalue took Ranami's face in her hands and kissed her cheek. "I was. But it gave me time to think. Tythus let me out."

Ranami buried her face in Phalue's chest, holding her close. "I'm just glad you're out. That everything still happened as planned."

Not quite as planned, but this wasn't any place to tell her that. I gave Gio one last glance and then tapped Ranami's arm. I was nearly done here – I could go back to the rebel hideout and check on Mephi. My boat was still hidden in the harbor nearby, ready for me to take it out to sea. The Ioph Carn would still be looking for me, and each day the blue-sailed boat traveled farther away. "I'm sorry to interrupt, but I've done what I've promised. I believe you have information for me."

Ranami gave Phalue's arm a reassuring squeeze and then turned to me. "Yes, though I warn you it may not be what you expected."

"I don't care." I didn't. I'd done what she'd asked. I'd done what those men and women had asked, rescuing their children. There had to be something at the end of this road, some reward.

"The boat made landfall at Maila according to reports we've received."

My mind went blank. Maila was on the north-eastern edge of the Empire. It would take weeks to get there. I'd only been on this island for three days, and I'd been sure I was close. "That's impossible."

"It's not an ordinary boat," Ranami said. "And there may be two of them. We're not sure. But what we are sure of is that one of them is moored at Maila."

I'd heard the stories. Maila was surrounded by jagged reefs. No one went there, though every Imperial navigator knew where it was – so they could avoid it. Why would a boat land there? Why would *this* boat land there? What she'd said finally registered. "What do you mean it's not an ordinary boat?"

"There are stories. I don't know how true they are, but it's said the boat is made from the wood of a cloud juniper."

"Don't tell me lies; you owe me the truth." Yet when I looked at her I couldn't detect any falsehood. Cloud junipers were all under the care of the cloudtree monks. Cutting one down would be more than just blasphemous. It meant incurring the wrath of an entire religious order. Either the boat was older than the monks or there had been a cloud juniper they hadn't known about. Around us, the rebels moved, pulling the curtains from the window, taking the gilt vases from the floor. Phalue directed them, going through the room and searching out its needless luxuries. I struggled to think.

"You have no reason to trust me," Ranami admitted. "But I have no reason to lie."

Maila. I didn't even know if I could make it past those reefs. I had to try.

"Wait," Ranami said as I turned to leave. "I have another choice to offer you."

I should have left; I should have told her to keep her words behind her lips. But maybe a part of me was tired and scared, and the thought of sailing all the way to Maila made my bones ache. I didn't know what I'd find. I stopped.

"Help us. This island isn't the end of things. We can't just take back our freedoms here. We need to end the Empire if we're ever to all be free. No more constructs, no more trepanning, no more fear of enemies that will never return."

"It's not my fight."

"The woman you search for – how long has it been?"

I squeezed my eyes shut, feeling anger rise within. "It doesn't matter."

"It's been years, hasn't it? If she was taken by that boat, she's not coming back. No one comes back, Jovis."

"And what would you have me do?" She didn't hear the warning in my tone.

"Go to the heart of the Empire. Infiltrate the palace. If you have any hope of finding out what's happened to her, you'll find it there. That boat goes to Maila – it always ends there – but it goes to Imperial too."

"So I help you overthrow an island's governor, and now you want me to go to Imperial and spend whoever knows how long there so you can overthrow an Empire. What's in it for me? Life satisfaction?" She started to speak, but I raised my voice to speak over her. "You're no different from the Empire or the Ioph Carn. You all use people to get what you want. You might even think you have noble motives. But what I want, what I've always wanted, was just to find Emahla and bring her home. What care have you for that when you have your ideals?"

Ranami pursed her lips, her expression pained. "I'd care about it more if it were a thing that was possible. But you can't bring the dead back home."

"Don't speak of her as though she is dead!" I brought my foot down on the floorboards. The tremor I hadn't even realized had been building inside of me released. It radiated out from me like the ripple in a pond. It toppled everyone in the room to the floor.

Phalue rushed to Ranami's side to help her up.

Easy enough for her to make these sorts of plans when she had the one she loved with her. She had a life to build here, a purpose. She didn't know what it was like to exist with a hole where a person had once been.

I strode from the room and no one stopped me.

The city was changed from when I'd set out that morning. Word had traveled quickly, it seemed. Revelers filled the streets by light of lanterns; merchants passed out free cakes, even to the gutter orphans. I wondered how festive they would be when they realized that changing rulers didn't mean the end to all problems. Not that I could fault them for it.

It was well into the night by the time I made it back to the rebels' cave. I rushed through the opening, squeezing through so quickly that my shirt ripped. "Mephi!"

I thought he would still be in the main hall, stretched out by the fire. Instead, he came scampering up to me like he'd never been at death's door. He pushed his head beneath my hand, twining around my legs, his tail wrapping around my waist. I dropped to my knees and wrapped my arms around his shoulders. "I thought you might die."

He tolerated my hug for a moment before squirming away from me. "Good?" he said.

I gave him one last scratch around the ears. "We're leaving."

39

Sand

Maila Isle, at the edge of the Empire

The branches of the mango tree spread overhead like the canopy of an umbrella. Sand studied the leaves, the wan sunlight filtering through, the sound of rain pattering against their broad surfaces. She knew the exact juncture she'd fallen from. The rest was hazy. Somewhere along the way she'd cut her arm on a branch or on the bark. She walked around the perimeter of the tree. Something had changed here, and it hadn't been just the cut. Sand had been hurt before, they all had. There was something else.

Dead leaves gathered at the base. She kicked at them and they stuck to her sandaled feet. A few steps away, a mango rotted on the ground.

A flash of white caught her eye. There, near the rotting mango. Sand went to it, knelt. It was wedged in a small puddle; it had been raining frequently these past days. She reached into the water and plucked it from the mud. It was the size of her thumbnail, though longer and narrower. It could have just been a piece of rock, but when she brought it up to her eyes and wiped away the mud with her shirt, there were markings on it. Scratches?

No. Writing.

Her fingers trembling a little, she held it up to the gash in her arm. They were the same length.

"Sand." Shell stood several paces away, a spear in his hand. "Coral thinks she saw sails on the horizon. It's time. Leaf is gathering the others."

Sand rose to her feet, pocketing the shard. "Everyone knows the plan?"

"The net is in place. We're ready."

Not that it would matter if they were not. The boat was coming, and they didn't know when it would come again, or if they would still be free of the fog that always threatened to cloud their minds. Sand felt for the knife at her belt. It wasn't a spear, but it was all she had. "Let's go."

They left the mango grove behind. In the distance, a low rumble of thunder sounded. The rain was light and Sand knew it wouldn't turn into a real storm for some time yet. She'd lived a life with memories and her own purposes. She wasn't sure how long it had been or what had happened to her to lead her here to Maila, but sometimes when she was still and thinking, a memory would wend its way through her mind. That dining hall with its vast ceiling. The murals. The cloud juniper doors and the tall, handsome man in his silk robes. Heat rose up her neck as she followed Shell through the trees. She'd known that man intimately. And he hadn't only loved her, he had shown her things – secret things.

The memories hadn't made clear exactly what. But she had to believe there was a life for her away from Maila. A man like that wouldn't want an ugly woman of no importance like Sand, but perhaps ... ? Perhaps they had once meant something to one another.

"Are you all right?" Shell asked.

She'd fallen far behind, lost in her own thoughts. She hurried to catch up. Now of all times was not the moment to get caught up in dreams and memories. They had this one chance to take the ship, and she was mooning about. "I'm fine."

The sound of their footsteps faded into the rain drumming against the forest canopy, the high, sharp calls of birds. Hope had tightened her throat. She swallowed past it. "Shell, have you ever had memories of a life before this?"

"No," he said. He used the butt of his spear to shove a branch aside.

A little part of Sand withered. Perhaps she was mad.

A few more steps, and Shell cleared his throat. "But I've had dreams. I suppose they could be memories if they were real. But what's real here?"

"I don't know." Her hand snaked into her pocket, closing around the shard with the strange writing.

"I don't remember much of them. But sometimes, when I wake up, I have this impression. It's like staring at a sunset for too long and then looking away. You can still see it on your eyelids." He took in a deep breath, climbed up a rock. "For me, I think I smell fresh ginger. And I feel this warmth on my hands, like I'm near a fire. There's this comfort in my heart and in my bones. I think it's a man and a woman that I love, and they're both with me. There's a child." He shook his head, and his lank hair dripped. "I don't know any more than that. I don't know where I am, what I do for a living, what their names are, what *my* name is. How can I think of it as any more than just a dream?"

"Mine are different," Sand said. Shell's recollection might be a painting of a few brush strokes, but hers were like the scenes of a play. "I don't know my name, but I see everything as though through my own eyes." She wasn't sure how to further explain, so she didn't.

They spoke no more until they reached the cove. Leaf had found it a few days after they'd started looking. Maila was not a large island. The plan had come together after that, with a good deal of help from Coral. They couldn't be like pirates, using their numbers to storm the boat and throwing its captain overboard. Instead, they had to get what they wanted with a series of steps, like approaching a frightened animal sideways.

The first step: making sure the boat couldn't leave.

Coral, Frond and Leaf were here already, along with four others. They'd been able to clear the fog for more of the inhabitants, but most inevitably fell back into it after a day or two. Only the nine of them had been able to stave it off.

It had been enough to make the net. They'd all neglected their daily chores in order to set this trap. Coral and Frond already stood in place on the rocks, ropes in hand.

"How far off?" Sand called.

Coral pointed to the horizon. Her eyes must have been sharper than Sand's to spot it earlier, because Sand could only just make out the blue sails. "We'll have to stay hidden," Sand said to the rest of them. "Make sure they don't see us until the boat is well into the cove. On my signal, raise the net. The rest will go as we've discussed."

The others nodded. Sand went to her spot in the trees overlooking the cove. Shell went to the rocks on the beach. Coral and Frond ducked behind outcroppings. When they all were in place, the cove looked mostly undisturbed. As long as the captain of the boat didn't look too closely, they wouldn't be any the wiser until it was too late.

Sand found herself reaching into her pocket again and wrapping her fingers around the shard.

It was bone. The answer came to her all at once. Maybe it was the feel of it in her palm, but she wasn't crouched in the trees anymore, the seagrass obscuring her form.

She was in a library, shelves climbing close to the ceiling. A row of windows, high up, let in the light. The man stood in front of her, his back to her. Even without seeing his face, she knew who he was. Her heartbeat quickened. He looked upon the shelves, his hands clasped behind his back. "This is everything," he said, his voice echoing from the walls. "This is all the knowledge I have."

Memory-Sand strode to a shelf and ran a hand across the book bindings. The smell of old glue and paper rose from their spines. "I want you to teach me."

"We pass this knowledge down linearly," the man said, still not looking at her. "Father to son to daughter to son."

"Family," memory-Sand said. "Am I not now your family?" She took one creeping step toward him, and then another.

He turned to face her then, and though he gave her a forbidding look, she was not afraid. "They said I could have married more advantageously than you."

Memory-Sand felt her lips curve into a smile. "There's still time, you know. You can tell everyone you've made a mistake. Nullify the marriage. Go marry one of those dull women your advisers put before you."

He reached out a hand to touch her cheek. "You're too clever."

"As are you." She kissed the base of his throat, took his hands in hers and kissed those too. "You had to know, the way I did, that we would end up this way."

He sighed and kissed the top of her head. "My knowledge is your knowledge. And I could use the help."

"The Alanga coming back to haunt your kingdom?"

"It's not a joke, Nisong. I know people are restless with the rule of the Sukais, but there will come a day when they need us. You see the traces of them all around you and in our cities; how can you mock their existence?"

"Hush," memory-Sand said. "You know I believe you." She twined her fingers in his hair.

And then he was leaning down to kiss her, wrapping his arms around her, his warmth suffusing her. Heat and excitement electrified her veins.

A salty breeze gusted across her face, bringing with it the rain. Sand blinked. She wasn't in her husband's embrace. She was on Maila, in the forest near the cove, her knees damp from kneeling in the mud.

The blue-sailed ship was near. This close, she could see the dark wood of its deck. A cloaked figure stood near the stern, robes billowing in the wind. They didn't seem to notice the salty spray of the waves or even take heed of the rolling ocean. They moved with the boat as though they were a part of it. Sand had spoken with all the island occupants of their time at sea. All of them had vague memories of this one master of the boat and no other crew.

Sand glanced at the beach. Her compatriots were still hidden. They'd have only the one chance at this.

She watched as the boat navigated through the reefs, trying to mark its path as best she could. If they were able to commandeer it, they'd still need to breach the reef on their way out. Shell had surveyed the shoreline, and everywhere he'd looked he'd seen the reef. No wonder this was the only ship that came here. As the ship sailed into the cove, Sand quieted her thoughts. She needed to focus on what was happening here and now.

The only person visible on the entire deck was the cloaked figure. When they moved, it was all at once. Flowing from the stern to the bow, pulling on ropes, unwinding them. Sand couldn't follow the movements. It was as though the person had more than two arms and legs. At last, they heaved an anchor overboard and then disappeared below decks.

Nothing happened for a little while after that. Sand shifted in her spot in the seagrass. Her knees and back ached, but she didn't dare move too much.

The figure reappeared. This time, with others. Men and women lined up on deck. Sand felt her pulse pounding at her throat. Had that once been her, standing on that deck? Several of them stepped onto the rowboat, and the figure stepped into it after, lowering it with the pulleys into the water. Once they'd rowed to the beach, the men and women stepped out, and the cloaked figure rowed back to the boat.

The men and women stood still as statues on the beach, their gazes blank and straight ahead.

Two more trips, and then there weren't any more men and women on the deck. Sand waited until the rowboat had beached itself, her breathing shallow. And then she stood and shouted at the top of her lungs, "Now!"

Coral and Frond stood, pulling on their ropes. A net rose from the water. Both of them ran to the trees, wrapping the ropes around sturdy trunks, pulling them taut so that the net blocked the way from the cove. At the same time, two of the others ran toward the cloaked figure with a rope strung between them. The figure drew a knife from their belt, ready for an attack. But the two Maila people threw the rope over the figure and then turned to run back up the beach. The rope caught the figure just below the knees, sending them toppling to the sand. Above, on the cliff, Leaf was pushing a boulder over the side. He had his back to it so he couldn't see what was happening below.

The boulder fell.

Sand flinched. It didn't crush the master of the boat as they'd planned. But it pinned an arm to the sand. It was enough.

She rose from her spot in the seagrass and went to meet the others on the beach. The men and women the figure had brought to Maila still stood there, dressed in simple, mismatched clothes. It was downright eerie. They didn't look at her; they didn't look at one another. But as she passed them, they started to move. They walked up the beach, single file, heading toward the path.

"Should we try to wake them?" Coral asked.

Sand shook her head. "Let them go. We can try later." She knew where they would go to. The village. It was the trek they all must have taken at some point. She strode toward the boulder, unease building in her belly.

Leaf ran down from the cliff, breathless. "I meant to crush the person," he said. "But I couldn't look or else I wasn't able to move the boulder at all."

None of them could directly enact violence. "At least we were right about there being only one," Sand said. The net at the end of the cove would have stopped any others.

The hood of the cloak had fallen to the sand. The figure beneath looked like a man, though not any man Sand had ever seen. One arm was pinned, but *three* arms still lay free. They pushed at the boulder, and as she watched, the stone moved a little. "Coral," she barked out. "Sit on the boulder."

Coral, to her credit, moved to obey without asking questions.

The cloaked man grunted as she sat, and lay back on the beach. The rain had subsided to a light drizzle, and he blinked against the moisture.

"Who are you?" Sand asked.

He looked to her, his dark eyes solemn. "I am like you."

She barked out a laugh. "I don't have four arms, stranger. You brought these people here. You brought us here. Where did you come from?"

He said nothing.

Sand held back the next question and just watched him. She wanted to ask where she had come from, where all of them had come from. "Shell, can we use the rope to—?" Her throat caught. The thought caught with it. No, it seemed restraining this man was also out of the question. No violence, no restraint. What was more cruel though? Tying him up or leaving him here to die without food or drink on this beach? She held out her hand, sweating. "Give me the rope, Shell."

He handed her the rope.

It took all her concentration to tie the stranger's three remaining hands together. She had to focus on that fact – that tying these hands would allow them to remove the boulder. Every so often she had to stop to wipe the sweat from her brow and to still her trembling hands.

"Sand," Coral said from atop the boulder, "what do we do now? We have the boat; we have its captain captive."

Sand stood, her legs weak. On the horizon, the waves crashed against the reef. "We figure out how to escape." She wiped her palms against her shirt. "And call me Nisong."

40

Lin

Imperial Island

Something scratched at the shutters. I turned over in my bed, my eyes still bleary. I'd spent half the night on the floor by the door before dragging myself back to bed and crawling beneath the covers. Everything felt hopeless. My father had made me. He knew every aspect of who he wanted me to be.

My dead mother.

No, wait. She wasn't my mother. And he wasn't my father. He was the Emperor. I was Lin, but I was not the Emperor's daughter. I burrowed beneath the covers. I didn't know what I was.

The scratching sounded at the shutters again, followed by squeaking.

It was Hao, the spy construct I'd rewritten. I could see the shadow of it between the slats. Automatically, I reached for the drawer where I kept the nuts and pulled one out. Dragging myself from bed seemed easier when I was doing it for someone else. The little spy construct stopped scratching as I approached the windows. I slid the nut between the slats. Little claws tickled my fingertip as the construct took the nut.

My father would never love me in the way I wanted or needed him to. The grief of it filled me, overflowed. It felt like a wound that would never close. All my life I'd spent trying to earn his approval, and the only way I could have done so was by being someone else.

My construct outside squeaked again.

Dutifully, I retrieved another nut and fed it through the shutters. My freedom was so close. Sunlight shone through the gaps in the shutters, scattering barred light across my skin. If I could only just—

The door was locked.

Something jolted inside me. But when had I ever let that stop me? My father's room had been locked. All the doors in the palace had been locked. I'd still found my way through them. What was I doing, moping in this room? There had to be a way out.

The only thing I had to look forward to now was the Emperor "fixing" my memories, making me into some pale facsimile of his late wife. I'd lose myself anyway.

I slammed a shoulder against the door. The wood had no give to it. I tried pulling at the handle; I tried throwing a chair at it. I only managed to scratch the wood. I tried the shutters next, pulling and pushing at them, trying to break them. I pried at the wood slats until my fingers ached.

There had to be a way. There was always a way. I sat back on the bed, trying to think of a solution. I was locked in here alone, without any means to escape.

A scratching sounded at the shutters again. The spy construct, asking for another nut.

It was still there, even after I'd been flinging chairs about the room. Hope surged in my breast.

"Wait right there," I said to the spy construct.

I took another few nuts from the desk drawer. Hao would obey my commands without them, but the nuts had brought the construct back to me at this critical time. Perhaps they would provide extra incentive.

I held the nut so the construct could sniff it. "Hao, tell me how the shutters are locked."

Hao sat on its haunches, whiskers twitching, clearly confused.

I tried again. "These shutters. What is on the outside?"

"Outside the shutters is the palace, and the palace grounds, and the city, and the island—"

"Yes, I know." I squeezed my eyes shut. There had to be a better way to ask. Numeen and all his family had given their lives. They'd believed I would help them. The least I could do was to make sure they'd not died in vain. "Tell me, other than the corner furnishings and the hinges, is there anything else attached to the shutters in front of you?"

A long silence.

For a moment, I thought I'd confused the poor beast again, but then Hao spoke. "There is a bar."

I pressed my nose to the slats, trying to see it. "Can you lift it?"

The construct's shadow moved as it stretched up on its hind legs. A scratching, then a pause. "No."

"Can you bring another construct here? I have more nuts." I held my breath. My father could have ordered the constructs away from my room; he could have ordered them not to help me, but he'd never shown any construct consideration beyond issuing commands. To him, they had no free will at all.

But Hao had proven differently.

The construct didn't respond; it scurried away. I leaned my forehead against the shutters, setting the nuts in a row on the windowsill.

Did my father think I had no free will either? He'd made me. Perhaps to him, I was just like a construct. He could put me in a room and expect I'd stay there.

"Back." Hao's nose nudged at the shutters. Another, larger shadow was next to it. I caught a glimpse of brown fur and black, shiny eyes through the slats in the shutters.

"Hello," I said to the other construct. "Do you want a nut?" I held one just out of reach. Its little claws scrabbled at the wood, its whiskers twitching as it sniffed. "All you have to do is help Hao here lift the bar on the shutters."

The creature sat back on its haunches.

But I'd done this before. "What harm can it do? You've not been commanded to leave the bar alone. Just this one task and I'll give you five nuts. That's a bargain, don't you think?"

It didn't move toward the bar, but it didn't run away either.

"Six nuts?"

One more nut was all it took to tip the scales in my favor. Both constructs reached for the bar. The wood squeaked as they pushed it out of place, the shutters pushing inward briefly.

And then the bar was free and I opened the shutters. The cool, damp air had never felt so good against my face. My little spy construct leapt inside. I counted out six nuts for the other construct and watched as it stuffed them into its cheeks. There was power beyond that carved out by commands. Shiyen might have created me, but he didn't *know* me.

I gathered my things, half-formed plans running through my head. I couldn't take my father on alone. Even unlocking his doors I'd needed help. He had too many constructs – watching, guarding the walls, awaiting his orders. My father might not have truly known me, but I knew him. He'd had no doubt he could keep me in my room. He wouldn't have moved right away to fix Mauga and Uphilia; they still worked after all, and he had Ilith to repair. And me. His broken wife. If I was right about him, I still had Mauga and Uphilia. I had my little spy. I tucked the engraving tool into my sash pocket. They wouldn't be enough. But there was someone else who might help me.

I started to second-guess my plan when I was clinging to the roof tiles, a light drizzle beading on my eyelashes. Ahead of me, the spy construct sprang to the peak of the roof as though it were merely out for an afternoon stroll. I'd sent Hao through the halls of the palace, but there were simply too many servants and constructs this time of day to make my journey safely. Not that this was any safer.

When at last I slid off the roof and onto a balcony, my arms were ready to give way. This was the right room. I just had to hope he was here.

I rapped on the door lightly. It swung open.

Bayan's handsome face greeted me. Although, by his sour expression, "greeted" was a stretch of the word. "What are you doing here? Are you here to rifle through my things again?" He wrinkled his nose and glanced up. "Did you climb here?"

"No, idiot, I flew." I pushed past him into his room. Did I have to rebuild that fragile foundation we'd begun to form together?

He stared at me for a moment, but then closed the door.

"What do you remember?" I asked him.

"More than you."

I clenched my fists in frustration. "No. You don't get to do that. Not right now. I just spent the whole morning convincing constructs to act against their nature, and trying to figure out what it is the Emperor has done to me."

"You . . . what?"

"Do you remember the library? The Emperor striking you in the dining hall? The cloud juniper?"

His face, which had been a mask of contempt, crumpled. "Yes."

I closed my eyes, relief making me weak. I sank onto a nearby chair. "And after that?" The agony on his face told me all I needed to know. "You can tell me," I said, my voice low and soft. "We're not enemies, I promise."

He gave me a hopeless look. "There's a gap. I don't know what happened that night. I thought – maybe the sickness is coming back. Maybe I never really beat it."

"It's not the sickness. It never was." I couldn't think of how else to explain it to him, so I rose to my feet. I put a hand to his chest and felt his heartbeat below my palm, rapid and strong. "Try to relax. I'm not going to hurt you." Slowly, I pushed my fingers inside.

He went still, but by the way his panicked eyes held mine, I knew he could push past the stillness if he really tried. "How are you doing this?" He choked out the words.

I stepped away, hands held up, palms toward him. "Because we weren't born, Bayan. We were made. He made us. The night you don't remember? I found you in my room." The skin peeling away from his eyes, the sagging, lumpy flesh. "You were falling apart. He'd tried to change something in you, but he'd done it wrong."

"What's wrong with you? That's madness. A person can't fall apart." Despite his words, his face was still pale.

"A construct can."

He scoffed. "I'm not a construct." But he didn't sound sure when he said it. He waited for me to say something else. When I didn't, he waved a dismissive hand at me. "And what? You're a construct too?"

I met his gaze and held it. "He said he grew me. I don't know what that means."

He peered into my face. "You're serious."

"Why would I lie about something like that? You told me he

was growing people, that night you came to my room for help. You think I want to be something he's made? The Emperor wants me to replace his dead wife. He made me for that purpose. If I wanted to lie, I'd come up with a better lie, one I'd actually want to be true. Like my father named me his one true heir only a moment ago. I've come climbing over the rooftops to tell you." Perhaps it was a trifle sharper than I'd intended, but there simply wasn't time.

"If you're so clever, why'd he make me?"

I threw up my hands. "That's your business, not mine. Don't you have any clues? Has he said anything to you?"

Bayan stared at me, and I could see the panic lurking in his widened eyes, the tremor at the corner of his lips. "Only that I could be the heir if I tried hard enough. That I might one day replace him."

More pieces clicked together in my mind. "No," I said. "That's terrible." But I'd thought him and Bayan so alike. And now I could see the similarities in their faces – the high cheekbones, full lips, large, dark eyes. Oh, he had meant what he'd said. A replacement.

He bristled. "My ruling as Emperor would be terrible? For you, perhaps."

He didn't remember. "Bayan, he has a machine. It puts memories into your head. It must have worked better for you than for me. But he didn't give you his own memories, not yet. He gave you someone else's. He doesn't want you to rule as Emperor. He wants to rule as Emperor, for ever, in the body he's made for this purpose."

Bayan whirled away from me, pacing the length of his room and then back. "This is a trick meant to distract me from my goals."

I stuffed down my own panic. I had to convince him. "If I was trying to trick you, don't you think I would tell you something a little more believable? Think about the gaps in your memories. You know I'm telling the truth."

He collapsed onto his bed, his shoulders slumped, his fingers pressed to his temples.

Shiyen would have pressed harder, would have demanded that Bayan face the truth. But I wasn't the Emperor. "I laid in bed, useless, after I figured it out," I said softly. "I know I'm asking a lot of you, more than I asked of myself."

I watched him breathe, the rest of him unmoving, hoping he wouldn't turn against me. And then he glanced at me from beneath the curtain of his hair, giving me a weak smile. "But how high a standard is that really?" To his credit, he straightened – absorbing the information and standing against it. "What do we do to stop him?"

I wanted to weep with relief. I wouldn't do this alone. "I've taken two of his constructs. I think we can take the last two if we work together."

My spy construct sat on the bed next to me, alert, awaiting my instructions. I'd not told it to wait there. A made thing could grow and change beyond its original purposes.

I would show the Emperor: I'd grown beyond mine.

41

Jovis

Nephilanu Island

I knelt and packed my things in the room the rebels had assigned to me, heedless of any questioning looks. I had to get out of here. I had to get to Maila. Emahla might be there even now, looking out over the horizon, waiting for me to come for her. What would I tell her? That I'd given up for a time? That I'd fallen in with the Ioph Carn? There was nothing I could do to make it up for her except to rescue her.

Mephi pushed his head beneath my hand. "Calm, Jovis. I am here."

Without even thinking, I stroked his head, moving my fingers to scratch behind his ears. His words were clearer than they'd been before he'd fallen ill. My fingers stilled. The shiny nubs on his skull had been replaced with two budding horns. Only now did I notice that Mephi had not come out of his illness unchanged. He was taller, his face and legs longer. His tail had become bushier, the webbing between his digits more distinct.

I swiveled on the balls of my feet. "What happened to you? What made you sick?"

He shook his head. "Not sick. Just changing. It makes you tired. Very tired." His head drooped. "Couldn't help you. Sorry."

Changing. I stroked Mephi's cheek. "Don't be sorry. You've helped me more than enough." My fingers shook. I snatched back my hand.

"Jovis all right?"

Of course I wasn't all right. I couldn't ever be all right. I'd spent too long not getting to Emahla, running about, acting the part of the hero. I wasn't a hero.

She wasn't dead. She *wasn't*. She was waiting for me.

"No," I said. My eyes itched; heat gathered behind them. "I'm not all right. We need to leave."

Mephi tried to help, picking up clothes in his teeth and handing them to me – a little moist and worse for the time spent in his mouth. But I couldn't complain. I was shaking now. There was a tremor building within me, and it wasn't Mephi's magic. I could hear Ranami's voice, over and over: "She's dead."

No. I would know it if she were.

At last I had all my things in a bag. My hair curled in the moist air. I was a half-blooded smuggler, and I finally had the information I needed to rescue the woman I loved.

Mephi leaned against my leg, steadying me. "We could help here," he said.

I thought of Gio, who wanted to take the islands for his own, whose plans I did not know. I thought of Ranami and Phalue, who didn't know they'd already been betrayed, of the children being marched to trepanning rituals, of the gutter orphans who'd wanted to rob me. It was true: we could help here.

It didn't mean we had to. "No. Emahla. She is my priority."

Mephi made a small, confused noise. He didn't know her.

"You'd like her," I told him. "But she's in danger. She's been gone for seven years and now I know where she might have been taken."

"We go there?" He wound around me.

I didn't know. Maila was treacherous, and I wasn't sure I could slip past its reefs without crashing. "Yes." I put my hand on the floor, ready to push myself to my feet. Even this seemed an effort.

Mephi put his paw on my knee. "She is one. These people are many."

Everything terrible I'd been feeling over the past three days welled within me, overflowing. "I don't care about these people! They don't care for me except for what I can do. They don't know me. Emahla knows me. She loves me, and I've let her down for too long."

The creature didn't even look away or flinch. "I know you."

"Do you?" I jerked away from his touch and rose to my feet. But, Endless Sea help me, I stopped to check if he was following. He was, his head so low that my heart shattered a little to see it. But I couldn't stop now; if I did, I might not ever start up again.

The few rebels who remained in the caves watched me go, and said nothing.

My boat was where I'd left it, hidden behind some rocks on the shoreline. Mephi slipped into the water, graceful as a sea lion. I waded into the water as he scrambled aboard. The ocean had cooled with the migration of the islands north-west, and the chill of it seeped into my shoes. I stripped off my wet clothes once I was aboard, put on dry ones and hauled up the anchor.

Mephi lay on deck near the bow of the ship, his head between his paws. He watched as I readied the boat to leave, as I tested the wind. Most times, when I'd rebuked him, he'd either ignored me or taken it with the irrepressible good humor of a puppy.

This time, he lay apart from me, as though his heavy heart had anchored him to the bow.

I couldn't keep thinking about everyone else.

The wind was good. It would take a long time to reach Maila, but the sooner we left, the sooner we'd arrive. I'd have to figure out the reef on the way. "No more stopping," I muttered into the night. The moon was full, and enough to see by. "No more sad stories about children who need to be saved, or regimes that need toppling. We go straight for Maila."

Mephi only huffed out a sigh and looked toward the horizon.

I remembered the dreams we'd told each other. I would be an Imperial navigator, and she would sell pearls. Emahla had stopped collecting clams at the beach and had started diving for pearls when she'd turned fifteen. She could hold her breath for far longer than I could, and never seemed afraid of the depths beyond the shoreline. "Sometimes," she'd told me as we'd lain on the beach together, "I think I've reached the part of the island where it stops sloping out and starts falling straight into the darkness. At some point, even after that, they must slope inward. The islands float in the Endless Sea. I wonder if any diver has seen the bottom of an island?"

"You'd be the first," I'd said, pulling her into my arms and kissing her brow.

She'd laughed and pushed me away. I still remembered the jasmine scent of her, the touch of her thick black hair against my neck. "I'd drown."

"There is no one as clever as you, as smart, as strong." I'd buried my fingers into her hair.

"You are *such* a liar." But she'd smiled as she'd kissed me.

Darkness had begun to cloak the sky. I couldn't see the stars. I hadn't been lying to her. She *was* smart, and clever, and strong. She'd never needed me. She'd chosen me.

If there'd been a way to escape her fate, she would have found it. She hadn't. It had been seven years. No one else who had disappeared had ever returned.

I told a great many lies to others, and I told a great many to myself. This perhaps was the greatest lie of all. Emahla is alive. She is waiting for you. She needs you to rescue her. It was the only thing that kept me getting up in the morning, that kept me from giving up and giving myself over to the Endless Sea or the Ioph Carn.

My legs folded beneath me, my knees sinking to the deck. "Mephi," I whispered.

He was there, beside me before the tears even began. I clutched at his fur so tightly I was sure I must have hurt him. But he didn't move, steady as a cloud juniper.

She was dead.

All these years spent searching and wanting. It didn't matter if I found her; I had no power to bring the dead back to life. All my life stretched ahead of me – without her. I forced myself to face it, to push the lie aside. "I don't know who I am," I said, my fingers digging into Mephi's undercoat. "I don't know what to do."

"When I was in the water," Mephi said, "I didn't know where to go. I had to find someone to help me. I swam to you because I knew you would help me. I know who you are." He nuzzled my shoulder. "You are the person who helps."

Was I? I'd been finding reasons to rescue these children without ever having to commit myself to the cause. Someone had saved me, but no one had saved Onyu. No one had saved Emahla. I felt their absences every day I kept living. Sometimes one was enough.

Sometimes it wasn't.

I could help all the children who were so much like my dead brother. I could help the shard-sick and the people who loved them. I could help the people stolen away by the Empire's constructs. I had the power to save more than just one here, one there. If I simply tried, I could do more than chase whispers of Emahla; I could go to the heart of the Empire and take a stand against it. I could believe in this, and it wouldn't be a lie. I wiped the tears from my cheeks, though the ache in my chest remained. Some wounds would never heal. "It sounds like a lonely life, Mephi." No one was telling the truth to anyone else. Even the Shardless Few was fractured.

"No." Mephi rested his chin on my shoulder. "Not lonely. I am here with you."

I reached up to rub his cheeks. The shore was still close; it wouldn't take long to get back. Somewhere in the darkness lay the Shardless hideout, filled with people who yearned to break free. I couldn't save all of them. I couldn't. But I could save more than my fair share. I pushed myself to my feet. "Then it's settled. Let's go topple an Empire."

42

Lin

Imperial Island

We went first to gather Uphilia from her lair. Bayan crawled up the roof tiles after me. "You did this once already?" he said.

"Yes."

"You're a little bit mad, you know that? I wonder –" He huffed out a breath and reached for the next handhold. "– if your mother was like this."

I wished she'd been my mother, but she was not. She'd seemed like a normal enough young woman in her journal, but she'd aged before she'd married my father. Something must have changed between that time and when they'd wed. Bayan didn't say anything after that, only put his head down and concentrated on the climb.

The broken ironwork piece was still there on the eaves. When I peeked over the edge of the roof, I could see Uphilia curled in her alcove, her tail over her nose and her wings tucked to her sides.

"Uphilia," I whispered to her, "you must come with me." I wasn't sure why I whispered, except that I was unsure of my own work. If I hadn't altered her commands correctly, she'd awaken and send up an alarm. Or Father – the Emperor – might have already altered her commands back. Her ears twitched, but that was all. The wind had swept my voice away.

This wasn't the time to let fear rule me. I tried again, louder, more sure. "Uphilia, awaken and come with me."

She rose, stretched her wings and sprang from her alcove. With a quick turn of her wings, she was on the rooftop, amber eyes looking into mine. She did not send up an alarm.

Behind me, the spy construct squeaked in surprise.

"No," I said, putting a hand behind me. "We're on the same side now."

"Even with Uphilia and Mauga, can we take on Tirang?" Bayan asked. "Tirang is strong and has war constructs at his disposal."

"If you have a better idea, tell me when we're back on solid ground." We returned to Bayan's balcony, Uphilia in tow. "We can remove shards from any constructs attacking us. Subvert some if we have the chance. I'll tell you how I rewrote the commands for the spies. I suspect the war construct commands are written in a similar way. We can do this. The constructs are strong, but we have more knowledge. We can control them. All we have to do is get through them to the Emperor."

"Yes, easy enough." He was speaking this way because he was scared. I knew these feelings.

"I never said it would be easy."

Bayan rubbed at his arms, as though trying to wipe away his fear. "I'm sorry. I know you're right. And if I'm ever to have a life worth living, this is the way through to it. I thought things were hard enough when I had to compete with you for your father's approval. This is ... toppling an Emperor. It's something your ancestors would have done. Or the Alanga."

"Again, I am not one of the Sukais. I am a facsimile."

"You're as close to a Sukai as one can get nowadays." Bayan shook his head. "Let's get Mauga and do this before I change my mind."

I took his hand in mine. Our fingers twined together as naturally as breathing. "Thank you," I said.

He didn't say anything stupid this time, only looked at our hands. With his expression solemn, the resemblance to the Emperor became more pronounced. The Emperor had built a younger copy of himself, cobbled together from who knew how many people. Yet Bayan was different. He gave my hand a squeeze. "I am sorry we couldn't have been friends."

"There's still time."

The smile he gave me was half-rueful, half-wry. "So she says, before they go into battle against their very creator."

I squeezed his hand back. "There is always time."

We slipped into the hallway together, after sending the spy construct to scout the way, Uphilia on our heels. As we stepped toward Mauga's room, the scent of his lair growing in my awareness, Bayan's palm slipped against mine. I wasn't sure if it was my sweat, or his. Either way, we both gripped tighter. If I'd put aside my pride, if I'd figured things out earlier, we might have seen past the rivalry the Emperor had set upon us. He'd manipulated us both, and I'd fallen prey to it. I might have been able to save Numeen and his family. But I couldn't change what had happened, no matter how much I wished it. And oh – how I wished it.

Mauga was awake when we entered, sitting on his haunches, straw scattered beneath him.

Bayan's support gave me courage. I did not whisper, or creep forward like a mouse. "Mauga, you must come with me."

He blinked and then lowered himself to all fours. "I knew you would come for me."

Uphilia stepped to my side, stretching her wings and resettling them. "It's time."

"I need to find my father," I told the constructs. "I need to set everything right." As much as I protested, as much as I kept telling Bayan I was not a Sukai, the identity was pressed too deeply into my bones. I'd find a way to leave it behind someday – if I lived through this.

"He is in the dining hall with Tirang," Mauga said, "plotting a war against the Shardless Few."

"Ilith?" Bayan asked.

Uphilia shook her head, as though she'd bitten into something distasteful. "No one knows."

Hopefully she was still incapacitated in her lair. The engraving tool that Numeen had given me was still in my sash pocket. "I'll need you to cover for me from time to time," I told them. "The more time I get to rewrite the commands of basic war constructs, the more we'll have on our side."

"And if we win?" Bayan said it like he was starting to believe we could.

"We bring back the servants, the soldiers. We open up the palace again. We treatise with the governors and form alliances. We become strong again. The rest ..." I thought of the shards within Bayan that even now were draining the lives of the Empire's citizens. I didn't know how to reconcile that with who Numeen had wanted me to be. He'd wanted me to stop the trepanning rituals, to provide succor to the people. I closed my eyes, hoping for a vision of the future that made sense. I found only darkness behind my eyelids and my heartbeat pounding like a drumbeat in my ears. But there were rooms I'd not been in yet, and secrets I didn't yet know. Perhaps I'd find answers there. "The rest we will have to figure out."

The march to the dining hall felt an eternity. The one servant we saw went pale as she spotted us, retreating into a room, her head bowed over her basket of linens. I'd reclaimed my hand from Bayan's grip and had fished out the engraving tool. He held his own in his hand like a weapon. His was much more elaborate than mine, carved with vines up and down the handle. Uphilia padded beside us, her footfalls silent, and Mauga strode behind, his bulk a comforting presence at our backs.

For Numeen. For his wife, his brother, his children – his family that he'd entrusted me with.

Bayan waited at the dining-hall door. This was my plan, so this was my move to make. The trick, I thought, was not to think about it at all. I took in a breath, opened the door and stepped inside.

Shiyen, the Emperor, stood over the table, leaning on its surface. Tirang loomed behind him, his wolf's snout pointed at the map, his clawed ape's hand holding the edge flat. Both of them looked up as I entered, my engraving tool in hand. A flash of surprise crossed my father's face, so quickly I barely saw it. It was enough to know – I'd not met his expectations.

This time, I yearned to break them.

As Bayan, Mauga and Uphilia filtered in after me, understanding smoothed Shiyen's features. "I locked you away. You . . . you are not supposed to be here," he said slowly.

"No, I am not. But I'm not who you think I am."

"That's because I need to fix you. It's not your fault."

I straightened. "I'm happy as I am."

Shiyen sneered. "You don't know what happiness is. You don't know what sadness is. I grew you in a cave beneath this palace from stolen bits of flesh. I put memories into your head. You are my creation. You are mine."

I was not. But the only language he understood was violence. "Mauga. Uphilia. Kill Tirang."

They rushed forward. I felt Bayan's arm, pressed against mine, trembling. I might have been ignored by Shiyen, but he'd suffered Shiyen's wrath much more often.

Shiyen slammed a hand on the table. "*Ossen!*" he shouted. The word echoed from the walls. Even as Mauga and Uphilia rushed at Tirang, I heard the drum of distant footsteps.

I'd never expected this to be as simple as killing Tirang, but the confirmation of it made me quail.

Tirang seized Uphilia in his jaws, and Mauga slammed his massive bear-shoulder into Tirang's chest. With a contemptuous glance at me, Shiyen plunged his hand into Mauga's side. The construct froze.

"What now?" Bayan said.

"What else?" I sounded braver than I felt. "We fight."

I strode toward my erstwhile father, my engraving tool held at the ready. Even though I'd studied hard, I knew his library of knowledge was greater than mine. But he was weaker and sick, and I had the strength of youth.

Tirang dropped Uphilia and turned to me, a growl in his throat. Before he could swipe at me, Uphilia sprang from the ground and seized his calf in her teeth.

I grabbed Shiyen's hand and yanked it from Mauga's body. He'd already closed his fingers around a shard. The bones of Shiyen's wrist squeezed together, frail as a songbird's legs. He grunted as I wrested the shard from his fingers, glanced at it and pushed it back into Mauga where it belonged. Mauga shook his head and bared his teeth.

"Lin!" Bayan called from behind me.

I looked to find Bayan trying to hold the door shut against a tide of constructs. He lost the battle as I watched and war constructs flooded into the room — wide-eyed creatures of teeth and claws. "Turn them!" I cried out. "The way I showed you."

He thrust his hand into a nearby construct, but he could only handle so much at a time. I threw my father to the floor and ran back to the doorway, my free hand held in front of me. The first war construct I encountered, I pushed my fingers inside its chest. When it froze, I crouched in its shadow, using its body as cover as I plucked the shard from inside of it and rewrote its contents. Behind me, I heard the tap of my father's iron-tipped cane as he pushed himself to his feet.

Something snarled, close to my ear. I whipped my head up. The golden eyes of some giant cat met my gaze. The construct's heavy jaw and long teeth sent a jolt through my veins, my heart kicking at my ribs. It stalked one step closer and I slammed the shard back into the construct I crouched beneath.

"Protect me," I commanded it.

It met the cat-thing with its teeth bared and I rolled away. I grabbed another construct's hairy leg. As soon as it stopped to growl at me, I pushed my hand into its chest to pull the correct shard out. I heard yowling as the other two constructs tussled. Two others had stopped in their rush and were approaching me.

I had to keep ahead of it, to keep turning enough so I had protection to turn more. And there was my father to worry about, with his own power to contend with.

Teeth sank into my arm as I finished carving the new command into the shard. A smaller war construct with the face of some sharp-toothed fish. I pulled my arm away and felt flesh tear. Pain flared, a burning sensation, the warmth of blood trickling toward my hand. I shoved the shard back into the construct above me. "Protect me," I commanded.

I dared a glance at Bayan. He was still near to the door, but he was holding his own – one construct in his control and another he was working on. He wasn't as quick as I was, but he seemed to be managing.

Too many constructs stood between us – at least twenty of varying sizes. Behind me, my father had risen to his feet. If I kept trying to go to Bayan to help, I'd be giving Shiyen time to wreak more havoc. I didn't know what else he had in store. Ending this quickly was the best way to protect us both.

I pivoted toward the Emperor.

He had Mauga in hand again. Tirang was still standing, although blood flowed from a wound on his shoulder. A gift from Mauga's jaws. One of the constructs I'd turned disappeared beneath the onslaught of three others. I couldn't make it there with only one construct protecting me. I grabbed for another one, my breath tight in my throat, pain running up my arm.

I turned it quickly.

"Lin, help!" Bayan cried out.

He was pinned beneath a construct. Both the constructs he'd turned were lying on the floor, blood pouring from their throats. He was pushing his hand into the chest of the construct holding him down, but his fingers didn't move past the skin. He was panicking, unable to keep up with the pace.

I couldn't turn back, not without losing everything we'd come here to do. And I wouldn't make it in time.

"Protect Bayan," I said to the construct I'd just turned. I didn't have time to see if its help sufficed. I'd left myself vulnerable. A war construct that was mostly wolf stalked toward me from the right. The remaining construct I'd turned was occupied keeping two others away from me to my left.

I put my hand out at the ready, hoping I could react quickly enough to plunge my hand inside the wolf construct before it could attack me. I didn't have surprise on my side; this construct looked me straight in the eyes.

It leapt.

A squeak cut through the air. Hao dropped from the ceiling beams and landed on the wolf construct's head. The wolf construct snapped its jaw shut on empty air as the spy construct clawed at its eyes.

My heart leapt into my throat. I hadn't told the spy construct to help me. I'd forgotten it was there at all – it was too small. No one, it seemed, was too small to turn the tide.

Father was finishing an engraving. Uphilia, bleeding, darted at Tirang's feet. She was no match for him. She wouldn't last much longer. And then Shiyen pushed his engraving into Mauga's flesh.

Mauga turned. I could feel the difference in the air as he awoke. He seized Uphilia, and his clawed hands that I'd thought so slow and lazy tore her neatly in two. Blood and bone shards spilled from the halves of her broken body. My mouth went dry. It was what would happen to me if I lost this fight. I leapt to the side to dodge a bite, grabbed the dog-snout of the attacking construct and thrust my hand into its body.

It couldn't have been that long, but it felt like I'd been fighting for a lifetime. My injured arm burned and numbed in turns. I turned the dog-snout construct, and then another. It was all I could focus on. But then Mauga began shuffling toward me, and I knew I'd have to come up with some way to turn him back. I had no idea what my father had written into his commands. All I saw was a brief flash of triumph on his face – one that sent ice through my veins.

"Bayan!" I called out. I heard no response. He could have been injured, or dead, or too busy with his own battle to respond. I hoped he'd caught my meaning. I'd need time to figure out what the Emperor had done, because we couldn't afford to have Mauga against us.

For Numeen, for his family, for all the rest of them.

I ran toward Mauga, my fingers tight around my engraving tool. He saw me coming, his brown eyes narrowing. He swiped. I leapt to the side and ducked beneath the swing. Claws caught in my hair briefly, sending a shiver up my spine. Before I could straighten, his other paw caught me in the hip. I felt my flesh tear, the blow sending me tumbling. My vision hazed, the world spinning around me. I licked my lips, tasting copper. A musky, manure smell filled my nostrils.

Get up.

Mauga's foot appeared in my vision. A piece of straw was stuck between his toes. I tried to focus on it, get my vision cleared. Somewhere behind me, Bayan shouted. I couldn't tell what he said.

I was Lin. I was not the Emperor's daughter, but I was stronger than he knew. I would not die here. I would not become his wife.

Gathering all the strength left in my limbs, I launched myself to my feet and pushed my hand into Mauga's chest. Pain bloomed across my body, radiating from my arm and hip. Grimacing, I ran my hand across Mauga's shards. There were too many of them. It would take me too long to find the one Shiyen had altered. I closed my eyes. "I'm sorry, Mauga." I seized a fistful of shards and yanked them free.

Mauga froze.

The second construct I'd turned still protected me, though it was bleeding from multiple wounds and looked about ready to fall apart. I grabbed another construct.

I could see Bayan out of the corner of my eye, working furiously to change the war constructs over to our side. Uphilia was dead now. But I could feel the tide turning. If we could just take out Tirang, we'd win. I turned two more constructs.

A long, low growl sounded from the doorway.

Bing Tai leapt into the room and seized Bayan by the neck. Blood spurted.

I felt as though I watched through a lens from far away, my lips numb. Bayan didn't scream, Bing Tai's teeth clamped around his throat. When Bing Tai let go, Bayan dropped to the ground, his body limp. The constructs he'd turned ran about, purposeless, attacking both my father's constructs and one another.

Bing Tai ran at me from one side. From the corner of my eye, I saw the ruddy fur of Tirang.

Bing Tai growled.

And suddenly, I wasn't in the dining hall anymore. I was in the library, Bing Tai laid out before me. My hands moved of my own accord. It was me, yet not me. I was sorting shards into rows, laid out on a silk cloth on the floor. I brought one up to my eyes and examined the command.

"It's quite complex." I knew the voice that echoed from the shelves. A hand came to rest on my shoulder. Shiyen.

"Yes, well, why do something simple if I have the capability for more?" I kissed the hand. "This will be for both of us. A guardian. A personal protector." I started pushing the shards into Bing Tai's body.

The memory rushed away from me and I was back in the dining hall, blood seeping from my wounds. Bing Tai stood over me.

"Kill her," Shiyen called out. "I can grow another."

Bing Tai hesitated.

The shard I'd held in front of my eyes blazed back into my mind. *Ossen Nisong en ossen Shiyen*. Obey Nisong then obey Shiyen. Nisong took precedence, and I resembled her. I held some of her memories.

"No." I pushed myself up, my heart and bones aching. I remembered the way Bing Tai had backed away from attacking me when I broke into my father's rooms. I'd thought my father had commanded him to protect his family; now I knew that his wife had created Bing Tai. And much as I wanted to be my own person, some of her identity was mine. Even as he growled, I put a hand out. I stuffed down all the fear, all the uncertainty. I touched his nose and the beast stilled. "I know you, Bing Tai. You are mine."

I met my father's gaze as my war constructs brought down Tirang and savaged him. "Kill Shiyen."

Bing Tai turned and charged toward my father, my creator, my one-time husband.

He sank his teeth into Shiyen's neck. The room erupted into chaos.

I collapsed once more, the *drip drip drip* of my blood on the floorboards like the remnants of a storm that had long since passed.

43

Jovis

Nephilanu Island

By light, Mephi's changes seemed even more pronounced. His back was waist-high now; his brown fur thicker. A patch of hair on his chin had begun to grow longer, giving him something of a beard. I scratched it absently, and he closed his eyes. "Very good," he rumbled.

Ranami had been pleased to see me return, Gio even more so. I knew now, though, that their motivations differed. Ranami was a believer in the cause. Gio had his own plans, and I didn't know what they were. Ranami drew me aside. "Here." She pressed a package into my hands. "You'll need a way to get messages to us. There's a code in there; study it. There's also a fair approximation of the Imperial seal. At the docks is a woman who sells steamed bread. She flies a white flag at her stall. Give the messages to her, no one else. Send us as few as possible, but keep us updated. If you need help, let us know. She'll pass messages back to you."

I hesitated before whispering back to her. "Gio was going to kill Phalue. Keep your eyes open and watch your back."

She gave no indication she'd heard me, but then I'd not expected her to.

Gio's parting message was far more cryptic. "Keep Mephi close," he said. "You'll need him."

I studied his face. As far as they knew, Mephi was merely a beloved pet. Gio knew more, though I didn't know how.

"Did you say anything to Gio?" I asked Mephi.

His eyes opened. "You said not to say anything."

"Did you?"

"No." He turned from me, bounded to the railing and dove into the ocean. He did that a lot now. The first time he'd done it after he'd come out of his sickness, I'd panicked, counting time as he remained beneath the waves. At last, when he'd popped his head above the water, a fish in his jaws, I'd nearly wept with relief. Mephi was providing me with more food now than the other way around. He ate ravenously, but was a proficient hunter. He'd even once returned with a squid, its tentacles still wriggling as he'd tossed it aboard. I'd cooked it and shared it with him, and he'd hummed with pleasure.

I feared for him less now that he was so much larger. There were bigger and more dangerous things in the Endless Sea, but Mephi was quick as a dolphin in the water. His fur slicked against his skin, forming a smooth, thick barrier. And I couldn't loom over him like an anxious mother for ever.

The wind ruffled my hair. The rebels had suggested I straighten it before going to the palace, but I wasn't keen on hiding who I was. I'd gotten into the Navigators' Academy and had graduated without hiding my heritage. I wasn't a fool. I'd only been a fool over Emahla, and love addled everyone's mind. It had addled my heart too, leaving an ache that I felt would never fade. I'd clung to her memory for so long. I didn't know what life was like without hope of finding her, but I would have to find out.

The rain had increased the closer I sailed to Imperial. I'd been fortunate this morning, with no rain as of yet. By the look of the skies, I wouldn't be lucky for long.

Mephi scrabbled back onto the deck, a large fish in his mouth. He began to devour it, organs and all. He stopped, his bloody muzzle pointed to the north. I followed his gaze. There, in the distance, I saw the green, sloping mountains of Imperial. He looked to me, his whiskers twitching. "Plan?"

I ran a hand through my hair. "I don't know." I'd thought of this over and over. I didn't want to leave Mephi again, and despite my misgivings about Gio's motives, his words rang true to me. How would I explain this at the palace? What could I offer?

They'd know I was Jovis. The Emperor or one of his lackeys had ordered the portraits of me made. If I was to keep my appearance and keep Mephi, the only way I could infiltrate the palace was as a prisoner. It could still work. They'd find me harder to kill than they'd first considered. And I had information they'd want. I knew where Kaphra and all the highest Ioph Carn were hidden.

It was the only plan I had. "I give myself up," I said to Mephi. "I offer my services."

He strode over to me and pressed his forehead against my hip. "We do it together. I've done things they wouldn't like too."

"So you have." I ruffled the fur on the top of his head. His language skills seemed to be improving.

It began to rain in earnest as we arrived at Imperial's harbor. I pulled on an oilskin jacket, though rain still blew beneath the hood and trickled down my neck. Mephi trotted beside me, leaning his head back and opening his mouth to catch the rain. He licked his nose and shook his head, showering me with even more moisture. "At least one of us is enjoying the weather," I said.

He huffed something that sounded like a laugh.

I paid the dockworker construct and headed into the city. Imperial was lavish by any island's standards. The buildings rose several stories, all topped with tiled roofs. After the rebuilding, Imperial had been the first city to rise. It showed in the sculptures that adorned some of the stoops and the gutters. I kept Mephi close to me. In this weather, he could be mistaken for a dog. And people here were used to all the Emperor's constructs. Another strange creature didn't warrant much attention.

I leaned on my staff as I climbed the streets toward the palace. How would I do it? Knock on the great doors and ask to see the Emperor? I could look for one of those posters and take it with me in case anyone was unsure of who I was. I glanced up.

And my heart froze. A figure walked up the street ahead of me, cloaked in dark gray. It was unnaturally tall, just like the one I'd seen on the blue-sailed boat. Had the blue-sailed boat been in the harbor? I hadn't looked for it, and the weather had obscured the other ships. Around us, people went about their business, glancing into the figure's hood and then looking away, their heads down.

"Hey," I called out. "You, in front of me."

The figure didn't stop or even pause. They climbed the slope faster, broad shoulders moving as they pumped their arms.

"Wait! I need to talk to you."

But the figure only moved away, toward the palace. I wove through the people in the streets, rain running into my eyes. So many times I'd seen that infernal boat, only to have it slip away from me despite my best efforts. I couldn't let this be the same.

"Jovis." Mephi trotted beside me. "Need me to—?"

"Hush." I patted his head to soften the blow, and glanced around at the people in the streets. He took my meaning and kept his tongue behind his teeth. "We should hurry. Stay with me."

I broke into a jog to keep up, my legs still unsteady from the sea. The earth felt like it rolled beneath me, disorienting me with every step. As soon as I began to run, the figure did too. Of all the things in the world and in the depths of the Endless Sea – of course this wouldn't be easy even when I was so close. I gritted my teeth. I'd had to scrounge and scrape for every clue I'd found; why would this be any different?

The palace walls loomed ahead, the paint and plaster chipped in places, revealing the stone beneath. The red gates were closed and took more than one person to open. Beyond, I could see green-tiled rooftops. If I could back this person against the palace walls, if I could send Mephi to cut them off on the other side ...

Before I could give Mephi the command, the figure crouched at the base of the palace walls, and leapt. Hands clutched at the top of the wall, and then another pair of hands joined the first pair, propelling the cloaked figure over the ramparts.

I skidded to a halt, breathless. Two pairs of hands. This wasn't a person. It was a construct. Ranami had been right. My answers lay here, in the very heart of the Empire. All constructs were under the command of the Emperor. Whatever had happened to Emahla, it had started with him.

I knelt at the base of the wall, the sound of my breathing filling the hood of my coat, rasping and harsh. What could I do against an Empire? It had been a hopeless task from the beginning.

Mephi's face appeared in front of me. He peered into my hood. "We go over?" he said, his voice quiet.

I looked at him and then the wall. The places with the stone exposed provided some handholds. My bones began to thrum. I had the strength to make it over. "Get on my back and hold on," I told Mephi. I grunted as he clutched at me, but I could bear his weight. I strapped my staff to my back and began to climb.

The ramparts, when we arrived, were eerily silent. No one

stood there. The governor's palace at Nephilanu had been a fortress in comparison. I scanned the palace grounds. Empty except for one figure, cloaked in gray. With the magic humming in my veins, I could catch them. I hesitated. Something here felt wrong. The place didn't just feel run-down; it felt abandoned. What had the Emperor been doing when he'd been holed up behind his walls? Outside them, his constructs ran the world. I couldn't remember the last time anyone had spoken of the Emperor even venturing into Imperial City, much less beyond. Or, for that matter, anyone being invited into the palace. When I'd been younger, things had been different. Envoys went to Imperial regularly and were sent away awed by what they'd seen – an Emperor and his wife, both at the height of their power. He had an heir, I knew, but no one had much to say about her.

I climbed halfway down the walls and let go. A little of the magic leaked out as I landed, sending a tremor through the earth and shaking the walls. When I turned to look for the gray-cloaked figure again, they were running toward the main palace building.

Not this time.

Mephi clambered from my shoulders, and I put all my strength into running. Each step I took was a bound, the broken cobblestones of the courtyard passing in a blur beneath me. Mephi ran beside me, ears flattened to his skull. We passed empty buildings, halls that hadn't been used in years. Ahead, the figure tried in vain to outrun us.

At the palace steps, I caught the edge of their cloak.

The construct whirled as the cloak fell away. Rough gray cloth wrapped around the creature's limbs and body. Four spindly arms snapped out, looking like nothing so much as the giant jaws of some insect ready to attack. The legs were too long, as was the face. The pale skin there had been stitched together without care or concern for how it might look. Dark eyes sat too high on the construct's face; a large, thin-lipped mouth with pointed teeth seemed to take up the entire lower half.

But I was too angry for fear to seize hold of my heart. "What did you do with her?"

"Who?" The construct's voice rasped like sandpaper. It backed up another step toward the doors.

"You took her from the only life she ever wanted. She had plans. She had things she wanted to do. You took that all away from her. You took it all away from me." Words spilled out of me, words I'd not had an outlet for. I vomited them forth. "Seven years ago. Anau Isle. You left nineteen coins on her bedspread."

"Fair price paid," the construct said. "The Emperor is not unfair." It took another step back.

Mephi growled and slipped away from me. He padded up the steps and cut off the construct's escape.

I drew the steel staff from my back. "Tell me what happened to her."

The construct tilted its head as though calculating figures. It looked at me. "No."

The thrumming in my bones exploded into my body, sending heat and fire through my veins. I leapt forward. The construct met me, its four hands moving quicker than any person's. Before I could even land a blow, it had pulled four knives from somewhere on its person. They flashed like lightning against the cloudy sky. It blocked my staff with two knives, the other two snaking toward my torso.

Mephi seized the construct by the calf, sinking his teeth into its flesh. It howled, and I used its brief distraction to spin my staff and strike it hard on one wrist. The hand opened, sending the blade skittering down the steps. Three blades left. Three blades too many.

I'd fought against Imperial soldiers, but the ones sent to enforce the Tithing Festival were young, inexperienced. They seldom encountered any resistance, so why send hardened soldiers? This construct moved in a way I was unfamiliar with, long limbs flowing with the grace of an egret darting for prey. Even as the blade fell down the palace steps, the construct's arms moved. I blocked two with my staff. The third seized the end of my staff and held it as the fourth sliced across my chest. I felt the cloth and skin part, the stinging of the rain as it ran into the wound. Mephi circled, searching for an opening. I couldn't underestimate this foe. The Emperor's war constructs were simple creatures. It seemed he'd put more work into this one. I had no idea of the commands written into this creature, what knowledge it had been given.

I jabbed experimentally with the end of my staff. The construct caught it before I could ram its belly. Mephi, as though reading my mind, darted in, teeth aimed at the other leg. Without even glancing behind, the construct flourished its three blades at Mephi, forcing him back. I pushed the thrum to the bottom of my feet, stomped.

The steps trembled. The construct tried to steady itself on its spindly legs. The injured one gave way, sending the construct to its knees. Both Mephi and I leapt forward. I struck another wrist. The construct snarled, its fingers still tight around the blade. I struck again. This time, the construct's fingers opened.

I felt the impact before I felt the pain. A punching sensation struck my thigh. I glanced down to see the handle of a knife embedded in my leg. The construct yanked it free. There was the pain now, a symphony to the lone instrument of the gash across my chest.

Mephi let out a strangled cry. Panic pulsed through me. Mephi had seized another of the construct's arms at the elbow, but the construct had been able to twist its arm, hooking the blade into the soft flesh of Mephi's ear. It tore the blade free, leaving a bloody mess of the ear. Both of us drew back, alert, assessing the damage.

I couldn't put much weight on my injured leg. Mephi's ear hung limp against the side of his head. The construct only had two blades left. And then the creature *grinned* at me. It was an unsettling expression on a thing that was supposed to be only following commands written into its shards. I lifted my staff, preparing for an attack. But the construct whirled. I struck it on the back, too late.

It plunged both blades into Mephi's shoulders.

Mephi's cry tore my heart in two. The thrumming built in my chest like the rumbling of thunder from an approaching storm. My awareness of the water around us sharpened. Without even thinking, I *reached*. The rain around me stopped, mid-fall. I gathered the droplets, pulling them from the air and then the ground. All I could think was how this creature had hurt Mephi and I needed to end it. A wave of water formed, crashing into the construct with the force of the ocean against a cliff.

The construct fell away from Mephi, carried down the steps with the waterfall. I leapt after it.

When I knelt on its chest, my staff held against its neck, it held no more blades in its hands. "What happened to her?" I cried out. "You took her. What do you do with them?"

A cough erupted from the construct's throat; a blood-tinged foam touched its lips. "I do nothing. I bring them here."

I pressed harder. "What happens to them after you bring them? Tell me."

The construct gritted its teeth. "If I tell you, you swear to let me go."

"I swear it," I said.

"They go to the Emperor for his experiments. This woman you

seek – if it was seven years ago she was taken, she is long dead."

I thought I'd accepted it; I'd thought I could move on from this. But hearing it, knowing now it was true unleashed a wellspring of grief. The rain around me seemed to fall harder. I would never see her again, and never was a longer time than I could ever comprehend.

I rose to my feet, my fingers clenched around my staff.

"You promised," the construct said, trying to wriggle free.

I put a heel on its chest. "I am not a construct. I can lie whenever I choose." I brought the staff down hard on the construct's head and felt the crack of its skull. I collapsed, the weight of sorrow pressing like a heavy hand upon my chest. I'd come all this way, had left behind my family, had given up my career – and I would have done so much more, anything. But I was too late. I'd likely been too late by the time I'd found the silver coins across Emahla's bedspread.

Mephi whimpered.

My friend was still alive. I still had responsibilities here, things I needed to do. When I sat up, I saw Mephi standing near the top of the palace steps, his head low, blood mixing with the rain and dripping from his jaw. The two knives jutted from his shoulders. He glanced at me and wheezed. "Not good."

I went to him and pulled my tunic over my head. Carefully, I pulled the knives free as he hissed, then tied my tunic tight around the wounds. I scratched him under the chin. "Can you walk? We need to get you some help."

"I can walk. Slowly." His nose found the wound in my leg. "You?"

"Slowly," I said. I surveyed the empty palace grounds, the lack of guards at the door. "Something's not right here. No people, no constructs except for that one."

My staff tight in my hands, I climbed the steps with Mephi and tried the door. It swung open at my touch, revealing an empty entrance hall, the lamps unlit. I stepped inside, conscious of the rain and blood I dripped onto the floor. Scenes of peacocks and mountains were painted between the pillars against the walls. A faded mural graced the wall above the steps, men and women hand-in-hand. Their gazes seemed to be fixed on me.

"Keep close," I said to Mephi, twining my fingers into his fur.

We climbed the steps of the entrance hall and ventured into a dark hallway, our footsteps echoing.

A voice emerged from the darkness, sending the hairs on my arms on end. "Who are you?"

44

Lin

Imperial Island

I lay on the floorboards as the constructs destroyed one another above me. My father's and Bayan's attacked one another, heedless of which were meant to be friend or foe; mine attacked my father's. I heard the click of footsteps, and then Bing Tai's cold nose touched my cheek, a huff of warm breath gusted across my forehead.

I'd won.

Bayan was dead. Numeen and his family were dead. And here I was, still alive and more alone than I'd felt since I'd first awoken to chrysanthemums painted on the ceiling above me. I rolled onto my belly and pushed myself to my feet. Only the simple war constructs were left, and Bing Tai. As I watched, the last of my father's was taken down. The dining room, a mess of overturned chairs and broken furniture, fell into silence. Above, rain pattered on the tile roof. I pressed a hand to the wound on my shoulder, grimaced and tore my sleeve off to fashion a makeshift bandage. The wound across my belly was shallow enough. I'd have to clean it later.

"Bayan?" My voice trembled in the empty air. I shouldn't have even tried, but hope clung to my bones. No one answered. I limped over to where he'd fallen.

He lay on his back, his gaze fixed on the ceiling, his throat torn open. I didn't realize I was kneeling until I was crouched at his side, my hands hovering helplessly over his neck. He was a construct. There had to be a way to repair him, even now once he'd died. If I did repair him, he'd be a new construct, no memory of me or his life before. Whatever magic my father had used to put memories into my mind and into Bayan's, it was an imperfect magic I did not know.

I strode to my father's fallen form next, still cautious, still not quite believing he was dead. The surviving war constructs had settled where they stood, sitting on haunches or lying on the floorboards, watching me. Bing Tai followed me, guarding my back. Shiyen lay face down, blood pooling beneath him and staining his robes. I knelt and touched his neck. His skin, papery thin and gray, had already begun to cool.

With some pain and effort, I turned him over. Sightless eyes stared at the ceiling. I'd have to send out missives announcing his death. The governors would expect a grand funeral, but I could ask for privacy. Even though Shiyen hadn't been to the other islands since he was young, they'd met him. They hadn't met me. I'd have to spend some time establishing diplomatic ties. And there was the larger matter of the constructs. The simpler ones would turn mad, sowing chaos. The more complex ones – I wasn't sure. The Empire I'd inherited was already fraying at the edges, and this would only tug loose more threads.

A glint caught my eye. The chain of keys around my father's neck. I unfastened the clasp and pulled it free. I still hadn't found the place where he'd so often disappeared to. There was that door in the old mining shaft, the one that looked like it had seen some use. I steeled myself and patted down my father's corpse.

Something small and solid was tucked into his sash pocket. I reached inside and pulled forth a small, golden key. Somehow I knew – this would open the door in the tunnel.

I should rest. I should call forth the servants from wherever they'd hidden during the battle. I should clean my wounds and change my clothes. But the pull of unveiled mysteries was too strong for me to ignore. Had his wife been so curious as well? The trek to the old mining tunnels seemed to take a lifetime. I kept touching the walls, each footfall a reminder that this palace was mine. These floors, these walls were now my property to do with as I willed. Bing Tai kept pace with me, and I leaned on him when I felt I didn't have the strength.

I took a lamp from the wall and entered the tunnels beneath the palace, pulled along as though by a rope. My father, occupied by some other task, hadn't taken the time to repair the guard constructs I'd disabled. Neither of them bothered me as I passed.

The door in the tunnel was where I remembered it, small and nondescript. I pulled the key from my sash pocket and tried it in the lock. It slid in easily, as if it had been used a thousand times. I stepped inside.

The room beyond was dark, my breath echoing off distant walls. I took the time to light the lamps by the door, and only then did I get a decent look at the room. It was more a cave than a room, vast and rough-hewn. A thick vein of witstone ran through the ceiling. A pool filled half the room, and as I watched, water dripped from above, sending ripples across the surface. In the middle of the space, next to the pool, stood a number of strange machines, tools and tables. The whole place smelled earthy and warm, like freshly roasted chestnuts.

This. This was where he'd disappeared to all those long days.

I ran my hand over the metal tables, the instruments. Some I recognized – scissors, needles, knives of various shapes and sizes. Others, with grasping claws and serrated edges, I did not. I wondered if he'd used these tools to build both me and Bayan. A glint of gold caught my eye. I turned to see a small shelf lined with various objects. On one of the bottom shelves was a silk cloth. When I pulled it free and unfolded it, I felt recognition stir in my chest. It was painted with golden chrysanthemums.

A little awed and apprehensive, I brought it close to my face. The chrysanthemums hadn't been on the ceiling. In the haze of my first awakening, I'd mistaken this cloth tented above me as something much farther away. When I put my nose to it, the soft floral scent sent me tumbling back through time, to a moment when I'd gasped awake, chrysanthemums in my vision and a chill at my back. He'd made me here. I laid it back on its shelf, my fingers lingering. Books with blank bindings lined the other shelves, and when I picked them up to leaf through them, the pages were filled with my father's handwriting and sketches. Others were filled with handwriting that looked like my own.

I turned to examine the rest of my father's laboratory. A low hum caught my ear. Among the tables, close to the pool, was a wooden chest. A contraption lay on top – a metal band with thin silver wires running from it and into the box. *His memory machine.*

The lid was heavy, and lifting with my one good arm proved almost too difficult for me to manage. Inside, gears worked and strange liquids bubbled. A brazier for witstone, covered in a glass dome, was nestled into one corner. The whole thing smelled of cloud juniper. I had no idea what all the parts did, how it worked. But with the books the Emperor had written, I could learn how to operate it. I could bring Bayan back. He would wake, a little confused, a lot annoyed. He might sneer, or roll his eyes, and wonder aloud how long it had taken me to bring him back to life. "I could have done it more quickly," he'd claim. The thought made me smile, even as my eyes prickled with tears.

Glass and rubber tubes protruded from the side of the chest, snaking across the stone floor and into the pool.

I rose to my feet, wondering what purpose these tubes had and where they led. The water had a reddish hue, and was so dark I could barely make out anything in it. But there was a shape. For a moment, I thought it might just be a log, or some rock formation. I squinted.

It was a face.

He's growing people. I heard Bayan's voice in my mind again, his eyes wide, his flesh melting. Cautiously, I approached the edge.

The body in the water was not mine, and some small part of me felt relief. I had no other self to contend with. But as I grew closer, I recognized the full lips, the strong jaw, the high cheekbones. The face of the Emperor lay in stillness below the surface, eyes closed.

I remembered my father's limp, the fresh wound on his foot one of my earliest memories. I remembered his words when he'd confronted me in my room. "You must understand, by the time I figured out what to do, my wife – she was too long gone. I'd burned her body, sent her soul to the heavens." It had not, it seemed, been too late to use a piece of himself to grow a body.

Bayan, then, was an earlier experiment, something that could be used simply to spur my ambitions. I frowned. None of the tubes led to the body. It floated unattached, suspended in the pool.

Something else in the water moved.

I froze, all the hairs on the back of my neck prickling. "Bing Tai." He padded to my side and sat but seemed otherwise unperturbed. He'd likely been down here before with the Emperor or his wife. Marginally comforted by his lack of concern, I fixed my gaze on the widening ripples. A pale shape, like some cave fish, glided beneath the water's dark and ruddy surface. As I watched, it rose.

It wasn't a fish at all. A snout broke the surface, and then a head, and then a chin, large as a horse's, came to rest on the stone next to the chest. One cerulean eye rolled from within the skull to look at me. A translucent eyelid blinked. The creature had some patches of thick hair, though most looked as though it had fallen out. It had a face like a cat's, but with a longer snout, whiskers twitching as it exhaled. Two spiraling horns rose from its skull, just over its ears.

It let out a low moan. I leapt back. I couldn't see the whole of it beneath the dark surface, but judging by the head alone, it would be as tall as my waist.

But it didn't seem to have the strength to do any more than moan. Rubber tubes ran from the chest into the creature's shoulders and neck. I couldn't see the contents – whether they carried something into or away from it. Water pooled beneath its head. Its rough breathing sent a spray of water across my slippers.

Another moan, this time softer.

"My father did this to you." My voice, low as it was, echoed from the cavern walls. My father's memory machine. This creature had been hooked to it for at least the last five years. Something in it was the key to making the machine work. I'd not seen an animal like it before, but then, I'd not been to all the known islands.

The eye rolled back into the creature's head, both eyelids sealing shut. It slid back into the water, its exhaled breath leaving bubbles in its wake.

I wasn't a fool. I knew suffering when I saw it. My father had always been single-minded in his goals; everyone who stood in his way was expendable. Everyone who helped him was expendable.

This was *different*. I could learn to use the machine, restore Bayan, let the creature go.

Numeen's shard still lay within my sash pocket. It was light as a piece of driftwood, yet I felt the weight of it, a weight I felt I could never unburden myself of.

I'd told him I wouldn't be like my father. I'd told him I would make things better. Even as the creature suffered underwater, out of sight, I would know it was there.

I was Lin. I was the Emperor. And I could not let cruelty drive my actions.

I knelt and tore loose the tubing from the chest. Blood and some white, milky liquid seeped from the ends. I cast them onto the cave floor and watched the water.

For a while, I thought even this small kindness might have killed the creature. It was in a weak and sickly state; any change to its circumstances might be a shock to its body. But then the surface bubbled, and a pale shape rose from the darkness.

It bobbed to the surface and scrabbled at the stone. I went to help it, forgetting for a moment about the wounds on my shoulder and belly. I felt the wound in my shoulder open a little as I grasped the creature's leg, as I pulled it out onto the stone. Before it could react, I tugged the tubes loose from its body. Each was a little thicker than my finger and left gaping holes in the beast's flesh.

My instinct was to run, to back away, to stand at a distance to see what the creature would do. But its head came to rest on my shoulder in a strange sort of embrace.

Something shifted within me, the same sense of wonder and hope I'd felt upon unlocking the first of my father's doors. Was it the trust she'd shown in me? The simple touch of her chin to my collarbone? Whatever it was, it drained away all the bitterness I'd felt at never receiving my father's affection, at never being enough. For this creature, I was more than enough. I was everything. I found myself putting a hand on her neck – I knew in my bones it was female – and whispering into her ear, "It's all right. I'm here. You're safe."

She breathed out a shuddering sigh, like a terrified, exhausted lamb finally laying down to rest.

"Come on, you don't need to be in the dark anymore." She limped with me from the cavern, Bing Tai at our heels.

By the time we'd emerged into the palace proper, a few servants had begun to slink out from their hiding places, tiptoeing through the halls as though expecting to find monsters at every turn. They weren't much wrong.

"You." I beckoned to the first servant I saw. She bowed low, her head nearly level with her waist. Despite her obeisance, I could see the tension and fear in every line of her body. Doubtless she expected I might decide to kill the witnesses to my apparent patricide. Let them spread their gossip. I needed a fearsome reputation if I was to hold the Empire. "Fetch me parchment and pen and bring it to my room." I had proclamations to write.

My beast – I'd already begun to think of her as mine – leaned against me. I wanted a bath.

"Thrana." Her name. She needed a name.

Thrana chirruped and nudged my arm with her nose. I scratched the base of her horns.

"Bing Tai, follow."

I'd have to find another servant and ask them to accompany me to the bath house, to fill the one remaining working bath there. The proclamations would be next. I'd have to find a way to clean the dining hall, to dispose of the bodies. No matter how tired I was, how heartbroken, I'd get little sleep tonight. I made my way toward the entrance hall and froze, dread rising in my breast.

I could see the edge of the faded mural, the Alanga hand-in-hand stretched across the wall.

Their eyes were open. They'd been closed the last time I'd seen them, only a day ago. No one would have had the chance to paint them open, and there was no discernible fresh paint. What could it mean?

Someone stepped into the hallway. He wasn't dressed in servant's clothes. Blood dripped from his limbs and onto the floor. My hand tightened around Thrana's neck. And then a creature appeared beside him. I blinked, trying to believe what I saw. It was smaller than Thrana, with much more fur, but it was the same sort of creature. How could I never have seen one before and now had encountered two in one day?

Without intending to, I called out. "Who are you?"

45

Ranami

Nephilanu Island

Ranami watched Phalue settle into her role as governor with the ease of an otter learning to swim. She seemed born to the role, a brash and honest leader with enough humility to ask for help when she needed it. She asked Ranami for help often, sending missives to her apartment by the docks, asking her respectfully to make the trek to the palace to offer her counsel.

The distance between them was more than physical.

This was what Ranami had been working toward with the rebellion, yet she'd told Phalue more than once that she did not want to be a governor's wife. And she knew, every time she went to the palace and offered her counsel, that Phalue wondered where that left them.

Ranami crumpled the latest missive in her hand as she strode up the path to the palace. She wasn't sure herself where that left them. The words Jovis had spoken to her before leaving still echoed in her mind, drumming against the inside of her skull as surely as the rain drummed against the hood of her cloak.

She couldn't trust Gio. Gio wanted Phalue dead. However inadvertently, she'd brought this danger upon Phalue, had even encouraged it. Although the rebels now seemed content with Phalue's governorship, guilt still tugged at Ranami's heart. She'd pushed Phalue to this, to imprisoning her own father. It didn't sit lightly with Phalue, and Ranami could see the strain each time she looked at her.

She stuffed the missive back into her pocket. "Please come to the palace. I need your advice." That was all it said. No mention of the matter. No playful, loving sign-off at the end. Just those words and the official governor's seal on the outside. Half-disbelieving, she'd turned it over, expecting to see more words. Nothing. Not that she deserved any more.

The guards at the palace gates recognized her without her having to explain what she was doing there. They waved her in. In the courtyard, a retinue of workers and guards were dismantling the fountain. One of the guards smiled at her. Tythus, Phalue's sparring partner.

"It's good to see you back here," he said. He left his work at the fountain.

She glanced at the stone being broken apart and hauled away. "The fountain?"

His expression sobered. "Opened its eyes again. Phalue asked me to take it apart and remove it. She's not superstitious but, well . . ." He shrugged, as though that explained it. "What brings you back?"

"She wants my advice," Ranami said, flashing the crumpled missive. "Nothing more." The people would whisper about the fountain again, but its destruction would hopefully put rumors to rest. Still, Ranami wasn't quite sure what to make of it herself.

Tythus fell into step beside her. "I doubt that. She talks a lot when she spars. Lets off steam in more than one way, I suppose."

Ranami felt a trickle of curiosity. "She talks about me?"

Tythus laughed. "Constantly." He fell silent for a moment as they strode into the palace. "I don't agree with her all the time, and until recently I wouldn't have even said she was a friend. But Phalue tries very hard to do the right thing."

Rain dripped from her hood onto her collarbone. She threw back the hood of her cloak and shook her hair loose. "I know."

"You know the way from here?"

"Is she in the governor's suites?"

"Yes."

Ranami strode past Tythus and made her way to the stairs. She'd give whatever advice Phalue wanted, and she wouldn't cry. These things so often ran their course, didn't they? People grew apart, decided they were no longer meant for one another. It had happened for Phalue's mother and father. It had happened for Ranami's mother and father, long before she'd even been born. And Phalue had always moved from one woman to the next until Ranami. Perhaps she'd go back to that. Perhaps she missed it. As the governor, she'd have her pick. There would be women lined up to court her. The thought made Ranami more miserable than she'd thought possible.

She supposed, in the end, they'd had a good run together. They'd toppled a corrupt governor, and that was more than most could say.

She knocked at Phalue's door with the ghost of a smile on her lips.

Phalue's voice emanated from within. "Enter."

Ranami drew herself up, took in a deep breath and turned the doorknob. She'd give her opinion with all the impartiality she could muster. She owed Phalue that much at least. But when she opened the door, she had to blink several times to adjust to the dim light.

Lanterns had been placed on the floor, their flames low and inviting, casting everything in gold. Bowls had been placed at intervals, filled with water, white lilies floating atop their surfaces. Phalue sat by the window, the soft light from a cloud-covered sun limning her outline. She had a stack of books on the bench beside her, piled in a tower that reached her chest. She wore her leather armor, the set that Ranami so often admired her in.

It couldn't have been comfortable.

Phalue set her palm on the stack of books, her expression solemn. "I read them. All of them. I would have called for you sooner, but it took me some time."

Hope blossomed in Ranami's chest, unfolding gently as a flower in a wet season rain. "I never expected you to."

"But you asked me to. That should have been enough. I always thought you asked too much of me, but I'm beginning to understand: you never asked enough."

Ranami tried to gather herself. The flowers, the lanterns — they could be for someone else. Phalue had summoned her here for advice, not a reconciliation. She would have said she wanted to reconcile in her missive, wouldn't she? But the tears had already gathered in her eyes. She wiped them away with the flat of her hand, embarrassed. "I'm not sure what to say."

Phalue rose and strode between the lanterns to Ranami. Each step made Ranami's heart leap. Hesitantly, Phalue lifted a hand and touched Ranami's cheek. "I wasn't sure if you would come if I asked you for more." Her breath gusted warm across Ranami's cheek. "It's hard to remake one's view of the world, to admit to complacency. I thought remaking myself for you was hard enough, but doing that was something I wanted. I didn't want to realize how much I've hurt the people around me, and that's what confronting my beliefs meant. We all tell ourselves stories of who we are, and in my mind, I was always the hero. But I wasn't. Not in all the ways I should have been. Can you forgive me?"

Ranami laughed through her tears. "Can *you* forgive *me?* I shouldn't have pushed you."

Phalue brought her other hand up, cupped Ranami's cheeks. Ranami felt her pulse pounding at her neck, the way it had the first time they'd ever kissed. She'd known then that things would come between them, but she couldn't have stopped if she'd tried. She closed her eyes, her chest aching. She heard the creak of Phalue's armor as she bent, a sweetness rising in her throat to burst like honey on her tongue. When her lips brushed against Ranami's, it was like the sealing of a letter — a promise that could not be unwritten. She wrapped her arms around Phalue's broad shoulders, tangled her fingers in her hair. She sank into Phalue's embrace, her legs weak beneath her. This was *home*.

Phalue pulled back a little, brushing the damp hair from Ranami's cheeks. "You promised me before that you'd live here at the palace with me if I helped you. I won't hold you to that promise."

"I'll do it," Ranami said, breathless. She clung to Phalue like a woman drowning.

"No," Phalue said, shaking her head.

For a moment, Ranami's heart dropped to the soles of her feet. She couldn't gather a breath to speak.

"I want more than that," Phalue said. She took Ranami's hands in hers. "You said you never wanted to be a governor's wife, and I understand that now. You didn't want to be a party to the way this island has been run. You didn't want to contribute to the pain you saw and experienced. But I will do better. And I want to do better with you at my side. Ranami, will you be my wife? Please?"

Ranami pressed her forehead to Phalue's, grinning so hard

that her cheeks hurt. "Is this the tenth proposal? The eleventh?"

"I would propose a thousand times if I knew you'd say yes in the end."

"You're governor now. I shouldn't let you debase yourself so."

Phalue squeezed her hands. Her voice was soft, breathless. "Is that a yes?"

Ranami had thought their love would end in disaster. It still might. But she was willing to take the chance. "Yes."

46

Jovis

Imperial Island

The woman emerged from the dimly lit hallway, looking as worse for the wear as I felt. She'd wrapped a makeshift bandage around a wound in her shoulder that seeped fresh blood, and her tunic was slashed across the middle and bloody. She looked exhausted, dark circles beneath her eyes, her black hair hanging limply around an unremarkable face. In spite of her injuries, there was a reserve of strength behind those eyes. My gaze dropped to her feet and I saw fresh spatters of blood on the hem of her pants. Somehow, I doubted that blood was hers. I leaned on my steel staff like a walking stick. *Kill her!* my mind screamed. The wrongness I'd sensed in the palace seemed to follow her like a cloud.

I might have attacked except for the creature at her side.

It was taller than Mephi by at least a head, though its back was hunched in pain and its chin low. Several bandaged wounds on its shoulders were stained with blood. Though its horns were longer than Mephi's, it was almost entirely bald, random patches of thick hair sprouting from its belly, back and cheeks. By the possessive way this woman draped her arm about its neck, this creature was hers in the way Mephi was mine. I didn't know what that meant.

"Who are you?" she asked again. "And what are you doing here?" Her voice traveled to me as though through a rolled piece of parchment.

A thousand lies filtered through my mind. An Imperial soldier. A guard. A friend? No, that was beyond idiotic. I didn't know who she was, or where she stood in the palace hierarchy. I didn't know what chaos had occurred here, or if she had the same powers as I did.

I tried the truth. "My name is Jovis. I'm a smuggler."

Her brow furrowed as she glanced down. "I know that name." Her gaze met mine. "The folk songs. You're the one who's been smuggling the children away from the Tithing Festivals."

"That's me. Jovis from the songs." We could have been two strangers meeting on the street, not two people who'd recently won what had clearly been difficult fights. I looked her up and down again, trying to get an idea of who she might be. Her tunic, before it had been shredded, looked hand-painted. She wasn't a servant. It was the only clue I had.

"Again, what are you doing here? The gates—"

"Were not guarded," I smoothly finished for her.

She pursed her lips. "Ah. Of course. They wouldn't have been."

I shifted from foot to foot, my breath short. I couldn't seem to take in enough air. "I was here to turn myself in."

The look she gave me was incredulous and very clearly stated, "Are you addled?" And then a construct prowled from behind her, a growl low in its throat.

"Quiet, Bing Tai," she said.

A sinking feeling started in my chest. Mephi looked up at me as though he could sense it. "Very bad?"

"Yours can talk," the woman said. It was more an excited statement than a question.

"Excuse me," I said, because I had the feeling I might know who she was now, "but do you mind if I ask who you are?" My mouth felt stuffed with cotton. Were the lamps dimming?

She straightened, her chin held high. "I am Lin Sukai, and I am your Emperor."

The hallway began to spin. "That is ... that is not what I expected." My knees gave way and the world went black.

47

Lin

Imperial Island

I started with the small things. A bath, calling for a physician to stitch my wounds and Thrana's, a simple proclamation to Imperial and all the known islands that my father was dead and I was now Emperor. I'd hired guards to man the walls immediately. I had the coin. What I didn't have were constructs. I felt a little of the paranoia my father must have felt – how could I trust men and women I did not know?

But I hadn't had much choice.

I shifted on my chair, my pen poised over paper as I deliberated what I should say. I didn't have the benefit of Ilith's network anymore. I had no idea what was happening beyond Imperial, and that ignorance could kill me. I needed to ask the governors how their islands fared while seeming like I already knew.

And after the awakening of the mural, I needed to ask: what other Alanga artifacts had awakened? Had there been any other signs? I needed to study those books in the library, to gather defenses. I didn't know the Sukais' secret for defeating the Alanga. That had died with the Emperor. But somewhere in the library, among all of Shiyen's experiments, there had to be clues. Next to me, Jovis lay stretched on the couch, his companion curled at his feet, alert and watching.

I'd had the servants and the physician tend to both the smuggler and his beast. I'd watched with fascination as his wounds and his companion's had healed more quickly than I'd thought possible. And then I'd noticed mine and Thrana's doing the same. I had so many questions, ones it seemed he might be able to answer.

"Is this what you do for all criminals who turn themselves in? I would have turned myself in much earlier had I known."

I dropped the pen and twisted in my chair.

Jovis had opened his eyes and was watching me. He lifted a weak hand. "You should work on your posters. There's something about 'Any persons harboring this individual will be hanged' that seems rather threatening." His companion crept to his face and sniffed his cheeks. Jovis squinted and waved him off. "Are you checking to see if you can eat me yet, Mephi? Regrettably, I am not dead."

I studied him as he scratched his beast's cheeks. I think he knew I was watching him, but he kept his gaze low, let me look. Despite the songs, he seemed unremarkable. A little taller than average, with a rangy build and sun-darkened skin. A light spray of freckles ran across his nose, disappearing into the thick, curly hair at his cheekbones. There was Poyer blood in him, I'd have sworn it. As he rubbed his companion's undamaged ear, I saw the tattoo on his wrist – the mark of an Imperial navigator. I'd expected someone grand, with shoulders like mountains and arms thick as pillars. He looked too thin, too plain, too *tired* to be a hero. Yet he'd defeated scores of soldiers if the songs were to be believed.

I wasn't sure what to believe.

But when I'd exited the palace doors, I'd seen one of my father's constructs dead at the base of the steps. I'd not seen its kind before. Its unnatural height, its four arms and the scattered blades had given me pause. Jovis must have killed it. I supposed I should be glad that he had, for if it had been responsive to my father's call, and had made its way inside – I wasn't sure if I'd have had the strength to defeat it, even with Bing Tai at my side.

"What do you plan to do with me?" he said, still not looking at me. He stroked the top of Mephi's head. "Your father would have had me hanged. Publicly, of course. No use putting up such a fuss about an errant smuggler if you're not going to follow through and show everyone that you will."

"I'm not planning on hanging you." I should have held that back, should have made him guess, but I was too tired for games. "I want to know everything you know about your companion – Mephi."

"Mephisolou is his full name," he said. "Mephi is his nickname."

"A grand name," I said. Mephi trilled a happy response. "I believe Thrana is the same sort of creature. Where did you find him?"

"He was in the water by Deerhead Island when it sank." Something seemed to fall away from him as he spoke, as though he'd drawn back a curtain I hadn't realized was there. He told me how he'd plucked Mephi from the water, how he hadn't wanted him at first, how he'd let him go. And then miraculously Mephi had come back. Little by little, he'd become more than just an animal, but a companion he couldn't see himself being parted from.

Thrana lay on the ground and rested her head in my lap. "I found Thrana in my father's laboratory. I think he experimented on her." I didn't mention the other body I'd found growing in there. I'd left it, unsure whether removing it from the pool would wake it up. A matter to be dealt with at a later time. I stroked the bare skin of Thrana's neck, gently running my fingers over the wounds the physician had stitched shut.

"She'll need you to help her get better," Jovis said.

Our eyes met. I felt an odd rapport with this man who'd shown up inside my palace. "Stay here," I said impulsively. "My rule has just begun. I need help. I want to stop the Tithing Festivals, and I need to find a way to change things, to make them better. Pardoning you would be a symbolic beginning."

He raised an eyebrow. "Your father wanted me dead, and you want me to work for you?"

No matter what we'd shared, I could never confess that I was not my father's daughter. I was something so, so different. I watched his face as I spoke. "My father lived in fear – of the Alanga, of his governors, of the very people he claimed to protect. He hid himself away and conducted experiments, and let everything fall apart around him. I loved him, but he could not love me. Whatever you might think of me, of my station, I am not my father. I do not fear the people. I am Lin Sukai and I will remake this Empire."

Jovis had a face like my father's – immutable as a wall when he chose it to be so. I wasn't sure what thoughts lurked behind that expression. Mephi chirruped and leaned his chin on Jovis's shoulder. "A very good."

Jovis's face softened as he pressed his forehead to Mephi's. He took in a breath and let it out, his eyes closed. He turned to look at me again. "Yes. I'll help you."

His words held the weight of some ages-old bargain, as though we were more than just one young man and one young woman, battered and bruised, trying to puzzle out the best path forward.

"Good," Thrana cooed out.

48

Jovis

Imperial Island

Things could have gone much, much worse. The Emperor could have decided to have me hanged. She could have ordered her constructs to tear me apart. Or she could have sent me away, which considering my current state of mind, would have been worse. Emahla was dead. Whatever experiments the prior Emperor had conducted on her, she was gone. It hurt my heart to think of her here in this palace, alone, living out her final days in pain and anguish. I wished I'd been there for her, as she'd always been for me.

But grief was a wave I could keep my head above.

I tugged at the collar of the jacket Lin had gifted me. If I'd thought the soldier's jacket an ill fit on Deerhead, this one fit even more poorly – despite the perfect measurements. It was dark blue and gold brocade, with golden buttons shaped like chrysanthemums. The high collar had just enough room around it to let my neck breathe, and it fell to mid-thigh. Lin had given me a golden sash to match, with a ring of keys hanging from it. Captain of the Imperial Guard was an odd title for a smuggler, a onetime Imperial navigator. She'd played up that second part in the proclamations, and downplayed the first. Either way, if I'd wanted a giant sign pointing out to the Ioph Carn where I resided – I'd gotten it. At least they'd hesitate to strike at me here, in the seat of the Empire's power.

I'd sent a missive to my mother and father the day before, letting them know where I was, what I was doing and that I was safe. I thought often of how it would be when they opened it, my mother's eyes filling with tears, my father holding the letter to his chest. I already knew what their response would be: when could I come see them, when could they come see me, this was what had been happening on our little island, the people who had left and died, the people who had married, the children who had been born. Life had been passing by while I'd been chasing a ghost.

"Sir, are you ready?" A servant stood in the doorway, his hands clasped. Lin had begun to hire more servants, and had ordered the buildings of the palace grounds to be repaired. Workers filled the walls, plastering and painting, cutting fresh wood. The faint scent of mud and sawdust seemed to fill the air, dust particles floating in every sunbeam. This seemed as much a symbol of rebirth as her hiring me on as Captain.

"I'm ready," I said. "After you." I followed the servant, Mephi bounding at my side. And that was the biggest problem. I'd arrived at the palace expecting hostility. I'd been at odds with the Emperor from the beginning. This Lin Sukai, this daughter that few had seen since she'd been young, she claimed to want something different. It was the same thing the Shardless Few claimed to want. A better life for everyone on the islands. Gio had other motives. Did Lin? I wasn't sure.

I strode through the hallways, trying not to gape at the murals, at the carvings, at the gilt inlay. The governor's palace at Nephilanu had been so gaudy as to seem cheap. This palace carried the weight of history in it, the art carefully cultivated, each piece complementing the next.

We made our way to the palace entrance hall.

The doors had been thrown open. The weather was auspicious for the wet season: faintly cloudy, breezy but without the scent of rain. Lin stood at the top of the steps, resplendent in the Emperor's fiery phoenix robes, the headdress nearly dwarfing her small, wiry frame. Guards surrounded her, mostly newly hired, though she did not seem worried. Thrana sat at her side. In the last several weeks, the fur had begun to grow back on the bare patches of skin. She still looked worse for the wear, and she was still far too thin, but she was beginning to seem intimidating.

As I approached, I could see the crowd beyond Lin, gathered inside the palace walls. The public hadn't been allowed inside the palace walls for the last twenty years. Even at this distance, I could see hope on their upturned faces. I stepped to the Emperor's side and the crowd roared. Someone in the midst of the crowd began to sing the folk song about me; several others joined.

Could a person die of embarrassment?

All my limbs felt too long and rangy, my skin too blemished, my hands too rough and cracked. Songs were not written about people like me. People like me weren't honored in ceremonies and given a lofty position by Imperial decree. I should have been a navigator, Emahla waiting for me at home, one or two children running about her feet. I closed my eyes briefly, waiting for the wave to pass me by. That was not my life.

This was.

"Kneel," Lin said. Her voice resonated through the courtyard, filling the space. She held a medallion in her hands.

I knelt. Mephi sat beside me.

"Jovis of Anau, former Imperial navigator, I offer you the

position of Captain of the Imperial Guard. Know that this position carries with it great responsibilities. You must swear your fealty to me, to the Empire, to all the known islands. For you are not a leader of men, but a servant of them."

I focused on my feet, blinked and then gathered the courage to look her in the eyes.

Her eyes – heavy-lidded, but rimmed with lashes so thick and long – stared back down at me. There was something familiar in them, something I recognized. It was like a word I knew but couldn't remember.

"I swear it," I said. The words didn't seem to come from my mouth, but from some deeper place inside me. They resonated into the silent crowd. Even as I said the words, I knew I lied. I'd promised Ranami I'd infiltrate the palace, that I'd send them information. I couldn't be loyal to both the Shardless Few and the Empire.

As Lin nodded, as she placed the medallion over my neck, I realized what had been bothering me.

Her eyes looked just like Emahla's.

49

Sand

Maila Isle, at the edge of the Empire

isong sent Shell and Leaf out in the rowboat over the next several days. They scouted the reefs, trying to find the passage the boat had traveled through. The blue-sailed boat had arrived and departed over and over without crashing upon the reefs. There was a way in and out.

Leaf sketched out the reefs onto pieces of bark with charcoal. They'd set up a camp on the beach where they'd taken the boat. Here, their minds seemed to fog less. There was something about the routine back at the village that lulled them back into a stupor. With the boat in the cove and the salty spray hitting their cheeks, they knew the truth. None of them had been here for ever.

"The passage is narrow," Leaf said. "But if we are careful, and we work together, we can sail safely from Maila."

"And go where?" Coral asked. She didn't say it as a reprimand; she sounded genuinely curious.

"South," Nisong said. "South and west." She'd seen it in one of memories – a map. A brief flash of it, but she'd noted where Maila was. If they went south-west, they'd spot another island.

Leaf nodded, jotted something down on his piece of bark. Nisong wasn't sure how she'd become the leader of this group, but somehow she'd slid into the role. It seemed to fit her the same way her new name did, comfortable as an old cloak. With the name came a conviction: there was a place for her outside this island. A place where she lived in a palace and her words held import. She closed her fingers around the shard in her pocket, knowing now what it was.

She was a construct. They were all constructs – built by the Emperor's hand. The memories she couldn't explain, but their inability to think of or enact violence she understood. They'd been made this way, commanded by the shards within their bodies. And one had torn free of hers – the one that allowed her to tear free of the fog and to bring others with her.

She hadn't told them yet. She'd have to at some point, but she wasn't sure when was the right time. And she didn't know their limitations, or her own.

Rain pattered against the roof of their makeshift hut. A few drops made their way through, sizzling as they hit the stones around the fire.

"Should we take any of the others?" Frond asked.

Nisong shook her head. "We can't keep them out of the fog. They'll keep falling back into it, and on a boat, that could be dangerous."

"But we don't know what's causing the fog," Coral said. "It could be the island itself."

It wasn't, but she couldn't tell them that.

And then the world seemed to tilt. It took Nisong a moment to realize the world wasn't actually tilting. Something in her perception was shifting. Leaf fell. Coral put out a hand to the wall of the hut to balance herself. They were feeling it too, this shockwave emanating from the center of her being.

As quickly as it had come, it stopped.

"What was that?" Leaf said. He scrambled to his feet.

Nisong still felt herself, yet something had changed within her. She wasn't sure what, but she knew it as surely as she knew she was missing two fingers. She waved away their concerns. "I don't know. But we should keep planning."

Despite the apprehension on their faces, they obeyed. "What should we do with the creature who was sailing the boat? It's still trapped beneath the boulder and it hasn't died," Coral asked.

"We kill it," Nisong said. The words fell from her without hesitation.

They all stared.

She tried again. "We kill it."

"The fog is gone," Frond said.

He was right. For the first time in her memory, Nisong's mind felt bright. She couldn't sense any cloudiness threatening on the horizon. For a moment, they just sat there in silence, all of them lost in their own thoughts. Nisong could think of violence. She could think of it with a clarity and intensity that surprised her. She wanted to hunt down whoever had left them all here, whoever had abandoned them to live these automated lives until death. She wanted to put her hands around their throat. She wanted to squeeze until their eyes bulged and their face purpled. Until they gasped out one last breath, bloody tongue protruding. The thought sent a flush of heat through her chest.

She swallowed.

The one who created them either was dead or had released them from their commands. She could think about violence now. She could easily remember that she had not been on Maila for ever. She had no urge to collect mangoes.

Coral cleared her throat. "The others—"

"Bring as many as we can," Nisong interrupted. "Shell, figure out how many we can take aboard if we plan for rations for thirty days and nights."

"Nisong." Leaf touched her arm, his dark eyes concerned. "If we get out of here, we can always come back for the rest."

"We will come back for the rest, but right now we need as many as possible," she replied. In her memory, she'd made a construct. There were others like them, built for one purpose or another, and now they'd all be without their commands pressing on their minds. They'd all be without a leader.

"What for?" Leaf said.

She could feel the weight of them watching her, waiting for her response. She breathed in deep.

"We're building an army."

The story continues in...

THE BONE SHARD EMPEROR

Book Two of The Drowning Empire

Keep reading for a sneak peek!

Acknowledgements

It's been a long road. And like most (successfully concluded) journeys, I did not undertake this one alone. I owe a debt of gratitude to many, many people, without whom this book would not be published, including:

James Long and Brit Hvide, my editors at Orbit and the whole Orbit publishing team. You've helped me put a fine polish on this book and to make this longshot dream of mine a reality. I cannot thank you enough.

My agent, Juliet Mushens, who through her notes, has taught me oodles about character, plot and pacing. Your insightfulness, hard work and dedication are awe-inspiring and unparalleled.

All of the Murder Cabin crew: Thomas Carpenter, Megan O'Keefe, Marina Lostetter, Tina Smith/Gower, Annie Bellet, Setsu Uzume, Anthea Sharp/Lawson and Karen Rochnik. Your feedback has been invaluable, and our yearly get-togethers are always invigorating (and a little frightening; it IS the Murder Cabin after all).

My beta readers for this book: Greg Little, Steve Rodgers and Brett Laugtug. I pored over all your notes and really appreciated your reassurances that this book might actually be . . . good?

Alvaro Zinos-Amaro, for being a listening ear and offering suggestions when I was puzzling through a couple of plot points.

My writing groups in Sacramento: WordForge and Stonehenge. You never stopped believing in me through all the books I've written, and that belief helped keep me going. I could never disappoint such wonderful people.

Kavin, Kristen, Mom and Dad, who all read various versions of this book and picked out logical inconsistencies. Your enthusiasm has meant the world to me. Stewarts! Stewarts! Stewarts!

John, my husband, whose endless support could buoy a lead weight in stormy seas. Celebrating the sale of this book with you will always be one of the highlights of my life.

And Mrs. Schacht, my fifth-grade teacher, whose praise of my story about a clay falcon come to life made me think, "Maybe I can be a writer?" May every daydreaming child have a teacher as wonderful as you.

extras

orbit

meet the author

Photo Credit: Lei Gong

ANDREA STEWART is the daughter of immigrants and was raised in a number of cities across the United States. Her parents always emphasized science and education, so she spent her childhood immersed in Star Trek and odd-smelling library books.

When her (admittedly ambitious) dreams of becoming a dragon slayer didn't pan out, she instead turned to writing books. She now lives in sunny California and, in addition to writing, can be found herding cats, looking at birds, and falling down research rabbit holes.

Find out more about Andrea Stewart and other Orbit authors by registering for the free monthly newsletter at orbitbooks.net.

interview

One of the central themes of The Bone Shard Daughter *is identity. Every challenge Lin faces – whether it's learning bone shard magic, her sibling rivalry with Bayan or trying to remember her past – is rooted in her sense of self, who she thinks she is, and who she wants to be. Was this exploration of identity something you wanted to develop from the start, or did it happen naturally as you began telling Lin's story? And how have your own experiences shaped Lin's struggles?*

Identity as a thematic element was something I'd wanted to explore from the beginning. Lin desperately wants to live up to who her father thinks she is, even though she feels more and more this isn't who she wants to be. Yet at the same time, who she wants to be feels unattainable. I grew up in a family that emphasized the importance of STEM subjects. My parents were both immigrants and wanted to see me do well – which to them meant studying something "practical." I struggled balancing living up to expectations with my own pie-in-the-sky dreams of being an author.

Revolution is another major theme of the book, and one that resonates strongly given the political upheaval in the real world over the past decade. Do you think fantasy fiction is at its most powerful when it reflects our own world in this way, or does the power of fantasy lie in the exact opposite – escapism?

As the popular meme suggests: why not both? I think the power of fantasy lies in combining escapism with a reflection of real-world issues. There are so many possibilities available to us in fantasy that I think it can allow writers to cast a different light on issues or to explore different aspects of them – aspects that people might not normally think of. There's a rhythm to stories that we don't have in the real world. Stories circle back. Stories make sense even when exploring senselessness. There's safety in that – and it can lower defenses we might otherwise have and make real-world issues feel less overwhelming.

Looking Medusa in the eye might turn you to stone, but you can get a good, long look at her by using a mirror.

The bone shard magic is such an interesting concept – it's almost like magical computer coding! Were there any specific influences that gave rise to this brand of magic?

There are a few things that influenced this brand of magic. I've always been fond of logic puzzles, and I knew as I developed this system of magic that it would be a little like computer coding. My spouse works as a software engineer and his explanations of the problems he'd run into during the day were always fun to listen to. And the first science fiction book I read was *I, Robot*, which lays out three rules of behavior for robots and then goes on to show how those rules can be twisted. In my day job, I worked as a compliance officer, which involved me referencing a lot of official documents and doing my best to interpret their intent. I thought about all these things when I was writing. In particular, I find the fallibility of language – any language – really interesting. You may intend to say one thing, and for that thing to be immutable, but there are always loopholes or gray areas.

Staying on the theme of worldbuilding, the world you've created has some fascinating elements – like the migrating islands! How did this element of your worldbuilding come about?

I like the idea of the land we live on being uncertain in some way, and the depths of the ocean never-ending. In some ways, it's just a more extreme version of our current world. In an empire of these moving islands, everyone has to adapt. Trade is affected by which end of the empire you're on and whether you're briefly in a different season, people have to learn complicated navigational systems, and things that sink out on the open sea will never be seen again.

The Bone Shard Daughter *is a book rich with mysteries: Lin's missing childhood memories, what manner of creature Mephi really is, how Sand and her fellows came to be on their island, what happened to the Alanga and so on. Do these secrets and questions reflect your own love of a good mystery?*

I've always loved reading books that unfold mysteries in ways that can surprise you but also make you feel really smart if you figure them out just before the reveal. Mysteries can be a way that the reader and author interact – the author lays out the clues and the reader gets to play a bit of a guessing game until *ta-da!* the answer is revealed. So I knew when I wrote this book I wanted to attempt the same thing.

The way the mysteries are slowly revealed feels like the skins of an onion being slowly stripped off to reveal another layer beneath, which suggests careful planning on your part. Is this true – did you sketch out all the major events of the book in detail before you wrote it? Or did you throw caution to the wind and make it up as you went?

I'm definitely a planner! So the major mysteries and reveals in all three books are things I've planned out from the beginning. Not everything is sketched out in detail, and there are smaller things I discover on the way, but the big events are all predetermined. I want to make sure that I've laid the groundwork so that readers can go back and see all the breadcrumbs on the way. That's hard to do without proper planning!

Which character did you enjoy writing the most? And what scene from the book is your favorite?

This is like asking me to choose a favorite child! I love different aspects of all of them: Lin's intelligence and ability to work through problems, Jovis's lightheartedness combined with his deep grief, Ranami's fierce nature, Phalue's big heart and Sand's determination. I think Jovis was quite fun to write sometimes; I also get amusement from my own jokes and almost certainly think I'm funnier than other people do.

My favorite scene to write was the scene where Lin and Jovis meet. Their storylines take them in vastly different directions, but I always knew those storylines would converge by the end of the book, so it was hugely rewarding to finally get there and to write their reactions to one another.

Writing is hard work! What was the most challenging aspect of writing The Bone Shard Daughter*?*

I think the most challenging aspect of writing *The Bone Shard Daughter* was making sure all the storylines lined up and complemented one another. I was juggling several different viewpoints, and I never wanted the reader to feel like they wanted to skip anyone's particular chapters. I wanted to make sure I was drawing the reader through the book at the right pace and drawing them in at the same time.

You've spoken before about your long journey to becoming an author – the many manuscripts you've written, the two novels you finished that didn't find a publisher. Determination and hard work are obviously important to becoming a published writer, but what other advice would you offer to a writer hoping to be published one day?

The biggest piece of advice I'd have other than persistence is to befriend other writers, especially other writers at the same stage you're at. Writing can be a lonely, solitary activity. Combine that with the vast number of rejections you can expect, and it gets a bit depressing! Having a group of friends who you can commiserate with and exchange critiques with, as well as cheer on and be cheered on by in return, is invaluable.

Finally, can you give us a teaser as to what we can expect in the next book, **The Bone Shard Emperor?**

Definitely more magical creatures and constructs, mysteries revealed, a deeper look at bone shard magic and where it comes from, more exploration of the past, reckoning with damaging legacies, bigger battles and a couple new characters!

if you enjoyed
THE BONE SHARD DAUGHTER

look out for

THE BONE SHARD EMPEROR

Book Two of The Drowning Empire

by

Andrea Stewart

Andrea Stewart returns with **The Bone Shard Emperor,** *the second installment of this unmissable, action-packed, magic-laced fantasy epic.*

The Emperor is dead. Long live the Emperor.

Lin Sukai finally sits on the throne she won at so much cost, but her struggles are only just beginning. Her people don't trust her. Her political alliances are weak. And in the northeast of the Empire, a rebel army of constructs is gathering, its leader determined to take the throne by force.

Yet an even greater threat is on the horizon, for the Alanga—the powerful magicians of legend—have returned to the Empire. They claim they come in peace, and Lin will need their help in order to defeat the rebels and restore peace.

But can she trust them?

Lin

Imperial Island

I'd thought I could set things right in the Empire if only I'd had the means. But setting things right meant weeding a garden gone wild, and with each new weed pulled, two sprouted in its place. It was so like my father not to leave me an easy task.

I clung to the ceramic tiles of the rooftop, ignoring the soft whimper from Thrana below. There was little privacy in the palace of an Emperor. Servants and guards walked the hallways; even at night there was always someone awake. My father had strolled the hallways of his own palace at all hours with impunity; no one had dared to question him, not even me. It probably helped that he kept more constructs than servants, and the servants he did keep regarded him with terror. I wanted to be a different kind of Emperor. Still, I hadn't counted on having to sneak around my own palace.

I wiped the moisture from a rain-slicked tile with my sleeve and pulled myself onto the peak of the roof. It seemed a lifetime ago that I'd last climbed up here, and though it had in fact been a few short months, my muscles felt the lack of activity. There had been administrative matters to deal with first—hiring servants, guards, and workers. Repairing and cleaning out the buildings on the palace grounds. Restating some of my father's commitments and abolishing others.

And always there were people watching me, wondering what I

would do, trying to take my measure. Constructs were unquestion-
ingly loyal and could always keep secrets. People were different.

Somewhere below me, Jovis, my Captain of the Imperial Guard,
paced the hallway outside my room, his beast, Mephi, beside him.
He'd insisted on taking on this duty himself, and though he did
sleep at some point, he only did so after he'd had another guard
relieve him. Having someone stationed outside my door at all hours
made me grind my teeth. Always he wanted to know where I was,
what I was doing. And how could I blame him when I'd tasked
him with my safety? I couldn't very well order him and his guards
to leave me in peace without sufficient reason. My father had been
known to be ill-tempered, eccentric, reclusive. How could I give
that order without appearing to be the same?

An Emperor was beholden to her people.

I sat on the peak of the roof for a moment, taking in the damp
air, the smell of the ocean. Sweat stuck my hair to the back of
my neck. Some of the rooms I'd discovered in the aftermath of
my father's death were pointlessly locked. One filled with paintings, another with trinkets—gifts from other islands. These I set
the servants upon to clean and to organize, to display in the newly
renovated buildings.

There were other rooms I dared not let anyone else access. I still
didn't know all the secrets that lurked behind these doors, what the
things I'd found meant. And prying eyes made me wary. I had my
own secrets to keep.

I was not my father's daughter. I was a created thing, grown
in the caves beneath the palace. If anyone ever found me out, I'd
be dead. There was enough dissatisfaction brewing with the Sukai
Dynasty without adding this to it. The people of the Phoenix
Empire wouldn't suffer an impostor. In the courtyard below, two
guards patrolled. Neither looked to the roof. Even if they had, I'd
only be a dark shape against a cloudy sky, the rain that drizzled into
their eyes obscuring their vision.

I crept down the other side, making my way to a window I knew
was still open. The night was warm in spite of the clouds and the

rain, and shutters were often left open unless we were in a true gale. Only a few lamps were lit when I slid from the edge of the tiles, my feet finding the sill.

There was an odd comfort in creeping through the hallways of the palace again, my engraving tool and several keys hidden inside my sash pocket. It was familiar—something I knew.

I couldn't help but peer around the corner to see the door of my room. Jovis was still there, Mephi next to him. He was showing the beast a deck of lacquered cards. Mephi reached out with a webbed claw and touched one. "This one."

Jovis sighed. "No, no, no—if you play a fish on a sea serpent, that means you lose that turn."

Mephi tilted his head and sat back on his haunches. "Feed the fish to the sea serpent. Make the sea serpent your friend."

"That's not how this works."

"It worked on me."

"Are you a sea serpent?"

Mephi clacked his teeth. "Your game makes no sense."

"You said you were bored and wanted to learn," Jovis said. He started to tuck the cards back into his pocket.

Mephi's ears flattened against his skull. "Wait. Waaaaait."

I pulled back, keeping an ear out for footsteps. Playing cards while guarding the Emperor's room wasn't very professional, no matter all of Jovis's insistences that he needed to protect me. I supposed I'd done this to myself, hiring a former member of the Ioph Carn and a notorious smuggler as Captain of the Imperial Guard. But he'd saved hordes of children from the Tithing Festival and earned a great deal of goodwill from the people.

And goodwill was something I had in short supply.

I made my way to the shard storeroom, ducking down side passages or behind pillars whenever I saw a guard or a servant. Swiftly, I unlocked the door and slipped inside. I moved through muscle memory, taking down the lamp by the lintel, lighting it, striding to the back of the room. There was another door there, carved with a cloud juniper.

Another lock, another key.

I descended into the darkness of the old mining tunnels below the palace, my lamp casting the sharp edges of the walls into stark relief. The constructs my father had placed to guard the way were dead, disassembled by my hand once I'd had the strength. The constructs still scattered across the Empire were another matter. All were commanded to obey Shiyen. And now that he was gone, their command structure had fallen to pieces. Some had gone mad. Others had gone into hiding. None of them had a master now, except Bing Tai.

At the fork in the tunnels I veered left, unlocking the door that blocked the way. I'd often wondered what my father was doing when he disappeared behind his locked doors. I still didn't exactly know.

The tunnel opened up into a cavern, and I lit the lamps scattered throughout. A pool filled part of the cavern, a workstation was set up next to it. There were bookshelves, a metal table, baskets of tools I didn't recognize. And the chest that held my father's memory machine. It was here I'd found Thrana, submerged in the pool, connected to that machine. As I did every time I entered this cavern, I checked the water. My lamp reflected off of the dark surface; I had to squint past that to see into the water below. The replica of my father still lay in the pool, his eyes closed. After the first rush of relief came that familiar pang. He looked so much like Bayan—or, I supposed, Bayan had looked so much like him.

But Bayan had died helping me to defeat my father, and there was no bringing him back. I was proof of that. My father had grown me from the parts of people he'd collected throughout the Empire, tried to infuse me with the memories of Nisong, his dead wife. It had only partially worked. I had some of her memories, but I wasn't her.

I was Lin. And I was Emperor.

I whirled, suddenly sure I'd heard something. A footstep? The scuff of shoe against stone? The lamps I'd lit behind me illuminated only stone and water; the only sound I could hear was my heartbeat thundering in my ears. In that one instant of blinding panic, I could feel everything being taken away from me—my years of hard work, the nights spent reading about bone shard magic, the courage I'd had to gather to defy my father—all of it dissolved in a moment of discovery. I was getting paranoid, hearing things where there was nothing. How could someone have followed me down here without the keys? The doors all locked again as soon as they latched shut.

Several of the books and pages of notes my father had gathered lay spread across the metal table. I was reluctant to move them to my rooms, where servants might see them. These were the weeds I was trying to pull: the Shardless Few, the sinking of Deerhead Island, the leaderless constructs, and the Alanga. There were answers here, if only I could find them. It was finding them that was difficult. My father's notes were scattered, his handwriting messy. In spite of the three locked doors, he wrote as though afraid someone else might find these books. Nothing was straightforward. Often he referenced notes he'd written previously, or other books, but without naming where those notes could be found or the titles of the books. I was trying to assemble a puzzle that had no picture.

I drew up the chair and flipped through page after page, a headache forming quickly behind my eyes. A part of me thought if only I read enough, if only I read it enough times, I'd figure out my father's secrets.

So far, all I'd been able to gather was that islands had sunk before, a long time ago. Knowing that more than one had sunk back then and so far we'd only seen Deerhead Island fall made sweat gather on my palms. I still didn't know what had caused Deerhead to sink, or when or how I might expect another island to drown. And the Alanga—another thing my father would have told to his heir. Who were they, and what could I do to fight them off?

My gaze strayed to the memory machine.

There had still been liquid in the tubes when I'd disconnected it from Thrana. I'd gathered the milky fluid into a flask. In his notes, my father had mentioned feeding the memories to his constructs and to me. He'd seemed dissatisfied with his first attempts, reluctant to disassemble the constructs that might be carrying his dead wife's memories but unhappy with how little they seemed to understand of Nisong.

I wasn't sure what he'd done with those constructs, but the more pressing matter was where the memories were stored.

I'd corked the flask, placing it on the table with the books. I'd gotten as far as uncorking it and sniffing the contents. But always I stoppered it again, searching Shiyen's notes for more concrete evidence that the memories were in that fluid. Was I getting that desperate, to consider drinking it without knowing for sure? For all I knew it could be some sort of lubrication for the machine, poisonous and not meant to be consumed.

But some of that had come from Thrana. I wasn't sure of the connection—where he'd found her, what sort of creature she was. She was like Mephi, and Jovis had found him swimming in the ocean after Deerhead's fall.

There was nothing toxic about Thrana.

Ah, I was making excuses because a part of me just wanted to drink it. I wanted to know. I couldn't be sure whose memories might be in that fluid, but I had an idea. Shiyen had been old and ill. He would have been trying to gather his memories, to place them within his replica before he died. I hadn't discovered until the end that he'd grown me to replace his wife, and had grown a replica of himself down here too. This was to be the end result of all his experimentation: him and Nisong together, young again, ruling as Emperor and consort for as long as they wished.

I was looking for answers, and some of those answers might be in the flask. The Phoenix Empire stood on a knife's edge. What was I willing to do to save my people? Numeen had told me they needed an Emperor who cared. And I cared. I cared so much.

I seized the flask, uncorked it, and lifted it to my lips before I could change my mind again.

The liquid was cold, though that didn't mask the taste. Copper, sweetness, and a strange, lingering aftertaste that filled my mouth and clung to the back of my throat. I swiped my tongue over my teeth, wondering if I should have tasted it before swallowing. Perhaps it was poison. And then the memory swept over me.

I was here, still in this chamber, though it looked different. Three more lamps were lit in the working area, and Thrana still lay in the water. My hands adjusted the tubing leading into the memory machine. Liver spots scattered across the backs of my palms, tendons pressing against skin. I pushed too hard, my hand slipped and hit the side of the chest. Something jolted loose.

"Dione's balls!" Frustration welled within me. Always one thing after another. Get something into place, another thing falls out of place. The only thing I had to live for were these experiments. My chest ached as I thought of Nisong, of her dark eyes, her hand in mine. Gone. I felt around the bottom of the chest, pushing the hidden compartment back into line.

My gaze flicked involuntarily to the other end of the cave.

And then I was back in my own body again, wondering if that was what it felt like to be my father. Strangely astonished that he had such strength of feeling at all. I'd always known him to be cold and distant.

He really had loved Nisong. I wasn't sure why that surprised me. Perhaps it was because, no matter how hard I'd tried, I could not get him to love me.

In the memory, a hidden compartment had come loose from the chest. Experimentally, I struck the side of the chest with the flat of my palm. Nothing jolted loose, but I put my hand where I remembered my father's hand pressing the wood back in.

There was something there. A small rectangle where the wood felt slightly raised. I struck the chest again.

This time, it came loose. A drawer slid partway open. I pried it the rest of the way out. Inside rested a tiny silver key.

I wasn't sure whether I wanted to laugh or to cry. Always my father kept so many secrets—secrets within secrets within secrets. His mind was a maze even he couldn't find his way out of. What if he had truly raised me as his daughter? What if he'd put aside his foolish quest to live on in another body, to bring his dead wife back to life?

The key was cold when I picked it up, the tiny teeth at the end sharp. I'd unlocked all the doors I could find in the palace. This belonged somewhere else.

My gaze flicked to the other side of the cave. He'd looked over there when he'd pushed the drawer back into place. I hadn't thought there was anything there, but perhaps I hadn't looked closely enough.

I lifted my lamp. Stalagmites blocked my path to the other side; I had to weave between them like a deer through bamboo.

At last, I reached a clear area against the wall—the spot I'd seen my father looking at. As I cast my gaze around, my heart sank. There was nothing here, just stone and the flash of crystal in the walls. I'd walked over here before; I wasn't sure why I expected anything different.

Secrets within secrets.

No, there was something here. He'd glanced at this spot, and I'd been experiencing his memory. There'd been a reason for it, I could feel it. I dropped to my knees, setting the lamp down and feeling around on the ground.

My fingers found the smallest crack filled with dirt.

I set aside the key, pulled my engraving tool from my sash pocket, and used it to clear the dirt from the crack in the stone. Someone had chiseled a piece of stone away and then replaced it. There was something here; I hadn't been wrong.

The engraving tool bent as I used it to pry the stone loose. My fingernails ached as I wedged them beneath the slab, pulling until it came free. Dirt shook loose, catching the lamplight. I peered inside the cavity and found a hatch with a keyhole.

What would my father have kept that necessitated four series of locked doors? The key slid into the lock easily and turned with a soft click. The hinges to the hatch were well oiled; it opened soundlessly. When I swung my lantern over the hole, all I could see was a ladder descending into the dark.

There could be anything down there. I crouched down, lay on my belly, and lowered both the lantern and my head into the hatch.

It was difficult to see very far into the cavern below with only one lamp, and upside down at that. The ladder was long, the bottom farther than I'd first thought. But I could make out shelves against one shadowy wall.

Well, I'd come this far, hadn't I? And it wasn't as though I was going to go back and ask Jovis to accompany me into my father's lair. I'd defeated my father; I could climb into a dark hole by myself. I pushed myself back up, tucked the engraving tool back into my sash, gripped the lantern's handle between my teeth, and set my feet upon the ladder.

The air felt even cooler in this lower cave than in the cavern with the pool. It had a musty petrichor scent, though I couldn't detect any excess moisture. It was a relief to finally touch ground again, to take the lamp from my jaw, which had already begun to ache.

I shook out the tension in my shoulders. There were perhaps more books down here, more notes, more puzzle pieces I could lock together. I pivoted, lifting the lamp.

And found its light reflecting from two monstrous eyes.

if you enjoyed
THE BONE SHARD DAUGHTER
look out for
THE MASK OF MIRRORS
Rook & Rose: Book One
by
M. A. Carrick

Darkly magical and beautifully imagined, **The Mask of Mirrors** *is the unmissable start to the Rook & Rose trilogy, a rich and dazzling fantasy adventure in which a con artist, a vigilante, and a crime lord must unite to save their city.*

Nightmares are creeping through the city of dreams....

Renata Viraudax is a con artist who has come to the sparkling city of Nadežra—the city of dreams—with one goal: to trick her way into a noble house and secure her fortune and her sister's future.

But as she's drawn into the elite world of House Traementis, she realizes her masquerade is just one of many surrounding her. And

461

*as corrupt magic begins to weave its way through Nadežra, the
poisonous feuds of its aristocrats and the shadowy dangers of its
impoverished underbelly become tangled—with Ren at their heart.*

1

The Mask of Mirrors

Isla Traementis, the Pearls: Suilun 1

After fifteen years of handling the Traementis house charters,
Donaia Traementis knew that a deal which looked too good to be
true probably was. The proposal currently on her desk stretched
the boundaries of belief.

"He could at least try to make it look legitimate," she muttered.
Did Mettore Indestor think her an utter fool?

He thinks you desperate. And he's right.

She burrowed her stockinged toes under the great lump of a hound
sleeping beneath her desk and pressed cold fingers to her brow. She'd
removed her gloves to avoid ink stains and left the hearth in her study
unlit to save the cost of fuel. Besides Meatball, the only warmth was
from the beeswax candles—an expense she couldn't scrimp on unless
she wanted to lose what eyesight she had left.

Adjusting her spectacles, she scanned the proposal again, scratching angry notes between the lines.

She remembered a time when House Traementis had been
as powerful as the Indestor family. They had held a seat in the
Cinquerat, the five-person council that ruled Nadežra, and charters
that allowed them to conduct trade, contract mercenaries, control
guilds. Every variety of wealth, power, and prestige in Nadežra
had been theirs. Now, despite Donaia's best efforts and her late
husband's before her, it had come to this: scrabbling at one Dusk
Road trade charter as though she could milk enough blood from
that stone to pay off all the Traementis debts.

Debts almost entirely owned by Mettore Indestor.

"And you expect me to trust my caravan to guards you provide?" she growled at the proposal, her pen nib digging in hard enough to tear the paper. "Ha! Who's going to protect it from them? Will they even wait for bandits, or just sack the wagons themselves?"

Leaving Donaia with the loss, a pack of angry investors, and debts she could no longer cover. Then Mettore would swoop in like one of his thrice-damned hawks to swallow whole what remained of House Traementis.

Try as she might, though, she couldn't see another option. She couldn't send the caravan out unguarded—Vraszenian bandits were a legitimate concern—but the Indestor family held the Caerulet seat in the Cinquerat, which gave Mettore authority over military and mercenary affairs. Nobody would risk working with a house Indestor had a grudge against—not when it would mean losing a charter, or worse.

Meatball's head rose with a sudden whine. A moment later a knock came at the study door, followed by Donaia's majordomo. Colbrin knew better than to interrupt her when she was wrestling with business, which meant he judged this interruption important.

He bowed and handed her a card. "Alta Renata Viraudax?" Donaia asked, shoving Meatball's wet snout out of her lap when he sniffed at the card. She flipped it as if the back would provide some clue to the visitor's purpose. Viraudax wasn't a local noble house. Some traveler to Nadežra?

"A young woman, Era Traementis," her majordomo said. "Well-mannered. Well-dressed. She said it concerned an important private matter."

The card fluttered to the floor. Donaia's duties as head of House Traementis kept her from having much of a social life, but the same could not be said for her son, and lately Leato had been behaving more and more like his father. Ninat take him—if her son had racked up some gambling debt with a foreign visitor...

Colbrin retrieved the card before the dog could eat it, and handed back to her. "Should I tell her you are not at home?"

"No. Show her in." If her son's dive into the seedier side of Nadežra had resulted in trouble, she would at least rectify his errors before stringing him up.

Somehow. With money she didn't have.

She could start by not conducting the meeting in a freezing study. "Wait," she said before Colbrin could leave. "Show her to the salon. And bring tea."

Donaia cleaned the ink from her pen and made a futile attempt to brush away the brindled dog hairs matting her surcoat. Giving that up as a lost cause, she tugged on her gloves and straightened the papers on her desk, collecting herself by collecting her surroundings. Looking down at her clothing—the faded blue surcoat over trousers and house scuffs—she weighed the value of changing over the cost of making a potential problem wait.

Everything is a tallied cost these days, she thought grimly.

"Meatball. Stay," she commanded when the hound would have followed, and headed directly to the salon.

The young woman waiting there could not have fit the setting more perfectly if she had planned it. Her rose-gold underdress and cream surcoat harmonized beautifully with the gold-shot peach silk of the couch and chairs, and the thick curl trailing from her upswept hair echoed the rich wood of the wall paneling. The curl should have looked like an accident, an errant strand slipping loose—but everything else about the visitor was so elegant it was clearly a deliberate touch of style.

She was studying the row of books on their glass-fronted shelf. When Donaia closed the door, she turned and dipped low. "Era Traementis. Thank you for seeing me."

Her curtsy was as Seterin as her clipped accent, one hand sweeping elegantly up to the opposite shoulder. Donaia's misgivings deepened at the sight of her. Close to her son's age, and beautiful as a portrait by Creciasto, with fine-boned features and flawless skin. Easy to imagine Leato losing his head over a hand of cards with such a girl. And her ensemble did nothing to comfort Donaia's fears—the richly embroidered brocade, the sleeves an elegant fall

464

of sheer silk. Here was someone who could afford to bet and lose a fortune.

That sort was more likely to forgive or forget a debt than come collecting...unless the debt was meant as leverage for something else.

"Alta Renata. I hope you will forgive my informality." She brushed a hand down her simple attire. "I did not expect visitors, but it sounded like your matter was of some urgency. Please, do be seated."

The young woman lowered herself into the chair as lightly as mist on the river. Seeing her, it was easy to understand why the people of Nadežra looked to Seteris as the source of all that was stylish and elegant. Fashion was born in Seteris. By the time it traveled south to Seteris's protectorate, Seste Ligante, then farther south still, across the sea to Nadežra, it was old and stale, and Seteris had moved on.

Most Seterin visitors behaved as though Nadežra was nothing more than Seste Ligante's backwater colonial foothold on the Vraszenian continent and merely setting foot on the streets would foul them with the mud of the River Dežera. But Renata's delicacy looked like hesitation, not condescension. She said, "Not urgent, no—I do apologize if I gave that impression. I confess, I'm not certain how to even begin this conversation."

She paused, hazel eyes searching Donaia's face. "You don't recognize my family name, do you?"

That had an ominous sound. Seteris might be on the other side of the sea, but the truly powerful families could influence trade anywhere in the known world. If House Traementis had somehow crossed one of them...

Donaia kept her fear from her face and her voice. "I am afraid I haven't had many dealings with the great houses of Seteris."

A soft breath flowed out of the girl. "As I suspected. I thought she might have written to you at least once, but apparently not. I...am Letilia's daughter."

She could have announced she was descended from the Vraszenian goddess Ažerais herself, and it wouldn't have taken Donaia more by surprise.

Disbelief clashed with relief and apprehension both: not a creditor, not an offended daughter of some foreign power. Family—after a fashion.

Lost for words, Donaia reassessed the young woman sitting across from her. Straight back, straight shoulders, straight neck, and the same fine, narrow nose that made everyone in Nadežra hail Letilia Traementis as the great beauty of her day.

Yes, she could be Letilia's daughter. Donaia's niece by marriage.

"Letilia never wrote after she left." It was the only consideration the spoiled brat had ever shown her family. The first several years, every day they'd expected a letter telling them she was stranded in Seteris, begging for funds. Instead they never heard from her again.

Dread sank into Donaia's bones. "Is Letilia here?"

The door swung open, and for one dreadful instant Donaia expected a familiar squall of petulance and privilege to sweep inside. But it was only Colbrin, bearing a tray. To her dismay, Donaia saw two pots on it, one short and rounded for tea, the other taller. Of course: He'd heard their guest's Seterin accent, and naturally assumed Donaia would also want to serve coffee.

We haven't yet fallen so far that I can't afford proper hospitality. But Donaia's voice was still sharp as he set the tray between the two of them. "Thank you, Colbrin. That will be all."

"No," Renata said as the majordomo bowed and departed. "No, Mother is happily ensconced in Seteris."

It seemed luck hadn't *entirely* abandoned House Traementis. "Tea?" Donaia said, a little too bright with relief. "Or would you prefer coffee?"

"Coffee, thank you." Renata accepted the cup and saucer with a graceful hand. Everything about her was graceful—but not the artificial, forced elegance Donaia remembered Letilia practicing so assiduously.

Renata sipped the coffee and made a small, appreciative noise. "I must admit, I was wondering if I would even be able to find coffee here."

Ah. *There* was the echo of Letilia, the little sneer that took what should be a compliment and transformed it into an insult.

We have wooden floors and chairs with backs, too. Donaia swallowed down the snappish response. But the bitter taste in her mouth nudged her into pouring coffee for herself, even though she disliked it. She wouldn't let this girl make her feel like a delta rustic simply because Donaia had lived all her life in Nadežra.

"So you are here, but Letilia is not. May I ask why?"

The girl's chin dropped, and she rotated her coffee cup as though its precise alignment against the saucer were vitally important. "I've spent days imagining how best to approach you, but—well." There was a ripple of nervousness in her laugh. "There's no way to say this without first admitting I'm Letilia's daughter…and yet by admitting that, I know I've already gotten off on the wrong foot. Still, there's nothing for it."

Renata inhaled like someone preparing for battle, then met Donaia's gaze. "I'm here to see if I can possibly reconcile my mother with her family."

It took all Donaia's self-control not to laugh. Reconcile? She would sooner reconcile with the drugs that had overtaken her husband Gianco's good sense in his final years. If Gianco's darker comments were to be believed, Letilia had done as much to destroy House Traementis as aža had.

Fortunately, custom and law offered her a more dispassionate response. "Letilia is no part of this family. My husband's father struck her name from our register after she left."

At least Renata was smart enough not to be surprised. "I can hardly blame my gra—your father-in-law," she said. "I've only my mother's version of the tale, but I also know *her*. I can guess the part she played in that estrangement."

Donaia could just imagine what poison Letilia's version had contained. "It is more than estrangement," she said brusquely, rising to her feet. "I am sorry you crossed the sea for nothing, but I'm afraid that what you're asking for is impossible. Even if I believed that your mother wanted to reconcile—which I do not—I have no interest in doing so."

A treacherous worm within her whispered, *Even if that might offer a new business opportunity? Some way out of Indestor's trap?*

Even then. Donaia would burn Traementis Manor to the ground before she accepted help from Letilia's hand.

The salon door opened again. But this time, the interruption wasn't her majordomo.

"Mother, Egliadas has invited me to go sailing on the river." Leato was tugging on his gloves, as if he couldn't be bothered to finish dressing before leaving his rooms. But he stopped, one hand still caught in the tight cuff, when he saw their visitor.

Renata rose like a flower bud unfurling, and Donaia cursed silently. Why, today of all days, had Leato chosen to wake early? Not that fourth sun was early by most people's standards, but for him midmorning might as well be dawn.

Reflex forced the courtesies out of her mouth, even though she wanted nothing more than to hurry the girl away. "Leato, you recall stories of your aunt Letilia? This is her daughter, Alta Renata Viraudax of Seteris. Alta Renata, my son and heir, Leato Traementis."

Leato captured Renata's hand before she could touch it to her shoulder again and kissed her gloved fingertips. When she saw them together, Donaia's heart sank like a stone. She was used to thinking of her son as an adolescent scamp, or an intermittent source of headaches. But he was a man grown, with beauty to match Renata's: his hair like antique gold, fashionably mussed on top; his ivory skin and finely carved features, the hallmark of House Traementis; the elegant cut of his waistcoat and fitted tailoring of the full-skirted coat over it in the platinum shimmer of delta grasses in autumn.

And the two of them were smiling at one another like the sun had just risen in the salon.

"Letilia's daughter?" Leato said, releasing Renata's hand before the touch could grow awkward. "I thought she hated us."

Donaia bit down the impulse to chide him. It would sound like she was defending Renata, which was the last thing she wanted to do.

The girl's smile was brief and rueful. "I may have inherited her nose, but I've tried not to inherit *everything* else."

"You mean, not her personality? I'll offer thanks to Katus." Leato winced. "I'm sorry, I shouldn't insult your mother—"

"No insult taken," Renata said dryly. "I'm sure the stories you know of her are dreadful, and with good cause."

They had the river's current beneath them and were flowing onward; Donaia had to stop it before they went too far. When Leato asked what brought Renata to the city, Donaia lunged in, social grace be damned. "She just—"

But Renata spoke over her, as smooth as silk. "I was hoping to meet your grandfather and father. Foolish of me, really; since Mother hasn't been in contact, I didn't know they'd both passed away until I arrived. And now I understand she's no longer in the register, so there's no bond between us—I'm just a stranger, intruding."

"Oh, not at all!" Leato turned to his mother for confirmation.

For the first time, Donaia felt a touch of gratitude toward Renata. Leato had never known Letilia; he hadn't even been born when she ran away. He'd heard the tales, but no doubt he marked at least some of them as exaggeration. If Renata had mentioned a reconciliation outright, he probably would have supported her.

"We're touched by your visit," Donaia said, offering the girl a courteous nod. "I'm only sorry the others never had a chance to meet you."

"Your visit?" Leato scoffed. "No, this can't be all. You're my cousin, after all—oh, not under the law, I know. But blood counts for a lot here."

"We're Nadežran, Leato, not Vraszenian," Donaia said reprovingly, lest Renata think they'd been completely swallowed by delta ways.

He went on as though he hadn't heard her. "My long-lost cousin

469

shows up from across the sea, greets us for a few minutes, then vanishes? Unacceptable. Giuna hasn't even met you—she's my younger sister. Why don't you stay with us for a few days?"

Donaia couldn't stop a muffled sound from escaping her. However much he seemed determined to ignore them, Leato knew about House Traementis's financial troubles. A houseguest was the last thing they could afford.

But Renata demurred with a light shake of her head. "No, no—I couldn't impose like that. I'll be in Nadežra for some time, though. Perhaps you'll allow me the chance to show I'm not my mother."

Preparatory to pushing for reconciliation, no doubt. But although Renata was older and more self-possessed, something about her downcast gaze reminded Donaia of Giuna. She could all too easily imagine Giuna seeking Letilia out in Seteris with the same impossible dream.

If House Traementis could afford the sea passage, which they could not. And if Donaia would allow her to go, which she would not. But if that impossible situation happened...she bristled at the thought of Letilia rebuffing Giuna entirely, treating her with such cold hostility that she refused to see the girl at all.

So Donaia said, as warmly as she could, "Of course we know you aren't your mother. And you shouldn't be forced to carry the burden of her past." She let a smile crack her mask. "I'm certain from the caterpillars dancing on my son's brow that he'd like to know more about you, and I imagine Giuna would feel the same."

"Thank you," Renata said with a curtsy. "But not now, I think. My apologies, Altan Leato." Her words silenced his protest before he could voice it, and with faultless formality. "My maid intends to fit me for a new dress this afternoon, and she'll stick me with pins if I'm late."

That was as unlike Letilia as it was possible to be. Not the concern for her clothing—Letilia was the same, only with less tasteful results—but the graceful withdrawal, cooperating with Donaia's wish to get her out of the house.

Leato did manage to get one more question out, though. "Where can we reach you?"

"On the Isla Prišta, Via Brelkoja, number four," Renata said. Donaia's lips tightened. For a stay of a few weeks, even a month or two, a hotel would have sufficed. Renting a house suggested the girl intended to remain for quite some time.

But that was a matter for later. Donaia reached for the bell. "Colbrin will see you out."

"No need," Leato said, offering Renata his hand. When she glanced at Donaia instead of taking it, Leato said, "Mother, you won't begrudge me a few moments of gossip with my new cousin?"

That was Leato, always asking for forgiveness rather than permission. But Renata's minute smile silently promised not to encourage him. At Donaia's forbearing nod, she accepted his escort from the room.

Once they were gone, Donaia rang for Colbrin. "I'll be in my study. No more interruptions barring flood or fire, please."

Colbrin's acknowledgment trailed after her as she went upstairs. When she entered the room, Meatball roused with a whine-snap of a yawn and a hopeful look, but settled again once he realized no treats were forthcoming.

The space seemed chillier than when she'd left it, and darker. She thought of Alta Renata's fine manners and finer clothes. Of course Letilia's daughter would be dressed in designs so new they hadn't yet made their way from Seteris to Nadežra. Of course she would have enough wealth to rent a house in Westbridge for herself alone and think nothing of it. Hadn't Gianco always said that Letilia took House Traementis's luck with her when she left?

In a fit of pique, Donaia lit the hearthfire, and damn the cost. Once its warmth was blazing through the study, she returned to her desk. She buried her toes under the dog again, mentally composing her message as she sharpened her nib and filled her ink tray.

House Traementis might be neck-deep in debt and sinking, but they still had the rights granted by their ennoblement charter. And Donaia wasn't such a fool that she would bite a hook before examining it from all sides first.

Bending her head, Donaia began penning a letter to Commander Cercel of the Vigil.

extras

Upper and Lower Bank: Suilun 1

Renata expected Leato Traementis to see her out the front door, but he escorted her all the way to the bottom of the steps, and kept her hand even when they stopped. "I hope you're not too offended by Mother's reserve," he said. A breeze ruffled his burnished hair and carried the scent of caramel and almonds to her nose. A rich scent, matching his clothes and his carriage, and the thin lines of gold paint limning his eyelashes. "A lot of dead branches have been pruned from the Traementis register since my father—and your mother—were children. Now there's only Mother, Giuna, and myself. She gets protective."

"I take no offense at all," Renata said, smiling up at him. "I'm not so much of a fool that I expect to be welcomed with open arms. And I'm willing to be patient."

The breeze sharpened, and she shivered. Leato stepped between her and the wind. "You'd think Naděžra would be warmer than Seteris, wouldn't you?" he said with a sympathetic grimace. "It's all the water. We almost never get snow here, but the winters are so damp, the cold cuts right to your bones."

"I should have thought to wear a cloak. But since I can't pluck one from thin air, I hope you won't take offense if I hurry home."

"Of course not. Let me get you a sedan chair." Leato raised a hand to catch the eye of some men idling on the far side of the square and paid the bearers before Renata could even reach for her purse. "To soothe any lingering sting," he said with a smile.

She thanked him with another curtsy. "I hope I'll see you soon."

"As do I." Leato helped her into the sedan chair and closed the door once her skirts were safely out of the way.

As the bearers headed for the narrow exit from the square, Renata drew the curtains shut. Traementis Manor was in the Pearls, a cluster of islets strung along the Upper Bank of the River Dežera. The river here ran pure and clear thanks to the numinat that protected the East Channel, and the narrow streets and bridges were clean; whichever families held the charters to keep the streets clear of refuse wouldn't dream of letting it accumulate near the houses of the rich and powerful.

But the rocky wedge that broke the Dežera into east and west channels was a different matter. For all that it held two of Nadežra's major institutions—the Charterhouse in Dawngate, which was the seat of government, and the Aerie in Duskgate, home to the Vigil, which maintained order—the Old Island was also crowded with the poor and the shabby-genteel. Anyone riding in a sedan chair was just asking for beggars to crowd at their windows.

Which still made it better than half of the Lower Bank, where a sedan chair risked being knocked to the ground and the passenger robbed.

Luckily, her rented house was on Isla Prišta in Westbridge—technically on the Lower Bank, and far from a fashionable district, but it was a respectable neighborhood on the rise. In fact, the buildings on the Via Brelkoja were so newly renovated the mortar hadn't had time to moss over in the damp air. The freshly painted door to number four opened just as Renata's foot touched the first step.

Tess made a severe-looking sight in the crisp grey-and-white surcoat and underskirt of a Nadežran housemaid, but her copper Ganllechyn curls and freckles were a warm beacon welcoming Renata home. She bobbed a curtsy and murmured a lilting "alta" as Renata passed across the threshold, accepting the gloves and purse Renata held out.

"Downstairs," Ren murmured as the door snicked shut, sinking them into the dimness of the front hall.

Tess nodded, swallowing her question before she could speak it. Together they headed into the half-sunken chambers of the cellar, which held the service rooms. Only once they were safely in the kitchen did Tess say, "Well? How did it go?"

Ren let her posture drop and her voice relax into the throaty tones of her natural accent. "For me, as well as I could hope. Donaia refused reconciliation out of hand—"

"Thank the Mother," Tess breathed. If Donaia contacted Letilia, their entire plan would fall apart before it started.

Ren nodded. "Faced with the prospect of talking to her former sister-in-law, she barely even noticed me getting my foot in the door."

"That's a start, then. Here, off with this, and wrap up before you take a chill." Tess passed Ren a thick cloak of rough-spun wool lined with raw fleece, then turned her around like a dressmaker's doll so she could remove the beautifully embroidered surcoat.

"I saw the sedan chair," Tess said as she tugged at the side ties. "You didn't take that all the way from Isla Traementis, did you? If you're going to be riding about in chairs, I'll have to revise the budget. And here I'd had my eye on a lovely bit of lace at the remnants stall." Tess sighed mournfully, like she was saying farewell to a sweetheart. "I'll just have to tat some myself."

"In your endless spare time?" Ren said sardonically. The surcoat came loose, and she swung the cloak around her shoulders in its place. "Anyway, the son paid for the chair." She dropped onto the kitchen bench and eased her shoes off with a silent curse. Fashionable shoes were *not* comfortable. The hardest part of this con was going to be pretending her feet didn't hurt all day long.

Although choking down coffee ran a close second.

"Did he, now?" Tess settled on the bench next to Ren, close enough that they could share warmth beneath the cloak. Apart from the kitchen and the front salon, protective sheets still covered the furniture in every other room. The hearths were cold, their meals were simple, and they slept together on a kitchen floor pallet so they would only have to heat one room of the house.

Because she was not Alta Renata Viraudax, daughter of Letilia Traementis. She was Arenza Lenskaya, half-Vraszenian river rat, and even with a forged letter of credit to help, pretending to be a Seterin noblewoman wasn't cheap.

Pulling out a thumbnail blade, Tess began ripping the seams of Ren's beautiful surcoat, preparatory to alteration. "Was it just idle flirtation?"

The speculative uptick in Tess's question said she didn't believe any flirtation Ren encountered was idle. But whether Leato's flirtation had been idle or not, Ren had lines she would not cross, and whoring herself out was one of them.

It would have been the easier route. Dress herself up fine enough to catch the eye of some delta gentry son, or even a noble, and marry her way into money. She wouldn't be the first person in Nadežra to do it.

But she'd spent five years in Ganllech—five years as a maid under Letilia's thumb, listening to her complain about her dreadful family and how much she dreamed of life in Seteris, the promised land she'd never managed to reach. So when Ren and Tess found themselves back in Nadežra, Ren had been resolved. No whoring, and no killing. Instead she set her sights on a higher target: use what she'd learned to gain acceptance into House Traementis as their long-lost kin...with all the wealth and social benefit that brought.

"Leato is friendly," she allowed, picking up the far end of the dress and starting on the seam with her own knife. Tess didn't trust her to sew anything more complicated than a hem, but ripping stitches? That, she was qualified for. "And he helped shame Donaia into agreeing to see me again. But *she* is every bit as bad as Letilia claimed. You should have seen what she wore. Ratty old clothes, covered in dog hair. Like it's a moral flaw to let a single centira slip through her fingers."

"But the son isn't so bad?" Tess rocked on the bench, nudging Ren's hip with her own. "Maybe he's a bastard."

Ren snorted. "Not likely. Donaia would give him the moon if he asked, and he looks as Traementis as I." Only he didn't need makeup to achieve the effect.

Her hands trembled as she worked. Those five years in Ganllech were also five years out of practice. And all her previous cons had been short touches—never anything on this scale. When she got caught before, the hawks slung her in jail for a few days.

If she got caught now, impersonating a noblewoman...

Tess laid a hand over Ren's, stopping her before she could nick herself with the knife. "It's never too late to do something else."

Ren managed a smile. "Buy piles of fabric, then run away and set up as dressmakers? You, anyway. I would be your tailor's dummy."

"You'd model and sell them," Tess said stoutly. "If you want."

Tess would be happy in that life. But Ren wanted more.

This city *owed* her more. It had taken everything: her mother, her childhood, Sedge. The rich cuffs of Nadežra got whatever they wanted, then squabbled over what their rivals had, grinding everyone else underfoot. In all her days among the Fingers, Ren had never been able to take more than the smallest shreds from the hems of their cloaks.

But now, thanks to Letilia, she was in a position to take more.

The Traementis made the perfect target. Small enough these days that only Donaia stood any chance of spotting Renata as an imposter, and isolated enough that they would be grateful for any addition to their register. In the glory days of their power and graft, they'd been notorious for their insular ways, refusing to aid their fellow nobles in times of need. Since they lost their seat in the Cinquerat, everyone else had gladly returned the favor.

Ren put down the knife and squeezed Tess's hand. "No. It is nerves only, and they will pass. We go forward."

"Forward it is." Tess squeezed back, then returned to work. "Next we're to make a splash somewhere public, yes? I'll need to know where and when if I'm to outfit you proper." The sides of the surcoat parted, and she started on the bandeau at the top of the bodice. "The sleeves are the key, have you noticed? Everyone is so on about their sleeves. But I've a thought for that...if you're ready for Alta Renata to set fashion instead of following."

Ren glanced sideways, her wariness only half-feigned. "What have you in mind?"

"Hmm. Stand up, and off with the rest of it." Once she had Ren stripped to her chemise, Tess played with different gathers and drapes until Ren's arms started to ache from being held out for so long. But she didn't complain. Tess's eye for fashion, her knack for imbuing, and her ability to rework the pieces of three outfits into nine were as vital to this con as Ren's skill at manipulation.

She closed her eyes and cast her thoughts over what she knew about the city. Where could she go, what could she do, to attract the kind of admiration that would help her gain the foothold she needed?

A slow smile spread across her face.

"Tess," she said, "I have the perfect idea. And you will love it."

The Aerie and Isla Traementis: Suilun 1

"Serrado! Get in here. I have a job for you."

Commander Cercel's voice cut sharply through the din of the Aerie. Waving at his constables to take their prisoner to the stockade, Captain Grey Serrado turned and threaded his way through the chaos to his commander's office. He ignored the sidelong smirks and snide whispers of his fellow officers: Unlike them, he didn't have the luxury of lounging about drinking coffee, managing his constables from the comfort of the Aerie.

"Commander Cercel?" He snapped the heels of his boots together and gave her his crispest salute—a salute he'd perfected during hours of standing at attention in the sun, the rain, the wind, while other lieutenants were at mess or in the barracks. Cercel wasn't the stickler for discipline his previous superiors had been, but she was the reason he wore a captain's double-lined hexagram pin, and he didn't want to reflect badly on her.

She was studying a letter, but when she brought her head up to reply, her eyes widened. "What does the *other* guy look like?"

Taking the casual question as permission to drop into rest, Grey spared a glance for his uniform. His patrol slops were spattered with muck from heel to shoulder, and blood was drying on the knuckles of his leather gloves. Some of the canal mud on his boots had flaked off when he saluted, powdering Cercel's carpet with the filth of the Kingfisher slums.

"Dazed but breathing. Ranieri's taking him to the stockade now." Her question invited banter, but the door to her office was open, and it wouldn't do him any good to be marked as a smart-ass.

She responded to his businesslike answer with an equally brisk nod. "Well, get cleaned up. I've received a letter from one of the noble houses, requesting Vigil assistance. I'm sending you."

Grey's jaw tensed as he waited for several gut responses to subside. It was possible the request was a legitimate call for aid. "What crime has been committed?"

Cercel's level gaze said, *You know better than that.* "One of the noble houses has requested Vigil assistance," she repeated, enunciating each word with cut-glass clarity. "I'm sure they wouldn't do that without good cause."

No doubt whoever sent the letter thought the cause was good. People from the great houses always did.

But Grey had a desk full of real problems. "More children have gone missing. That's eleven verified this month."

They'd had this conversation several times over the past few weeks. Cercel sighed. "We haven't had any reports—"

"Because they're all river rats so far. Who's going to care enough to report that? But the man I just brought in might know something about it; he's been promising Kingfisher kids good pay for an unspecified job. I got him on defacing public property, but he'll be free again by tonight." Pissing in public wasn't an offense the Vigil usually cracked down on, unless it suited them. "Am I to assume this noble's 'good cause' takes precedence over finding out what's happening to those kids?"

Cercel breathed out hard through her nose, and he tensed. Had he pushed her patience too far?

No. "Your man is on his way to the stockade," she said. "Have Kaineto process him—you're always complaining he's as slow as river mud. By the time you get back, he'll be ready to talk. Meanwhile, send Ranieri to ask questions around Kingfisher, see if he can find any of the man's associates." She set the letter aside and drew another from her stack, a clear prelude to dismissing him. "You know the deal, Serrado."

The first few times, he'd played dense to make her spell it out in unambiguous terms. The last thing he could afford back then was to mistake a senior officer's meaning.

But they were past those games now. As long as he knuckled under and did whatever this noble wanted of him, Cercel wouldn't question him using Vigil time and resources for his own investigations.

"Yes, Commander." He saluted and heel-knocked another layer of delta silt onto her carpet. "Which house has called for aid?"

"Traementis."

If he'd been less careful of his manners, he would have thrown her a dirty look. *She could have* led *with that.* But Cercel wanted him to understand that answering these calls was part of his duty, and made him bend his neck before she revealed the silver lining. "Understood. I'll head to the Pearls at once."

Her final command followed him out of the office. "Don't you dare show up at Era Traementis's door looking like that!"

Groaning, Grey changed his path. He snagged a pitcher of water and a messenger, sending the latter to Ranieri with the new orders.

There was a bathing room in the Aerie, but he didn't want to waste time on that. A sniff test sent every piece of his patrol uniform into the laundry bag; aside from the coffee, that was one of the few perks of his rank he didn't mind taking shameless advantage of. If he was wading through canals for the job, the least the Vigil could do was ensure he didn't smell like one. A quick pitcher bath in his tiny office took care of the scents still clinging to his skin and hair before he shrugged into his dress vigils.

He had to admit the force's tailors were good. The tan breeches were Liganti-cut, snug as they could be around his thighs and hips without impeding movement. Both the brocade waistcoat and the coat of sapphire wool were tailored like a second skin, before the latter flared to full skirts that kissed the tops of his polished, knee-high boots. On his patrol slops, the diving hawk across the back of his shoulders was mere patchwork; here it was embroidered in golds and browns.

Grey didn't have much use for vanity, but he did love his dress vigils. They were an inarguable reminder that he'd climbed to a place few Vraszenians could even imagine reaching. His brother, Kolya, had been so proud the day Grey came home in them.

The sudden trembling of his hands stabbed his collar pin into his thumb. Grey swallowed a curse and sucked the blood from the puncture, using a tiny hand mirror to make sure he hadn't gotten any on his collar. Luckily, it was clean, and he managed to finish dressing himself without further injury.

Once outside, he set off east from Duskgate with long, ground-eating strides. He could have taken a sedan chair and told the bearers to bill the Vigil; other officers did, knowing all the while that no such bill would ever be paid. But along with stiffing the bearers, that meant they didn't see the city around them the way Grey did.

Not that most of them would. They were Liganti, or mixed enough in ancestry that they could claim the name; to them, Nadežra was an outpost of Seste Ligante, half tamed by the Liganti general Kaius Sifigno, who restyled himself Kaius Rex after conquering Vraszan two centuries past. Others called him the Tyrant, and when he died, the Vraszenian clans took back the rest of their conquered land. But every push to reclaim their holy city failed, until exhaustion on both sides led to the signing of the Accords. Those established Nadežra as an independent city-state—under the rule of its Liganti elite.

It was an uneasy balance at best, made less easy still by Vraszenian radical groups like the Stadnem Anduske, who wouldn't settle for anything less than the city back in Vraszenian hands. And every time they pushed, the Cinquerat pushed back even harder.

The busy markets of Suncross at the heart of the Old Island parted for Grey's bright blue coat and the tawny embroidered hawk, but not without glares. To the high and mighty, the Vigil was a tool; to the common Nadežran, the Vigil was the tool of the high and mighty. Not all of them—Grey wasn't the only hawk who cared about common folk—but enough that he couldn't blame people for their hostility. And some of the worst glares came from Vraszenians, who looked at him and saw a slip-knot: a man who had betrayed his people, siding with the invaders' descendants.

Grey was used to the glares. He kept an eye out for trouble as he passed market stalls on the stoops of decaying townhouses, and a bawdy puppet show where the only children in the crowd were the pickpockets. They trickled away like water before he could mark their faces. A few beggars eyed him warily, but Grey had no grudge against them; the more dangerous elements wouldn't come out until evening, when the feckless sons and daughters of the delta gentry prowled the streets in search of amusement. A pattern-reader had set up on a corner near the Charterhouse, ready to bilk people in exchange for a pretty lie. He gave her a wide berth, leather glove creaking into a fist as he resisted the urge to drag her back to the Aerie for graft.

Once he'd passed under the decaying bulk of the Dawngate and across the Sunrise Bridge, he turned north into the narrow islets of the Pearls, clogged with sedan chairs. Two elderly ladies impressed with their own importance blocked the Becchia Bridge entirely, squabbling like gulls over which one should yield. Grey marked the house sigil painted onto each chair's door in case complaints came to the Aerie later.

His shoulders itched as he crossed the lines of the complex mosaic in the center of Traementis Plaza. It was no mere tilework, but a numinat: geometric Liganti magic meant to keep the ground dry and solid, against the river's determination to sink everything into the mud. Useful . . . but the Tyrant had twisted numinatria into a weapon during his conquest, and mosaics like this one amounted to emblems of ongoing Liganti control.

On the steps of Traementis Manor, Grey gave his uniform a final smoothing and sounded the bell. Within moments, Colbrin opened the door and favored Grey with a rare smile.

"Young Master Serrado. How pleasant to see you; it's been far too long. I'm afraid Altan Leato is not here to receive you—"

"It's 'Captain' now," Grey said, touching the hexagram pin at his throat. The smile he dredged up felt tired from disuse. "And I'm not here for Leato. Era Traementis requested assistance from the Vigil."

"Ah, yes." Colbrin bowed him inside. "If you'll wait in the salon, I'll inform Era Traementis that you're here."

Grey wasn't surprised when Colbrin returned in a few moments and summoned him to the study. Whatever Donaia had written to the Vigil for, it was business, not a social call.

That room was much darker, with little in the way of bright silks to warm the space—but warmth came in many shapes. Donaia's grizzled wolfhound scrambled up from his place by her desk, claws ticking on wood as he trotted over for a greeting. "Hello, old man," Grey said, giving him a good tousling and a few barrel thumps on the side.

"Meatball. Heel." The dog returned to Donaia's side, looking up as she crossed the room to greet Grey.

"Era Traementis," Grey said, bowing over her hand. "I'm told you have need of assistance."

The silver threads lacing through her hair were gaining ground against the auburn, and she looked tired. "Yes. I need you to look into someone—a visitor to the city, recently arrived from Seteris. Renata Viraudax."

"Has she committed some crime against House Traementis?"

"No," Donaia said. "*She* hasn't."

Her words piqued his curiosity. "Era?"

A muscle tightened in Donaia's jaw. "My husband once had a sister named Letilia—Lecilla, really, but she was obsessed with Seteris and their high culture, so she badgered their father into changing it in the register. Twenty-three years ago, she decided she would rather be in Seteris than here…so she stole some money and jewelry and ran away."

Donaia gestured Grey to a chair in front of the hearth. The warmth of the fire enveloped him as he sat down. "Renata Viraudax is Letilia's daughter. She claims to be trying to mend bridges, but I have my doubts. I want you to find out what she's really doing in Nadežra."

As much as Grey loathed the right of the nobility to commandeer the Vigil for private use, he couldn't help feeling sympathy. When he was younger and less aware of the differences that made it impossible, he'd sometimes wished Donaia Traementis was his mother. She was stern, but fair. She loved her children, and was fiercely protective of her family. Unlike some, she never gave Leato and Giuna reason to doubt her love for them.

This Viraudax woman's mother had hurt her family, and the Traementis had a well-earned reputation for avenging their own.

"What can you tell me about her?" he asked. "Has she given you any reason to doubt her sincerity? Apart from being her mother's daughter."

Donaia's fingers drummed briefly against the arm of the chair, and her gaze settled on a corner of the fireplace and stayed there long enough that Grey knew she was struggling with some thought. He kept his silence.

Finally she said, "You and my son are friends, and moreover you aren't a fool. It can't have escaped your notice that House Traementis is not what it once was, in wealth, power, or numbers. We have many enemies eager to see us fall. Now this young woman shows up and tries to insinuate herself among us? Perhaps I'm jumping at shadows... but I must consider the possibility that this is a gambit intended to destroy us entirely." She gave a bitter laugh. "I can't even be certain this girl *is* Letilia's daughter."

She must be worried, if she was admitting so much. Yes, Grey had suspected—would have suspected even if Vigil gossip didn't sometimes speculate—that House Traementis was struggling more than they let on. But he never joined in the gossip, and he never asked Leato.

Leato... who was always in fashion, and according to that same gossip spent half his time frequenting aža parlours and gambling dens. *Does Leato know?* Grey swallowed the question. It wasn't his business, and it wasn't the business Donaia had called him for.

"That last shouldn't be too hard to determine," he said. "I assume you know where she's staying?" He paused when Donaia's lips flattened, but she only nodded. "Then talk to her. If she's truly Letilia's daughter, she should know details an imposter wouldn't easily be able to discover.

If she gives you vague answers or takes offense, then you'll know something is wrong."

Grey paused again, wondering how much Donaia would let him pry. "You said you had enemies she might be working for. It would help me to know who they are and what they might want." At her sharply indrawn breath, he raised a hand in pledge. "I promise I'll say nothing of it—not even to Leato."

In a tone so dry it burned, Donaia began ticking possibilities off on her fingers. "Quientis took our seat in the Cinquerat. Kaineto are only delta gentry, but have made a point of blocking our attempts to contract out our charters. Essunta, likewise. Simendis, Destaelio, Novrus, Cleoter—Indestor—I'm afraid it's a crowded field."

That was the entire Cinquerat and others besides...but she'd only stumbled over one name.

"Indestor," Grey said. The house that held Caerulet, the military seat in the Cinquerat. The house in charge of the Vigil.

The house that would not look kindly upon being investigated by one of its own.

"Era Traementis...did you ask for any officer, or did you specifically request me?"

"You're Leato's friend," Donaia said, holding his gaze. "Far better to ask a friend for help than to confess our troubles to an enemy."

That startled a chuckle from Grey. At Donaia's furrowed brow, he said, "My brother was fond of a Vraszenian saying. 'A family covered in the same dirt washes in the same water.'"

And Kolya would have given Grey a good scolding for not jumping to help Donaia right away. She might not be kin, but she'd hired a young Vraszenian carpenter with a scrawny kid brother when nobody else would, and paid him the same as a Nadežran.

He stood and bowed with a fist to his shoulder. "I'll see what I can discover for you. Tell me where to find this Renata Viraudax."

Follow us:

f **/orbitbooksUS**

🐦 **/orbitbooks**

▶ **/orbitbooks**

Join our mailing list
to receive alerts on our
latest releases and deals.

orbitbooks.net

Enter our monthly
giveaway for the chance
to win some epic prizes.

orbitloot.com